CASTLE IN THE GLOOM

Castle in the Gloom

Paul Ruffin

UNIVERSITY PRESS OF MISSISSIPPI / JACKSON

Author's note: The circumstances and characters of this book are purely fictitious. Any resemblance to people living or dead or to any actual circumstances resembling those in this narration are coincidental.

www.upress.state.ms.us

The University Press of Mississippi is a member of the Association of American University Presses.

Manufactured in the United States of America

08 07 06 05 04   4 3 2 1

Library of Congress Cataloging-in-Publication Data

Ruffin, Paul.

Castle in the gloom / Paul Ruffin.

p. cm.

ISBN 1-57806-618-2 (cloth : alk. paper)

1. Kidnapping victims—Fiction. 2. Mentally ill women—Fiction. 3. Wilderness areas—Fiction. 4. Automobile travel—Fiction. 5. Marital conflict—Fiction. 6. Married people—Fiction. 7. Texas—Fiction. I. Title.

PS3568.U362C37 2004

813'.54—dc22   2003025289

British Library Cataloging-in-Publication Data available

FOR SHARON

Whose spirit is this? we said, because we knew
It was the spirit we sought and knew
That we should ask this often. . . .

—WALLACE STEVENS

ONE

Encroaching twilight deepened the gloom of the little opening we were parked in, and as far as I could see ahead, the road wound back through darkening trees that seemed to swallow it, their limbs arching out from either side, in places meeting to form a solid canopy and leaving me with the chilling notion that I was looking down the barrel of a shotgun. Buffeted by an occasional gust that funneled down the road from the north, the car sat quietly, engine ticking as it cooled. For long minutes I stared straight out past the hood toward the end of the raw, red gash cut by recent rains. It ran straight across the pebble driveway and ended where heavy grass took over like a great bushy eyebrow, and beyond the grass thick brush and woods began again. Then I looked over at my wife, who had said nothing.

Except for two littered and lonely crossroads where dumpsters overflowed with trash from county households, it was the first break in the trees we'd seen in miles and the only one that had what looked like an occupied house sitting in it. Any other time I'd have zipped right past it without looking, probably wouldn't even have seen it. With a crippled car and an anxious woman, it was an oasis in the wasteland.

I couldn't see her eyes through the dark lenses of her sun-shades, but I could read her face well enough to know that it had lost the gladness that flared there when we crept around the curve and saw the old white building, behind which the sun was just wallowing down in the trees for the night like some big soft orange thing in a nest. I didn't pay too much attention to the house—I just hoped someone was at home.

"Well, it's a place," I said. "It may not look like much, but it's been cleared of trees and vines, it has a driveway, and I'm sure they've got a phone. And they have curtains in the windows."

She rose in her seat and looked out over the hood. "Some driveway. Maybe an Army all-terrain vehicle could use it. Can't you get any farther off the road? You're almost on the asphalt on this side. Somebody's likely to bang into this thing."

"Best I can do without sliding into that cut."

"Why would anybody let their driveway get like that?"

"I don't give a damn about their driveway. What I'm interested in is their phone."

"If they've got one," she said.

"Everybody has a phone these days. Stop being so cynical."

"Everybody has one in their *car* these days," she sniped, "except you." Her chin was thrust out and a little to the side. She was always cute when she was angry.

"And you."

"You're the one driving. You're supposed to have the phone."

"I've already—"

"I know. You dropped it in the toilet."

"Shit happens."

"In the *toilet*, just like the rest of your miserable life."

I turned to study the depth of the ditch beside us. "Just shut up about the cell phone. You could have brought one. We've got other things to worry about."

"You don't . . . ," she started. Then: "By the way, there is no *we* anymore. Did you forget again?"

"Yeah. I forgot again."

"Well *don't*. I'm me and you're you. There is no *we* anymore."

"Is that as plain as you can make it?"

"You don't know that anybody lives here," she said. "I don't see any signs of life, and I don't see any lights. There ought to be lights already, at this hour. The place doesn't *look* lived in. Put your damned glasses on so you can see the place, Tommy. This driveway hasn't been used in forever, no tracks along the shoulder here, and surely whoever lives in that place—if anybody does—doesn't drive *that*." She pointed to an old rusty green truck parked beneath a lean-to at one end of the building. I couldn't tell for certain, but it looked as if the far hind wheel rested on boards. Something had roosted on the cab and left long chalky streaks down the sides and back.

I couldn't see much detail without my glasses, so I took them out and slowly wiped them on my shirtsleeve, then put them on and looked past the building. "That's a pasture behind it," I pointed out. "Look at how the grass has been eaten down beyond that fence. It's some kind of farm or ranch."

"That building looks more like a barn than a house," she said, "maybe a place where they keep feed for animals. Or maybe the animals themselves."

"Well, maybe the animals have got a phone."

"Har, har."

I took my glasses off and put them back in my pocket and faced her. "Look, Annie, I don't need my glasses to tell that it's the first spot we've come across in miles and miles that doesn't have trees growing up to and over the road. We can't keep creeping along on that spare. It'll be full dark soon, and if we don't get help, we're going to be stuck out here. Somebody's *got* to live here."

She studied the little clearing. "This place is downright spooky, Tommy. I don't like it. Why don't we limp on a little while longer? There must be something farther on."

"What happened to your enthusiasm of a few minutes ago? Where's the 'I closed my eyes and wished for a miracle and it happened'?"

"I take it back," she said. "It's like most things that look good at first. When you get a chance to consider them more closely, they turn out disappointing. Sort of like most men I've known."

"Let up," I said.

"Let's go on."

"Annie, how long has it been since we saw any building at all that looked habitable?"

She kept her head turned away from me, toward the trees. "At the speed we've been going, we couldn't have covered more than eight or ten miles, and I didn't see any houses *or* trailers that looked like they had people in them. Frankly, I haven't seen anything the whole trip that *I* would live in."

She took the map off the dash and unfolded it, studied it a few seconds, then thrust her finger down. "Look here, captain." She was pointing to a large green area. "You have plopped us down in the middle of a national forest. A *national forest!* Do people live in national forests?"

I laughed. "Of course they do. It just means—"

"But what *kind* of people? Have you noticed that the houses or trailers or whatever the hell they are out in here don't look much different from those dumpsters we saw back there? *Everything* is a dump. *East Texas* is a dump, and I hate it with a passion. At least farther west you can see the sky. Damn it, come to think of it, I hate *all* of Texas with a passion. Texas reminds me of you."

"Thank you, kind person." I squared in the seat to face her. "The fact is, you hate *everything*, but not with a *passion*. It's more like vile, cold, bloodless reptilian disdain, contempt, whatever word you want to use, and it's the very worst kind of hatred, because there's no antidote for it and no cure. You're consumed by it to your icy core."

"And you are just an ordinary, very typical male asshole." She turned to look behind us, then down the road ahead. "Tommy," she said quietly, "I say we go on and try to find a safe place before it's pitch dark."

"We're not out for real estate, damn it, Annie, and even if this were an exotic Hilton, with palms and a pool and little men in white running around serving pink drinks with umbrellas, *you'd* bitch about it."

"Put your glasses on again, Tommy, and *really* look at the place. This is about as far from a Hilton as you can get. It looks more like a junkyard. And I'll tell you something for sure."

"What's that?"

"No *woman* lives there. There's not a flower or identifiable shrub around that house or barn or whatever it is."

"I see some kind of shrub." A small green bush with a smattering of yellowed leaves grew very near the doorway.

"The operative word is *identifiable*, Tommy. That doesn't look like any shrub I know anything about. No rosebushes, no vines climbing up the walls. Nothing."

"I don't care if there are four redneck *men* living there, growing nothing but mildew. All we need is to use a *phone*. Now, I say I get out here and take a shot at it. If nobody's home or nobody lives here, then I'll try to drive a little farther. But if that little popcorn-fart spare blows, we'll likely never see civilization again. We can just sit here in the car and the vines and woods will eventually swallow us up and someday a road crew'd find our bones, and if we get out and try our luck thumbing on the highway, wolves will get us, or rednecks, or a logtruck will run us down."

"More good cheer. And another reference to rednecks and logtrucks. Thanks." She turned in her seat and looked again down the road in the direction we had come from. "We could just wait here for someone to come along. Surely somebody lives back in here, somebody who drives a vehicle. I mean, this damned highway is supposed to have *traffic* on it. That's what highways are *for*. We could flash the lights at them. Three times, you know, like an SOS, let'm know we're in trouble."

"Should you be using *we*?"

"Oh, go to hell!"

"By the way, Annie, exactly how many vehicles would you say we've passed or been passed by in the last hour?"

She sat a few seconds and thought. "Two logtrucks and a pickup. A blue logtruck and a red one. The blue one had pine logs on it and the red one had some kind of hardwood, probably oak."

"Both had pines."

"Bullshit. I'll bet you didn't even notice what color they were."

"The logs?"

"No. The damned *trucks*."

"Neither did you," I said.

"Did too. Blue and red. I just said so."

"I doubt it."

"So what color were *they*?"

"I don't give a God—"

"I don't mean the trucks. I mean the drivers. Blacks or whites driving?"

"Yes," I said.

"That's not an answer."

"Sure it is. It was blacks or whites."

"Could have been Hispanics, or Orientals."

"Maybe," I said, "but—"

"Black guys driving both, rap blaring from the blue one. No antenna on the red one, and I doubt that a tape deck or CD player'd last long on those logging roads."

"Just shut up about it, Annie."

"Two redneck men were in the pickup, with a child between them. A little girl, blond hair with long bangs. A gun on a rack behind the seat. It was a two-tone blue Ford F-250 with half the grill missing, a rusty home—or *trailer*—air conditioner in the bed and a big black and brown dog on top of it—the air conditioner, not the truck. Maybe a rottweiler, but because of a little white spot on his left front leg I'd bet it was mixed-blood. Texas plates on all three trucks. No inspection sticker on the blue logtruck. What else would you like to know? Like what caliber the gun was?"

"Now *you're* the one talking about rednecks and logtrucks. And I've got no way of checking to see whether you're lying or not about what you think you saw. Lighten up, Annie. You don't have to constantly remind me that you've got your attention on everything but me. I know you don't want to be here."

"I don't want to be *anywhere* with you. By the way"—she looked down the darkening road behind us again—"I wonder where those people in the pickup were from. Surely they live out here somewhere."

"Or they were going home in the other direction. And let me remind you that you didn't *have* to come."

"Don't start that crap. I will not go through it again. You exercised your little extortion play and I'm here. I don't like it, and I won't like it until I'm back in Shreveport Sunday. Now, how about trying to get us out of this mess before there's no light left?"

"I thought you wanted to wait until someone comes along."

"Surely someone will. I mean, Tommy, it is a frigging *highway*, with concrete and signs. It's where people *drive*. The concrete starts at a town and ends at a town, and people drive vehicles along it. It's what they're *for*."

"Asphalt."

"What?" She stared at me through her sunshades.

"The highway's made out of *asphalt*. How's that for observation? And I can *prove* it."

She slammed the dash. "I don't give a good Goddamn whether it's made out of concrete or asphalt or peanut butter or yellow bricks or that gluey sawdust they roll corny-dogs in—people *drive* on it. Somebody has to come along it sooner or later."

"Well, do you want me to get out and stand there with your scarf to wave someone down, or should I sit in the car or—"

"I don't care how you get their attention," she said. "Throw yourself in front of them if you have to. Just get somebody to *stop*. Or drive on. I don't give a damn what you do—just do *something*."

"These people out here would probably just run right over me, then say, 'Wonder what that bump was back yonder?' and go on. I think I'd rather flash the lights at them if they're coming from the south and hop out and lean around from in front of the car if they're coming from behind us. But I'll bet you anything that nobody'll stop, even if they do come along."

"Do you want me to get out and do the stopping, Tommy? Maybe I could loosen this blouse up some, undo three or four buttons, or slip on a dress and show some thigh. . . . I've got a short bright-green one back there in the trunk that would do the trick. Ooooh, it sure worked on a guy I was out with a few nights ago."

"Who cares about you and your dates? If you got out there, either we'd get a couple of redneck guys, who'd just snatch you up and take you off, leaving me here with the car, or a redneck woman, who'd be jealous and run over you. I'd better do it."

"If the guys looked pretty good, like that one in the gray T-shirt at the Dairy Queen back there, I might just let myself be taken. I don't see anything wrong with leaving you out here for the wolves."

"Let's get serious about this thing, Annie. What if we wait for somebody to come along and nobody does—or nobody stops—in the next thirty minutes or so, which is about all the light we have left? We're going to be stuck out here."

"Eventually Jane and Tony would send somebody for us."

I dropped my head forward onto the steering wheel. "Annie, I didn't tell Jane exactly when we would get there, just sometime early evening, probably around dark, and they would expect us to come down 59. They've got enough on their minds without worrying about when we're going to get there. And even if they did get worried and send somebody to try and find us, how the hell would they know to look out *here*?"

"There you go with that *us* stuff again," she seethed. "*You* are the one who did all the arranging, *you* are the one who didn't stick to the regular highway, *you* are the one who decided on this colorful route. There it is. Look right there." She tapped on the windshield, her finger pointing to the little map drawn in the grime of the hood by the service station attendant back in Lufkin. "*You* are the one who refused to use my map and couldn't follow his and *you* are the one who ran over whatever the hell it was that blew out the tire. *You* are the one who didn't bring a phone. *We* are somewhere on that snaky-looking road on the hood, broke down and lost, and not God Himself will be able to find us in this wilderness in another half hour. And *I* didn't have a bloody damned thing to do with it. I tried to get you to go on down 59, but *noooo. . . ."*

Her eyes were burning at me through the sunshades. "What kind of damned fool tries to follow a map drawn on the hood of a car by a mouth-breather who still sweeps off aprons at service stations at thirty-five or forty or however the hell old he was—somewhere between thirty and eighty, I think we could safely say—and hasn't washed his hair in weeks and doesn't have as many teeth as he has fingers? He didn't have enough sense to tell you the number of the highway, for God's sake, Tommy—'Just foller the signs to Trinity,' he said. Sounds like some religious message you'd find nailed up on a tree out here in God's country, right under *Jesus Saves. Foller the road to Trinity for Salvation.* According to this *paper* map here—"

"You know, he's exactly the kind who'd come along and pick you up if you got out there to flag somebody down, and exactly what you'd deserve if you were fool enough to try to do it. How'd you like to run off with *him*?"

"Well, he could handle a *broom*. Might be handy to have around. Bet he keeps his place tidier than yours."

"His *place* is probably one of those dumpsters we passed or one of the trailers earlier, which didn't look any better than the dumpsters." I pointed back out to the tracing on the hood. "I thought he was clear enough with his directions. And he *did* label 94 on the hood."

She smacked the map. "All I know is that we are *lost* in a national forest. *For-est*, Tommy. Think of that word. *For-est*. Woods. Deep, dark, and getting-darker-by-the-minute *woods*. Now, if you can get that tire fixed somewhere, we can weave our way out of here, if you'll follow *my* directions. When we hit 2262, we can turn left and go on over to 59—and we should come out well south of that roadwork on 59—"

"Which is exactly what I told you we were going to do."

"—or turn right and hit 287, which will lead us back to 94, the highway that we're supposed to still be on."

"The bloody hell with 94," I said. "When we get up and moving on four good tires, we're going over to 59 and heading south."

She slapped the map again. "Look, it is getting *dark* and I am starving to death. I've had nothing but that little milkshake back in Nacogdoches. Tommy, you'd better get us out of this mess fast."

"Come on, Annie, ease up."

"Ease up, hell. I shouldn't even be in the same state with you, much less in the same car." I could feel her eyes glaring at me. "And why don't you carry a regular kind of spare, one that you can *drive* on?"

"It's what came with the car."

"Hooray," she said. "Detroit saves a dime and we get swallowed up in the Big Thicket. I just wonder how many people have disappeared forever because of one of those tacky little spares."

I slipped on my glasses and pointed to the big green blob on her map. "This is part of the Davy Crockett National Forest. The Big Thicket is farther east."

"I really don't care about the names of East Texas wilderness areas, Tommy. All of East Texas is a wilderness area to me, a *big thicket*, even parts of downtown Houston. What I do know is that we are in the middle of a jungle, a wilderness—call it what you will. And we are not *sightseeing*." She tried to fold the map, got it wrong, then tried again, and finally tossed it onto the dash, where it lay flared open.

"You didn't fold that right."

"I may not be able to fold one," she snapped, "but I can sure as hell *follow* one."

I removed my glasses and slipped them into my pocket. "Take your shades off—the sun's down."

"I'll take them off when I get good and ready. Now why don't you try to figure out how to get us out of this mess that *you* got us in? If you don't think that waiting for someone to come along is the best thing to do, and you are determined not to drive on down the road, then march yourself up there to that house or barn, or whatever the hell it is, and see whether anybody lives there."

I looked ahead past the clearing and saw nothing but a tunnel of trees and through the rearview mirror the closing dark. I wanted to reach out and pat her hand and tell her that things would be fine, but my wife was just any other stranger now, as if I had picked her up at a truck stop, only a pick-up would have been friendlier.

"Maybe a highway patrolman will drive by," I suggested.

She snorted. "Get *real*. They don't even know this trail is out here. What would they patrol out here for? There is nobody for one to catch and ticket." She yanked the map off the dash, opened it, and flattened it on her lap.

"Annie."

"Look here, Tommy." She jabbed at the map with her forefinger. "You can barely *see* this road on the map. I had to squint to make the number out. Now, 357 connects Lennard and Apple Springs and no-damned-where-at-all, as if those towns were any-damned-where-at-all. They aren't even *towns*, just crossroads where there may or may not even be a dumpster. And a dumpster does not a town make. Then 357 runs into 2262, which connects no-damned-where-at-all to no-damned-where-at-all. I don't even know why these roads are in here, unless it's for logtrucks. No highway patrolman has been in these parts since God *invented* the highway patrol or Texas Department of Public Safety, or whatever they call themselves. Highway *petroleums* is what Goober back there called them." Her face was a fierce red.

I nodded toward the white building. "I've made up my mind. We're not waiting in the car for someone to come along, highway patrolman or redneck or whatever, and neither one of us is going to stand on the road to flag anybody down. And I'm not moving this car another inch. I'm going to go up to that house to use the telephone while I can still see how to get over there without breaking a damned leg in that moat."

"Fine, then. Just *do it*. Get out and go see whether you can use their phone. It's getting *dark*, for God's sake, Tommy. We don't want to get stuck out here in this wilderness after dark. And start the car. It's hot in here."

"Roll down the window."

"Not on your life. Not out here."

I cranked the car and turned the air conditioner fan on high. "There you are. Now cool down. Adjust it to suit yourself."

Staring out across the road toward the darkening wall of trees that came right up to the edge of the asphalt, she looked like a frightened child with the scarf still pulled tight over her hair. Beside her left ear a little trickle of blond spilled from under the edge.

"You sit tight," I said. "I'll be right back."

"Just where the hell would I *go*?" I heard her say as I closed the door.

I motioned for her to lock the doors, then put my glasses on so that I could see the way and scrambled down and across the cut. A fine red silt had washed from the shoulder of the road and formed deep pools of mud along the outer edge of the drive-way—we were parked right in the middle of one of them—then overflowed into the ditch. At the bottom the goo came up over the edge of my shoes, and I almost lost my left one trying to pull my right foot free. When I had managed to scramble up the other side, my feet sank into the thick layer of pea gravel that coated the drive, and little pebbles stuck to the mud on the bottoms and sides of my shoes. I moved in slow motion, like a moonwalker in weighted boots.

I shook one foot, then the other, but the pebbles still clung. "Damn!" My feet felt like lead. I must have looked like a fool to her. I certainly felt like one. Well, hell, there was certainly no way I could be heroic in her eyes. I'd lost that chance a long time ago. And I doubted she would be amused.

I clumped down the drive and squared myself to the doorway, leaned and knocked three times on the frame, waited a few seconds, then knocked again, this time more vigorously. I stepped back and looked for signs of life. Nothing. So leaning forward, supporting myself with my left hand on the door frame, I hammered with my right fist on the door itself until my hand hurt. The damned thing must have been solid wood, three inches thick, or steel. I could hear the booming echo in the room behind it.

The wind was whistling around the corners of the building and moving in waves across the high grass that grew right up to the edge of the gravel drive. As gusts rode the grass down on the highway side of a fence that joined the back side of the lean-to, a stretch perhaps thirty or forty feet wide, pieces of junk bobbed up like flotsam of a wrecked ship rising to the surface of some forgotten sea—an old refrigerator and hot-water heater, a couch, a set of bedsprings, two dining chairs with red plastic cushions, some large odd shapes I couldn't make out. Certainly enough stuff out there to furnish a house. Colorful pieces of paper and cardboard were scattered everywhere, cans, little cartons from fast-food places. There was no way to imagine how much stuff lay beneath the surface.

I took off my glasses and burnished them with my handkerchief. "Damn, what a dump," I said quietly to myself. I put the glasses on again. Annie was right about the little shrub growing by the door—it didn't look like anything I'd ever seen either. It was thorny as hell though. Some sort of quince maybe.

On the other side of the fence and as far down the slope toward the woods as I could see, the grass seemed to have been gnawed right down to the earth itself, and I saw what looked like the inverted hood of a car with some kind of big birds around it, but it was too far and too dark for me to be certain what I was seeing. Chickens or turkeys. Maybe even buzzards. I had noticed some outbuildings as I approached the house but paid no attention to them.

Up close now, I could see the heavy coats of whitewash on the front of the building, so thick that the paint-filled mortar joints were smoothed out almost level with the concrete blocks, as if some child had made a crude cake and plastered it with icing. Old settling cracks angled out from the top of the door and from above and below the window frames, stairstepping where they followed the joints. The windows, the kind that open with little handles that operate a screw drive and swing out from butt hinges, were caked with paint and apparently hadn't been opened in years. They had straps of steel across them, riveted to form latticed burglar bars, and behind them hung cheap print curtains like the sort of thing country women used to get feed in and after the feed was gone made dresses and tablecloths from.

I lurched to the nearest window and tried to look in, but it was dark inside and the curtains were tight, so I went back and hammered the door again, this time with my left fist, and yelled the traditional "*Hello. Anybody home?*"

I heard something. A lock clicked, the knob rotated, and the heavy old door creaked open until the little security chain at eye level jerked tight. In the evening light I could see nothing beyond the door frame.

"Uh," I spoke to the dark crack, "howdy, there. Sorry to disturb you, but we—I've got a problem here." I pointed toward the car. "Had a blowout—"

"Who *are* you?" The voice was low and raspy, vaguely female, like that of a woman hardened into her late years. She sounded like she needed to cough.

"Just a traveler. We've got a problem."

"Who's *we*? You got a mouse in yer pocket?"

"My wife and I. She's in the car." I pointed.

"What's yer name?" the voice insisted.

"Tommy. Tommy Carmack."

"What you want?"

"Well, like I say, I've got a problem. I need to use your phone." I could see nothing of the woman who was talking. "I need to call my auto club, get somebody to come out here and bring me a tire."

"How come you ain't got one of them portable telephones?"

"I—it's back home. Got a bad battery."

"Is anybody with you?"

"I told you, my wife. She's in the car." I turned and pointed again.

"Can't tell much about her from here."

I squinted into the dark crack of the doorway but still couldn't make anything out. The sun lay in the woods down the slope behind the old building, and what afterglow there was shone on the trees behind and afforded no penetration of the gloom before me. There was no light on in the room—whoever was talking might just as well have been in another world.

I tried to scrape off my shoes but imbedded more pea gravel in the red mud that coated them.

"That mud's real sticky," I said.

"Stay out of it myself."

"Uh, ma'am, suppose I could use your phone?"

The only answer that came back was some sort of shuffling on the floor, like a large animal moving.

"Ma'am?" I leaned toward the dark crack and placed an open hand on the door. "I'll kick my shoes off, come in there in just my socks, if that's what's bothering you. I know you don't want this mud on your floor."

"I can't tell nothin' about whoever's out there."

I nodded toward the car, settled beside the old washed-out scar like a crippled beast on its left front, where the absurd little spare just barely held the bumper off the ground. I could see Annie's pale face against the dark interior—she sat stiff and her sunshades stared straight ahead.

"My wife," I said, still looking at the tilted car. "That's just my wife."

"Tell'r to get out and come on up here."

"To tell the truth," I said, "she's pretty tired and disgusted with things. We're from Shreveport. Been a long trip. All I want to do is—"

"Shrevesport?"

"Shreveport, yes'm."

"Louisiana?"

"Yes'm." *Shreveport where the hell else?*

"Where you headin' to?"

"We're uh—we're going to Houston."

"Houston?"

"Yes'm." Then I added, "Texas."

"I know where Houston's at," she said. "Y'all must not though. What're you doin' back in here?"

"Ma'am?"

"This ain't the way to Houston. S'posed t'go 59. That's the way to Houston. Any fool ort to know that."

"We took a back way."

"I rekkin you did." A cackle came from the dark crack. "About as back a way as there is. Shrevesport to Houston. Lordy. . . ."

"A guy in Lufkin told us which way to go. Drew us a map on the hood of the car." I pointed.

"Well, he's out of his skull to send you back in here. That or you ain't follered his map and done got yerself lost. This ain't no way to Houston." She spat through the crack in the door. "Eventually you'd get there, I rekkin, but you'd be a sight older when you did. Better turn around and head back out to 94 and head east, hit 59 at Lufkin, or go on down till this road dead-ends and turn left and it'll lead you over to 59."

"Ma'am," I said, "I'd *love* to turn around and drive out of here, but we are broken down." I pointed to the car again. "Can't you see how we're down on the left front? I've got one of those little temporary spares on, and it's low on air, and I'm afraid we—" I sighed and spread my hands. "Look, it's getting dark. All I want to do is use your phone, have someone from Lufkin to come out here and get us up and going."

"Tell'r to get out."

"Ma'am?"

"Tell yer lady to get out and come on up here."

"I told you—"

The voice came back quick and harsh: "She don't get out, you ain't comin' in. Ain't no man comin' in here without his woman is with him. Tell'r to come on up here." The door had not moved.

"Ma'am," I tried again. "Your telephone, ma'am. I'd just like to use your *telephone*. To call my auto club."

"Like I said, she don't get out, you don't get in. Ain't that simple enough for you? Did I go too fast?"

It was the kind of voice I had heard before, from aging women working in smoke-filled truck stops, generally smokers themselves, whose every sentence seems designed to be punctuated with a cough, though this woman did not cough. I kept wanting her to, to clear the thickness from her throat.

I shrugged my shoulders. "OK, OK, I'll go and ask her. But she's not going to be happy about that mud." I pointed to my shoes.

"I ain't happy about it neither," she said, "but I live with it. Now tell'r to get out and come on up here."

I shrugged again. "OK, I'll be right back."

I clumped to the car, walking around a rectangle of concrete from which rusty pipes stuck, this time skirting the deeper, wider part of the gash, leaping across the narrower end. Annie's sunshades followed my progress.

Her window was halfway down. The engine was still running. "Well, what did you find out? It took you long enough."

"Nothing much. There's some old woman in there. That's all I know for sure."

"What'd you do, try to sell her a policy, or proposition her? I thought you'd forgotten about me."

"She asked me some questions."

"What kind of questions?"

"Just questions, Annie. I'm a stranger."

"You sure are. You've been strange a long time. Will she let you use the phone?"

"I don't know."

"What do you mean you don't know? What did she say? You talked to her. What did she *say*?"

"She wants you to get out and come on up to the house."

Annie nodded toward the building. "She calls that a *house?* This place looks like something out of Erskine Caldwell. *Tobacco Road* or *God's Half Acre.*"

"*God's* Little *Acre,*" I corrected her. "*Little,* not *half.*"

"Whatever," she said. "I'm no judge of size, but I damned sure know a white-trash hovel when I see one. You've got your glasses on. Look at it."

"I've already looked at it," I said.

But I turned and studied the place closely for the first time from her perspective. It was obviously an old converted country store, one story and flat roofed, perhaps sixty feet in length, the same in depth, with a shed at one end, beneath which the old pickup was parked. Besides the steel-latticed windows in front, at the end I could see one small window up high, barred like those you might see on old jails in country towns, the kind cowboys would tie ropes to and jerk out with their horses to help a friend escape.

There was no way to determine when the structure had been painted last, though it had to have been ages ago. The roof was flat, with pieces of metal flashing lapping over the walls, and long dark streaks from rainwater reached all the way to the ground. Even in the failing light I could see faint lettering beneath the paint over the door: *Autrey's Grocery.* There was another line below it, but the paint was too thick for me to make it out.

The sorry land, clumped with brush and occasional small trees, sloped back to a wall of woods, perhaps two hundred yards distant, that transcribed an arc, as if someone had clamped a half-moon cookie cutter down in the forest and chopped out a clearing. A barbed wire fence, with hogwire stretched along the lower three strands, came up to the corner of the store on the end that I could see and joined the back of the lean-to. Two rusty barrels for trash incineration sat just behind the building, and an old paintless barn slouched halfway down the slope, flanked by a couple of smaller weathered outbuildings. Way down by the woods I could see some sort of dark animals with their mouths to the ground, though I couldn't imagine that they were finding much forage. The stretch of grass between the fence and the highway was tall and lush and littered with trash, but beyond the fence the grass was clipped like some mowing machine, set to its lowest cut, had run across it. This wasn't a farm or a ranch or even a decent homestead. I didn't know what it was. But surely whoever lived there had a telephone.

I leaned my hands on the roof of the car. "It was a store and service station at one time. Autrey's Grocery, the painted-over sign says." I pointed to the concrete island. "That's where the gas pumps were."

"Who cares where the gas pumps *were? Were* doesn't count. We *were* in Shreveport earlier today, but we're not now. Besides, we don't need gas." She pulled the knot on her scarf tighter. "All we need is a damned phone. And I don't see why I've got to get out."

"I guess she just wants to meet you," I said. "Maybe she hasn't seen another woman to talk to in a while. Maybe—"

"Tommy, I am in no mood to socialize."

"Why the hell can't you be pleasant for once?"

"Because I'm lost in a jungle, because I am hungry, and because *you're* here! And I'm not getting out of this car. If she wants to meet me, she can come out here. I'm not walking in that mud."

"Annie, she was adamant—if you don't go up there, she won't let me in to use the Goddamned phone."

"That's crap, Tommy."

"Annie, she's an old woman, apparently by herself, and she's afraid to let a strange man in to use her phone. If his woman's along, she'll feel more comfortable about it. I can understand that. Why don't you try seeing it from her perspective?"

She burned at me through the shades. "I am not your *woman*."

"Well, I told her you were. *Are*. That you're my wife. Now come on and get out of the car, Annie."

I grabbed the handle and pulled, but she'd kept the door locked. "Damn it, Annie. Come on. She's watching us." I let the handle go. "If I didn't want you to get out of the car, you'd bust your ass getting out."

She crossed her arms. "You might have something *there*."

"Annie, please. Let's pull together on this one. It's almost dark. Neither of us has had any food. . . . Look out there." I pointed to the wall of woods across the road. "And that old woman's probably beginning to wonder whether you're my wife or not."

She turned and looked at the woods again, then back at me. "Well, *I* sure as hell don't have to wonder about it." She reached and snatched her purse from the backseat. "All right, I'll go, damn it."

"Uh, do you need to fix your face first or something?"

She glared at me. I could tell, though I couldn't see her eyes.

I pointed at the purse. "I'm talking about the purse. Why do you need the purse?"

"I'm not leaving my purse out here." She opened the door and swung her legs out but stopped short of dropping her feet into the thick red mud. She swept her legs back into the car.

"Tommy, how about looking in the trunk in my carry-on bag and getting my old sneakers?"

"I'll be Goddamned if I'm going into that trunk for sneakers. If I open it for anything, it'll be for a shot of JD. I could use a drink."

"Don't you dare touch that stuff," she said. "If she smells whiskey on you, she sure as hell won't let us in."

What I wouldn't have given for a deep, searing shot of straight JD on my empty stomach. It would have been like a jolt of electricity firing through my veins. Two shots and I wouldn't have cared where we were. Three and I'd have forgotten it had been three years since I'd touched my wife.

"Then I'm not going into the trunk," I said. "I got my good shoes muddy and you can get *yours* muddy. We can wash them off later." I smiled and held out my arms. "Would you like me to carry you?"

"No thanks." She swung her legs back out and put her feet down into the mud. "Asshole."

"Annie."

"What?"

"You notice anything odd about this scene?"

"Yeah. I notice lots of things odd about it. For one thing, I shouldn't be in it."

"That's not what I'm talking about. The engine's still running. How about rolling up your window, turning the Goddamned car off and locking it, and giving me the keys?"

"Why, you worried about somebody *stealing* it?" She raised her window and leaned back on the seat, killed the engine, and yanked the keys out. She slapped them into my hand and swung her legs out again.

"Watch the mud," I said.

She glared at me again with her face. I could just imagine what her eyes looked like behind those dark lenses. "Jesus, what a mess." She stood up and her feet sank until the mud all but covered her little black flats.

"Oh, God, Tommy, look at that."

"You'll get over it. The mud'll wash off. Now come on. And take those damned sunshades off. It's too dark to go on looking cool." I reached to assist her, but she shoved my arm away.

"Just leave me alone." She slammed the door and tiptoed around the front of the car.

"Did you lock it?"

"Yes."

"Why are you *tiptoeing*? The mud's already covered your shoes."

"Jesus Christ." She stood pointing at her feet. "Look at this stuff. These shoes are brand new! Eighty bucks. The leather'll be *ruined*."

"As far as I am concerned, your shoes are a low-priority item right now. You want me to help you across this?" I pointed to the cut in front of her. "Or you can go out there around the shallower end."

"No. My shoes are already covered, so I'll just slog on across right here."

"Fine, go the hell on. Hope you sink to your knees."

She stood teetering at the edge of the gash looking over at the building, craning her neck. "Do you think there're dogs here?"

"How do I know whether she's got dogs or not? I didn't see one or hear one. Usually if they have dogs, they're the first thing you hear. A dog would be a fool to tangle with you, though, the mood you're in."

"Well, I don't want to get across the Grand Canyon and then have a couple of hounds tear my legs off before I can get back to the car."

I nodded toward the house and the narrow crack in the door. "The woman is right there watching us. Surely to God she's not going to let any dogs eat us. Now, will you relax and go on across?"

She rolled her jeans up a couple of folds, balanced like a skier, and slid down one side of the cut. When she started up the other, she slipped and fell with one open hand onto the mud. She protected her purse with the other arm, clutched it to her chest the way she would a baby. Her pretty little ass was high in the air.

"God-*damn*, I hate this." She righted herself, looked at her mud-caked hand and splattered jeans, and climbed out the other side. When she turned to wait for me, her face was red with anger. She looked like a little girl in a home movie who's been caught on film doing something ungraceful. I wanted to laugh at her, but I didn't. It had been so damned long since she'd done anything to make me laugh that I knew she wouldn't understand, so I just thought briefly of the time right after we were first married when she knocked one of those enormous theater Cokes off onto her chest and lap, almost a quart of the syrupy stuff, and how we had snickered about it the rest of the movie, then made love in the car in the driveway when we got home. I could still remember the feel of that sticky Coke between our bellies.

Then, again, she looked pathetic. Here was a woman I had loved deeply for over eight years before things fell apart, a woman still as beautiful as she ever was, maybe more now that the years had put a bit more character in her face, as they say. In the middle of a deep forest in East Texas going somewhere with a man she didn't love anymore—in fact, a man she hated now more than ever for stupidly getting her into this mess. She looked frightened and helpless in her rolled-up jeans and gingham blouse and muddy shoes, her sunglasses and scarf, a purse hugged to her chest like a baby, her mud-coated hand held out in appeal. She looked like a helpless little pixie.

"What are you looking at?" she whispered harshly. "Would you please come on?" She had her back to the building.

"I'm watching that big black dog behind you."

She spun her head and stepped back toward the cut.

"Just joking."

"You sonofabitch!"

I eased down the slope and slogged across the ditch. When I clambered out and reached to take her arm, she shook loose and walked ahead of me, stopping several feet short of the cracked door. Little pebbles completely coated her shoes. They looked like those red candied apples rolled in nut chips that you buy at a county fair.

"Like your shoes," I whispered, stepping in front of her. "They go well with your scarf."

"Fuck you," she snarled out of the side of her mouth.

"Maybe later," I whispered and leaned and knocked and squinted into the dark opening. "Ma'am, I'm back."

There was no sound from the doorway, so I gestured toward Annie, who stood mortared to the driveway behind me.

"This is my wife, ma'am. OK?"

Still no sound.

"Jesus, Tommy," Annie whispered. "Are you sure you talked to somebody?"

I ignored her. "Ma'am, may we use your phone?"

"It take'n you long enough to get back over here," the voice from the doorway said. "Bring'r on up a little closer. It's gettin' dark and I cain't make'r out."

The afterglow was almost gone now, and it was indeed getting dark, so I reached and grabbed Annie's arm and pulled her up beside me. She had taken a tissue from her purse and wiped her hand clean. She put the tissue back into her purse.

"This is my wife, Annie, OK?"

A gravelly laugh came from the doorway. "Annie Oakley?"

"No ma'am, her name—"

She cackled. "Got yer gun with you, Annie?"

"Sweet Jesus," Annie said aloud. "My name is—"

"Her name is Annie . . . *Ann*. I call her Annie. I just said OK after. . . ." I felt like I was talking into a cave. My voice echoed back.

"Annie Ann or Annie Oakley? Which is it? And what she s'posed to be, a movie star?"

"Ma'am?" I asked.

"Them sunglasses. And thatere bandanner over her hair. And a name like Annie Oakley. She looks like she come out of some kind of movie. A cowboy movie. Y'ain't armed, are you, Annie Oakley?"

"No." Annie was not amused. Her face was aimed at the doorway, but I could not tell where her eyes were looking. Her jaw was clenched, her lips drawn in a straight, tight line.

"No ma'am. Annie—just *Annie*—likes to travel looking like this. I think it's an image thing."

I could feel the heat rising higher as we stood in silence before the door. For a few seconds there was no reply from the old woman, but she was mumbling something. Then a light blazed on above my head and another came on at each corner of the building, trapping us in a crossfire of brilliance.

The voice came harsh and loud: "Now, Mr. Tommy whoever you are and Miss Annie Oakley—"

"My name is not Annie Oakley." She spoke defiantly into the glare, like someone addressing the sun.

"Well, whatever yer name is, I want y'all to lace yer fingers together, both of you, and put yer hands on top of yer heads."

I just stood there.

"What—" Annie had her head cocked to the side, still with those damned sunglasses on.

"Do it! Then get on yer knees."

"Ma'am?" I leaned and squinted toward the doorway.

"Now, you listen here, lady—" Annie started. "I am not. . . ."

The door opened a little wider and I saw something long and dark edge out, as big as the end of a broom handle. "Folks, you two ain't on yer knees time I count three, yer gon' be real sorry.

You look at what's sticking thoo this here door and you'll see it's the barrel of a mighty big pistol. Now, *down!*"

I just stood there frozen, with my mouth open—I could imagine Annie in the same pose.

"I tol' you to get down on yer knees. *Now!* One. Two. *Three.*"

Before the word *three* was out of the old woman's mouth, I had reached and grabbed Annie's blouse and yanked her down with me and we were kneeling in the gravel like supplicants. She offered no resistance, simply crumpled like clothes with the body removed.

How long we knelt in the gravel in silence staring at the dark opening, I cannot say, but it seemed forever. Nothing moved along the highway, nothing made a sound except for the razz of insects in the woods and somewhere far off a dog barking. High above us, zigzagging across the stars, were satellites carrying on the business of the civilized world, and a hundred miles in any direction there were movie theaters and restaurants, people just getting in from work, some already laughing and drinking and eating, making love, having a good time. There we were on our knees, strangers in a strange land, with our hands on our heads and an enormous pistol pointing at us. I wanted to look over at Annie, to tell her that all this would come right, but I didn't dare move or say a word. Scenes from the movie *Deliverance* kept flashing in my head.

The voice came back. "All right, big boy—usin' one hand at a time, empty yer pockets out on the ground there, and do it real slow, like cold syrups. And you stay on yer knees, both of you. Remember that this here .44 makes a hole the size of a dime goin' in, but it'll take off the back of yer skull on the way out. They holler-points. I bet Annie there can tell you about bullets, can't you, Cutie?"

Annie said nothing while with dreamlike slowness I removed the car keys and ChapStick and change from my pants pocket and laid them on the gravel before me.

"Everthang. Back pockets too." She bumped the barrel of the pistol on the side of the door for emphasis.

"Yes'm." I eased the wallet from my pocket and held it out toward her. "Can I keep my handkerchief?"

"No," the voice said. "Put it and the billfold in the pile and then turn yer pockets inside out." She motioned with the pistol.

"What in God's name—"

"You shut yer mouth, Annie Oakley. And you quit usin' the Lord's name in vain. I'll get to you d'rectly."

I laid the wallet and handkerchief beside the other stuff. "There. That's all I have. I swear."

"You *already* lyin' to me," she said. The gun barrel motioned to my shirt pocket, where my glasses case was, so I took the case out and laid it in the pile.

"Sorry," I said. "I didn't know that counted."

"Them pens too."

"Yes'm." I removed the two ballpoints and laid them across my handkerchief.

"That all you got?" the voice asked.

"Yes'm. That's everything."

"You sure?"

"Yes'm. Can I keep my glasses? And my watch?"

She pointed the pistol at my left-front pocket. "I don't guess them matters, but I tol' you to pull the pockets out, turn'm inside out. Now do it."

I looked at Annie, whose sunshades were fixed on the pistol, then reversed my pockets, one at a time.

"Look like you got little ears hangin' off of you, don't it?" the old woman asked. I still had not seen her face. "Like a Indian in from a war party, got ears hangin' off of him all over. Scalps and thangs."

"I'm glad you're entertained," I said.

"You shut yer smart mouth and reach and dump Annie Oakley's purse right there longside yer stuff."

"Woman—" Annie clutched her purse when I reached for it, so I gave it a tug. She held on. "This is *my* purse, old lady, and I don't have anything in it that could threaten you. Now, will you please just put that gun away and let us go on? We'll just drive off—"

"Don't give me a reason to kill you right here at my front door," the old woman said. "I can shoot you both right thoo the head and wouldn't no court in the land do a thang to me for killin' you. This is Texas and it's dark and I got a right to pertect my castle. Texas is real funny about people that comes in off the road messin' around yer place after dark. You turn that purse *aloose*."

"Yeah," I said quietly. "Texas is *real* funny."

"Why not just let us *leave*?" Annie still clutched the purse. She looked toward the car. "Please, lady, just let us get up and turn around and walk away from you and your . . . your *castle*."

"Ma'am," I said softly, "we'll just leave and not say a word to anyone about the pistol. It's just a mistake. We know that. It's dark, you're just frightened, you felt threatened."

The muzzle of the .44 inched farther through the door. I could see a hand now, an old pale, liver-splotched hand with horny fingers.

"I ain't scared of nothin', ain't *threatened* by nothin'," the voice said. "Not with this here .44 in my hand I ain't. Now dump that purse."

I snatched the purse from Annie, unzipped it, and emptied its contents in an arc in the gravel between me and the threshold: the soiled tissue, lipstick, keys, compact, brush and comb, coin purse, checkbook, credit-card folder, fingernail file, pens, breath mints, a pack of Spearmint, address book, a packet of tissue, paperclips and a lamp finial, a little plastic Ziploc bag full of coupons. Grocery coupons! How absurdly useless it all looked spread out there, trappings of another world. I could see strands of her blond hair interwoven in the bristles of her brush. *Two* tubes of lipstick, one the color she had on and one a couple of shades darker, a little jar of rouge. I hadn't seen what she carried in her purse for so long that for a few seconds I just stared at it.

"Shake it out good," the voice said. The hand motioned with the pistol. "Unzip them little pockets inside and shake it out agin."

"I will not stand for this," Annie seethed. "You cannot treat people like this."

"You want to bet yer skinny little butt on it? Now, big boy, I done tol' you to dump out them pockets."

"Let it ride, Annie." I unzipped the little inside pocket and held the purse up by a bottom corner—it was one of those fancy ones, a Coach, brown leather, nice and expensive—and shook it vigorously. Two little squares of folded notebook paper tumbled out, a ring case, then an open pack of gum, followed by a single flat condom packet with a picture of a man and woman holding hands and laughing on the front. I looked at Annie. She kept her face toward the gun.

"Jesus Christ." I threw the purse on the ground and slapped it against the door facing. "There now, by God, there's nothing else in it." Then to Annie: "Or do you have a whip and handcuffs in a separate compartment?"

"Watch yer mouth, young man," the old woman said. "We don't take the Lord's name in vain out here. And neither do you. I don't want to have to keep tellin' you." She angled the pistol barrel toward the little packet. "That what I thank it is?" She cackled and snorted. "Uh-huh, sho' nuff. Used to be just boys and men toted them thangs. Guess I been stuck out here so long I don't know what women's s'posed to carry these days."

"What now?" I asked.

She looked at Annie. "You totin' anythang on yer body, little lady?"

"Not a thing." Annie thrust her hands into her pockets and inverted them, front and back. "You want to frisk me?"

"You got a smart mouth too," the voice said. "Take that bandanner off of yer head. And them shades."

"What have *they* got to do with anything?"

"Annie, do as she says," I hissed. "Just take the Goddamned thing off your head, *now*. Or have you got rubbers hidden up there too?"

She flashed me a vicious look. She didn't seem at all innocent now.

The old woman cackled again. "Sounds like that he's got more sense than you got. Now do what he says and take them shades and that bandanner *off.*"

Annie hesitated, then raised her hands and unfastened the scarf and yanked it off. She wadded it up and threw it in the pile in front of us and snatched off her sunshades and they clacked onto the gravel.

"Anything else you want me to take off?"

"Watch yer tone, little lady. I'm in charge here and I'll let you know what I want you to do and when to do it."

"Cool it, Annie," I said.

"Arright," the old woman said, "spread out that bandanner and put all yer stuff in it and tie it up and hand it to me."

"Hers too?"

"Yeah, all of it, yers and hers. Just pile it up and tie it off and give it here."

"For what?" Annie asked. "What are you going to do with our stuff?"

"Just hush, Annie. We have to do what she says."

I spread the scarf out into a square and gathered Annie's things with mine, then heaped everything in the middle of it, pulled the corners together and tied them and held the bundle toward the crack in the doorway. Faster than a snake striking, a hand shot out and took the bundle, hefted it, pitched it into the dark room, then the hand came back and snatched the empty purse.

"Ma'am." When I spoke, the barrel fixed on me. "We're not armed, I assure you. This is all we're carrying. We're just a couple traveling and in trouble, and we need to use your telephone. But we'd just as soon be on our way, if it's all right with you."

Silence. Long, unearthly silence. I could hear Annie's shallow, fast breathing, sounds of night birds and insects in the darkening woods, and in my temples the throb of my heart, like a muffled war drum. I kept hoping for the whiz of tires on the highway, even the rumbling of a damned logtruck, anything, anyone.

"OK, take them filthy shoes off, both of you." The voice was steady, low, and firm. The door closed slightly, the safety chain rattled, and the door swung halfway open and remained there.

I looked at my mud-caked shoes, then at Annie's. She had compliantly pushed one flat off with the toe of her other shoe, but seemed uncertain how to work the other flat off without getting her fingers or other foot muddy. I reached my foot over and pried off the pebble-studded flat.

"Thanks," she said quietly.

I couldn't even see my laces for the mud. "Uh, have you got anything, a towel or something, I can wipe—"

"Just get them shoes off. They the least of yer worries."

I spread my hands and stared at where her face should be. "I'd like to, but—"

"Get them shoes off now and then crawl in here on all fours, slow, *real* slow."

"You mean," I asked the dark doorway, "you want us to *crawl* in there? On all fours? Like *animals*?" No answer came back. I turned and looked at Annie, whose hair had fallen over her face so that I could not see her eyes. She had dropped down and was waiting on hands and knees behind me, her face toward the ground.

"Tommy," she whispered through the curtain of hair, "what are we going to do? I can't go into that room."

I turned around and rose into a sitting position and wedged

my shoes off without bothering with the laces. "I don't see that we have any choice," I whispered. "All our stuff, including the car keys, is in that room now, and she's got an awfully big gun on us. We've got to do as she says. Just hold it together. We'll be all right."

"Tommy, I'm scared now. I'm really scared." Her fingers were dug into the pea gravel like someone clinging to the side of a mountain. She was trembling.

"Y'all shut up that talkin' and crawl in here. I'm a-losin' my patience." She flipped off the lights and we were in total darkness.

I dropped down on all fours and crept forward until I bumped the door, which swung on open with a creak, and crossed the threshold with my hands, then my knees. When I had reached what seemed to be a reasonable place to stop—though I had nothing whatsoever to base that judgment on in the dark room—I ceased crawling and felt Annie touch one of my feet. I could hear her rapid breathing, could feel her breath on my calves, where my pants legs had ridden up above my socks. And I heard more—could it be the old woman?—the inhaling and exhaling of ano-ther creature, almost an excited pant.

I finally said, "Lady, would you please turn on a light and let us get up? We're not here to do you any harm."

The voice came back dry and hard and close to my right ear. "You just stay down on all fours and don't you move muscle one when I turn it on. I'll have this gun on you. And Duke'll have a eye on you."

Then the light blazed, at first so intensely bright that I had to close my eyes and gradually open them to the details of the room. At an inner doorway the old woman stood—maybe seventy, maybe over eighty, so punished by whatever forces had dogged her life that her face looked like weathered stone—what I could see of it—where it stared coldly past the sight of the .44. Her left hand was sliding down the wall from the light switch. Beside her, his eyes fixed on mine, crouched an enormous black and silver dog.

"Well, sir, they don't look all that dangerous now, do they, Duke?" She leaned down and patted the dog's head. "You can set up, if you want to, but stay where yer at. You make a quick move and this gun or Duke one'll get you. He's pure-blood German shepherd, and I trained him to kill myself."

She was a short woman, skin snuff-colored like smoked meat, her build slight, and I marveled at how the tiny arm holding that revolver could manage such weight for so long. Her wizened face reflected years of savage East Texas sun and probably cigarette smoke, but the eye that studied us was bright, almost dancing, as if she were glad that finally someone had come in off the road, uninvited or not. Heavy straight gray hair draped across her head and fell over half her face, and when she spoke she moved her head from side to side, like a bird, hair swinging with the motion of her head. First one eye examined us, then the other.

When she spoke, I could see that her teeth were dark yellow, almost brown. The room smelled heavily of stale cigarette smoke.

She was dressed in an old sleeveless gray shift that draped loosely from her shoulders by wide straps. I could see the dark hair of her armpits. Though she was thin, she had no muscle tone at all—great rolls of flesh hung from her upper and lower arms, as if she had simply pulled her skin, two sizes too large, up over her skeleton and let it hang however it would. There was no ankle definition in her legs, which fell from the shift like thick cylinders of mottled marble. She wore house slippers with little roses on them.

I sat back and looked at Annie, still on all fours, but with her stark-white face lifted. I could read in it nothing but childlike terror and confusion. The light application of makeup I noticed earlier in the day seemed to have evaporated, leaving a half-dollar size trace of rouge on each cheek and lips as pale as the inside of her upper arm. The sunshades had left two angry-looking little indentations on either side of her nose and slight rocker-shaped depressions under her eyes. She had not taken them off all afternoon.

Jesus, I hadn't seen her face up close for so long. For a few seconds I stared at her, still incredibly lovely, almost untouched by time, as if she had simply shrugged off the last few years of stress that put streaks of gray in my hair and wrinkles around my eyes and mouth. Her hair was much shorter than I'd ever seen it, but still almost shoulder-length, the way it had been cut in early photographs. Her pale-blue eyes were wide with wonder as she took the place in, like a forest nymph trapped in a witch's hovel. When she swept her eyes my way, she seemed to look right through me.

We were in a large room, what once had obviously been the main part of the store. The ceiling was made of interlocking squares of decorative stamped metal, painted over so many times that details of the floral design were barely visible. Old Coca-Cola coolers, thickly coated with white paint, lined one wall, and above them hung calendars and cardboard advertisements of products that could not have been sold there in over thirty years: tires whose names I did not know, odd-sounding oils and gasolines, chewing gum and candy, snuff and cigarettes. The women in the ads wore clothes from decades before, and their men, with carefully coifed hair and most with thin mustaches, some with splendid hats, sported striped double-breasted suits. No calendar had a date later than the sixties.

The room was scattered with cheap furniture bearing the scars of years of use and obvious marring by a large animal allowed to roam freely and sprawl wherever he wished—an old couch, heavily soiled, against one wall, at its ends simple tables painted an ivory color by someone using a heavy-bristled brush, probably the same person who last whitewashed the building. In front of the couch lay an oval braided rug, shredded in dozens of places where apparently the dog had scratched, and on it sat a coffee table, very plain, made of dark wood and burdened with almanacs and farm journals. An ashtray, thick with ashes and littered with butts, sat on a stack of magazines, and our little bundle of property and Annie's purse lay at one end of the table.

In a corner a stainless steel beer barrel, the kind you rent for keg parties, stood with a simple plywood circle for a table surface, a bright-green ceramic lamp burning atop it. Plain board shelves were anchored to the concrete-block walls with angle-iron braces opposite the coolers, and on the shelves sat crude pots and bowls—natural clays, some painted blue or green—along with a variety of cheap vases, depression glass, and old soft-drink bottles and oil cans, many of whose shapes and labels I could not recall. A garish hubcap collection hung on either side of the front door, strung out and down like small bright shields on the wall of a medieval castle, some delicately crosshatched with wires, others bold and solid, with fierce-looking hubs that any charioteer would have been proud of. One hubcap had been converted to a clock, its hands dead at fifteen until three.

Along two shelves lines of home-canned vegetables stood, squat soldiers at attention, three ranks deep: tomatoes, green beans, pickles, corn. There had to be well over a hundred jars in all, their little brass rings sparkling like crowns, not stained and dusty and forgotten looking, the way I remembered my grandmother's jars of food. Like they were wiped clean every week. Or had just been put there. As frightened as I was, my stomach remembered that it had not had food all day. The canned goods made me feel a little better about things—surely someone who canned vegetables like my grandmother wouldn't kill a couple just because they knocked at her door and asked to use the phone.

In another corner sat a large rolltop desk whose surface was covered with every sort of paper imaginable, from bills to newspapers, most yellowed with age, and the faded covers of gardening magazines jutted out of stacks here and there. A manual typewriter, one of the old Underwoods that a good-sized child would have trouble carrying, crouched gray with dust on the writing surface, and it was obvious by the uneven keyboard tabs and jammed keys at the strike point that the last person who tried to type there had given up in utter frustration and left the machine to languish. Beside the typewriter sat a metal rotary file with a few cards sticking out at odd angles, grimy with handling. Everything about the desk had the look of disuse and abandonment, as if whoever owned it knew it was there but deliberately avoided touching it, for fear of animating ghosts.

Above the desk, on either side of a framed auburn-haired, blue-eyed Christ—his sad, waxen chiseled face fixed straight ahead—two sepia pictures hung on wires from nails driven into a mortar joint: a man and woman austere of countenance, their defiant and ferret-like eyes riveted on the camera as if they too held weapons and would not hesitate to use them. I could see no more family resemblance between these flat, fading people and the old woman with the enormous gun in her little blue-veined hand than I could between them and the gaunt-faced man hanging between them.

The old woman coughed and spat into a can by the doorway. "You about thoo lookin' the place over? You act like you plannin' to buy it . . . or *steal* it." She had the gun leveled at my face, the hammer back, her finger across the trigger. I could see the gray heads of bullets in the cylinder. The dog watched one of us for a few seconds, then the other, perhaps waiting to see which one twitched first, whereupon he would spring for the throat. From time to time I could hear deep down a growl or whine as he eyed us.

"Ma'am," I said, "would you please put the gun up? We can't do you any harm." Annie had moved close behind me and leaned against my back, trembling. She made small gasping sounds like someone, I swear, in the raptures of making love.

"You can't be too sure these days." She eased the barrel down until it pointed at my knees. "There's so much meanness goin' on. And you, little lady, you get out from behind him to where I can see you." She brought the pistol back up and aimed it at Annie, who turned my hand loose and crawled to the side.

"Would you mind telling us what this is all about?" I asked her. "All we wanted was to use your telephone. We're no threat to you."

"Defendin' my castle is what it's about. Guardin' my propty. You two pilgrims come up here at dark out of nowhere and stop and bang on my door and look in my winder and ast to come in, and I don't know who you are or nothin' about you. Tellin' me yer from Shrevesport and on the way to Houston and this not even the road to Houston don't make a lick of sense. I could've killed you at the door, you know. Robbers run in pairs, or ain't you heard? Bonnie and Clyde? You ever heard tell of them?"

I swept my eyes around the room. "They robbed banks. This is no bank." Visibly trembling, Annie was looking at the canned goods.

"Ain't no tellin' what people might think I got here. Used to be a store, you know—lotsa money made here."

"Lady, we're not interested—"

"By the way, I ain't got no telephone. Lemme set you straight on that."

"No *telephone.*" Annie's voice squeaked, distant and hopeless and resigned. "No *telephone.* We went through all this and—"

"You don't have a *telephone*?" I asked.

"At's right. Why do I have to keep repeatin' myself to y'all? Can't you hear? Don't need no telephone. Got nobody to call and don't want nobody a-callin' me. Telephones is a nuisance and a unnecessary expense."

I shook my head and looked at Annie. Her eyes met mine then

returned to the pistol. "Then why in bloody hell did you bring us in here?"

"Mister, you stop yer swearin'. You knocked on my door is how come I let you in."

"But you knew all I wanted to do was use the phone."

"I never knowed *what* y'all wanted, from the get-go. But it's too late to worry about that now. You are inside now—"

"We'd be happy to leave," I said.

"That ain't a option." She pointed the .44 at my head again. "Now, I still ain't sure about y'all, so I got to check you out to see that you ain't got no hidden weapons."

"What do you mean?" I asked her.

"What I mean is, I don't know what you got under them clothes. You might have a pistol or knife or God knows what strapped to yer body. Pull up yer shirt."

I shrugged and lifted my shirt and turned around on my knees. Annie looked away. "Satisfied?"

"Matter of fact, I ain't. I want you to take all yer clothes off and I'll shake'm out and see that you don't have no weapons on you. Far's I'm concerned, you are Bonnie and Clyde right now. Robbers."

"Lady, this is plain bullshit." I started to stand up, then locked eyes with the dog, who seemed to want me to make some sort of move. I sat back onto my calves and spread my arms. "Lady, we don't have any weapons with us. We're a married couple going to Houston for the weekend and that's all. We don't—I don't own a damned gun or even a knife that couldn't be found in any kitchen. We're just—"

She shook her head. "You are inside of my castle now and I

ain't takin' no chanch on you." She worked the pistol up and down. "Now, you stand up, big boy, stand up real slow and take yer clothes off and lay'm right there in front of you." She looked at Annie. "You just stay where yer at till I'm satisfied with him."

I stood up, then tried again. "Lady, I really don't think this is necessary. Look." I put my hands out and turned around twice, then pulled my shirttail up and turned again. "There's no weapon here."

"Don't matter what *you* say. I'm in charge here, me and this .44 and Duke, and we say we ain't a-takin' no chanches on you. Don't you get the pitcher? You got to do what I say for you to do. Like Simon Says. And Simon says that you better get them clothes off. But tuck yer pockets back in first—you look ridiculous with them pockets hangin' out."

With a sideways glance at Annie I unbuttoned my shirt and let it slip off my shoulders to the floor. I regretted the extra weight I'd added around my middle since she last saw me without a shirt. I pushed my pockets back in. The old woman nodded and pointed the pistol at my belt and made a downward motion, so I unbuckled and slid my pants down to my socked feet.

"Step out of'm and kick them and that shirt over here to me."

I did as she instructed and then I was there with nothing but my Jockeys and socks on in front of an old woman I had never seen before and my estranged wife, who had not seen me without clothes in over three years. The day had been fairly warm and the room was hot, but I felt a chill over my legs and back and chest. I wondered whether Annie felt it too.

Like someone at a garage sale the old woman picked up the

shirt and pants and shook them and held them out to the light, then, apparently satisfied that I had not smuggled in some sort of weapon to slice her throat with, dropped them to the floor in front of her.

I pointed to my Jockeys. "Is it necessary to pull *these* off?" I glanced at Annie, but she turned away.

She motioned with the pistol and cackled. "Naw, I purty well know what kinda gun yer a-carryin' in there. Bet Annie Oakley does too." She looked at Annie and cackled again.

I tried again. "Ma'am . . ."

"What caliber is he, Sweetie? Is he a long-barrel or a snub? How many times a week you get to pull the trigger on that thang?" She cackled again. I kept my eyes on Duke. "I had a husband one time myself, for nearly a whole year. He had a *cannon* down there. Trouble was, he shot it in ever woman he seen that would let him get close enough. My daddy almost shot *him*, but I tol' him he wudn't worth the bullet it'd take to kill'm. The Good Lord take'n care of 'm soon enough anyhow."

"Ma'am, can I put my clothes back on?"

"When I say so you can. And pull them socks off. Never could stand to see a man wearin' undershorts and socks. Plain tacky. You got a choice—socks or shorts."

I yanked my socks off and pitched them over onto the pile.

"Now, get back down on yer knees." She turned to Annie. "Yer go, little lady."

"Ma'am?" Annie squeaked.

"Yes'm, you got to stand up and take yers off too. Like I say, I ain't takin' no chanches. Now, get'm *off*."

On my knees, I had turned to face Annie. "Tommy," she implored.

"I don't guess you've got any choice, Sunshine."

She gave me a strange look. I realized that I had used a pet name I hadn't called her in years, one of those early-marriage terms of endearment that couples use just between themselves.

"Stand up and get'm off." The old woman waved the pistol.

Annie stood and unbuttoned the top two buttons of her gingham blouse and stopped. "I just can't do this, lady. I'm sorry, but I just can't do this."

"Oh yes you can. Ain't nobody here but me and yer husband and Duke. Yer husband prolly sees you without clothes ever day and Duke don't care one way or the other—I doubt that you'd look all that good to him nekkid, even on all fours. Besides, I got this gun on you and I am tellin' you to take them clothes off. So do it."

"My husband—" Her eyes were brimming.

"Just do it, Annie."

Two more buttons and she stopped again and looked at me. "Tommy, this is so humiliating."

"Just *do* it," I hissed.

"Tommy, don't watch," she said quietly.

"What do you mean, tellin' yer husband not to watch? He's got a right to watch." The witch had taken a step toward us, waving the pistol around her head. "These modern marriages don't make no sense atall to me. Tellin' yer husband not to watch you take yer clothes off. You sure had yer eyes on him when he take'n *his* off! I wish I had a man around that I could watch undress and that wanted to watch me take *my* clothes off. I wish I had a man, *period.*"

She pointed the gun at Annie's head. "You don't know how lucky you are, havin' a man that wants to take a look at you. Now, you get them clothes off before I forget myself and blow you to Kingdom Come!"

I glanced at Annie, but she had her head down, weeping. Her shoulders were heaving as she struggled with the buttons on her blouse.

"Kingdom Come," she muttered and snuffled. She just stood there fumbling with the buttons. "Just where in the hell *is* Kingdom Come? I have heard that all my life, and I just do not know where—"

"Annie, shut up about that and do what she says before she shows you where it is. Get your mind on what you are doing."

"And you, sir, are to watch her. This is my house and I'm in charge here and what's fair's fair. She watched you get nekkid, and you are goin' to watch her. Now get on with it."

Annie gave me another look, quick and angry, concentrated on the buttons, and yanked her blouse off and dropped it to the floor in front of her. She glanced at me again, then at the old woman. The faint spots of rouge had blossomed now into violent full-blown roses.

I met Annie's eyes, then allowed mine to drop down her neck to her wonderful cleavage and on to her flat stomach. The memory of our stomachs covered with syrupy Coke came back full force.

"And I don't give a shit where Kingdom Come is, except I think I'd prefer it to this hellhole."

"You better watch yer filthy mouth, little lady, or you'll find out where it's at."

"Stop looking at me, Tommy," she snapped.

"Get that brassiere off too," the old woman said.

"M—ma'am?" Annie looked at me again, then back to the old woman. "What could I carry in my *bra*? A grenade? A machine gun? A Goddamned Sherman tank?" She stamped her foot. "You—nobody can make me take *all* my clothes off. Nobody."

The old woman scowled, then laughed and swung the revolver about her head. "*I* can. I can make you take ever stitch off and wish you hadda done it sooner. I can make you do anythang in the world that I want you to do. I pull the strang, you jump. You hear me now? And you stop swearin' and takin' the Good Lord's name in vain in my house. I *mean* that."

"Lady," Annie shouted, "what could I carry in my *bra*?"

I knew very well what she carried in her bra, and for the first time I began siding with the old woman. It was as if we had drifted off into some sort of absurd hunger-induced dream, the hag no more a real part of this scene than a phantom monster conjured out of the gloom who would disappear the minute I willed it. She had the power to make Annie undress, and I wanted to see my wife's breasts, I wanted to see what three years had done to those small, wonderfully sculpted creamy breasts with the little nipples that stuck out hard and red when she was excited. "Right on!" I wanted to shout.

Annie had tears in her eyes. "Lady, can't you just *search* me? I have nothing on my person—"

"Take thatere brassiere off before I make *him* do it." She motioned toward me.

Annie moved her hand around behind her back, then dropped it to her side again. "I'm sorry, but I can't do this. You let him keep his shorts on."

"And I may let you keep *yer* underpants on, but that brassiere and everthang else is a-comin' off!"

"Please, lady—"

The old woman pointed the gun toward me. "You, then, Tommy—or whatever yer name is—you go over and take the thang off of her before I have Duke do it."

"Uh, lady. . . ." I stayed on my knees.

She reached up and pulled her hair from her face until one eye glared at me. "Are you two crazy or *what?* You are in my house and I got a gun on you and when I tell you to do somethin', you gon' *do* it. Now, mister, you get up from there and go over and take that brassiere off of yer woman." She pointed the pistol from me to Annie.

Tears were streaming down Annie's red face. "Oh, never *mind,* I'll do it myself." She reached around and unfastened the bra, a lacy white one with pale blue trim, and slipped it over her arms. She dropped it on top of the blouse at her feet.

"At's better," the old woman said. She pointed the pistol at Annie's chest. "I can kinda understand why you'd be ashamed to take it off. You ain't totin' much."

I stood looking at Annie, who was very much aware of my attention. Torn between fascination at seeing her body again and uncertainty over where this night was going, I didn't quite know what to do. The dream was getting better.

"Stop staring at me, Tommy!" She crossed her arms and covered her breasts.

So I turned away and studied the shelves of canned goods, waiting for the next instructions from the old woman.

"Now, take them pants off."

"Oh, Jesus." Annie was looking at the ceiling as if she expected divine intervention. I watched out of the corner of my eye as she unbuttoned her jeans and worked them down her thighs and off.

"Kick'm over here."

Annie glanced at me, then scooted her clothes over to the old woman, who nudged my pile of clothes next to Annie's, then kicked the stack into the corner.

Finally I couldn't stand it anymore. I turned and faced her and swept my eyes up her legs and across her chest, then back down. *Oh, my God, it's been so long since I've seen her body. How could I ever have walked away from something like that?*

I swear she looked as young and delectable as ever standing there in those pale-blue bikini panties, the same blue that trimmed her bra. Matched. She always matched her underwear anytime she left the house, no matter what she was wearing over it. Jesus! Her legs were so incredibly perfect, her breasts, stomach, and thighs—I would have seized her in a breath but for the old woman, with the gun and the silent dog at her side, and Annie, who would have killed me herself before she would allow me to touch her again. She was so perfect in every detail, so beautiful, an intricately carved little wood nymph with nothing but panties on. God, how I wanted the old woman to order her to take *them* off.

"Would you please stop staring at me?"

"She *told* me to look."

"You're *staring*. And you've got your glasses on. If you're going to stare at me, you could at least take your glasses off."

"I'm just—"

"You let him look, little lady. You sure act strange to be his wife." Her face was quizzical. "Somethin' wrong with yer marriage?" She shook her head, steadied her gaze at me. "You two *are* married, ain't you?"

"Yes ma'am. We're married. I promise."

"We are married," Annie confirmed.

"Where's yer rangs at?" She pointed the pistol at my left hand. "You married, you ort to have rangs."

"I'm having it resized," I lied. "Mine and hers both. But hey, look—you can see where the rings were. Go on, look at my wife's ring finger."

Annie nodded vigorously and held her left hand out. The old woman leaned and squinted and, apparently satisfied, said, "Well, y'all sure act awfully strange to be married."

"This is just such a strain on us," I said.

She sized us up again. "Whatdaya figger, Duke. They look dangerous now?" The dog growled low in his throat.

"Can we get dressed?" Annie looked at the pile of clothes in the corner. "And leave?"

The old lady shook her head. "No ma'am, Annie Oakley. I got yer clothes and I know you ain't goin' to steal me blind and take off down the road nekkid. I'll give yer clothes back when I'm good and ready. Y'all might as well settle down and relax. You ain't goin' anywhere tonight."

"Oh, my God," Annie whispered.

"What do you mean? What exactly do you intend to do with us?" I had forgotten about Annie's body.

"You're not going to let us *leave*?" Her voice was thin and child-like. "You're going to make us stay here, like prisoners?"

The old woman leaned against the wall and dangled the .44, training it first on me, then Annie. "Like I tol' you, y'all might as well shut up and rest easy. You *are* prisoners, and you ain't goin' nowhere tonight. And what I decide to do with you is up to me, ain't it? I never ast you to stop at my place and bother me—you done it on yer own. I coulda killed you right out there and let that gravel sop up yer blood and that'd been the end of it, but I let you live. That means that yer lives is mine, so I can do anythang I want to with you and you got no say in the matter."

For the first time I felt the flush of genuine fear. My eyes spun around the room, hesitated on the door, built like something for a fortress, then on the barred windows.

"I just might have all kinds of plans for the two of you. I don't get compny in here very often."

When Annie moaned behind me, I whirled to catch her as she dropped to her knees, head thrown forward. We reached the floor together and her back was heaving as she gasped and sobbed like a child whose world has gone terribly wrong. For a crazy instant I wanted to say that I was sorry for the son of a bitch I had been, that if we made it through this I would make things right with her, that my life had been nothing but shit since we had separated. But I said nothing and did nothing but hold her to me on that hard floor, hold her and stroke her soft blond hair while the wild old woman and her dog looked on.

TWO

I phoned her. I had to. When an old friend calls and tells you you're needed and that someone you're not sure you want to talk to or be with anymore and who sure as hell doesn't want to have anything to do with you is needed too, you don't fret over etiquette. You do what you have to do. So I called her. What I would have done if I had gotten that damned machine of hers, I don't know—she might have phoned me back, might not have. She picked up on the second ring.

She answered with enthusiasm, so it was obvious she was expecting a call, but certainly not from me. I had already put down a couple of stiff ones—you don't call a woman you once loved and still might but who you know doesn't care a damn about you anymore and hasn't for years without getting yourself up for it. It was good to hear her voice, and in spite of the whiskey, or maybe because of it, my heart was thrashing.

I don't fathom how that happens. It's like a jolt of electricity. If I were seeing her naked or something, or if we had parted on amicable terms, I could understand it, but feeling the ambivalence I did about her and not knowing how she felt about me, just hearing her voice after all that time shouldn't have done much of anything. But, then, really, I didn't just hear her voice—I saw her face and body, I felt her next to me. You can't shut that kind of thing off. You'd like to, but sometimes you can't. It just happens.

"Hi, Annie. It's me." I was white-knuckling the receiver.

"Hi, *hell*. Tommy, how did you get my number?"

"Jesus, Annie, you haven't heard from me in—however damn long it's been—and all you can ask is how I got your number? No mild curiosity about *why* I would call you?" The nervousness cleared up fast when that bitch edge cut in.

"That's what I'm asking and all I'm asking. You are just fool enough to try to sell me a policy." I could hear her tapping something on the desk surface, a pen, letter opener maybe, and I could imagine the set of her face, the chin thrust out and slightly to the side, her perfect little teeth clamped together in a fine white porcelain line like the blades of some sort of chopping machine that would as soon shear off my balls as clip a piece of celery. I tried to imagine what she was wearing, whether she was sitting there with just her panties and an old shirt on, the way she used to lounge around the house. But I didn't ask.

"Annie, it doesn't matter how I got the number. I need to talk to you. It's important. Otherwise I wouldn't have called. And it's not about a policy."

"I hope not," she said. "So what *is* it about?"

"Will you talk to me for a minute?"

She was silent a few seconds, then said, "I asked you what this is about, so fire away, tell me what's on your mind, but it had *better* be important. And *quick*. Somebody's coming by to pick me up at six-thirty."

"I'll be quick." I squinted at my watch to make out the time, then reached for my glasses, but they were not in my pocket. *God-damn it, can't see shit.* I reached and raked my hand along the desktop, scattering pens and pieces of paper.

"What are you doing?"

"I'm trying to find my fuc—I'm trying to find my glasses."

"Why? You're talking on the phone with me. You can't see me anyway. Bet you wish you could."

"You don't know what I wish," I said.

Then her voice came in strong: "Fran! Frances had to have given it to you. Damn it. Didn't she?"

"What?"

"My number. Frances gave it to you, didn't she?"

"No," I lied. "I've got my ways. Fran had nothing to do with it." I kept feeling for my glasses along the top of the desk.

"That's crap. I know she gave it to you. Whatever, you've got it now and you've got me on the phone, so go on with whatever's on your mind, but be quick about it. And you'd better not call back here again. You'll just get the machine. I don't know when I'll learn not to answer the damned thing."

"It's a deal, Annie. Now how many times have I called you—" I leaned and slid the bottle over to my glass and unscrewed it, quiet-ly poured a couple of inches in. It was a goofy notion, but I didn't want her to hear it gurgling. *Now, where the hell are my glasses?*

"Numbers of times don't count. It's the fact that you had the gall to call at all."

"That has a nice ring to it," I said.

"Tommy, speak your mind and hang up. I don't have time to mess with you. I'm standing here dripping."

"Dripping what? It's sure as hell not charm."

"Water's what I'm dripping. From a shower. I just got out of the shower. What's it to you?" She was drumming the receiver with her fingers.

She was right—I did wish to see her. "It's *nothing* to me. You sure got to the phone quick if you just got out of the shower."

"Would you please get to the point and quit worrying about how I got to the phone? For all you know, I've got one *in* the shower. Tommy, what's this about? I mean it. I'll hang up if you don't get on with it."

I reached and slugged my whiskey again, slouched in the chair and said simply, "Annie, this is serious." The room was beginning to swim with whiskey warmth, so the glasses really didn't matter.

"So serious you're drinking again?"

"I never quit. But how—"

"I heard you pouring and I heard the ice clinking in your glass. I've heard it enough to know the sound, Tommy."

Jesus, she could always hear what I didn't want her to hear. I could talk to her face to face for an hour and she wouldn't hear a word, but let me be off in a back room on the phone and she'd hear from the kitchen every word I said, even when I whispered. And the only time I ever poured a drink that she didn't know about, she was not at home. She could hear me twist off a cap, with a handkerchief over it to mute the sound. Damnedest thing.

"Annie, Allison's in the hospital."

"Allison?"

"Yes, Allison."

"Allison Hunt?"

"Yes, *our* Allison."

She knocked something over on the desk, took a deep breath and asked, "Tommy, what's wrong with her?"

"I got a call from Jane this morning. She left a message with my secretary while I was on break and I called her back. Allison got thrown by a horse yesterday, out at some friend's ranch near Conroe. The kids were riding horses and something spooked the one Allison was on and—"

"How bad, Tommy? How bad is she hurt?"

I shrugged, then realized how stupid that was. It was like suddenly she was in the room with me. "I don't know exactly."

"Well, didn't Jane—"

"Annie, she's hurt bad, that's all I know, all Jane had the time and composure to tell me. She was real upset."

"Why did she call you and not *me*?"

"Probably because she had my *number*."

"She could have called Frances. She knows her. Or *you* could have given it to her."

"I just got the number, Annie. Forget about that. It's Allison we're talking about here."

There was silence on her end, then, "What else did she say?"

"The bottom line is that Allison has asked for us, for you and me, and I just thought—I thought maybe you'd like to go down there."

"*Asked* for us? I mean, Tommy, she's not dying or anything—"

"I don't know. I told you what Jane told me and that's *all* I can tell you."

"Go when?" she asked.

"I don't know. As soon as possible. Tomorrow maybe?"

"Do they have her in Houston?"

"Yes, Texas Children's. She was in the ER in Conroe, but they moved her to Texas Children's."

"Well, that sounds encouraging, you know, that they could move her over there."

"Maybe, maybe not," I said. "Will you go down there with me?"

Silence. Long silence. Then, "Tommy, I've got to think about this. Jesus, Jesus. Just hang on and let me think this out."

Besides her parents, we were the first people to see Allison Marie Hunt alive, the first to hold the tiny thing, all red and snuggly and sweet-smelling, as newborns are. We sat in Jane's room when they brought her back from Neonatal clean and wrapped in a pink flannel blanket, passed her back and forth and pressed our lips and cheeks to her face, and for years after that instant of bonding she had seemed as much ours as theirs. Before we left Jane's room that afternoon we were blessed with godparenthood. Jane and Tony even gave her Annie's middle name, Marie.

This was back when we lived there in Houston, not long after my graduation from Memphis State and our marriage. I was working with a big insurance agency downtown while Annie finished a master's in interior decorating at the University of Houston. We met the Hunts at an antique show, became close friends, and visited each other often, occasionally taking long fishing trips together off Galveston, so we took a special interest in Jane's pregnancy and the little girl who came.

For nearly four years Allison was the closest thing to a child that we ever had, and we were with her every holiday and at least a weekend each month, taking her to the zoo, to movies, anywhere and everywhere she wanted to go. We lavished expensive gifts on our little blond godchild, would have bought her the world. She was, quite simply, the finest, most beautiful, most delightful child we could ever have asked for, and because of her we felt no real urgency to try for our own. Nights when we lay limp and damp after making love we would admit to ourselves that any child who didn't live up to Allison—and no matter how much we resisted the temptation, our child would be measured against her—would be a disappointment. So we waited and we loved Allison as our own.

Allison fulfilled us, Allison was our single brightest joy, and when we moved to Shreveport for my new job, nothing left a deeper emptiness in our hearts than the loss of that child. For months afterwards we spoke of seeing her fade from our vision as we drove off that gold-brown late October, the little blond girl with both arms waving, her face slick with tears, saying good-bye to people who loved her as much as they had ever loved anyone or anything. And seldom a day went by that one of us didn't mention her.

For the next three years we visited as often as we could, especially at Thanksgiving and Christmas, we sent gifts on the usual occasions, and at least once a year Jane and Tony brought Allison up to visit. But in time the visits grew fewer, as they do, supplanted by letters and phone calls and photographs. Allison found friends at school, had different needs, and we simply grew apart from her, though we still called her on holidays and on her birthdays, and she was often on our minds.

Maybe it was the gradual loss of Allison that led to the end of the marriage. As the child faded ever so slowly from our lives, we tried harder and harder to have our own Allison, consulting one physician after another as we failed to conceive. The harder we tried, the deeper our frustration when month after month nothing happened, until finally, late in the fall of our eighth year together, Annie missed a period, then two, and on a brilliant December afternoon, two weeks before Christmas, we sat on the steps and removed the piece of paper towel from around the slender test tube—we wanted it to be a surprise, though we both knew, the way couples know such things—unwrapped it the way you would a Christmas gift, and saw the bright little ring.

Then came the miscarriage, followed by months and months of frustration and bitterness as we tried again and again, each blaming the other, and the doctors offering neither explanation nor solution. We fought and we bitched at each other constantly, and I started working late nights at the office, leaving her alone in the big house that she had decorated herself. Annie turned to food and alcohol, grew indolent and sloppy and heavier than either of us liked, and the office and the road became my home. She was someone I simply returned to after a week or two, like a stopover on the way to nowhere in particular. The passion between us disappeared, *poof*, as if suddenly the woman living in my house were a stranger, someone I had never cared for at all. And the pity was that neither of us seemed to want to bother with trying to patch things up. We had simply and resolutely fallen out of love.

When a series of suspicious phone calls showed up on our bill,

I admitted after repeated questioning that I was having an affair, my fourth. She seemed neither hurt nor annoyed by it, merely suggested that perhaps the time had come for us to split.

Which we did—I thought fairly amicably. She went to live with her mother a few months and we sold the house, divided the money and other assets, and moved into apartments on opposite sides of town, where there would be little likelihood of our running into each other. Annie took a job with a residential contracting company as an interior-design consultant, and I was promoted to a managerial position in my insurance firm. And there *our* life ended and hers and mine began. For simple convenience and for a number of financial reasons we decided to remain married for a while, though it was clearly understood by both parties, as legal phraseology goes, that neither would call or otherwise try to contact the other unless an emergency arose. In time we would take the formal step.

The couple of times during that period that we did communicate, we exchanged letters, very formal and stiff, almost as if attorneys had prepared them. Annie even got an unlisted number, so that if I should long for companionship in some late-night drunken reverie—as I had been given to in recent years—she would not be the one I would call. Allison's accident was an emergency.

While I waited for Annie to give me an answer, I kept fumbling around for my glasses and finally found them clamped between the pages of a cheap novel I'd been reading, a book about two couples trapped in a New England bed-and-breakfast during a snowstorm—lots of steamy sex scenes with partner switching and all. I put the glasses on, checked the time, flipped quickly through a little stack of yellow reminder notes, then studied the cheap venetian blinds through which the sun projected itself in slices. Cheap. Everything about my study and the rest of the apartment was cheap. Cheap because I didn't care, didn't have anybody to impress or please or give a damn about. I certainly could afford better. Books and magazines scattered everywhere, clients' file folders, several weeks of dust and grime coating the furniture, such as it was, and down a narrow hallway the kitchen, where I could see the heap of dishes in the sink, and, far back in a corner, next to the green tiles of the backsplash, three brown bottles, all empty or well on their way to being. Nothing to see worth wearing glasses for, so I took them off again and slipped them into my shirt pocket.

The women I brought home didn't really give a damn about the way the place looked or about my drinking or anything else. Losers in one way or another, each and every one, they were usually drunk when they got there and drunk when they left and drunk all in between. The bedroom was about all they saw, and there weren't that many of them. I'd just about lost interest in sex. Probably the drinking.

I tried to remember the last woman who was there, weeks ago, but I couldn't focus well on a face, just a name: Sarah. A middle-aged housewife I'd met at the office, having trouble with her husband, who'd dumped her, not knowing what to do about a life policy left hanging. A few drinks that evening, our legs touching under a table in the bar, and the next thing I knew she was trying to get her clothes on in my dark bedroom and stumbling out the door. I'm not sure we even got around to *doing* anything, but from the looks of the bedroom the next morning, we had sure as hell tried. Her bra was lying under a chair in the corner.

I hadn't heard from Sarah again and didn't care. Hell, how can you care when you can't even see a woman's face and don't remember her last name? I put her bra in my underwear drawer, just in case we did get together again. There were two pairs of women's panties in there too, from months ago. Panties without faces and names to go with them, panties just left behind in the sheets or on the carpet, where I found them the next morning or a day or two afterwards. Almost every woman I'd brought there had left in the dark and left something behind, something not worth keeping.

I shuddered and put my glasses on again and reached and closed the blinds. The little slices of sun were cutting right through my brain.

"Annie, Annie. You've got to talk to me. Let me know. Will you go with me to Houston?"

She was fumbling with something on the desk. I could hear papers rustling. Then silence, then rustling again.

"Goddamn it, Annie, are you checking your datebook or calendar or what? This is not a social call. I'm glad it's not long-distance—I'd have to float a loan."

"You can *drown* alone, for all I care," her voice came back.

"Didn't know you were listening. That was quick."

She sighed into the phone. "I—Jesus, Tommy, this is a bad time. I'm just not sure I can get away right now."

"We don't get to choose these times, Annie. They just happen. My God, woman, get a focus on this."

"Tommy, this is crazy. I don't know you anymore, and you don't know me . . ."

"But *we* know *Allison*, Annie. We've got to go."

"I don't have to do anything with you, Tommy. There is no *we* anymore. There's me and you, no *we*."

Bitch. Silence on the line again as she studied what to do. I could hear tapping again, something metal on glass.

"Annie, what the hell are you doing?"

"I'm trying to figure out *what* to do," she said. "I've got several things going on, places to be, Tommy. My life's not dead and empty the way it was with you and the way yours probably is now."

Bitch.

"I'm going to call Jane."

"Annie, Allison's hurt bad. Jane said that she asked for us. The bottom line is we've got to go. We just don't have any choice."

"I sure as hell have a choice about whether I go with *you* or not."

"Annie, I'm not an ogre. What do you think I'm going to do to you?"

"Look, let me call you back. Give me a few minutes. I've got some calls to make. I've got to think about this."

"OK, but try to let me know soon. It'll take me all morning to get things squared away at the office—it's not a good time for me either—but we should be on the road by early afternoon, get there just at dark. It'll take . . ."

"I know how long it takes. We drove it enough. Back then." Her voice trailed off.

"Just wanted to remind you. Pick you up around two-thirty?"

"I haven't said I'm going."

"Annie, I don't see that either of us has a choice. If that child has asked for us, then *we* are going."

"Oh, I'm going to see Allison. I just don't know whether I'm going with *you*."

Bitch.

After a few seconds she said, "I'll call you back."

"Do you have my number."

"You're listed, aren't you?"

"Yeah."

"So what's the problem? I've finally learned to read."

Bitch.

I hung up and finished my drink, emptied the rest of the bottle in the glass, and went to the kitchen to get some more ice.

"Bitch," I said to the refrigerator, swinging the freezer door open, "all you Goddamned women are alike." I rattled up a handful of ice and dumped it in my glass, then ran my hand down the front of my pants and winced. "A cold hand on our balls is what you finally amount to, you bloody bitches!"

I sat back down at the desk and tried to concentrate on some paperwork I desperately needed to do, but my head was killing me, so I turned off the light and slouched in the chair, dangling the whiskey glass from one hand, glasses from the other, waiting. The sun was savage against the blinds. I could feel its heat searing through the closed slats.

I picked up the novel I'd been reading, but the thing had grown tedious, so I pitched it back onto the desk and waited. And waited.

It seemed like an hour, but in less than ten minutes the phone rang. It was Annie.

"Jane says it's bad, Tommy."

"You called her?"

"Of course I called her. I told you I was. You don't seriously think I'd believe anything *you* said, do you?"

"Jesus, you are something. What'd she say about the injuries?"

"Head and neck are involved, maybe spine. That's all Jane had time to tell me. She was home from the hospital to get some stuff for Allison. They're still doing tests on her, everything you can imagine—X-rays, CAT scans. She's in and out of it, but when she's been alert she's asked for us."

"I told you that. Are you going with me?"

"Yes, I guess so." I could hear an exasperated sigh. "I mean, I don't have a choice about going. Jane said Allison thinks we're still married—"

"We *are.*"

"Well, that's a textbook application of the word *technicality.*"

"So you're going?"

"I guess it's best."

"I thought so too," I said.

"Well, mark that one on your calendar. It's the first time we've agreed on anything in years."

"It's logged," I said.

"You know, Tommy, I could catch a plane and meet you down there at the hospital."

"Jesus, Annie, somebody'd have to pick you up. They're not going to have time for that."

"I can afford a Goddamned taxi. I'm working, you know."

"It's the logistics of it. Things are going to be confusing enough. Why don't you just ride down with me? It's not like we'd suddenly be back together again or anything. You don't even have to talk to me on the way."

"We'd be in the same car," she said.

"Annie, don't get the idea that I'm trying to pick you up or something or that I'm looking forward to being in the same car with you for five hours. Just do whatever the hell you want to do, but make up your mind and let me know something."

"Ten hours," she said.

"What?"

"Five down, five up. Ten hours. Even an insurance salesman ought to be able to calculate that."

"Why don't you just call me back when you've made up your damned mind, but be quick about it."

"Don't hang up, Tommy. Let me look at something."

While she looked at whatever she was looking at, I leaned and poured another stiff bourbon from a new bottle into the little button-size chips of ice. I didn't really give a damn whether she heard it or not. It's amazing how fast warm whiskey can melt ice. If she didn't want to be in the same car with me for five hours, or ten hours, fine. Bitch. Bloody cold bitch.

Her voice came back. "My car's got an electrical problem—the Check Engine light won't go off—and I don't want to take a chance with it until somebody's looked at it, but I could rent one and follow you down. What about that?"

"If that is what you want to do, fine. If I terrify you that God-damned much, Annie, fine. Rent a car and let me know where to meet you and we'll convoy down."

"You don't scare me at all, Tommy." She slammed something on the desk.

"Annie, we can be adults about this. But if you persist, go ahead and rent a damned car. Where do you want me to meet you? What time?" I wanted to add *bitch* in there somewhere, but I didn't.

After a few seconds of silence she said, "All right, I'll ride with you. It'll just be simpler. What time do you want me to be ready?"

"I'll pick you up around two or two-thirty. We ought to be able to get in there well before dark."

"Say two, and I'll expect you at two-thirty. You've always been late. I suppose you know where my apartment is."

"Yes, unless you've moved in the past few months."

"Same place. The Castlemaine Apartments. And you don't have to get out. Just pull up by the curb. I'll be at the curb at two-thirty. I'll be out on the corner by that big poplar, Durango and Stewart. Do you know where that is?"

"Yeah." I knew exactly where, though I'd never seen the corner when I wasn't drunk. Not long after she moved there, I'd even parked down the street and watched a couple of nights, hoping to catch sight of her, wondering who she was out with.

"All right, Tommy, I'll be there waiting on you, but I've got to be back here by mid-afternoon Sunday. OK? I've got—it's important that I be back then. I've got a function Sunday evening."

That meant she had a Goddamned date she didn't want to miss. "Yeah," I said, "I need to get back too."

"Jesus, Tommy, I hope Allison's all right."

"Me too, Annie. Me too."

At almost three-thirty I pulled up in front of her apartment. She was waiting at the curb beneath the big poplar with her purse and carry-on and a small clothesbag. Jesus, she was slim and pretty in her tight jeans and gingham blouse, wearing sunshades, her hair pulled back under a scarf. On the strip of bright green lawn in the dappled shade of the tree she looked like a delicate little lost forest nymph a moviemaker might create to be rescued by a passing prince. I sat for a few seconds studying the architecture of her body and her pixie-like face, wondering just how big a fool I'd been to let her get away. I don't know what I expected her to look like after all those months, but I didn't think she'd look *that* good. Face, body, everything, and so impeccably dressed, as if she had tried to match even the scarf and sunshades with the outfit that she wore.

She held up the bags and mouthed, "*What?*"

I hopped out. "Sorry." I opened the trunk and offered to help her with the bags. She brushed me aside and stowed the carry-on.

"Where the hell have you *been?*" She held up the clothesbag. "Can we hang this?"

"Sure." I offered to take it and hang it in the back of the car, but she hung it herself.

"I'm sorry I'm late, Annie," I said as I got in the car. "I got held up at the office. I tried to call around two-thirty. You been waiting long?"

"Yeah," she said, getting in, "nearly an hour. I've been standing at the curb for nearly a damned hour. You said two-thirty and I was under that tree at two-thirty. I felt like a hooker standing out there. Two carloads of boys came by, college students probably, honking and yelling, made the block twice. I thought I was going to have to go and call the cops to chase their little asses off."

"Oh, come on," I said, smiling, "you know you enjoyed the attention."

"You don't know what I enjoy, Tommy, and you have never been on time for anything in your life." She fastened her seatbelt. "You'd just better be glad it's not real hot."

"I am glad." I turned on the air conditioner as we drove off, headed south. I looked over at her. "You look nice."

"I've already been complimented, and by guys a lot younger and better looking than you. Did you call Jane and tell her when we'd get there?"

"I left word on her machine just before I left home. Told her we would probably get in right at dark."

"You've been drinking, haven't you?"

I nodded. She smelled it. She could always smell it. I might have a mild cocktail at lunch with the guys and she'd make some remark about liquor on my breath when I got home that night. Women have an incredible sense of smell. Or an incredible understanding of men. Or both.

"You're OK to drive, though?"

"Annie, I had some JD and water an hour ago. That's all. I'm fine."

"Where's the bottle?"

I pointed with my thumb. "In the trunk. Don't worry—I can't reach it."

"All right," she said. "You're OK, though? You don't need me to drive?"

"Hardly," I said, my hands very steady at the wheel. The vision of the beautiful wood nymph standing pale and thin in the shade of the tree was gone.

For the first few miles, as we cleared the heavy Friday afternoon traffic of Shreveport, we said nothing. She kept her face straight ahead or angled out the window to her side. Neither of us, I think, wanted to break the silence first.

As we flowed easily along in traffic on the little stretch of I-20 before cutting southwest into Texas, I looked over at her and said, "Why've you got that scarf over your hair?" I'd always liked her hair, a very light blond with a hint of red in it.

"I thought maybe you still had that goofy convertible. Didn't want my hair blown all to hell."

"Annie, I had that car for less than a year. Sold it the first decent offer I got. It was nothing but trouble."

"Another one of your little dreams, wasn't it?" She held her purse in her lap and played with the leather webbing of the strap like someone rubbing beads.

"Whatever, I got rid of it. This car has a top on it—you might have noticed—and you can, if you'd like, take off your scarf."

She turned to me with her very dark sunshades. "Look, when I decide I would like to take it off, I *will*."

"Annie, please, let's don't make this a three-day quarrel. Forget about the damned scarf. Wear it, if you like."

She turned her cold dark glasses on me again. "Thank you. I will."

A few miles west of Shreveport we angled off onto Highway 79 down into Texas, where in thirty miles or so we would hit 59, then mainline it into Houston. She opened her purse and took out a map and unfolded it.

"What's that?"

"Jesus, Tommy, I would have figured you had seen one before. It's a *map.*" She shook and flexed it to her satisfaction, then held it out to the light from her window.

"Smartass. What kind of map do you figure we need for this trip, as many times as we've made it?"

"That was a long time ago. I just wanted to make sure you're going right."

"Hell, I'm going right. We go down to Nacogdoches and hit 59 and head south to Houston."

"Wrong." She tapped the map with her finger. "We hit 59 at *Carthage.* We follow 59 on down through Nacogdoches to Lufkin, then to Houston. Thank God I brought the map." She folded it and got it wrong, the way people always do the first time or two.

"Want me to fold it?" I asked.

She slapped it flat and started over and got it wrong again. "Son-of-a-bitching things," she muttered. She flattened it once more and folded it, and this time it came out right.

"You're going to be contentious all the way, aren't you?"

"Not contentious," she replied. "Just *right.*" She turned her back to me and pulled her legs up onto the seat. "Have you got a full tank?"

I rolled my eyes. "Yes, Mommy."

"Now who's being the smartass?" She leaned and looked at the gauge.

"Plenty of gasoline, the oil was changed a week or so ago, transmission fluid's good for another year, Freon level's OK, brake fluid's been topped up, the tires are properly inflated. Hoses and belts are fine." I tapped the little square on the windshield. "Registration's good through March of next year. The inspection sticker's valid through May. Anything else bothering you?"

"I'll let you know," she said. "If you don't mind, I'd like to take a nap, now that I know that you are on 79." She curled up in the seat, facing away from me.

"Have a big date last night?"

She spun her head around at me. "Now, what the hell does that mean?"

"You seem to be so bloody tired. I just thought maybe you had a big date last night."

"Yeah." She turned and spoke into the window on her side. "Yeah, he was big. And good-looking and charming and well edu-cated. Good salary." She took a deep breath. "And he drove a Mer-cedes. S-class sedan. Expensive. Around eighty grand, he said. Pearl Black."

"Him or the car?"

"Funny. He was blond, tall, *very* long fingers." She reached and stroked the edge of the velour seat. "Don't you just love the smell of new leather?"

Big fucking deal. "Do I know him?"

"I don't know, *do* you?"

"Well, who the hell *is* he?"

"The guy I went out with last night. Who'd you think we were talking about?"

"Stop it, Annie." She could always slaughter me with word games. She used to *love* it. "I just wondered who you're dating."

She dropped her feet back to the floor and turned to face me. "Now, mister, it is none of your business who I'm dating. It might be a troglodyte working for a moving company or a hermaphrodite working for a circus or a lesbian working nothing but her tongue. The point is, it's not any business of yours. I date anybody I want to whenever I want to. We—you and me—are not together anymore. Hasn't the fact that we've lived apart for nearly three years sunk into your thick skull yet?"

"Well, we are, after all, still married."

"That is nomenclature, Tommy, not domestic status."

"Whew," I said, slapping myself on the cheek, "how quick you've become, and apparently you've been doing the Word Power sections of *Reader's Digest*."

"You're an asshole, Tommy, a simple asshole. I don't think either of us will have to look that one up. And I have *always* been quick."

I hushed after that and drove on in silence while Annie coiled onto the seat again and dropped off into an apparent doze. The nymph was gone for good.

From time to time as we headed southeast, then due south, I looked over at her curled up in her seat like a child in a heavy pout. All that was missing was a doll for her to clutch. She had rested her head against the corner of the seat and the windowsill and drifted off into sleep, her mouth slightly open, one hand resting on her thigh.

I watched her out of the corner of my eye, now and then turning to gaze directly at her, as if she were some woman I was seeing for the first time. My eyes lingered on her ring finger, where I could see the faint strip of flesh a bit lighter than the rest. My God, she'd been wearing her bands! She had probably taken them off that morning so that I wouldn't know that she wore them. Probably had them in her purse. She'd put them back on when we got to Houston, so that Allison could see them. I smiled and turned back to the road.

But it meant nothing that she'd been wearing the rings—guys were less likely to mess with her when she wore them. Women who weren't married sometimes wore wedding rings for the same reason. It was obvious that she wore them for no other reason. Still. . . .

I studied her some more as the traffic thinned out, leaving me with long stretches of wide, lightly traveled highway. Jesus, how splendid her face was—like fine porcelain—her small ears and nose, delicate cut of chin, the slightly pouty mouth, parted so that I could see the thin, perfect line of her teeth. A small bead of saliva collected in one corner of her mouth, but when I looked again it was gone. She was deep in sleep, the hand that she rested on her thigh no longer curled in a fist but flat, fingers relaxed. Where the blouse was buckled open between two buttons I could see the edge of her bra.

Christ, I thought, *what I wouldn't give to stop this car and pull her into the backseat.* The vision of the wood nymph was back, and I was feeling princely.

From the gearshift knob I inched my free hand down to rest on the edge of her seat, then back up, like a bird floating, hovering, or a shadow moved by the sun. I spread my fingers until one almost touched the back of her hand, almost but not quite, close enough to feel the warmth of her skin. If she'd been awake, even with her eyes closed she would have known how close I was. She would have felt my heat too. Finally, as lightly as a dandelion tuft drifting down, I allowed two fingers to drop onto the pale blue veins that ran back to her wrist, veins I had followed so many times before, yet I felt as if I were exploring the back of her hand for the first time. Her skin was surprisingly cool. How the hell can you feel heat when the skin is cool? There was no response. I caressed the veins, brushed like an eyelash across her knuckles, and with a spider's stealth moved my fingers to her thigh. I touched the tight denim of her jeans with the tips of my fingers and gently laid my hand out flat on her thigh, beside her hand, the way I had so many times when we traveled or when we lay in bed before sleep. My eyes on the road, I left my hand for long minutes resting there. Only that thin layer of cotton separated my hand from her smooth white thigh.

The heat of her leg so stirred me that suddenly I was ashamed of what I was doing, as if I had laid a lustful hand on a strange sleeping woman beside me on a park bench. I felt like a pervert. Cheap. Like I was touching the thigh of a sleeping stranger.

I moved my hand back to the gearshift, then put both hands back on the wheel, and concentrated on the road, which bore evidence of a recent rain. An early cold front had come down two nights before, roaring through like a long freight from dead north, a Canadian bitch of a blow, strewing debris across the streets and leaving houses powerless for hours, and even in mid-

September the air had had a faint chill to it that morning when I loaded the car. I knew that the evenings would be mild for a day or two, before summer reared again and pressed down on us with its oppressive heat until the fall and winter came down for good.

According to television weather the front zipped right down the state and out into the Gulf, leaving quite a lot of damage in Texas and Louisiana from flash flooding and wind gusts and a couple of small twisters. Rains had been heavy, and even as late as this morning some trailing gusty showers had been reported between us and Houston. As my tires hissed through patches of standing water, I noticed with some relief that skies were clear almost to the southern horizon.

North of Nacogdoches, as we entered a mild flow of traffic, Annie stirred and asked me where we were.

"South of Mt. Enterprise, headed into Nacogdoches."

She readjusted herself in the seat, flounced fretfully a couple of times, then sat up and looked ahead. "Is it raining?"

"No. Some showers came through earlier. Have a good nap?"

"It wasn't a nap. I have a headache. I was just resting my eyes from the glare."

"You didn't go to sleep?"

"With you driving? Get real."

"You were dead to the world, Annie."

"How would you know?"

"I lived with you long enough to know when you're faking."

"Oh, *yeah*. You left yourself wide open there, but I have enough class not to take advantage of you."

"Do you need to stop or anything?" I asked her.

"Maybe in Nacogdoches somewhere. I could use a bathroom, and all I had for lunch was a Coke. Maybe we could get something."

I shrugged. "Sure. Dairy Queen? Or—"

"A Dairy Queen'll be fine."

"Maybe we can find a Denny's, some sort of family restaurant."

"A Dairy Queen will do, Tommy. I don't need a family restaurant. We aren't a family, remember?"

A Dairy Queen it was. I found one readily enough and pulled in and parked. "Do you want to get out or do you want me to drive through, or should I go to the counter and get something to go? But you have to go to the bathroom."

"Jesus, I don't care how you do it, Tommy. Just *do* it. And you let *me* worry about when and where I need to go to the bathroom." She opened her purse and fished around and took out a wadded-up five and pressed it out on her thigh exactly where I had put my hand while she was asleep.

"Annie, it's on me. What would you like?"

She looked at me and continued to press the bill on her leg, as if she somehow sensed that my hand had been there. "No, no, let me get it. I can afford it." She held the five out to me. "And when you get gas again, I fill it up. Deal?"

"Hell's bells, Annie, stop acting like Little Miss Independent." I pushed the money away. "I know you can afford to treat."

"I insist," she said.

"Dutch, then, Goddamn it!" I snatched the five and got out and slammed the door, started across to the restaurant, then turned around and went back and jerked the door open and leaned down, one arm on the roof of the car.

"What the hell do you want me to *buy* with this five?"

Her dark glasses glared at me. "Glad you recalled that I hadn't placed my order. See whether you can remember what I might want."

I shook my head and thought a few seconds. "What? French fries and a Coke? A hamburger?"

"No."

She was toying with me, but there was no mirth in her face.

"I'm getting a damned corndog, something neat and easy to eat, and a Coke," I said. "Would that do you?"

"A corny-dog? You have got to be kidding. You don't remember *anything* about me, do you?"

"Hell, Annie, I didn't think you wanted me to remember anything about you. You sure don't want to remember anything about *me*."

"I remembered when I saw that Dairy Queen sign that you always liked those damned corny-dogs. Nothing but sweepings from the butcher's stall shaped into a weenie and rolled in sawdust thickened with Elmer's glue and dipped in hot lard until they look like they might be edible. I remember that. As a matter of fact, I am always reminded of you when I see a corny-dog."

"Annie, what do you *want*?"

"See whether your little pea-brain can figure out what I want."

I stared at the dark glasses. It was a fucking dominance game. That's all. She was trying to make me admit that I couldn't remember a simple thing like what she always wanted when we pulled into a Dairy Queen. And I couldn't. I had blanked out on it. Hamburger, hotdog, fries? The one thing I knew for sure that she didn't want was a corndog—and the only reason she hated them was that she ate three one time in West Texas on a very hot day and got sick and threw up all down the side of the car before I could pull over for her. Nachos? Onion rings? Hell, I just couldn't do it.

"I am not guessing at anything," I said, straightening up. "If you don't tell me right now, all you are getting is a corndog."

"Milkshake," she said simply.

"What flavor?"

She threw her head back and to the side in mock exasperation—at least I think it was fake. "You don't remember that *either*?"

"Vanilla's what you're getting!" I slammed the door.

"Chocolate!" she yelled as I was walking away.

Halfway across the parking lot I turned around and motioned for her to roll down the window. She leaned over and did it, glaring at me over the tops of her shades. "What do you want *now*?"

"I thought you had to go to the bathroom," I yelled.

She raised her head and fixed her cold dark glasses on me. "You just buy the food. I don't have to be reminded to go to the bathroom. And you sure as hell don't have to let everybody in East Texas know I've got to go. You go on and do what you have to do and let me mind my own business."

I shrugged and turned back toward the restaurant. "Bitch," I said. The nymph had turned back into an ogre.

While I was standing at the counter waiting for our order, she came in and walked past me toward the bathroom. "The car's not locked," she said as she went by. "You might keep an eye on it—I left my purse in there. And you left the keys in it."

"Yes'm," I muttered. "What kept you? You have to decide whether the place was good enough for you?"

She ignored me and walked between the booths toward the little door that led to the bathrooms. I watched her. Dear God, she still looked so *good*. Legs and ass and shoulders. Everything about her was classy. Always was. I just wished she had left that damned scarf in the car.

Out of the corner of my eye I noticed that I wasn't the only one watching her. Two rednecks over by the window were ogling and whispering and giggling. Damned lowlifes. They looked like loggers or plumbers or mechanics or something, bearded and greasy, one wearing a white T-shirt—or it was *once* white—the other a gray one. The one wearing the gray shirt had a package of cigarettes rolled up in a sleeve, a burlesque of what lived in and about the town and all over East Texas. Damned Li'l Abner cartoon characters.

I turned back toward the service area and gazed out across the field beyond, where two old rusty cars sat in high grass. The notion of someone like that laying a hand on her turned in my stomach like a bright steel blade. Troglodyte, she'd said. That's precisely what those two louts were, trogs. Trogs lusting after a forest nymph. Funny, but I couldn't remember ever thinking much about who might be making love to her, though many times with another woman I had fantasized Annie back into my arms, and there were times when we were married that I would pretend I was another man making love to her. Suddenly I was almost choked with rage at the idea that someone like one of those greasy bastards might be crushing his bearded lips against hers, running his hands over her, then taking her clothes off and . . . . I found myself trembling with jealousy that two white-trash cretins had looked at a woman I hadn't touched in years, that I had not one trace of claim on.

"Here y'are," the waitress behind the counter said. She slid my corndog to me in a little red woven plastic basket. Then the Coke and milkshake. She was old for a Dairy Queen waitress, lots of mileage on her, short and lean and leathery, skin the color of snuff, and I could tell by her eyes that she would cut a guy's balls off in a second.

"I wanted the corndog to go," I said.

"To go?"

"Yes. To carry out. To take with me. For the road. However you want to put it. Look, I told you that when I ordered it."

She cut her eyes up at me. "So I rekkin I forgot. But it ain't no problem. You want it in one of them little pasteboard boats so's you can put a galump of ketchup or mustard in there with it?"

"No. Just wrap it up. I don't want anything with it."

She scooped the corndog up with her hand, wrapped it in a napkin, and slid it into a white bag. "There y'are. Ready to go, to carry out, to take with you, for the road, not to eat on the premises, however you want to put it." She grinned and rubbed her hand on her apron front. "That sombitch is still bad hot, so watch yer mouth."

I handed her Annie's money. "Now, I want to pay for the milkshake with this five."

She dangled the five by a corner, the way you'd hold a dead mouse. "Where's this thang been? In yer shorts?" She cackled.

"If it's any of—my wife had it wadded up in her purse."

"I rekkin it's been wadded up somewheres." She smoothed the bill out by running it briskly back and forth on the edge of the counter. Satisfied, she held it up again. "You want to pay for the milkshake with this but not the corndog and co-cola?"

"No, just the lady's milkshake."

"At's *her* milkshake?"

I nodded.

"The lady that just come in and said something to you?"

"Yes. Her."

"At's yer wife?"

"Yes."

"You eatin' the corndog and drankin' the co-cola yerself?"

"They're for me, yes."

She held up the five. "And this here's yer *wife's* money?"

"Yes. What in hell is this inquisition all about? It's simple enough. Her money, that wrinkled five, is paying for the milkshake, which she's going to drink. I am paying for the corndog and Coke with *my* money. I will be eating one and drinking the other. What is the *problem*?"

"Look, I ain't just a waitress here—I *manage* the place. Mind if I shoot straight with you?" She was looking down into the register tray and making change from Annie's bill and bearing down on a great lump of some kind of red gum.

"No, what's wrong?"

"Whether she's yer wife or not, at's a classy-lookin' lady." She slid the money across to me, hardened her eyes at mine, and leaned forward until her face was not four inches away. "And, mister, you are one cheap shit."

"Look, you just don't—" But I didn't finish. She snatched the four dollars I held out and made change and slapped it on the counter, then turned to the drive-in window.

"One cheap shit," I heard her mutter. "Git them rangs done and on up here," she said to the cook, the top of whose head I could see bobbing around behind a divider, "and see can you do it quick." The other waitress, who'd just retrieved a basket of fries from the counter that separated the kitchen from the service area, was laughing her fool head off.

I snatched some napkins out of the black plastic dispenser and spread my fingers and scooped up the Coke and milkshake with one hand, the corndog bag with the other, and had turned to back out the door when I saw Annie coming through the door to the rear. She caught my eye, then walked up the other aisle, directly toward the two rednecks, flashing a quick smile at the one with the gray T-shirt as she passed. He smiled back, of course, and as Annie went by he pivoted his head like an owl, with the other fool looking on, mouth agape. They followed her out the door with their eyes. As I backed out, Gray Tee Shirt opened his mouth and flicked his tongue up and down and winked at me.

I hurried up beside her before she could get to the car. "Just why in God's name did you smile at those shitheads?"

She turned her dark glasses on me. "What are you talking about?"

"The rednecks in there. You smiled at them. They look like the ones out of *Deliverance*."

"You figure they'll pile in their truck and follow us?" she asked as she got into the car. She pointed to an old red pickup nosed up in front of the building. "I'll bet that beauty's theirs."

I stood behind her. "Do you mind taking your milkshake?"

She reached and took it. "Did I have change?"

"Yes, you have change. In my right-hand pocket. You can reach in there and get it with those assholes watching—" I nodded toward the restaurant. "Or you can wait until I've got a free hand and I'll give it to you."

"I'll wait," she said, and slammed the door.

I walked around, set the Coke on the roof of the car, and opened my door to get in.

She pointed to the corndog in my hand. "Would you mind terribly eating that thing out there?"

"What?" I was standing there with the door open, the Coke in one hand, the corndog in the other.

"How about eating your corny-dog out there?"

"This is *my* Goddamned car," I reminded her. "I'm not going to stand out here in the parking lot and eat this corndog. The whole point was to get something we could eat in the car and save time."

"Very well," she said, sucking hard on the straw of her milkshake until it collapsed, as they always do. She stopped and took a breath. "Come on in and have at it. But if I throw up all over your car from smelling that thing, don't blame *me*."

I recalled the pieces of cornmeal casing and wiener strung out down the doors and rear fender of our car that hot day just outside San Antonio and turned and slung the corndog from its bag toward the field of tall grass, got into the car, and balanced my Coke between my legs.

"Lose your appetite?" She jiggled the straw in the shake to break it up.

"Yeah, a Coke will do me. I drank a Slim-Fast before I left the apartment."

She pointed to the field as I backed out. "Some animal will die from eating that thing tonight. Maybe take it back to the family and kill the whole litter."

"Those two rednecks will be scrambling for it before we're out of sight."

"Nah. They had cheeseburgers and double fries, a big pickle each, apple pie for dessert, and large Cokes. Wouldn't have room for it."

"Damn," I said. "Onions? Pickles?" She had this incredible ability to register detail. "What was the logo on that white T-shirt?"

"It wasn't a logo. It was a blend of two colors of grease or oil, probably from a chain saw. They had sawdust on their shoulders—I thought it was dandruff at first. That grease spot looked like the face of Christ. A little Byzantine. Quite nice, actually."

She might have been lying, but every time I checked her out, she was right on target. She just never missed a thing.

"You didn't have to go to the bathroom?" she asked.

"Annie, I'll go to the bathroom when I need to. I'm not a child that you have to remind."

She nodded and sucked on her milkshake as I eased back onto the highway and headed south again. I sipped my Coke in silence.

"My change?"

"Oh, my God, woman." I rotated in the seat and fished the bills and coins out of my pocket and handed them to her. "I almost got away with it."

"Not a chance," she said.

A couple of miles south of Nacogdoches she asked, "Were you jealous?" I could tell by her relaxed cheeks that she was at long last getting something up the straw.

"What?"

"Were you jealous about those guys?"

"No. No, I was not—it wasn't jealousy. I have no right to be jealous of you. Disappointed is more like it. I just can't believe that you would stoop to their level." I lifted my head and scanned the rearview mirror to see whether the old red Ford truck was closing on us.

"Stoop to their level? You talk like I was eating with them, or eating *them*. I just smiled at them. And you can quit looking for them—if they were after anyone, they'd be after *you*. Remember, it wasn't a woman they got in *Deliverance*. It was Ned Beatty."

I shook my head. "Boy, have you stooped. Flirting with rednecks in a Dairy Queen."

"Yeah, just about as bad as working up Betty Dunbar at a Pizza Hut."

"What?" I stared at her.

"You were at that Pizza Hut on Central. A couple of months ago. I saw you."

"What is the point of this?"

"Betty Dunbar's the point. That's what *you've* come to. That's really high-class dating there. At a Pizza Hut with Betty Dunbar. That would be like me snuggling into the booth with one of those bastards back there and sharing a cheeseburger. She's a damned slut, Tommy. Since she divorced Johnny, she's rolled in the sack with every male in northwest Louisiana and probably northeast Texas, married and otherwise. An *old* slut at that. At least those guys were young."

"You don't know how old they were. Sawdust and grease and heavy drinking preserves'm. They might be fifty."

"No. The kind of life they lead makes'm look old at twenty. They were in their twenties."

"It's a wonder you didn't ask them," I said.

"Didn't have to." She drew some milkshake up the straw. "Heavy drinking hasn't preserved *you*, has it?"

Inside I flinched, but I didn't even look at her.

"Jesus, you got Betty Dunbar for a *pizza*, and probably just a one-topper. Do they make a Salami Lovers Special? She'd go for that in a heartbeat. 'Just lay the whole thang on top,' she'd say, 'I lak my meat in one big ol' piece, laid rim to rim.'"

"You are an absolute bitch, Annie." I glared at the dark glasses. "Betty and I were just having pizza. That's all. She's a friend, somebody to talk to."

"Getting a woman for a pizza, and probably a one-topper at that, ought to tell you something about her. And yeah, I'll bet her conversation was sparkling, all right—'Tommy, did you ever count how many slices of pepperoni is on one of these here thangs? Do you like them little salty fish? Wonder how they ketch them thangs and whur they catch'm at? Rekkin at's real cheese? What all kinda stuff you rekkin is in they sausage, Tommy?' Or when you finally got her home, 'How you want me to git, Tommy? On my back? Across the table? On my knees? Hang from the ceiling? Want me to take off all my clothes or do you want to take'm off yerself? You'll have to hep me with these industrial strength supports anyways. Want me to take out my teeth? I kin give you real good head without my teeth. You got a rubber? Better use a couple, since I ain't been by the clinic lately. And I 'spect you ort to have a life preserver on, case you fall in.'"

"You are one mean woman, and she happens to have all her teeth." I stared at the road.

"I guarantee you that half of the teeth in her head were made in a laboratory somewhere. Out of plastic or bone or whatever the hell they use. Deer antlers. Hog tusks."

"Just shut up, Annie. You don't know anything about Betty or anybody else I've been with."

"*Been with?* Bingo!" she said, "I knew it wasn't just pizza."

"Why don't you get off Betty?"

"I haven't been *on* her—you're the one."

"Bitch."

"Somebody told me she has coarse black hairs growing on her chest and around her nipples, like a man, like those rednecks back there."

"She does not have—"

"Bingo *again*! You'd know, wouldn't you? You are so fucking easy."

"I don't know how Betty got dragged into this. We were talking about you flirting with a couple of goofy-looking rednecks. You know, like it or not, I am to some degree responsible for you on this trip."

"Well, Jesus, Tommy, I didn't exactly strip and lie back and present a table spread for them. They smiled and I smiled. That's just being friendly."

"In this part of the country it's the same thing as a woman saying, 'Hey, comere, big boy, let's get it on.' The next thing you know, they'll be edging us over somewhere out here in the middle of nowhere and pulling you out of the car."

"Shi-i-i-t. Tommy Carmack, you are *jealous*. Jealous of a woman who couldn't care if you dove off an overpass onto a railbed and broke every bone in your body, then got run over by the next slow freight and cut in half. Mister, you don't have any rights to me, married or not, and you and your fucking jealousy can go to hell!"

"Just suck your milkshake," I said, a little embarrassed. "And clean up your language." I glanced over at her, fully expecting to see her face flushed with anger. Instead, she had a very thin smile. She was enjoying jerking me around.

"Maybe I should have asked one of them to take me on to Houston," she said after a few miles. "The one with the cigarettes rolled up in his sleeve would probably clean up all right and be fun in nicer clothes. I'd have to degrease him first, hose him down, rake out his beard, Lysol him maybe. Of course, the clothes wouldn't matter that much because they'd have to come off later anyway, or he could just keep on his T-shirt. I liked it. He was pretty cute. Had a nice gold chain running through his neck hair. He's the one I winked at."

"*Winked* at? I didn't see you wink at the guy. You really don't have a bit of sense, woman."

"It was a small wink," she said, "more of a twitch, so he may not have noticed."

"Oh, you can bet your ass he noticed."

"He really was kind of cute," she said. "The other one had some kind of sore under his ear, like maybe an infected tick bite, or a boil or something. Might have been just an ingrown hair. Playing around with him would be grosser than eating a corny-dog, unless it was in the dark or I was real drunk. But it sure would be nice to be able to look at that T-shirt every day and see the face of Christ."

"Annie, stop it."

"I could take a little bit of paint and touch the face up, make the eyes nice and blue, maybe lighten that auburn hair, work some thorns into it. We could make some real money off that shirt, him and me. These people down in here believe that about Jesus, that he had blue eyes and light hair and that he spoke modern English. Like he came from Milwaukee or someplace. You know, they buy these damned audiotapes of Jesus and prophets speaking—I've seen the ads in magazines—and I'll bet they believe it's actually Jesus and Paul and John talking. The people out in here are trapped in a time capsule. They haven't changed one little bit since they got here, except for the cars and trucks and aluminum trailers and the tools they use, and all that was brought in from the outside."

"You shouldn't knock their religion. It's the only thing that keeps them from killing each other."

"They *do* kill each other," she said. "And it's not so much religion as it is plain old superstition. Did you see that sign back there about AIDS being God's punishment for homosexuals? Like God, busy as He must be, got a little bored in His laboratory one day and decided to concoct something to kill off faggots. 'And I think I'll let it kill more blacks too, while I'm at it, and spare the good, straight-sex white people who worship me and tithe.'"

"Why don't you calm down? Finish your milkshake."

"How come you don't wear a beard and neat T-shirts?"

I ignored her and glued my eyes to the road.

Even when we were married and in love—at least I believe she was as in love with me as I was with her—she was given to merciless mind and word games. She loved my little demonstrations of jealousy, so at restaurants or bars or even in church she'd be especially friendly to young, nice-looking guys just to get my reaction when we got home—the reaction usually led, after quite a lot of sparring and sniping, to sex. I don't think that she was ever seriously flirting, at least not until the very end. Maybe not even then. No way to know for sure except for me to ask, and I wasn't about to do that. Even if I did, there'd be no way to know whether she would tell me the truth or not. It was apparent that she still knew how to play the game, only now she did it out of perverse pleasure rather than to spark healthy jealousy, and this time it certainly wasn't designed to lead to sex.

"The guy I've got a date with Sunday evening . . ."

"I don't want to hear this. Just suck your milkshake."

"Well, you're the one who brought up the wink. And by the way, I saw the sign that guy gave you. With his tongue. Maybe it was you they'd *really* like to do."

"I didn't figure there was a chance under the sun you'd missed that." I reached and turned the radio on and drowned her out with country music. She kept at the milkshake until finally I could hear her vacuuming the bottom, even over the radio. By that time we were approaching Lufkin. Oddly, we were already in a heavy line of traffic even before we got onto the first leg of the tortuous loop that would lead us back to 59 on the south side of town.

"Must have had a wreck or something." Ahead I could see people out standing on the shoulders talking it over. They'd get back in their cars after a while and move a few car lengths, then get out again and powwow.

Annie set her milkshake cup on the floor by her feet and squinted into the late sun. "Something sure has it stacked up. This is terrible. People who used to travel through here in wagons probably moved faster."

We'd inch along a few yards, stop, and inch along again, with more and more people turning and crossing the median and heading back the other way, presumably to follow another route to get to 59. Two helicopters flew past us low, headed south. I fiddled with the radio until I grew tired of country music, only once coming in on the tail end of something about a traffic jam in Lufkin. I asked Annie whether she wanted to try to find some news.

"Not really," she said. "Just turn the damned thing off. Whatever it is, we can't do anything about it."

"Still, I'd like to know."

She looked over at the family in a station wagon who'd been moving along beside us in the right lane. We'd move ahead a few feet, then they would, then we'd move side by side. "I feel like I've known these people forever. That little girl—" She nodded her head toward them. "That little blond-headed girl looks like Allison."

I glanced at the people and grunted, "Not much. Doesn't matter. By the time we're through Lufkin she'll be grown and married and have kids of her own."

"I used to wonder what it would be like to travel with kids on a long trip."

"It'd probably be hell. They look happy to you?"

"Not really. But we'll never know."

"About what?"

"Nothing," she said.

Time dragged on, and neither of us said anything for a long while. Stop and go, stop and go, mostly stop. In another hour, after we'd gotten maybe a quarter of the way around the west loop, I started feeling the Coke and told Annie that I was pulling into the next Quick Check or service station or whatever happened to come along.

"We need gas already?" she asked.

"No, I need a bathroom."

She sniffed and aimed her sunshades at me. "You are still like a little boy. I asked you back there in Nacogdoches whether you needed to go and you said no."

"That was over two hours and a pint of Coke ago, damn it. This is *my* car and I'll stop wherever and whenever I want to."

"Ooooh, don't get so excited. If you really intend to stop, though, you'd better get in the right lane."

I glared at her. "I know how to get off a highway."

"As slow as this traffic is, you could go to the restroom and then find yourself another corny-dog and actually eat it before you'd have to move the car up. Want me to take over while you run and pee behind a tree? My, I am rife with rhymes today. You bring out the poet in me."

"No, thank you. I'll find a place. And what I bring out in you is not the poet."

I smiled at the guy driving the station wagon and signaled that I needed to move over, and he yielded. It took nearly five minutes, but I managed to get in the right lane and after a very long quarter mile or so saw a service station that had bathrooms around on the side. It seemed like forever, but finally we reached the concrete apron in front of the station. It had been cordoned off with sawhorses and an orange ribbon at one end, where recent heavy rains had gouged under the edge of it, leaving a deep red cave. I eased in and parked by the gas island. Might as well fill up while we were there, though Houston couldn't be more than another three hours away and I had nearly three-quarters of a tank of fuel. Annie said nothing as I shut off the engine and got out, but when I uncapped the gas tank and started topping off, she rolled down her window.

"Shouldn't you go to the bathroom first? We wouldn't want you to wet your pants." She dangled a ten out the window. "Let me fill it up."

"Fuck you," I mouthed.

"In your dreams," she mouthed back.

I paid for the gas and bought a pack of gum, went to the bathroom, and got back in the car.

"Did you ask what the traffic is all about?" she asked.

"No."

"Jesus, Tommy. We've been in heavy traffic for miles and you didn't think to ask what was causing the problem?"

"No. I just forgot."

She pointed to the line of cars and trucks bumper-to-bumper. "How could you *forget*?"

"Even if we knew, what could we do about it?"

"Well, damn, Tommy, if we don't know what's going on, we sure as hell can't do anything about it."

"Whatever it is, we'll be around it soon."

She pointed to a guy sweeping debris from the apron. He had

been working from right to left in narrow rows, pushing small branches and leaves before him with a broom. He would work the little piles to the other edge of the apron and with a brisk shove jettison the lot off the edge of the concrete pad.

"Ask him," she said. "I'd just like to know."

"Oh hell." I nodded at her milkshake cup. "Want me to throw that away?" She handed it to me. "I'll be right back."

I got out of the car and trashed the cup, then walked over to the fellow, who, concentrating on his sweeping, was oblivious to me. He was whistling and chewing on something at the same time. *Now, how the hell can a person do that?* I got bad vibrations again, like those I had back at the Dairy Queen. This guy was probably in his mid-forties, his face leathery and lean, gray-streaked hair down on the soiled collar of his dark uniform. Even before I got within speaking distance I got a whiff of stale cigarette smoke and perspiration.

I stepped into his field of vision. "Hey."

"Hey yerself." He stopped sweeping and leaned on his broom handle.

Behind me I could hear the traffic stopping and starting, stopping and starting, and horns were blowing up and down the line. As far as I could see in both directions the southbound lanes were stacked.

"Excuse me, but can you tell me what all this traffic backup is about? Is there a wreck or what?"

He shook his head. "Naw, ain't no wreck, least not that I know anythang about. What it is is—" He pointed to the barricade at the other end of the apron. "You see them sawhorses?"

I looked behind me. Annie was messing with the map again. "Yes. It's obvious y'all had a washing problem here. This from the rain yesterday?"

"All damned week until this mornin'. Hell of a front come thoo too. Might near warshed us clean away." He pointed to the end where he'd been sweeping debris. "They's a hole gouged out over there eight feet deep where the water come acrost the ce-ment here and made a waterfall. What happened was some limbs and shit got caught acrost the two big pipes that come under us and that water didn't have nowhere to go to, so it come over the ce-ment here. Got within a inch or two of comin' in the station itself."

I nodded and pointed at the two lines of cars and trucks that stretched back out of sight. "And the traffic? What's that all about?"

"Well, it done the same thang to the highway. The state was workin' on 59 just south of town when that rain come in here and warshed away everthang they had done all summer. So now they got the reglar work plus having to redo what they done already did. Hell of a mess down there. Just rurnt the southbound lanes. So what they havin' to do is ease people goin' south over into one of the northbound lanes. Only trouble is, cars has wallered out the media so bad that people're gettin' stuck where they crossin' over, then they got to get *them* pulled out before traffic can move again. They been haulin' in some caliche to make the crossover better, and that take'n time too and held up thangs even more. Coupla fender benders too. Earlier. Got four wreckers standin' by down there. And then they got all of that northbound traffic comin' up out of Houston since it's a Friday. Like I say, it's a mess. Got more highway petroleums and shurf's debities down there to keep things movin' than you could shake a stick at, and it don't seem to be doin' a lick of good."

"So how long do you figure it'll take us to get to Houston?"

He pointed to an eighteen-wheeler a few yards south of us. "I seen that truck come around the curve back up there over a hour ago, and you can see how far he's got." He spit a streak of brown onto the concrete. "Ordinarily it wouldn't take you very long at all, but all that shit down there. . . ." He pointed south. "Ain't no tellin', really, but once you get around that bad place, you'll zip on in. Trouble is, you prolly fifteen miles from the prollem. And I'd caculate that to be three, four hours, if you real lucky. Glad I don't live thataway. Live back in there." He motioned with his thumb behind him. All I could see was a vast line of trees.

I scuffed my foot on the concrete. "Is there any way to avoid all that? I saw people turning around and going back the other way—"

"Them's the fools that don't know where the prollem's at. They goin' thoo downtown instead of around the loop here, figurin' on comin' out south of the bad place. Only they come out north of it, which just adds *to* the prollem, them tryin' to feed in on traffic that's already nose to ass. Them highway petroleums ought to ticket'm."

We had slowly worked our way back to the car, where Annie, with her window down, could hear what was being said.

"So you're saying that they're working on the highway south of town?" She was leaning out, holding open the map.

"Yes ma'am, that's what I'm sayin'. Workin' right into the night, right up until it gets so dark that they'll have to quit. Ain't no tellin' what it'll get like then. It's a hell of a mess. Yon't me to show you where the bad spot is at on the map?"

"The map's fine," she said.

I glared at her and shook my head.

She tapped it. "Can you show us a way around the road work?"

"Well, me, I'd just go a back way to Houston. The best way is 59 when traffic's movin', but it might be dark before you get around that bad spot, way them cars are movin'. Or tomar sometime. Me, I'd just go down here a mile or so to where that Zip-In is and take that next highway west, foller the signs to Trinity, then go on into Huntsville, where you'll hit Interstate 45. That'll take you right on in. I can't understand why more people ain't doin' that, unless they just don't know how bad thangs is south of town."

I took the map from Annie and held it out to him. "Can you show us how to go?"

"Yeah, but I don't need that. It's easy." He reached over and began drawing a crude map in the grime on the hood, thumping out landmarks along a tortuous fingerline of road and announcing them like a tour guide. When he was finished, he said, "Can you foller that?"

I nodded and looked at Annie, who had laid the map back on the dash. I couldn't see her eyes, but I could imagine what they were saying.

"It's the easiest way," the attendant continued, "and besides, I noticed from yer tags that y'all ain't from here. You'll get a better idea of what East Texas is like than you would goin' on in on the big highway. More to see. Ain't no service stations out in there much, until you get to Trinity, but I seen you get gas, so you won't need to stop for that. Coupla stores maybe. That's the way I'd go. Y'all gon' be passin' through part of the Davy Crockett National Farst out in there. Real purty country. Sometimes I thank it looks like Nam. Just bushes and trees."

I nodded and thanked him and got back in the car.

"Look out for them-ere cars when you try to git back into line, mister," Annie drawled. "Jesus, where do these people come from?" She snickered. "Highway petroleums. He called them highway *petroleums*. Did you hear that?"

"Oh, hell, he was joking," I said. "Lots of people call them that in fun. And, by the way, they come from out there in the trees," I said, pointing to the heavy woods behind the station, "that look like *Nam*, which rhymes with *Spam*, you probably noticed. You are about to enter the Big Thicket, or what's left of it—just the western edge." I pointed to the map. "What we've got to hit down here is 94. It weaves over to Trinity, where—"

"I know. I heard what he said, and I watched him draw that snake on the hood."

She pressed the map across her lap while I edged up to the highway and managed finally to plead an opening from a trucker.

"You know that he was the third redneck from *Deliverance*, don't you?" she said. "I wonder how he got separated from the other two."

"I don't know. But I could tell by the way he was looking at you that they had phoned ahead. You are their kind of woman."

"Thanks, bastard," she said. "I'll bet we could find you a

woman that would eat pizza with you nekkid, get ground beef and sausage and bits of olive and peppers in her navel and let you lap it out. Now, don't that make you horny and hongry?"

"Yon't some gum?" I held the pack out to her. "Hit's Big Red. Prolly got Louisiana hot sauce in it."

"No, thank you. I've got Spearmint right here in my purse, if I want gum. If'n you got a plug of tobakker, though, I'll take a chunk."

We laughed at that, and it felt good. It was the first time I'd laughed with her in years. But the laughing stopped soon enough.

"Tommy, I think we ought to stick to the main highway. It might take longer, but at least we can't get lost."

"No, let's try his way. We've got a full tank of gas and a little sun left. We've never seen much of East Texas—you don't learn anything about a place from traveling along its interstates." I folded the map for her and handed it to her to put away.

"Yeah, I know, hit's real purty country, jes' like Goober done tol' us," she said. "I jes' cannot wait to see thatere Davy Crockett National Farst with all them big trees and it jes' full of rednecks like him. Or the Veet Kong." This time there was a real bite to her words. She was not smiling. "*Nam*," she said. "Why do they always pronounce it that way? I'll bet you that his whole dumb life long he's never fought anything but rednecks, male and female, or been out of this *county*, much less the country, unless he's been in the pen—where is it, Huntsville?"

"Yeah. In and around Huntsville. Just ease up, Annie. Keep your sunshades on and your eyes straight ahead, and before you know it we'll be on I-45 heading into Houston."

"Yippee." Her face was like stone.

We crept along another half mile or so to the Zip-In and turned off to the west on Highway 94, drove through a dozen blocks of suburbs, and after a few miles of scattered homesites entered the shadows of tall trees.

THREE

When they venture off the interstates, as from time to time they must, travelers through Southeast Texas note even along major farm-to-markets a uniform bleakness to the land, not the kind of Texas they expect from what they've seen of it in the movies— vast, broad-sky stretches of wasteland that lie farther west, mesquite prairies broken by knobby hills thrust suddenly up, studded with cactus and scrub oaks and cedar and here and there a river valley with pecans and cottonwoods. Not the dusty cliché Texas of Hollywood swarming with cattle and blustery with men wearing cowboy hats and pistols, but the worst of what they know of the Deep South: low wooded hills and damp, mosquito-plagued bottomlands, clogged with undergrowth and virtually impenetrable beyond the shoulder of the highway, and sprinkled by small towns conjured out of the gloom, from which paved roads radiate like tentacles through the wilderness to other small towns, tentacles that do not possess the land and squeeze the life from it as roads do other places but hold it in a slack embrace, tentative, as a man might a woman, gently and with a seeming reverence. And along these tentacles, clinging like sea parasites, are trailers and small frame houses inhabited by the people who travel the thin black roads to and from work each day.

So perilous is the balance here that if left unattended these asphalt strips and the little homesites that lie along them would yield to the green gospel of the wilderness in a handful of seasons and even more quickly the dirt roads that branch from them like animal trails, sometimes as crossroads, sometimes alone, snaking off to single trailers or shacks or houses or to clusters of trailers where people have established their footholds against encroaching woods. As a cut on an animal reknits and furs over, any wound in the flank of this beast will begin to heal in days. In a year virulent brush and vines will absorb roads and fields, and in another year of suns saplings will tower where a house stood or a trailer crouched, where people slept and children played. In yet another, as the canopies close, no one would know, but for slabs of gray boards and a few brick piers and crumpled pieces of rusty tin back in heavy shade, that anyone was ever here.

But the people accept this tentative balance, wedged in the wilderness like a piece of flint, for it is their nature to strike deep and cling wherever they make their mark, that tenacity engendered when the fires of their precursors, pitifully few in number but bold of purpose, first threw human shadows against the wall of woods. Before those ashes had cooled, axes and saws were letting in the sun. Dead now by many years and buried in shallow, damp graves, claimed by the land they claimed, roots taking their flesh and the ribs run through, those strong flintlike men and women, fireformed by hard living and sharpened to a keen edge and with a vague destiny in mind, came to subdue this land of virulent forests and brush—they were the only kind of people who could.

For this land is and always has been a wilderness, in name and in fact, settled long ago by people running from something or toward something, but running, leaving whatever they had had in Louisiana or Mississippi or Alabama or beyond—dirt farms whose veneer of enriched soil had been sapped of nutrients over the years by those who knew no more of the way of growing things than what their fathers had taught them and their fathers before, trusting to elders and almanacs and the moon, abandoning their gray shacks to the next inhabitants, even poorer than they, who like sea creatures plundering hollow shells moved in and filled the void for a few years, scratched *their* brief histories in the thin soil, and left it even thinner, and left as well a few mounds with wooden markers or stacked stones when they moved on themselves toward some promise in the direction of the setting sun. Dirt farmers, ranchers, visionaries, debtors, and criminals, in search of land to clear and grow things on or to disappear into, leaving in that trackless waste not a trace for those in pursuit, the Law or Confederate scouts, Government troops, or God Himself—desperate or dream-struck or burning with religious zeal, they came to the East Texas forests, these westering people.

Uneducated, poor and ignorant and superstitious, lone horsemen came—their animals, one or two or a dozen, draped with all they owned—or families, their possessions rarely filling more than what a single wagon would hold after squeezing in women and children. They moved stubbornly westward, crossing rivers and swamps and creeks, pushing deeper into Texas until finally they broke from the piney woods onto deep black soil and saw more sky in its vast blue splendor than they imagined could exist. And some moved on even beyond, the loners, the deep dreamers, toward the sun that seemed no nearer in its setting. Others stayed on the flat, treeless prairie where the topsoil, almost the color of coal, ran deep, because to them black soil meant rich soil and rich soil meant a living.

But most, weary of the trail and bedazzled by the endless sky of these plains, merely shook their heads and said, "We have gone too far, we never knew there was so much sky, so much land without trees," and these stern people wheeled their horses and wagons around and headed back east, lashing hard the dazed and beleaguered mules and dull-eyed oxen until they had entered the forest again, and then even more, lest the wide prairie pursue them, retreating across the Trinity and losing themselves in the shadows of familiar pines and oaks and hickories and cottonwoods. But they ran not from fear, for these people were never likely to fear anything or anyone other than God, *their* God, who lived among trees. They could recall in Genesis no mention of prairies.

Here they found familiar game—deer and turkey, squirrels and hogs and bear—and soil not so very different from what they had left, a rich humus that ran deep as a man's forearm and would when cleared of trees and vines grow all that they had grown before. A shallow well could be dug to sweet water in less than fifty feet, and the winters were mild and summers no more savage than they had known. It was a land where cabin and barn would stand as solid against the elements as they had back in Mississippi and Alabama, and children and animals would thrive.

The people were at home in the great forest, and they were glad. They chopped out their farms and made a go of it, bothering no one and being unbothered, farmer and debtor and renegade, knowing that no one would trouble them here, since what they had few other men would want and only a man of mindless determination could keep, and chasing a man in this place of tall dark trees could lead to nothing but breathless despair. They cleared the trees and brush and built their modest houses of logs and hand-hewn planks and in time laid open with teams of mule and oxen fields rich with millennia of leaf mold, pulled stump and roots, and harrowed and sowed and grew their corn and cane and cotton and potatoes, raised hogs and cattle, and brought forth children, who in their turn chopped out little patches of their own. Or they lost themselves in the deep, dark swamps to live out their appointed time however.

And daily they gave thanks to the Great God who had delivered them unto this wilderness, for their faith gave them the purpose and the courage to come and the fortitude to stay. He was a God they understood and were at ease with, the God of trees, and He blessed them when they were deserving and punished them when they were not. They spoke with Him across their tables at grace and in their beds at night and at Wednesday and Sunday service in the little board churches where they worshiped, singing and clapping and talking in tongues, this God who looked over and protected them, whose son had died for them, a son not swarthy, with hair like the wool of the lamb, and with dark eyes, on his tongue the rattle of Aramaic, but a fair angelic form like their own strong blue-eyed sons, with straight, smooth hair that shone in the sun in tones of auburn or blond and whose language was very like their own. *In My image* rang in their minds, *in the image of My Father.* They embraced in principle and in fact the Trinity, as real to them as the brown river by that name that cut through the forest and their lives. A lonely people they were, except for Sundays, when they turned their backs on the wall of woods and mingled with others of their kind, knowing that even God had to have a day of rest from the green gospel and from serpents. Lonely and isolated and content with their solitude, they worked and they worshiped and they flourished, these strong people.

And in time life for most of them was good, and more came, and little towns sprang up, sometimes no more than feed stores and groceries and dry goods clustered at crossroads, sometimes enclaves where in timber buildings at first, then concrete and brick, bankers and attorneys and lawmen ensured the civility of the day and businessmen sold furniture and clothing and food, tools, feed for stock, seeds and fertilizers, and doctors attended the sick and injured and brought children into the world, ministers spread the Good Word, and morticians prepared cold and silent forms beneath their lights for the great eternal dark.

Seldom seen by the forest people they made their livings from, the little towns persisted, some with names derived from surrounding geographic features, like Bleakwood and Moss Hill and Sour Lake, some labeled by those who founded them or for men whose names flared brightly in the history of the Republic—

Crockett and Corrigan and Lufkin. Still others, like Beaumont, had names steamy with irony. Big towns and small, by the turn of the century East Texas was sprinkled with them.

Away from the towns life went on as it always had—men and women rose before the crack of sun and collapsed bone-weary not long after it lost itself over toward the wide prairies that some had seen and others merely heard about. They cleared and burned and plowed, planted, gathered and stored, laying in wood for the winter and laying by for another season. Their lives and the land inextricably wound together, their blood hammering to its rhythms, the people clung to their small clearings, beating back the vines and trees and freeing another acre when they could, always only one small step ahead of the wilderness that crouched, waiting for them to relax, to celebrate, or to convalesce, then sent a slender green probe, and another, feeding on itself as it reclaimed what was taken by axe and saw and plow.

In the winters life was slow, when the breath hung blue in the morning air and the woods were gray and stark, the vines furled for those few brief months, weeds in deep slumber. Gardens still yielded a green bounty, pork and beef hung from smokehouse rafters or lay in deep salt in wooden boxes, and the forest was rife with bear and turkey and deer, squirrels and rabbits. But the winters are short and shallow here and the weather turns all too soon to that long hot season of growth again, the earth rekindles, and they knew even as they lay down those first warm nights of spring that the wakening weeds and vines were slithering and grasping in the dark, inching toward the sun.

Then the northeastern forests thinned and a call came for timber—the hardwoods and pines of the Big Thicket—and railroads followed and the sleepy little towns burgeoned and rumbled, the thick grime of greed descended, with blaring trains and wailing sawmills whose fine yellow silt drifted over town and countryside. And men of the soil, unaccustomed to attention and to cash, whose estimation of land is based on what it will grow from the seeds they plant and the animals they put on it, were approached by men of timber, who showed them something the land could not yield them: bushel baskets of dollars. For the people, cutting trees was never anything but necessity—to clear a place for house and pastures and fields, and the trees that fell they put axes and saws to to shape into planks and logs for building, burning in fireplaces and stoves what they could not use.

And then came the cry for oil, as if what grew above the ground could not sustain the appetite of the men who now wanted what was beneath it, and those dark ugly stains the people saw from time to time in the bottomlands, that nuisance to clothing and skin, became a glorious symbol of wealth.

One by one the little men sold out to the big, and the land itself became a commodity, like corn and cattle, to be used and used up if need be, stripped of its trees, wrung dry of its oil, drilled and soiled and scarred. For the man of commerce, the man with coat and tie who convinced with a flourish of the tongue and flash of green, the land became his, but not his—the land was paper, folded and kept in a steel box in a vault in a dusty courthouse somewhere, the land was so many barrels of oil beneath the surface or so many board feet of wood above, but what the land was not was the man himself, for he cared little to see it or touch it, cared nothing for the fragrance of its springtime breath, its lush green of summer, the golds and reds of fall, and he did not wish to do daily battle with its vines and brush, or scrape its wintertime mud from his boots, and he did not wish to be buried in it.

As the oil and timber industry burgeoned, so too did the little towns, swelling with riotous men whose strong backs and arms and hands, conditioned by years of labor on Southern farms, now wrestled with drill stems and two-man saws or managed great teams of mules in muddy oilfields or in forests. The weathered men of simple dreams of getting by, whose notion of wealth was food on the table and shelter that would keep their family warm and dry, whose knowledge of money was limited to a damp clutch of dollar bills and change, flocked to the towns to work for pale men of big dreams and fat bank accounts that grew fatter by the year. They came and they worked, and for a long season East Texas, like a pulsing insect full of spring, thrummed with the rich, deep song of money.

Today the money is in the cities along the interstates, strung with the glitter of Wal-Mart Supercenters and malls and shopping strips, the crossroad towns left like drying empty locust husks fastened to the bark of trees, crumbling brick buildings with boarded-up windows and sunbleached, rainbeaten signs declarations of the long, persistent dreams of man. Streets once lined with fine houses and manicured lawns slowly succumb to encroaching weeds and vines as year by year the earth pulls the houses down into it, like some great green sponge, leaving a few bricks and slats of gray lumber, asphalt shingles and tin. For the people who were here are gone. Gone to the cities or back to the woods.

The forest goes on and the people go on, because neither has a choice. Along the winding, forested roads of the countryside, trailers and cheap houses abound, and around them, almost without exception, is strewn trash of all sorts, from beer cans to rusting cars and trucks, as if pride were a commodity ill afforded out here, better left in the cities and the suburbs, where there is time for civic concern. Here there is only work, always work, off somewhere else, in Houston or Beaumont or Lufkin, and travel to and from that work, leaving before the sun and weaving back in among the trees after it, with only the weekends and holidays for keeping back the jungle that flings itself against these little patches of defilement assaulting the walls of green. But driving long miles to work and back each day is better than driving a short while and living in or close to the city, where there are only passive trees, cropped and trimmed and anemic, and no land that smells of the creation itself, fecund and rich. And even after their travel to the cities is done, their official work over, some stay in the forest to wait out their days until that final slumber. And as they wait, they labor to hold what they have against the closing green. Work and rest from work and church—there is time for little more for these people. And even if modern economic urgencies make it impossible for them to earn a living from the land they are couched on, they want to touch it every day, as their parents and parents' parents did, and plant their little gardens, where at least there is room and time for tomatoes and peppers and squash. They can still live on it, this land, they can go to sleep with its sounds at dark and wake to its music with the sun, and they care little whether anyone understands what has drawn them here and keeps them here, any more than they care whether they understand it themselves. Mornings when they drive away to work, their anxious eyes sweep across the gash they have made in the wall of woods, and they note what needs attention the next weekend, what front is closing fastest on them.

They shun the broad, bright waters of the Gulf, which they can reach in only a few hours, in favor of the torpid streams, brown with sediment and pollution, that crawl through the wilderness, preferring catfish and crappie to redfish and flounder, and crawfish to shrimp. These people are descendants of the initial inhabitants, whose offspring could not wait to leave the hardscrabble life in the wasteland to work in factories in Beaumont or Houston, where modern houses could be had, with indoor plumbing and garbage pickup, where grass could be kept at bay with a mower. But these, the people whose blood flows with the same agrarian blood that brought the first of them here, have returned, driven by something deeper than they can understand, and here they will stay until their own children leave for the cities. And even then they will stay. And then the children's children will return, for the land is in the blood and the blood is in the land, and forever it will be so.

Back in here no one bothers with clipped lawns and bordered drives or concerns himself about trash in the yard, for who sees these little clearings are those whose places look the same or those whose opinions do not matter. Only here and there, once in a dozen miles or so, and usually nearer the larger towns, a little oasis of beauty pops up, as if conjured from the forest by some lost and lonesome good spirit passing through and desiring to leave something of herself to be remembered: a brick house or a trailer with clean-swept drive and mown grass and flowerbeds free of weeds and vines, white fences fresh-painted. But the traveler must look quick, for these rare visions are on him in a flash, like a pinch of fairy dust: ping, they are here—poof, they are gone.

And along these forest roads the traveler is struck by the preposterous absence of human life, western civilization reduced to the ribbon of asphalt he is rolling on, paced by wire-strung crosslike poles that lean and weave at the edge of the trees, and high above, against the pale deep blue of the sky, the chalky trails of planes and beyond them the invisible yet certain fact of satellites. And as he drives, he knows that the very air he moves through sings with human voices.

Signs abound, small hand-lettered rectangles leading to produce stands, with *cantaloupe* spelled a dozen ways, *peanuts* never spelled right, *seedless oranges*, letters angling and drooping or backwards, as if genetics were at work there too, and larger signs, whitewashed sheets of plywood with bold foot-high letters declaring *AIDS—God's Gift to the Wicked* or *Jesus Saves* or *Are You Washed in the Blood?* And the traveler thinks, *Hell yes, every Saturday night the women and children are drenched with it.*

Houses with junky yards, antique stores with a backdrop of rusty bedframes and rickety chairs and footed tubs, asplash with tawdry craftwork of wood and ribbons, dried flowers, and the boldest paints to be had. Stores old and abandoned with gas pumps squatting at attention, dutifully and patiently awaiting the cars that will never come again. Fences clotted with brush and grass and flotsam of every description left from the last high water. Trash everywhere, blown from trucks or thrown out of windows, abandoned furniture and appliances, tons and tons of trash.

And there are times when he feels as if he has surely left the known world forever and entered a desolation that, but for the road he is following and the intrusion of poles and wires, he would believe himself lost in a land of goblins and trolls, the towering trees coming right up to the edge of the narrow shoulder and arching out over the road to form tunnels of leaf and limb that entirely shut out the sun. He stares out past his hood into the deepening gloom and through his rearview mirror at the blacktop trailing out behind and wonders why he is there and whether and when he will see the real world again.

FOUR

As we headed west out of Lufkin, the sun was fierce in our faces, the highway a long narrow shimmer flanked by a line of trees far off at first, with a stretch of newly developed land between the road and woods, then closing. At the edge of town the traffic thinned until by the time the lanes narrowed to two and the flanking trees closed tighter we had only a couple of cars ahead of us and a pickup truck behind, the usual late afternoon traffic apparently having cleared. The driver of the car immediately in front, a pale-blue Chevrolet, looked up into his rearview mirror, then drifted over into the emergency lane, allowing me to pass. I nodded at the elderly man behind the wheel and threw up a hand as I went by. He nodded and smiled and stayed on the shoulder until the pickup behind me was also past him.

Annie turned and looked back at the Chevrolet, then at me. "What was that all about?"

"What?"

"Why did he move off the road to let you pass?"

"He didn't move off the road. He just moved over into the

emergency lane. And he did it because he was being nice. People in Texas do that. Or have you forgotten what it's like to be nice?"

She shook her head. "I don't remember—I don't remember much niceness in Texas at all."

"You have to be nice for people to be nice back. That's a fairly universal rule. Which is why—"

"Yeah," she said.

"It's a courtesy. If someone wants to pass you but can't for oncoming traffic, you move over to the emergency lane and let him by. It's just a courtesy."

The car now in front held to the lane, so I eased closer. The driver, a young woman, gave no indication that she knew I was behind her. Not much more than a car length from her bumper, I flicked my lights. I could see her raise her eyes and look through the mirror at me, then lower them. She doggedly stayed in the middle of her lane.

"Come on, damn it, move your ass over." I glanced at Annie, then pointed to the car ahead. "She's not doing fifty."

"She's being careful," Annie said.

"She's creeping."

It was one of those situations you get in on a country road where the person in front of you is obviously in a contemplative or contentious mood and wherever she's going she's in no great hurry to get there, and she's the only thing between you and open highway, which you can see just past her—but traffic from the other direction is scattered out just so that you don't dare try to make a run on her.

"Where in hell do you suppose this inbound traffic is going? People ought to be trying to get *out* of Lufkin, not in."

"You're getting a little close to her," Annie said. "According to the book I had to study to get my license, you are supposed to allow a car length between you and the car ahead for every ten miles per hour you are going."

"*I* am driving, and I studied the same book you did."

"Not very well, and I mean in both respects."

"I don't know of any other state where people routinely move over for you," I continued. "As a matter of fact, if you find someone in another state moving over for you, you'll generally find he has Texas plates on. Almost everybody does it here."

I eased closer still, but the driver in front was not budging from her lane. I flashed my lights at her again.

"She can't see your lights," Annie said. "You're too close."

"I could have flashed them for the last two miles and it wouldn't have made any difference. She can see them all right."

"Just won't move over, huh?"

"Won't move over. Bitch."

"She's not being courteous, you're saying."

"It's a woman."

She turned her head toward me. "I know it is a woman. I can see her hair. I can see almost every detail of the back of her head, you're so close. I can see her face in the mirror."

"Then what kind of bug is that just behind her left ear?"

"Smartass," she said. "What does the fact that it's a woman have to do with it?"

"It has *everything* to do with it. Women just won't do it. They won't move over for *anybody*."

"That's bullshit."

"They *won't*. Not one out of a hundred." I flashed my lights again. The driver held fast to her lane. "See. Not even when I ask her to. She'd die right there in that lane from old age before she'd move over for me. They're that way, women are."

"Shiii—" she said.

"Now where in holy hell do you suppose she's going that she's got no more enthusiasm for getting to than to drag along at fifty miles an hour?"

"Maybe she's going home to some grease monkey in a trailer and a couple of wailing kids wanting supper. We'll know when she gets to the road that leads to the trailer she lives in. She'll either turn off and go in and fix supper for the creep and kids or pop a finger at the trailer and take off like a jet and neither the grease monkey nor the kids nor us will ever see her again."

"God, what a poisoned mind you have. Don't you ever have pleasant thoughts?"

"Not with you around I don't."

The truck behind me was bearing down on my bumper, so I dropped back a few feet from the car in front, timed myself, and jammed the pedal, shooting around her and squeezing in just in front of an oncoming pickup. I wanted to throw her a little one-finger salute, but I figured it would just piss Annie off.

"That was *close*." She had her feet braced against the floorboard. Her lips were drawn in a tight, thin line.

"I'm driving." I moved onto the shoulder and let the pickup pass.

"I noticed." She relaxed her legs. "How nice of you to move over like that. I never saw that in you before."

I gave her a look.

"That woman was in the lane first, and she was ahead of you. She didn't owe you anything, you know."

"That's got nothing to do with it. It's a common courtesy."

"Yeah," Annie said, "like Texas has got courtesy all figured out and the other forty-nine states are just bassackwards. What a joke."

"All I know is that Texans will move over and let you pass and drivers in other states won't."

"They move over because they figure you'll pull out a gun and blow their heads off if they don't. I wouldn't call that courtesy, more like plain old fear out here on the wild frontier." She slapped the dash. "My, what a nice rhyme."

"Call it what you will," I said. "Just shut up about it. Didn't you bring anything to read?"

"I can't read with you driving. Can't concentrate."

She was silent a few seconds, then said, "I know why women won't do it."

"Won't do what?"

"Jesus, what an attention span. Why they won't move over."

"Why?"

"Why what?" she asked.

"Stop it, Annie."

"They won't move over because it's dangerous. Women are usually the ones with kids on board, as they say, and they're the ones who have to go home and fix supper and see that the kids get baths and get their homework done, and if something happened to them the whole family would just sit there in the trailer wondering where momma's at, how come momma ain't home to fix supper, then starve to death and decompose on the couch in front of the television, just seep right into the sofa, leaving nothing but bones for somebody to find. If they routinely moved over, it would probably mean the end of the Western World. There's all kinds of stuff over on that shoulder. It's rough, dangerous. Women've got more sense. That lane is for *emergencies*, which is why they call it an emergency lane, not for making a trip quicker for some asshole who doesn't have anywhere to get to except maybe the next beer joint. Besides, she might move over for some redneck in a pickup, who'd force her to stop, and then—"

"Got it all figured out, huh? That's not why they won't move over."

She shrugged and settled back in her seat, her face relaxed. "You don't know a Goddamned thing about women." She reached and brushed something off the dash. "And that's just *one* of your problems."

"I know when to leave one," I said.

She gave *me* a look.

"I know when to leave a woman."

"I know what you meant. That's real clever. But if you remember, I left *you*." She leveled her sunshades at me. "But why don't *you* leave *me* right now? Just pull over and let me out at the next town or, hell, *crossroads*, and I'll hitch a ride on into Houston."

"Bullshit. You wouldn't even *drive* down here by yourself. I can just see you on the side of the road, one hip thrust out, your thumb in the wind."

She kept her dark, cold glasses on me. "I told you my car has a problem. Just let me the hell out at the next crossroads. See how I do."

I snorted. "You are one tough cookie, one bad-ass little girl. Now just what do you figure would happen if I did leave you stranded in one of these little Godforsaken towns? Your daddy would probably come after me with a shotgun."

"All the more reason to let me out," she said. Her face was flirting with a smile, but she wouldn't let it come.

For the next mile or so she said nothing, just kept her shades directed into the glare of the road. We were in the countryside now, and the sun was sinking fast in the trees that converged ahead. It would be dark in an hour or so.

"I'd make it, you know," she said. "I'd probably beat you to Houston. You couldn't take that, though, could you?"

"Shiiiit." I reached over and picked up her arm at the wrist. Her hand dangled like a clutch of withered flowers, pale as marble, tiny blue veins. "The Iron Lady. You're not nearly as Goddamned tough as you'd have me believe. You'd end up in one of those dinged and dimpled pickups and spend the rest of your life in a trailer somewhere growing petunias in tire planters and old bathtubs, with those goofy-ass pink long-legged birds in the yard, and screwing a redneck with hair all over his back, a telephone lineman or a logger or something, and watching flies populate."

"Flamingos," she said.

"What?"

"The pink birds. They're called flamingos. But I'd prefer a statue of Elvis."

"Yeah, that'd be your speed. Yours and your redneck husband's."

She pulled her arm away. "At least he wouldn't be pushing

insurance, and he'd be getting what you're not and haven't for a while and never will again in this lifetime."

"Very funny. That's probably the only thing about you he'd enjoy. Did it ever occur to you that I just might not want—"

"Bull*shit*. You'd nail me in an East Texas second if I'd let you. We both know it."

"You're flattering yourself." I gripped the steering wheel hard.

She was actually smiling. "Oh, yeah, I guarantee you that if I asked you to pull off on one of these little dirt roads to screw, you'd do it so fast—"

"I'm getting plenty," I said. "And the best part is that I wake up beside somebody I want to share a cup of coffee with. And talk to."

"I've got a pretty good idea what you've been waking up beside," she said.

"You don't know a damned thing about me or my women."

"More than you think."

"Nothing at all."

"I just hope for your sake that you've been taking precautions."

"Thank you for your concern, but whether I have or not is my business, not yours."

She stared out the window a few seconds and said quietly, "I bet you'd just *love* to dump me in the middle of nowhere—"

"Yeah. It'd give you a chance to prove what you've been saying about yourself. Little Miss Independence."

"Not yet," she said.

"What does that mean?"

"Not *Miss* yet. But I'll start to work on it when we get back."

"Oh, fuck you."

She turned and gave me a sharp-edged smile that was not a smile. "And certainly not *that*." She turned her face back to the window and watched the sorry houses pass by. "God, I hate this—trees and cheap houses, trailers, the people. Texas in general. East Texas in particular. And *you*."

"Hate it, then, damn it. And hate me. But this train is going south—sooner or later. And you're not getting off. Didn't you bring something to read?"

"You've already asked me that. Since when are you concerned with my reading?" She pointed her thumb toward the back. "I've got a book and a magazine in one of my bags, thank you, but I'd prefer to watch the road."

"Fine," I said. "Count the stripes. Or maybe the trees. Or trailers. Or blessings, if you have any. Sheep. Hell, just count *something* and let me do the driving."

She crossed her arms and looked forward a minute or two, then turned her head back to the window. The nicer homes with well-kept lawns and neat outbuildings were gone now, supplanted by small frame houses and trailers that squatted in little clearings around which a line of trees formed a dark green barrier, thick and ominous. It was not pretty country.

It was a place of trees and the shadows of trees, country of a dying sun, boneyard of dead marriages. And a silent wife beside me, her eyes fixed through very dark glasses on the roadside, lips clamped in a hard red line that reflected in the window.

"It's obvious from the traffic," she finally said, "that nobody else is taking this detour. We should have stayed on 59."

"I told you, I'm doing the driving. So get off my back."

I could see clearly on the hood the little map the man had drawn, 94 the width of his index finger, running parallel with the length of the car in a mild dogleg, then a sharp turn to the west at Trinity and over to what he had said was I-45 at Huntsville, where we would head due south and in another hour or so be in Houston. What my eyes were fixed on, though, was the little fine-line road he had traced down to another small line that he said joined with 59 fifteen miles or so south of Lufkin, well below the problem area on the highway. I couldn't remember the number of the road, but he said it went south at Apple Springs, which was up ahead a couple of miles.

Annie had laid her head back on the seat and closed her eyes. They were still closed when I got to Apple Springs and made a turn onto the only paved road that went left and wound off down through a corridor of tall trees. The hell with telling her what I was doing. She would argue about it. Better to go ahead and do it, save the time and energy. We would come out south of the interstate work and be on our way to Houston again. Probably even before she woke up. If she slept. All I knew was that her eyes were still closed and she had stopped talking.

Here the road seemed to force itself through the wall of trees that loomed outraged and stunned to surrender by the narrow asphalt strip and the sheer audacity of the men who laid it there. It was trash strewn, as most rural roads are in areas populated by low-income families, and the presence of paper and plastic at a uniform height in the undergrowth suggested that it had been recently flooded. There was no traffic except for two oncoming logtrucks, empty, their trailers banging along like playthings, which I nervously squeezed past.

Annie stirred but didn't lift her head. Her pretty head. I studied out of the edge of my eye the graceful contours of her thighs. She was right about that much at least—I'd take her to the backseat in an East Texas second. Jesus. I felt myself getting aroused again. Jesus-H-Christ!

Trees and the shadows of trees. A dying sun. A ribbon of black road cutting through the wilderness. And beside me a woman who despises me.

What we struck with the left-front tire—I saw it at an appreciable distance, saw it but could not for the life of me avert the car from that certain collision, drawn inexorably toward it, mesmerized—was, I found out later, a metal bracket that probably bounced off one of the trucks. Much swerving and squealing and banging and clunking and we came to rest finally with half the car on asphalt, the other half on the narrow caliche shoulder that separated the road from a ditch that ran alongside it.

Annie sat staring at me through her dark glasses as I leaned my head on the steering wheel. The sun was lightly fingering the tops of the trees.

"Goddamn," I said quietly.

"What is going on?"

"We hit something."

"Hit something? What does that mean? Did we hit a deer? A cow? Did the car quit?"

"No. We had a damned blowout."

"Tommy, if this is some kind of joke—"

I lifted my head from the steering wheel. "Annie, I wouldn't make a joke about something like that. I ran over something and blew a tire."

"Well, aren't you going to see about it?" She had unbuckled and eased forward in her seat. "Everything looks fine to me. Are you sure you've got a problem?"

"Yeah, I'm sure. Like I said, we ran over something back there and we blew a tire."

"*You.* Not we." I could hear her light breathing, like a pant. She was frightened. "Shouldn't you get out and fix it?"

"Yeah," I said, opening the door. "You go on counting trees or sheep or whatever the hell you were counting."

"What I was counting was the moments until this trip is over."

"Hope you enjoyed your nap."

"I wasn't asleep."

"Bullshit." I got out and closed the door.

The tire on the left front was ruined. The treads had caught one leg of a steel bracket and flipped the other leg up, driving its tapered edge through the outer wall of the tire. It was still imbedded in the oblong gash.

"Aw, man." I stood back and studied the tire.

"Are we in trouble?" Annie yelled.

I nodded. My eyes moved past the car and to the wall of woods and undergrowth just beyond the ditch we were parked beside.

Annie slid over and rolled down my window. "Is it bad?"

"Yeah, it's bad." I squatted down and pried the bracket out of the tire wall and held it up. "This piece of steel went right through the side of the tire. Cut a hole this big." I held my finger and thumb five inches apart.

"You can't blow it back up?" she asked. "You know, those fix-a-flat-in-a-can things that you just screw on and—"

"Annie, the Goddamned tire's ripped open. It's blown out, not just flat. It wouldn't hold *concrete*." I motioned for her to hand me the keys.

She yanked them out of the ignition and threw them through the window to me. "I hope you've got an extra."

"An extra *what*?"

"An extra tire back there. You know, to replace the one that's blown up."

"Blown *out*," I said. "And it's called a spare."

"Whatever," she said.

"Of course I've got a spare," I said.

"Then shouldn't you get busy putting it on? It's getting late, Tommy, and we're in the middle of no damned where at all."

This was beginning to take on the tone of a terrible nightmare. I went to the trunk and after setting all our stuff on the roof of the car removed the spare, absurdly small in my hands, like something you'd put on a play car. One of those silly little temporaries that Detroit makes to save a buck or two. But at least it had air. Not much—it barely bounced when I pitched it on the pavement and reached for the jack and handle and lug wrench.

I started back around to the front of the car with my arms full like I'd just bought a load of groceries. Annie was studying the map she'd spread out on the dash.

"Are we still in Texas?" she asked as I passed by the window.

I ignored her and set down the spare and jack.

She slid over to my side and leaned her head out the window. "I don't understand. This road looks entirely different from 94. It's too narrow, for one thing, and—well, everything looks different. There're not even any stripes on it, and 94 ought to have stripes. The trees are right up to the road. And there's no traffic. And the sun's coming in from the right. It's not in our eyes anymore. Tommy, something's not right here."

I opened the door. "Move back over. I've got to get this car off the asphalt or some damned logtruck will run right over us." I cranked it and eased it over until we were completely on the shoulder.

"Tommy, this can't be right."

I shut the engine off and got out and dropped down and positioned the jack under the car the best I could. *Fuck you, fuck you, fuck you.*

"Tommy." She slid back over and opened the door and got out and leaned over me. "Tommy, are we still on 94?"

"We're aimed toward Houston," I grunted. "Isn't that what counts? Get back in the Goddamned car." Under my breath I added "Bitch."

She got back in. As I jacked I could hear her muttering in the front seat. Jesus, I was the one who should be annoyed. And I was. The jack kept angling dangerously as the car rose. Then it began sinking in the rain-softened shoulder. The harder and faster I jacked, the worse the angle got and the deeper the jack sank, so I started over. Three damned times.

"Tommy, what's happening out there?" I heard her ask.

Bitch.

Finally I forced the flange that had ruined the tire into the caliche and set the jack base on it, so that when I worked the handle and the weight of the car came full force, the jack held. It leaned, but it held the car off the ground. Hell of a note—the bracket that ruined the tire now let the jack work.

"Tommy," her voice came from the front seat.

Fuck you, fuck you, fuck you!

I broke the nuts loose and removed the tire. It was ruined, as surely as if someone had taken a broadhead axe and slashed the sidewall with it. I held it up for her to see, but she only glanced my way, then turned back to face the woods on her side. Jesus, sunshades are cold. I flung the tire to the ground and set about mounting the doughnut.

In another five minutes or so I had lowered the car and stashed the jack and ruined tire in the trunk. My hands were filthy, my pants and shirt smudged. I asked Annie whether she had any wipes in her purse.

"Wipes? I've got Kleenex."

"No. *Wipes.* Wet-wipes. Something I can get this grease and dirt off with before I set our stuff back in the trunk."

"Jesus, Tommy, I don't carry wipes. Women with babies and small children carry wipes. You may not have noticed, but I don't have a baby or small child."

"Fine," I said, "I'll get by." I went over to the ditch and scooped up some coffee-colored water and then scrubbed my hands with caliche and pine straw and got most of the grime off.

"You didn't get them very clean," she observed through her open window. "Don't you have a handkerchief?"

"Yes I do, but I'm not going to ruin it with this stuff."

"No, you'd rather ruin my stuff."

"Don't worry about your damned stuff. I won't mess anything up."

"Don't you have a rag or something back there in the trunk? Jerry Simms carries a rag and GOJO."

"I don't give a good Goddamn what Jerry Simms carries in his trunk."

"And he drives a Lexus."

Big fucking deal. Jerry Simms was a real estate dealer she dated for a while. Goofy-looking and dumb, even if he did carry GOJO and a rag in his trunk.

"A Lexus that probably has a big new full-size tire like the other four in the trunk, huh?"

"No," she said. "Just *one* big new full-size tire in the trunk. The other four are what the car rolls on."

At that I slammed my hands on the roof above her. "Goddamn it, Annie, I am in no mood for your word games."

She slammed her hands on the windowsill. "Well, mister, it might interest you to know that I am not in a very good mood right now either."

"Why are you worried about my hands anyway?" I asked when I'd walked around and gotten in the car. "You're not planning on holding one of them, are you?"

"Not on your life," she said.

"Then don't worry about'm."

I eased out onto the road and slowly accelerated, but the little tire roared and rumbled and complained against the asphalt—I might just as well have crept along on the rim—so I backed off and off until we were barely moving.

"Is this as fast as you can go?" She was sitting way out at the edge of her seat, her neck craned to see the road ahead.

"It's as fast as I *intend* to go," I said. "There's not much air in that tire. And besides, I've already had to use it twice. I don't think they were designed for that."

"Then why didn't you replace it?"

"I just never got around to it is why. It's not exactly the first thing you think about when you get a tire fixed. They just throw the damned thing back in there and you forget it until you need it again."

"It would be the first thing *I'd* think of," she said.

"Well, bully the hell for you. Maybe I'll remember it this time."

"You're assuming you'll get back home *this* time." She settled back in the seat and looked out at the trees that slowly slid past. "One thing for sure, I can count the trees now, as slow as we're going. As a matter of fact, I can out*walk* you at this pace. Why don't you just let me out and you can meet me in Houston some-time day after tomorrow."

"Then get the hell out and walk," I said. "You think I'm enjoy-ing this?" My voice rose until I was almost shouting. "It wasn't my Goddamned fault that that Goddamned piece of steel was in the Goddamned road."

"You didn't *see* it? Anybody should have been able to see some-thing that big. Why couldn't—"

"The point is that I *didn't* see it, Annie. If I had seen the damned thing, I would have dodged it. There might have been a time I would have screwed up a tire to get caught out in the woods with you, but that was a long time ago. . . . A sixty-dollar tire might have been worth it to me."

She snorted. "A *looong* time ago. And it certainly would have cost you more than a five-dollar pizza. You could have had Betty Dunbar even then for the price of a corny-dog."

"If you don't shut up about Betty, I swear to God that I will park this car and we'll spend the night on the shoulder. And, by the way, if you hadn't been out cold, you might have seen the damned thing."

"I wondered when you would figure out that it was my fault."

"Why don't we just talk about something else?"

The corridor we were traveling down settled into deeper shade as the sun slid farther behind the canopy of trees to our right, occasionally flinging little fingers of shocking bright light against the wall of trees on the other side of the road. At greater speed it would have been like a strobe tunnel.

"How far can we go on that doughnut?" she asked after a few hundred feet.

I shook my head. "I have no idea. A few miles. Not far. They weren't made to go far. They were made to get you to a service station."

"You heard what that guy said—there aren't any service stations out here."

"Well, maybe, Goddamn it, he was wrong. He did say there were a couple of stores."

"Well, maybe, Goddamn it," she said, "he was wrong."

She turned her head and squinted into the strobing shafts of sun. "You still didn't explain to me how the sun is over here now instead of in front of us." She looked down at the map and then at me. "The sun should be right in front of us or slightly to the left, but not over there." She pointed to the dark wall of woods to her right. "But this is Texas, after all, and the *sun* probably doesn't even act right here."

"What are you, the *navigator*?"

"Tommy, I'm just wondering about the sun. It ought to be in our face—and there ought to be *traffic*. And the road's too narrow. No stripes. Something's wrong."

"I took another road."

It got really quiet again, the only sound the noise of our tires against the pavement. The car was pitched down on the left front, as if we were going downhill. I kept my eyes straight ahead.

"Another road?" Her voice was flat and hard. I thought of that steel bracket. "This is not 94?"

"No." I pointed to the map on the hood. "The guy at the service station showed me another way. A little road that will get us there a lot quicker. We go south and hit 59 well on the other side of the road work. Should shave—"

"How the hell did we get on it? When did you turn off?" She had spun in her seat to look at the corridor of trees we had just passed through.

"Back a couple of miles," I said, "at Apple Springs, but—"

"I knew I shouldn't have closed my eyes. Why don't you just turn around and go back to 94?"

"It'll probably be just as close to go on now. Even if we could get back to Apple Springs, it's just a name on the map, a crossroads, and I didn't see anything that looked like a store there. We may run across a store or something up ahead."

"My God, Tommy, there's no store down in here." She pounded the dash. "There's nothing here but *trees*, billions and billions of *trees*. Turn around. Or let's just stop and call somebody to—"

"I don't have a phone. Do you?"

She gave me a long, steady gaze, then said, "You don't have a telephone? You don't have a cell?"

"It slipped out of my pocket and fell into the commode day before yesterday. Ruined it. I just haven't had a chance to get a new one yet."

"You don't have a *phone*?"

"No. How come *you* don't have one?"

"I do," she said. "It's on the kitchen counter. I just figured *you* would have one. God, Tommy. . . ."

"I doubt we'd get a signal down in here anyway—all these woods."

I kept the car at a steady pace on that gloomy forest road, my eyes alert and my ears attuned to the steady complaint of the little spare that I knew couldn't last much longer.

Annie spread the map across the dash and pointed. "Now, exactly where did you leave 94?"

"I told you, at Apple Springs. This cuts south there off 94."

"Put on your damned glasses, Tommy."

I eased the car over onto the shoulder and stopped, slipped on my glasses, and pulled the map onto the steering wheel. I traced 94 out west of Lufkin and found Apple Springs, where the fine black line headed off south.

"There," I said. "This is the road."

She raised her shades and squinted over at the map. "That? That is a *trail*. A forest *trail*. It doesn't even have a number on it. I can barely *see* it."

"Yes it does. Look." I pointed to a little number beside the road. "It's Highway 8."

"That's the distance between Alice Springs and that other little road down there."

I laughed. "*Apple* Springs. Alice Springs is in Australia."

She looked at me over the edge of her sunshades. "And we're just about that lost, Tommy. Probably be kangaroos ahead, and dingoes, or whatever they call those ugly damned dogs they have down there."

"The road has a number. All the highways here have one. I saw it on a sign right after we turned off 94."

"There is no number on the road. How could you take a road that doesn't even have a number? It's a wonder they don't show animal tracks on it. It's just a *pig trail*."

"Follow the damned thing north of 94—there's got to be a number on it."

She yanked the map onto the dash again and studied it a few seconds.

"OK, yeah, it's got a number—357. That's a good number for a road in Texas. Yes indeedy. It's a wonder somebody didn't put *magnum* after it."

"I didn't know you knew that much about guns."

"I don't, but I do see a movie occasionally, and 357 and magnum just seem to go together, like Colt and 45."

"All right. Notice that 357 goes down and hits another road that will carry us over to the interstate."

"It goes down and dead-ends into . . . 2262—my God, Tommy, it's an even *smaller* pig trail. I'll bet it's *dirt* and there are probably real pigs using it. Or kangaroos and dingoes."

"Annie, it'll be paved. All the roads on that map are paved now. We can go on 2262 over to 59 and we'll have a straight shot to Houston." I put my glasses back into their case.

"Oh yeah," she said quietly, settling back into her seat and re-folding the map. "Oh, hell yeah."

All a civilized man's life he finds himself compelled to try to impress females, puffing and strutting, from simian antics on jungle gyms and swing sets on dusty playgrounds to banging his helmeted head against other helmeted heads on Friday nights to leaving smoking rubber trails on asphalt, until finally, in control of his glands and with sufficient understanding of women to know what will and will not work to get their attention, he refines his courting ritual for the serious mission of securing a mate, having advanced beyond the bestial impulse merely to seize and hold.

But even when he has won his woman, he must continue the maddening business of impressing, through word and deed, keeping her interested and entertained, knowing that predictability and dullness are the twin barrels of doom for a marriage. For what purpose are estates and empires built, the glittering commerce of the world, why are wars fought and political careers pursued? Why but for men's urgency to impress women, for *women* are the commodity upon which everything human is based, the rest the frivolous fluff of a creature who presumes himself outside nature. When empires flourish in the sun and the powerful men who built them laugh in the teeth of destiny or dust settles on their ruins, the great men undone, the women are always there, before and after, in front of or behind—but they are always there, for this is the way of the world. The way it will always be. The way it *must* be.

And nothing is so enervating to a man as knowing that the woman he once called his cannot be impressed by anything he says or does, that her interest in him is as dead as old sand-covered ruins in some faraway desert. When he knows that the magic, if ever it existed, is exposed as a simple flourish of hands fast enough to fool only the eyes, for a while he carefully measures what he says and does in hopes of restoring it, pulling the curtain back across, reaching deeper in the hat for whatever exotic thing he may conjure, but he pulls out less and less until finally the hat is as empty as the wind across that buried desert empire and what is behind the curtain thin as ether. And when this happens a big part of him dies—the wolf—for man is a creature of conquest and must believe that there is something real for him to hunt and have at last, and when the wolf dies, all that is left is a shell inside which self-loathing echoes a long drawn-out howl.

I have never known time to pass more slowly than it did as my crippled car carried us deeper into that East Texas wilderness, the woman beside me despising me even more than she did when I had picked her up. There was nothing I could say or do to change anything either. She hated me on the surface and deep down. Through and through.

She refused to look at me now—her eyes were glued to the

road ahead, a road settling into dusk. About us the great dark trees loomed, their arms arching over, and it took little effort to imagine fancy gargoyle faces on them, teeth bared. The sun continued to fade, flashing across only the tops of the highest trees.

When a man finds himself unable to regenerate a woman's love, perhaps unable even to summon the love he once had for *her*, he feels at first a deep regret that saps his spirit as a dread disease does the body, debilitating it slowly until his very view of life is contorted by it, like the delirium of fever, and then regret evolves into anger, not so much toward her as toward himself for being unable to keep things together. For he knows deep down that almost always a marriage fails because of the man, to whom marriage is often little more than a convenience, a stopover on his way to other places, while to a woman it is everything, and though a man may stay with a marriage all his life, it is seldom so. His heart follows many drums.

Then the anger transmogrifies into loathing, again not so much toward her as toward himself, and he despises himself for what he has turned her into and for what he has become. He comes to realize and accept the fact that most sorry women are made that way by some sorry man, criminal and social statistics bearing out that truth. But by the time he comes to this truth, he is so confused by it all that he does not know what he understands or what he believes, and he simply does the best he can, poor son of a bitch that he is.

She broke the silence: "You are taking me into the very heart of darkness. This is not even real, Tommy, it's like a bad, bad dream.

Please turn the car around and head out of here before it gets dark. I'm getting scared."

"Annie, I can't—there's nothing behind us but where we've been and what we've seen and we haven't seen anything for miles. There wasn't anything before Apple Springs, there wasn't anything at Apple Springs, and there hasn't been anything between Apple Springs and here, unless you want to count trees and dumpsters and collapsed houses. We've got to go on, no matter how far. There's got to be something out here, a house or trailer or store or something."

"There's not even any traffic," she said. "There ought to be traffic. If you'll get us back to 94, at least there'll be traffic."

The words were barely out of her mouth when two logtrucks, heavily laden with tree trunks that stuck far out behind their trailers, cantilevered tips weaving and dancing like the tails of dragons, roared out of the gloom, peppering us with bark as they blew past, their airwash buffeting the car like some silly little boat in heavy seas. I braked and dropped the right wheels off onto the shoulder and turned on my lights.

"Christ!" Annie shouted. "They almost ran over us."

"Sonsofbitches. They were in one hell of a hurry."

"Yeah. Women may be slow, but you don't worry about them trying to run you over."

As we sat there idling and I struggled to get up the nerve to pull back onto the highway, a pickup shot out of the corridor ahead and passed us.

"Well, you got your traffic," I said.

"Yeah, but everything's headed *out* of here, like they're trying to get home before night closes on them. They must know something we don't know."

"Ease up, Annie, we'll come to something by and by. Start looking for lights."

"I can already see one," she said, pointing up.

I followed her finger. A tiny twinkling star hung directly above and before us.

"Well, it worked for the Magi," I said. "Maybe it'll work for us."

"I somehow don't think that the course of the Western World is going to be changed by this trip. I'd be happy enough just to be able to get back to where we came from." She folded the map resignedly and pitched it onto the dash, pushed some loose ends of hair back under her scarf, and adjusted her sunshades.

A logging road, and another, and still there were no houses, no stores, not even a mildewed trailer against the backdrop of trees. Nothing but woods and undergrowth and more woods, through which the narrow asphalt road crawled like a serpent. Not even an open field.

"There's a sign," Annie said, pushing forward in her seat. "There."

"I see it. It's just a highway number or something."

"A sign's a sign down in here." She lifted her shades onto her forehead and squinted. "I'd be happy enough if the thing told me something about Jesus, how he always saves the lost or something."

I put my glasses on, but before I could read the sign, she said in a flat voice, "Fifty-five. Speed limit fifty-five. That sign's not from Jesus, or if it is, He's got a better sense of humor than I gave Him credit for." She snorted. "I *wish* fifty-five. Fifty-five miles per hour or fifty-five miles in any direction from here or even fifty-five *years*—at least my barren, miserable, lonely life would be over or so nearly over I wouldn't give enough of a damn to worry about it. I'd have all my screwed-up, wasted years behind me."

"Settle down, Annie. Save your energy."

The sign slid past us. She was huddled in the seat now, with her legs pulled up beneath her and her face resting against the window. The shades were back in place. I couldn't tell whether she was crying or not, but she was far from being a happy camper. I wanted to reach and touch her, to reassure her, but I didn't dare. I frankly didn't know what to do or say to her. She might indeed just get out and walk.

"I see another sign," I said. It was a yellow one, which could mean anything, but as it slowly came into focus I could tell that it warned of a serpentine twist in the road ahead, as if at our speed a warning were necessary. A smaller sign beneath it read *30 mph*. Jesus, I could have made a U-turn with no danger.

"I guess that means snakes ahead, huh?" Annie said. "Why the hell not? Snakes and kangaroos and wild dogs and pigs and God knows what all. It is, after all, a *jungle*. Where is Tarzan when I need him?"

"You know what it means," I said.

"Well, do you intend to speed up to thirty or what?"

"Annie, relax. Just settle the hell down."

Her face in a little child's pout, she closed her eyes and stretched her legs out, then refolded them beneath her, dropping her head down into her open hands. I felt pity coming on again, but I knew the level of bitchery she was capable of and how close it lay to the surface, so I simply kept my eyes on the road, hoping somehow, for my sake as much as for hers, that beyond the next twist might lie some sort of deliverance. Through the trees overhead I could see more stars.

Around the last bend of the twist the road rose slightly and after a long dark passage through heavy trees suddenly the underbrush fell away and an opening yawned on my left. I saw beyond a barbed wire fence a field that sloped down and away toward distant woods and then a gravel drive and an old white building.

"Annie, look." I nudged her leg.

She raised her head and her eyes shot open and she sat forward in the seat. Her face was as eager as a child's. "It worked, Tommy. It worked. I closed my eyes and wished for a miracle and it happened."

"Bullshit," I said. "I wouldn't call that a miracle. And if I were trying to wish for a place, I'd have done better than that. Is it a house, or *what*?"

"It's a *place*, Tommy. Whatever it is, it's a *place*." She had pushed her shades up and was looking past me toward the building, where no lights burned but patterned curtains hung in the windows.

I had pulled over on the right shoulder and stopped to study the old building and driveway. "Well, I'm not sure this is something to celebrate."

"Drive over there and park, Tommy, and go use their phone. There are wires running into that building. They must have a telephone. This may be the only place we'll find on this Godforsaken road. Please try it."

"Maybe we ought to ease on a mile or two and see what we can find. We can always come back here."

She reached and seized my arm. "Tommy, you got us into this mess. Now you've got to get us out. Drive over there and ask to use their phone."

I put the car in gear and inched across the road and onto the pea gravel of the drive. A great gash stretched from one end of the apron to the other. It was just like the place in Lufkin where the culvert had stopped up and sent water over the concrete, only here there was no concrete, only clay and gravel, and it proved no resistance to the torrent that must have washed across it.

Careful not to slide into the cut, I opened the door and guided the car to a firm footing far enough off the asphalt that some fool in a logtruck wouldn't come along and destroy it. Annie was stretched forward in her seat, her neck craned like an eager child who finally sees the place the family has been driving toward all day.

FIVE

The way you might look at a dead animal in the road, the old woman craned her neck and studied Annie, collapsed like something made of rubber. She shook her hair to the side and squinted through a break in her bangs. "She faint, or what?"

"Yes'm, I think so." Annie was out cold, her head rolled back against my chest, her legs flung out on the tile floor, her lovely breasts on full display. I studied the details of her face a few seconds, noting that her color was still good, then leaned and kissed her on the forehead, on the cheek.

"Shain't hurt, is she?"

"No. I caught her. She's just out."

"Cold as a cucumber."

"Annie. Annie. Can you hear me?"

"She couldn't hear *thunder*," the crone said.

Annie continued her shallow breathing. I stroked her hair and whispered, but she was gone from that room and off somewhere else, in whatever vague place a person trips to in a faint. Her face was so incredibly beautiful, with only a hint of makeup left on her cheeks and around her eyes, her lips graced with a natural blush. There were few lines in her face, only very fine ones radiating from the corners of her eyes—I probably put them there—and her forehead was as smooth as porcelain. Jesus, time had been good to her. Her mouth was slightly open and I could see the edges of her perfect teeth.

"Well, see can you brang her 'round. I'll get some water or somethin'. You stay where yer at. Keep a eye on'm, Duke."

"We're not going anywhere."

"You can put hard money on that."

She turned and stepped toward a sink on the opposite wall of the room behind her. I could hear her opening a cabinet. Where the hell *could* we go, dressed in our underwear, Annie limp as a steamed noodle, and that dog watching? This whole thing had degenerated into some sort of ludicrous drama. I kept thinking how it would have appeared to somebody looking on, from the sight of us clomping up to the door in our nut-coated candy-apple shoes to that long, slow crawl on all fours into the dark room, then standing up and undressing in front of the wild old wicked witch. What a cast of characters. What a plot. And where in God's name was it going?

Impulsively I pulled Annie's head up and touched my lips to hers. It was like a lifeless kiss I stole one night when I was fifteen and sitting with a girl on her parents' front porch. We had had a busy afternoon in the park and were sitting on the floor of the porch with our backs to the wall of the house. She laid her head across my lap and after talking quietly with me a few minutes fell asleep, face up, her lips slightly parted. I could smell the tart sweetness of grape Kool-Aid. The light was on above the door, casting a pleasant glow over us, so I played with her hair a little while, shaping it this way and that, the way a beautician might, just seeing how she would look with different hair styles, then found myself wondering what it would be like to put my lips against hers, something I'd never even gotten close to doing with a girl before. I didn't have a sister, and my mother was as sexless as a stump, so modest that I had never so much as seen her in her underwear—girls were the greatest enigma in the world to me. The ones at school had always reminded me of twittering little birds, gracing the playground the way birds enchanted me with the mystery of flight.

That pleasant spring night of my childhood, with a great cloud bank off in the northwest rippling with lightning and all the crickets and frogs chanting about rain, my mind reeling, I raised my knees slightly off the floor, bringing the girl's face closer to mine, and arched over and, tightly puckered, pecked her lips. It was like touching my lips to the muzzle of a Coca-Cola bottle, a firm little ring and nothing more, just warmer. She did not respond, so I went down again, this time relaxing my lips like a mouth-breather and wallowing them against hers, the way I had seen people do it in movies. As her lips slackened against mine, I kept thinking that it was like kissing plastic fishing worms smelling faintly of grape Kool-Aid, all loose and slick and rolling around and utterly without life. I put my tongue against her teeth, then shot it in and out between them, quick like a snake, just touching her tongue, but she didn't wake up. Still playing my little game of tongue tag, I grew bolder and fumbled open two buttons on her blouse and eased my hand in and beneath her bra and cupped one of her small breasts, trapping the nipple between two fingers and lightly squeezing. At that point her eyes snapped open the way some dolls' eyes do when you lift them from a prone position, with an almost audible click, one minute pink lids, dead blank, and the next, two very bright accusing blue eyes with dark centers. She shoved away my face and hand and sprang from my lap and ran shrieking inside to tell her daddy what I'd been doing, but I was on my bike pedaling as fast as a boy with the greatest hard-on of his life can pedal and well in the next block before I heard the porch screen slam the second time, followed by the rumble of his voice. I never went back, and that girl never spoke to me again. But I didn't forget the feel of those lips or that breast with its hard little nipple.

Annie didn't stir. Her lips just rolled around against mine, warm but lifeless, and I guess I lost myself and held the kiss a little too long because the old woman loomed at the doorway and tapped the pistol against the facing.

"Come on back up for air, boy. You ain't gettin' nothin' there."

I raised my face from Annie's. "No ma'am, I don't guess so." She had no way of knowing that it was the first time I had kissed my wife in more than three years, and even if I got no more response than I'd have gotten from a Coke bottle or fishing worms, I wanted to kiss her again and again. And that was only the beginning of what I wanted to do to her. I continued to stroke her hair and stare at her breasts.

"You act like you seein' that woman for the first time. Y'all one strange couple—I'll say that for you."

"I'm just worried about her," I said.

"You really love that gal, don't you?"

I nodded, shifting her weight to my other arm. "Yes ma'am. I really do." The left one was dead asleep and had no more feeling in it than the big black pistol dangling from the old woman's hand. In her other hand she was holding a glass of water.

"She is a purty one, for sure, but she's got some kinda burr under her saddle. Acts like she's mad at the world. Y'all must of been fightin' or somethin' before you got here."

"It's a long story," I said.

"How you gon' get her out of it?"

"Ma'am?"

"How you gon' wake her up?"

"I'm not sure. I've never known her to faint before."

"Well, drag'r in the kitchen here and see can you get'r up in a chair and we'll try to get some water down'r. That ort to get'r goin' agin."

"How about just wetting a bathcloth or paper towels and let me see whether I can bring her around with that." Again I repositioned Annie across my left arm, which tingled but had recovered most of its feeling.

"Arright. But you better not move off that floor while I'm gone. Duke'll be watchin'. I'll be right back."

"I told you we're not going anywhere." I wasn't sure I *wanted* to go anywhere.

She turned and went down a hallway, toward the bathroom, I presumed, and I heard her rummaging in a closet and then the water running, but by that time I had pulled Annie's face close again and kissed her deep and long, my lips and tongue all over her slack mouth, my right hand stroking one breast, then the other. I had just begun sliding my hand down her stomach when I caught the dog's eyes. He had twisted his head to the side and cocked his ears the way animals do when they don't understand what's going on but might like to. The water shut off and the old woman came shuffling back. Suddenly I felt like a molester or a necrophiliac, something dark and ogre-like, and pulled my face away from Annie's and moved my hand to her hair again. If she had been awake, she would have felt something as hard as that pistol barrel against her back.

"Here y'are." She tossed me a wet rag and squatted in the doorway. "Rub'r face down with it and see can you brang'r out of it." She held the pistol in her left hand. I figured she could fire it equally well with either hand or foot. I sure as hell didn't want to have to find out.

The wet rag worked after a few seconds. I bathed Annie's forehead and cheeks, blotted her lips, then moved down her neck until she began to stir. I eased her into a more upright position. She blinked a few times, trying to focus on first the ceiling, then my face, and finally sucked in a deep breath and sat up. When she realized that she was essentially naked, deep color shot to her face. She pulled her arms across her breasts.

"God, Tommy, I fainted. I've never fainted before, at least not that I remember. How long—"

"Just a few seconds. I caught you when you went down. You didn't hurt anything."

"Thanks." She turned and looked at the old woman crouched

in the doorway beside the dog. "Can I put on my clothes now?" she asked, struggling to her feet. I rose with her and supported her by an elbow. She yanked it away.

Still squatting, the old woman pointed the pistol toward the pile of clothes. "Y'all can put on yer shirts is all, cover up some of that nekkidness."

"Why can't we just get *dressed*?" Annie had one arm across her chest, the other dangling over her crotch, like she was saluting a flag or something.

She wasn't the only one saluting. My shorts were still bulging. Annie hadn't looked down there, and I wasn't sure that she felt anything when she woke up. I was standing there with both hands cupped over it.

"Y'all sure are a modest pair. You can put yer shirts on is all."

"But—"

"No buts about it, little sister. Shirts is all. That way I know you ain't gon' try to get out of here tonight and go runnin' off down the road with my stuff."

"Your *stuff*? Jesus, lady," Annie said, "when are you going to get it in your head that we are not here to steal your things? We've already told you our circumstances."

"And I done tol' you about takin' the Lord's name in this house. His son's name too. You ain't to do it. Shirts is all." She reached and tossed Annie her blouse and me my shirt.

Annie spun her blouse on so fast I got only a glimpse before she buttoned it up. It was almost as long as a nightshirt. She saw me watching and gave me a hard look.

Luckily my shirt fell just below crotch level, so the bulge was covered. Only it wasn't so much a bulge anymore—it was more like a plastic fishing worm and subsiding fast. Looking down the barrel of a .44 magnum sometimes has that effect on a guy.

We took a seat at the kitchen table, one of those sturdy chromed-steel ones built during the fifties, with a red Formica top and matching chromed chairs with padded red plastic seats and backs. It was pushed against the inside wall with two chairs on one side and one at each end. She had motioned me into one at the end and Annie into the one beside it.

"I guess I was just hungry," Annie said. She turned and looked at the old woman. "You know, we haven't had anything much to eat all day."

"He won't *feed* you?" The old woman was leaning back against the cabinet with her elbows propped on the surface. The fingers of her left hand played lightly with the pistol, which she had laid at the edge of the sink away from the table.

"She got exactly what she asked for for lunch," I said. I was thinking about that old woman at the Dairy Queen. Somehow, when it comes to the way men treat their wives, women will always find a way to put an abuse or neglect slant on things.

"Where'd y'all eat at last?"

"In Nacogdoches," Annie answered.

"At a Dairy Queen," I added.

"Me, I wouldn't never eat in one of them places. The people that cook there are niggers and Meskins and white trash, and they spit in yer food just to get you back."

"Get you back for what?"

"Well sir, just for bein' better off than they are. I heard tell they put all kinds of stuff in yer food. It's *spite* is what it is."

"I thought you said *spit*," Annie said.

I gave her a look and shook my head *no*. "I don't think there's anything to that."

"Yessir, there is too. I heard tell one time—"

I shifted in my seat. "Ma'am, I'm sorry to have to change the subject, but what do you intend to do with us? Here we are sitting at your kitchen table with nothing but our shirts and underwear on and it feels damned weird—pardon the language—and I was just wondering what your plans are for us. It's dark and our car's—"

"I ain't got it figgered out yet exactly what I'm gon' do with you. I will d'rectly, and when I do, I'll tell you."

"What we'd really like to do is put our clothes on and leave."

"No ma'am, that ain't a option. Like I tol' y'all earlier, you are in for the night. Just pretend this is a castle and the doors has been shut for the night. I didn't ast you to come here, but you come, and you gon' be here till daylight. So you might as well shut up on that subject. You know, back in the olden days, people done that—somebody come along and ast to be let in, and if they take'n the traveler in, they never let'm go till the mornin'. Fed'm and locked'm up in a room till mornin'. That way they was in control. Didn't have to worry about the traveler breakin' in later and stealin' everthang. They was already on the inside of the castle, under lock and key. That's the way they pertected theirselves in them days."

I glanced around the kitchen. "Then why the hell let people in, if you're that scared of them? Why not tell them to go on down the road. If we'd had any idea we'd have a .44 pointed at us all night, we would have kept going."

"That's just the way it turnt out," she said.

I snorted. "These are not the *olden* days, woman. You are keeping us here against our will. It's against the law. It's kidnapping."

"Naw, it ain't. So shut up on that subject."

"Lady, please listen to me here," I tried. "We are on our way to visit an injured child in Houston. She has been asking for us. We've got to get to Houston. We do not have time to play your damned *kidnap* game."

Annie was looking at me, her eyes wide with fear again, and all I knew to do was formulate with shoulders and facial expression that universal look of *Damned if I know what's going on.*

"You could tell me any kind of tale just to get aloose. But it ain't gon' happen. Now, if y'all will shut up about the kidnappin' bidness, I'll see about gettin' you fed. You said yer hungry, right?"

I nodded at Annie and she nodded back. We nodded at the old woman.

"You don't spit in the food, do you?" Annie asked. I couldn't believe she said it. Her spirit was returning.

The old woman threw her head back and cackled. "Naw, the most I do is scratch my head and armpits over it, shed a few hairs, let Duke taste it first."

"Got a menu?" I asked. In just those few seconds something seemed to change. Like the mere mention of food introduced a softer element into the conversation.

Ultimately almost all the world's problems boil down to

hunger. A man with a full stomach is a man who's probably not going to cause you any grief—his mind turns to gentler things, assuming he's not drinking too or crazy or just a garden-variety asshole—and the most benevolent man in the world is a bear when he's hungry. He'll get mean, may even kill you, over food. Marx was wrong about religion—the real opiate of the people, of the world, is *food*. I'd bet that the last thing on the minds of most dying men is not women or memories of childhood or regret at having gotten themselves into a terminal condition, but *food*. There was a newspaper story one time about a guy named Shiflett who fell off a shrimp boat and drifted around for days in the Gulf off Florida holding onto a cargo flat he'd found, and when he was rescued, people asked him what he kept thinking about out there with hundreds of feet of water under him and miles of Gulf on all sides and shark fins zipping around him and his answer was simple: "Milk. I kept thinking about how I sure would love to have a big gallon jug of cold sweetmilk." Not women, not family and friends, not the emergence of a ship on the horizon, but a jug of cold milk. It could have been a hamburger or roast or chicken, but you can bet that it would have been food of some sort that his mind was on.

Not even a fool wants to die on an empty stomach and he shouldn't have to. A condemned man with the minutes ticking down to those final steps into the cold stark maw of the execution chamber is offered that one last meal, and whether he chooses pork chops or pizza or hamburger or fried chicken or softshell crabs, the authorities do their damnedest to put it before him, like that's the one decency that anybody's entitled to. And knowing that it's his last meal seems to make him even more desperate for it, and he eats it and sops his plate and wishes he'd be around for breakfast. Being properly fed should be the last dignity afforded us all.

The crone was smiling, with her fists on her hips. The pistol lay on the counter. "Y'all gettin' purty pushy, with there not no other place t'eat for miles." She was in a good humor, apparently happy that she had someone to talk to besides that damned dog. "What I got is some leftover turnip greens and cornbread in the oven, a little piece of ham. It's prolly still warm from supper. I could serve that up. I got all kinds of canned meat and stuff, and jars of beans and okry, just about any vegtable you can think of, rice, flour, salt meat—you name it and I got it. I'm a survivalist, you know."

"A survivalist?"

"Yes ma'am, I am. I can survive a year or two on what's in this house."

"Survive what?" I asked.

"Earthquake, flood, famine, plague, nukuler attack. You name it. But the question right now is what do y'all want t'eat?"

"Do you have anything to make sandwiches out of?" I asked.

"Right now I'll eat anything you have," Annie added. "Whatever you've got in that oven will do."

"I can make you tomater sanwiches, but they ain't much to'm. Like my daddy always said, tomater sanwiches are good, but they ain't enough to'm to make a little boy poot in church. He had a sayin' about everthang. He used to eat four tomater sanwiches for dinner and by supper time he was ready to graze thoo everthang on the table. Ain't got any perminter cheese made up. But I can fry up some ham, or some Spam—I got cases and cases of Spam—or I can make you some egg sanwiches. . . ."

"Egg sandwiches!" Annie slammed her hand on the table and shot it into the air like a kid in class waving to go to the bathroom. "I vote for egg sandwiches. But *he* might want a corny-dog."

"Ain't got the stuff for corny-dogs. Never could stand them thangs anyhow. My daddy used to like'm, though. He'd buy'm already battered in big boxes for the freezer and cook'm up and eat half a dozen at a time. Even sold'm in the store sometimes. He musta chunked enough of them little sticks out behind the house to build a barn with."

"What do you think they coat those weenies with?" Annie asked her.

"I got no idear. Like I said, I never liked'm. Cornmeal, I rekkin."

"You don't think it's sawdust?"

She narrowed the one eye I saw. "Might be. Looks like it. Come to thank of it, kinda tastes like it. All I know is, a butcher friend of my daddy's told me one time what all goes in them weenies. Daddy, he didn't want to hear it. Now, there's a story for you. They got lips and guts and sinuses and all kinds of stuff in'm, about anythang you can name."

Annie joined in: "Kidneys and liver and spleen, noses, hooves, adenoids, gums, eyes—"

"Y'all lighten up," I said.

"Just about anythang the average woman would thowe away from a butcherin'," the crone said.

"Corny-dogs," Annie said, giggling. "It's a man thing, like sardines. I never knew a decent woman in my life who liked either one." She reached her foot across and kicked me on the shin. That really surprised me. I tried to trap her foot with my legs, but she was too quick.

I swear she looked like a teenager. Her hair was tousled and cute as hell the way it fell across her forehead, and the color was up in her cheeks. Little pixie face. "I didn't know you liked egg sandwiches," I said.

"I haven't had one since I was a little girl. My grandmother used to fix them all the time for us when we were staying with her and she needed something quick and cheap and nutritious. Mother liked them all right, but she said they messed up too much in the kitchen and the whole point in making sandwiches was not to mess up the kitchen. I used to make them myself. I'd even eat them for breakfast sometimes."

I shrugged. "You just never told me."

"Well, it's not a subject that ever came up is all, Tommy. It's not like it was some kind of big secret I was keeping from you. I mean, couples don't sit around talking about egg sandwiches. If you want to know whether someone likes egg sandwiches, maybe you've got to just up and ask them."

"I know, but you'd think that as long as we were together—"

"You probably don't know that I like artichoke hearts either, do you?"

The old woman looked back and forth at us and broke in: "Y'all not together *now*?"

"Yes'm, oh yes ma'am. I misphrased myself."

"Yes, we're together," Annie said. "I'm at the same table with him."

I gave her a you-shut-your-mouth look. "She never mentioned

egg sandwiches while we—she's just never talked about egg sandwiches is all."

"Tell you what, Tommy, the next time I'm trapped in a car with
you on a long trip, I'll give you a complete rundown on egg sandwiches and any other kind of sandwich I like. Spam sandwiches,
grilled cheese, banana sandwiches, pineapple sandwiches, tomato
sandwiches. And on and on. OK? Right now I sure could do with
an *egg sandwich*." The mean edge was right under the surface,
almost at the point of breaking through.

The old woman smacked her hands together. "There y'are,
then. Tell'm straight. Egg sanwiches comin' up. Baked some bread
today—gon' be fresh."

"With mayonnaise and tomato and plenty of salt and pepper?"

"Yes'm. That's the way I always fixed'm. That the way you want
yers, big boy?"

I nodded. "That's fine. I don't recall ever having had an egg
sandwich, but I'll have mine the way you fix hers."

I kept trying to deal with this ludicrous image of somebody
putting an egg, uncooked and unbroken, between two pieces of
bread and then biting down on it and how awful that would be
with egg white and yolk squirting everywhere and dripping all
over the place and little bits of shell in your mouth. I mean, I
knew you didn't fix one that way, but that's what came to mind.

"That's sweet," Annie said, giving me a halfway warm look. "I
promise you'll like it that way."

"Where was you brought up at," the crone asked, "that you
never had egg sanwiches? Had to been somewheres north of
Virginia."

"No, Alabama and Mississippi," Annie answered. "His family

was just strange. He never had salad until he was in college. Never had shrimp or crab or anything but roast beef and pork and fried chicken, eggs and bacon and ham, until he married me. They were a really strange family, the whole bunch. If you listen and watch him, you'll see what I'm talking about. I still don't know why he never got egg sandwiches. Like I say, they were weird."

"Thanks," I said quietly to Annie, "now get off my back."

"What *did* y'all eat," the old woman asked, "besides beef and pork and—"

"Never *mind*." I motioned toward the range. "Just fix the egg sandwiches."

"That was about it," Annie said, "except for ice cream and watermelon in the summer."

The crone patted the pistol and looked shrewdly at us. "Now, in order to fix them sanwiches, I'm gon' have to turn my back on you. But you mind that dog is watchin', and I can have this pistol up and on you quicker'n you can say *Jack*."

I glanced at Annie and smiled. "You mean Jack *Robinson*?"

"Nossir, just *Jack*. Time I got *Robson* out you'd both be dead."

"We won't move," I said. I was feeling tightness in my chest again, and the color slowly left Annie's face. If only she'd put that damned pistol up. One minute I thought I could see the light at the end of the tunnel, the next the tunnel looked like a gun barrel with only the gray tip of a bullet showing.

She turned her back to us then and set about her business, first rummaging around for a black iron skillet that she set on an eye on the stove. Quick as a snake strike she swung a match across the countertop, firing it, and brought it close enough to the burner for the gas to poof and small blue and yellow flames fanned out under the skillet. In two ungodly long steps for a woman so old and short she swooped into the refrigerator for butter and mayonnaise and eggs, mystically balancing the quart jar, butter dish, and four eggs in her hands the way only a woman can do and delivering them safely to the side of the stove, where the skillet was beginning to hum with heat. A dollop of butter went hissing in and a mushroom-shaped cloud of thin white smoke rose like a ghost and engulfed her, billowed higher than her head, flattened on the ceiling, and curled back down in two arms as if to embrace her. One-handedly she cracked the eggs and dropped them into the skillet. The whites immediately firmed, sputtering and sizzling.

"Them yellers is gon' bust, but it don't matter with sanwiches. You want'm to bust. Otherwise the yeller'd drip out the sides and off the bottom of the sanwich when you bit in."

"Yes'm," I said. "I can understand how it might."

"My grandmother always poked them with the spatula," Annie said, "to make sure."

"They busted all right."

"She sort of worked the yellow in with the white. Almost scrambled."

"Yes'm, that's really the best way. Mixes the parts up better." She jabbed at the eggs with the spatula in short little strokes. "Now, my way is to put two eggs on each sanwich so that you don't end up with too much egg on one side of the sanwich and too much bread on the other. Them eggs kinda hang out the edges all the way around. I don't skimp on egg sanwiches."

"And I always liked the whites crispy around the edges."

The old woman cackled. "Yes'm, me too, me too. Gotta different taste when they're that way. At's the way they gon' be."

It has always been amazing to me how in a kitchen two women who have never seen each other before and who have nothing at all in common can fall into a conversation about food or people or home furnishings or clothes or whatever. I guess it's just familiar territory to them, neutral and inviting, and they'll set into a conversation the minute they arrive there. If I hadn't been along, I think the old woman would have forgotten all about the pistol and pulled up a chair at the table with Annie and they'd have started right off talking about the things that women talk about. Out in the shop or yard or in the living room a couple of men might stumble around a little bit about the weather or make a few passing remarks about cars or sports or tools, but unless they just happen to have the same kind of job or share a hobby, their conversation will go stone cold in five minutes. Unless they're drinking. Drop a third man into the equation and things will generally pick up again, especially if you throw in beer or whiskey or a deck of cards, and anywhere at all will do. Run a woman past them, and you've got a wolf pack on your hands, with whistling and lewd comments. It'll happen just about every time.

But a kitchen and two women—that's all it takes. Here was a lonely old woman armed with a .44 magnum and living in the Davy Crockett National Forest and a slender young woman from the bright outer world who'd probably never been that close to a gun before, much less had one pointed at her, not thirty minutes earlier absolute and utter strangers, mortal enemies, and likely to be enemies again in thirty minutes, and they were off on egg sandwiches. There is just something about kitchens and women.

Or maybe it's just women. Like what the old woman said about me not coming into her house unless my woman was along. As if the female somehow makes all the difference in the relative threat of a man. It's universally accepted that if two guys are approaching you on a sidewalk somewhere in a strange town, you go on mild alert, just in case, but if it's a man and woman, it looks right, harmless, and you nod and smile, no more ill at ease than you would be with a couple of toddlers passing you. She's the moderating agent in the man, you see. And women are just more inclined to resolve problems through conversation rather than through physical confrontation. That's a fact.

Maybe kitchens do help. If you had to choose any place in the house that seems to be symbolic of life and comfort and the most civil side of us, it's the kitchen. It might go back to the original kitchens, the old campfires that our hairy forebears gathered around—an almost sacred place of light and warmth where food was prepared and served and eaten and where people gathered at night against the awful dark, a place where whatever predators there were would not approach. And even if the kitchen's closed, with everything put away and it's cooled down and the lights are off, there's something comforting about it that you don't feel in other rooms in the house. Bathrooms and bedrooms and living rooms contribute to the myth of a house in their own ways, but nothing has the universal and collective appeal of a kitchen, an almost sedative effect, and I guess that's the way it is supposed to be.

I never in my life heard of a man killing another man or a woman or child in the kitchen, though there are probably far more dangerous weapons at hand there than anyplace else in the house. Knives and cleavers, icepicks. Your average butcher knife is just as good a weapon as a gun in close quarters—two steps and you can slice somebody's throat or gut him like a fish, kill him just as dead with that knife as a bullet and make a hell of a lot bigger mess. I suspect that there have been times when men have squared off in kitchens and one of them has held his hands out in appeal and said, "Let's take this outside in the yard or off in the den. We can't fight in no kitchen." The primary passion in a kitchen is hunger, and the kitchen's purpose is satisfying that hunger.

People don't even commit suicide in kitchens. They may blow their brains out in the den or living room or bedroom or cut their wrists over the lavatory or in the tub or hang themselves from the rafters of the shop or even do something really crazy like throw themselves out a second-story window onto the driveway, but somehow the kitchen just doesn't seem to be the place to die. I know that some famous poet stuck her head in an oven and gassed herself, but she was an exception. The kitchen is a place that makes you think about life and living. It's always the cleanest room in the house and in some ways it's as close to sacred as rooms can get.

I'll just bet that if the world's negotiators gathered around a table in someone's kitchen in just about any country you could name to talk things over, instead of seating themselves somberly and stiffly at a heavily oiled formal table in some official-looking room with dark paneling and portraits of dignitaries on the wall, international problems could be much more quickly solved. You know, somebody would say, "All right, after we get this taken care of, we're going to reach right over there and bring out the ham and cheese and make sandwiches and maybe open a couple of cans of that soup up there." They'd get the problem solved and then eat.

Whatever, there I was in this strange kitchen that because it was a kitchen actually felt as familiar as my own and I found myself utterly entranced by the sudden rapport between the two women engaged in an outrageous conversation about egg sandwiches. And I felt, naturally enough, like the odd man out.

"Do you have lettuce?" I asked.

"Lettuce?" they responded together.

"*What*?" I was mystified. "Is there some kind of law about using lettuce on egg sandwiches? I mean, will the concoction kill you, like catfish and milk?"

"Most people wouldn't even *think* of putting lettuce on egg sandwiches," Annie said.

"I thought all sandwiches went better with lettuce." You'd think I had asked for a layer of anchovies or something equally vile.

"Not less'n you live *way* up town," the old woman said. "Or way up *north*."

"Or are just plain weird," Annie said, grinning. "You'll have to forgive him. I told you about him and that family."

"Tomaters we got, not no lettis. Never knowed nobody in my life that eat lettis on egg sanwiches without they was showin' off. Egg sanwiches was invented by people in the country, where everbody grows tomaters and everbody's got eggs, but not many people, around here leastways, grows lettis. The weather ain't fit for it. You gotta brang lettis in from town. And these eggs, by the way, come from my own chickens, what they call free-range chickens, meanin' that they ain't been fed a whole bunch of chemicals and stuff. They eat all over the place. Them eggs is the real thang."

While she muttered and puttered about the stove and counter assembling our sandwiches, busy as anybody's grandmother, my eyes met Annie's, and what they found there was no longer the cold reptilian stare I'd seen earlier but a playfulness reminiscent of our early days together when such a look meant sex was certain later. The fear was even gone, though she swung her eyes from time to time toward the pistol. A set of old yellowed plastic salt and pepper shakers sat in the middle of the table. Annie reached and picked up the salt shaker and tapped my shin with her foot. She shook a little pile of salt onto the red table top and spread it out with her hand and printed something with her finger. I leaned to see what she had written.

OK, it said, upside down. She scooped the salt back into a pile and spread it out again. I nodded and smiled and leaned to write a reply.

"Y'all ort not to be playin' with that salt," the old woman said, watching out of the corner of her eye.

Annie grinned. "Sorry."

"Like my momma and daddy always tol' me, the kitchen ain't no place to play. You do that in the yard." She broke into a brown-toothed smile as she lifted a flap of egg out and ferried it over to a piece of bread she'd sliced off a brown loaf. "Or in y'all's case, in the bedroom."

Bullshit, I thought. Under different circumstances I would have had Annie laid across that table in a heartbeat.

Annie carefully scraped the pile of salt over to the edge of the table and into her other hand. "Sorry," she said to the old woman, who cupped a hand toward her and accepted the salt and threw it into the sink. "I spilled it."

"Ain't no prollem. I got cases of it." She finished up the sandwiches and put them on saucers before us.

"Maybe you should have thrown it over your shoulder," I said to Annie.

"Not on my floor she don't."

"Yes'm," I said.

"What y'all want to drank?"

We looked at each other and shrugged. "What you got?" I asked.

"Got co-colas, water, ice tea."

"Got any whiskey?"

"Nossir. Don't allow no whiskey in this house. Ain't been a drop in here since Daddy died. He kep' that stuff by the case."

"How about letting me go to the car? I'll be back, I promise. You can keep her for collateral." I nodded at Annie, who gave me a sour look. "I'll drink it out there in the dark if you want, not bring it in here." I swear I would have tilted back that half-gallon and swilled a quarter of it without taking a breath.

"Nope. I don't believe in that stuff."

"A Coke'll do," Annie said. I nodded.

I have to admit that egg sandwiches are good. Even when you're being held prisoner at the end of a .44 magnum wielded by the

Wicked Witch of the West in an old converted store in the middle of the Davy Crockett National Forest. But then, maybe that's why it was so good, not knowing whether it might be my last meal. Or maybe because I had been without food for so long. Or because I was sitting across from my beautiful wife, whose lips and breasts I'd just touched for the first time in three years, even if she was out concrete-block cold, whose wonderful body, covered by nothing but skimpy panties, was still poised in my mind. I wolfed the sandwich and slugged the Coke and would have asked for more of both but for the fact that things seemed to be going our way and I didn't dare risk changing that direction. While we ate, the dog sat in the doorway and constantly shifted his gaze between us. He got no egg sandwich. I would have fought him to death over mine.

The old woman had cleaned up the mess by the time we finished eating, but she never moved more than two paces from the pistol and from time to time readjusted it so that we remained aware that she knew precisely where it was. I handed her our saucers and empty cans and napkins and she smiled and thanked me.

"What now?" I asked. Annie had been quietly studying the details of the kitchen. Not that there was really that much to see. As kitchens go, it was pretty simple. A row of upper and lower metal cabinets, painted a dull blue with a paintbrush in some distant past, ran the length of one wall, broken only by a sink and the gas range, very old with sooty streaks around the oven door and up the front of the panel. A mixer squatted back in one corner, flanked by jars of fruit preserves and vegetables, all their little crowns aglitter, and at the other end of the counter were more jars, a few empty, but most newly filled. One of those old black antique oscillating fans sat, blades motionless, in front of them. She had apparently been very busy with canning.

The wall across from the cabinets, against which the table was pushed, was plain whitewashed concrete block with a calendar and spice rack and outlines of things that at one time had hung there but had been taken down, pictures or calendars, whatever. No one had bothered to remove the nails and screws on which they'd hung. One ghostly figure looked like an enormous bird, wings spread, with neck thrust out and down and legs in attack position, talons unsheathed, but the outline could have been left by anything. My imagination was in high gear.

There were two doorways behind Annie, the one through which we had come, the other apparently leading off to another part of the house, while at the other end of the room there was an outside door flanked by a set of double windows, their curtains tightly drawn.

The old woman had not answered, so Annie asked, "What are you going to do to us now? Make us get naked again?"

"Naw, you ain't totin' nothin' but what God give you. Gettin' nekkid is up to y'all later." She cackled and after wiping her hands with a white rag picked up the pistol. She leaned and pulled a chair over by the range, spun it around and sat down, her arms across the back, the pistol lightly resting on one forearm. "I rekkin we can *talk*, if y'all want to. I ain't had anybody here to talk to in a long time."

"Look, we didn't come here to talk," I started again, "we came here to try to use your telephone—"

"Which I tol' you I ain't got."

"Right," I said. "I understand that. *We* understand that. There are probably three people in this whole county who do not have telephones, and they are all in this kitchen. It has to be a record. So what we'd really like to do is *go.*" Annie nodded in agreement. "You've been kind to feed us and all, but we need to get on down the road to a phone. There is a little girl in a hospital in Houston who needs us, and there are people who'll be worried about us. Surely there are other houses or trailers not far from here where there's a phone."

She sighed and dropped her forehead onto the pistol and snapped it right back up, shaking her hair apart so that one dark eye looked out at me. "You back on that agin. I got no way of knowin' why y'all are back in these woods. I don't really know what it'll take to get it acrost to you that you and the little lady here ain't leavin' this here house tonight. I have done tol' you and tol' you, but it don't seem to register. It just ain't gettin' *thoo.* Like I am talkin' to stumps or mules, but even a mule listens better. I cain't make it no plainer. You come in here uninvited—"

"Uninvited, hell," Annie shot back, "you ordered us in here on all fours like a couple of animals. You *ordered* us. You *kidnapped* us."

"*Uninvited.*" She swung the pistol toward the front room. "After dark, with some crazy story about tryin' to get to Houston to visit a sick little girl, when any fool that's got a head between their shoulders knows you cain't get to Houston from here. At least not easy. And me not knowin' y'all and y'all's intentions from any thieves along that road out there. These woods is full of people that'll kill you over a glass of ice tea and take everthang you got that ain't bolted down to ce-ment. A woman livin' alone cain't take no chanches atall."

"Do we look like thieves?" I spread my arms wide.

"Not like any I ever seen. I don't thank you are thieves now, naw, but I still cain't be sure what you are or yer intentions are. You are *in* here now, in my castle, whatever you are, and you ain't gettin' out till mornin' light. So just shut up about that. I done fed you and I'm gon' give you a place to sleep."

Annie and I traded glances.

"I'mon put y'all in the storeroom tonight. You'll be awright in there. Won't nobody bother you and you cain't bother me. Mornin', less'n you do somethin' to make me change my mind, you can be on yer way."

"What do you mean, make you change your mind?" I asked.

Annie blurted, "Storeroom? What storeroom?"

"*The* storeroom. It's where my daddy used to keep stuff for the store. Mostly just boxes of junk in there now, but they's a mattress in there and a old sink with runnin' water. Ain't no hot water, but the cold'll do you, this still bein' summer and all. I'll let you visit the bathroom back there"—she motioned with her thumb toward the door at the end of the room—"before y'all go to bed."

"I am not staying in a storeroom."

"Yes ma'am, y'are."

"No I am not—"

"Just hush, Annie, let it go. Do you have a shower?"

"No sir. Got a tub, but the drain's rusted out and water goes all over the floor when you use it. Got somebody s'posed to fix it one of these days, but it won't hold water right now. This ain't no Hollerday Inn, you know. You can use the commode and wash up at the sink. Anythang else you want to do, you can do in the storeroom. They's some paper towels under the sink."

"I am *not* staying in a storeroom like some kind of livestock." Annie had her teeth clenched, with her lips in a fine white line.

"Oh yes you are."

"Look, how about us sleeping in the front room? Annie could take the couch and I'd just sleep on the floor beside her."

"That wouldn't hardly be no security for me, now, would it? You'd be aloose in the main house. Naw, you get the storeroom. But it ain't half bad. You can shove stuff around and make a nice pallet for yerselves. Like I say, you got water in there, and—"

"I'm not *staying* in a filthy storeroom tonight," Annie said, "what*ever* the hell it is."

"You ain't even seen it," the old woman said. "For all you know, it might be cleaner than this kitchen."

"I don't *want* to see it."

"Well, that is where you are gonna stay tonight." She thrust her chin out firmly.

"Now, you listen here, old woman." Annie had risen to her feet, hands balled on the table top, her cheeks ablaze, and I wasn't sure what was about to go down.

"Naw, *you* listen to the sound of this pistol cockin'." The old woman was on her feet too, with the pistol raised. She cocked it. Jesus, how loud those little ratchets and springs were in that kitchen. The barrel was level with Annie's face. I simply leaned back in my chair and turned my face away. I was beginning to have second thoughts about the safety of kitchens.

"Shoot me, then, Goddamn it, you crazy old witch, but I am not going to sleep with him in a storeroom that's probably crawling with roaches and spiders and rats."

"Annie, shut the fuck up and sit down." I reached and grabbed her wrist and forced her into the chair, then turned to the old woman. "And please, ma'am, put down the gun. We'll sleep wherever you say."

"They never was no doubt about it." She settled back down in her seat. "Y'all are a foul-mouth pair, I'll tell you that, and fools for cussin' me. And me with a pistol aimed at you. Just what kinda clay are you made out of, little girl? You mus' be from Missippi."

Annie was quiet in her chair. She was staring at the opposite wall.

"Tennessee," I said. "She's from a little town just southeast of Memphis, about a half a mile from the Mississippi line. But she was born in Mississippi, if that counts."

"And if it's any of your business," Annie said, jerking her head around to face the hag again.

"Anythang happens in this house *is* my bidness."

"Fine, but I'm not—"

"Shut up, Annie," I said. "Just shut up about it."

"And I'm not sleeping in the same room with *him*."

"You're sleepin' where I *tell* you to sleep. Now, *both* of you shut up."

"Nobody can make me sleep where I don't want to sleep,"

Annie persisted. "You might make me go in the room with him if you hold that big pistol to my head, but I don't have to *sleep* with him."

"Fine," I said, glaring at her. "Lie there all night with your damned eyes open. Or lean in a corner. See if I care."

"And I'm not going to lie down on the same mattress with him."

"I have been tryin' real hard to like y'all, but you are beginnin' to stick in my craw like a pinecone. You one of the strangest couples I ever met. Now, les' talk about somethin' else until it's time to go to bed. You can argue about it then, if you want to." She squinted at the barrel of the gun and lightly buffed at a spot with her finger. "But you are gon' do what I say."

"You—"

I reached and grabbed Annie's upper arm and squeezed. "No more, please. Just coast with this. It's her house and her gun and her dog, and we are in no position to argue."

"Never knowed anybody from Tennessee that was easy to get along with," the crone said. "Contrary, unaccommodatin' people is what they are. *Curious* people. And born in Missippi to boot. You never had a chanch, little sister."

"Get off of Tennessee," Annie said, "*and* Mississippi." She had her arms crossed and her face was fixed in a sour pout.

"You got a whole lot of grit. Remind me of myself."

"Yeah, for sure. You old bat—"

The old woman rose in her chair and lifted the pistol again. "You better shut up while you ahead. And while you still got one."

"Tell us a little bit about yourself." I thought I might be able to steer them off a collision track if I could just change the subject.

She settled back in her chair again and Annie relaxed a little in hers. "What you want to know?"

"Well, for one thing," Annie said, "what in God's—excuse me—what are you doing living in this place? It's not a regular house."

The old woman leaned and rested her chair back against the counter. The pistol dangled from her thin, blue-veined hand. "Use to be my daddy run a store here. I shut it down years ago when he got sick with the cancer and died."

"Where did y'all *live*?" Annie asked.

"We lived right here. That big room up there was the store part and we lived in the back. Momma died before he bought the store, died when I wudn't but six years old, so I don't remember much about her, only that she had dark hair and was real skinny. He was a farmer then, raised sweet pataters and corn and watermelons and stuff, and we lived back over torge Trinity a ways. When she passed on, the heart went out of his farmin' and he found out this store was for sale and I don't know how he done it but he bought it and me and him moved in. And it smack dab in the middle of the Depression.

"Made it work too, he did, and him with not a lick of bidness sense in the world until he take'n over the store, and then it just come to him, natural as teeth. We sold groceries and feed and cloth and just about anythang you'd want—gas and kerosene, harnesses, rope, butter and eggs and seeds and fertilizer. You name it, he had it. And he sold on credick, which meant that lots of people got stuff from him when they might coulda got it cheaper in town.

"The Depression might near wiped him out, but we got thoo

it—never did collect some of the money people owed us. I bet you they's two hundred people within twenty mile of here that still owes money for what they got here during the Depression and the war years after, but I'll never get a red cent of it."

"Did you go to school?"

"Yessir, I did. Thoo the second grade. Learned everythang I had to know to make do. Daddy needed me here too much to let it go on any longer. Didn't see much point in education anyhow, since he didn't have a single day of it that he ever told me about. But that wudn't all that unusual in them days. People went to work soon's they was big enough.

"He hired boys and men over the years to hep him out, but they always got dog-sorry after a while and started lazin' around or else stole stuff from him, and he'd have to run'm off. He beat the livin' tar out of one or two that stole stuff from him. Me, I could do the work of a man and didn't cost him nothin' extry, and I got up when he did and worked as long as he did, and he knowed I wouldn't steal from him because it would be stealin' from me too. So he take'n me out of school and I got my education right here."

"When did he die?" I asked. Her eyes seemed much softer now, as she moved back over the years, and I realized that here was a woman who probably hadn't talked to anyone in so long that what she was experiencing was something approaching pure joy. It was no wonder that she wasn't going to let us go anywhere until morning. The question was whether there would be any sleep at all that night.

"Like that I said, he come down with the cancer about—in

1980 to be exact. And he turnt as yeller as them egg yolks I was stirrin' in that skillet earlier and started losin' weight and in a few months he take'n to his bed for good and died real quick. Had somethin' called lymphobi . . . lymphomania—whatever it was. It started with *lymph*, I remember, because I kep' feelin' all *my* nodes reglar after that, thankin' maybe it could be passed on."

"Lymphoma," Annie suggested.

"At's it. Kilt him quick. Started in his belly and spread—" She laid the revolver on the counter behind her and moved her hands in a roiling motion across her torso from crotch to neck. "Spread all over his insides and eat him plumb up. Quick."

"They try anything?" I asked. "Radiation, chemo?"

"Too late. He wouldn'ta went thoo it anyhow. He thought at first it was the yeller jundice was all, but when the doctor tested him and tol' him it was the cancer, he come back home and went right on workin' until he got thin as a rail and couldn't stand up but a hour or two at a time and finally couldn't stand up at all—and down he went. Like a horse been hit with a .44 thoo the forehead. He didn't want no treatment. It was his time to go, and he accepted it, like the proper Christian that he was."

"What does being a Christian . . ."

"Annie," I cautioned.

"I just don't understand what you people—"

I swung my leg against hers. "Cool it."

She frowned and shook her head. "So your father went to be with his maker and then you had to run the store yourself?"

"Well, missy, that's where it got tough. My daddy might not have been a real smart man, but he could handle people. Knowed when to push and when not to, knowed the gray areas in dealin' with people. Me, I seen thangs more in black and white. So when he died, I take'n them books and they was a mess. They was more money on them books than the store and what was in it and all the land it was on was worth, so I just up and decided that them sorry folks that was draggin' around payin' on their bills was gon' pay up or I was gon' take'm to court. And they sure wudn't gon' get another red cent of credick. I mean, some of'm hadn't paid a dollar in years, not since before the War. I got out in the truck and started beatin' the bushes, turned some of the worst ones over to a collector out of Lufkin, and by George he could get blood out of a turnip, water out of a rock.

"Him and me collected a right smart of money on the newer accounts, the ones just a few years old, but the real old ones, them from the Depression and War and all, that money was just gone. Lots of them people dead or dead broke. Prollem is, when you make people do right, they always end up hatin' you. You treat'm good, do everthang you can to make thangs easy on'm, and then they up and decide they don't owe you *nothin'*. Like you owed *them* all that stuff they got. Well, we made them that had it pay what they owed and I never seen'm agin. Daddy's bidness was almost all credick, and when I called in the tabs and cut off the credick, them people never come back. Said they wouldn't deal with me, said I wudn't a Christian."

"Are you?" Annie asked.

"I believe in the Good Lord, if that's what you mean, but I don't thank that means that somebody that's got a store is supposed to *give* their stuff away. And I thank bad people're gon' go to hell and good ones to heaven, but I don't go to no church or anythang. We never did go to church after Daddy got the store. Sunday was for restin' is what he always said. At's the way the Bible puts it. And he'd get drunk and rest. I read outta my Bible and listened to the gospel over the radio and I watched some on TV—"

"You have *television*?"

"Course I do, little sister. Right there in that back room. Little bitty thang with rabbit ears and it ain't in color, but it does the trick. Cain't get nothin' but Lufkin—that's enough."

"What do you think about AIDS?" Annie asked. "Do you think it's God's revenge on homosexuals?"

"Annie." She was getting into her mean mode now and starting to pick at the old woman.

"You mean queers and such?"

"Yes, homosexuals," Annie said.

"I do. He's punishin' queers and niggers both. Gon' wipe the wicked right off this here earth, He is."

"Annie, drop it," I said. I kicked her hard with my balled foot and pointed at the massive pistol. "Did you use that gun to collect bills?"

"Naw. You cain't do that. Out here you'd just get y'self shot if you tried, or have to shoot somebody yerself. We put ever kind of pressure there was, though, right on to takin'm to court and gar-nasheein' their wages. I'm tellin' you, I got horses and cows and pigs and goats, two trucks and a car, even a travel trailer from one old man that lived down on the river. I wanted them books *square*. And we did square'm the best we could." She sighed. "But gettin' the books straight was my undoin.'"

"So you closed the store?" Annie asked.

"Had to. Them big shoppin' centers openin' up all over and Wal-Marts and stuff. Ever little ol' town has got a Wal-Marts now. This ain't that far from Lufkin, you know. And little old convenience stores ever few miles along the road. I never had a chanch. Especially after I'd made all them old customers mad at me."

"They had no right to be mad," Annie said. "They owed the money."

"At's right, missy. But owin' it and bein' tol' you owe it and have got to pay it is two different thangs. Especially when you start takin' stuff away from'm to settle their debt. Them people treated me like trash after I come down on'm. They wouldn't even wave when they drove by, much less stop. I know for a fact that lots of'm drove twenty miles out of the way not to have to pass here no more. And if one got in a bind and had to stop here to buy somethin', they'd go and get it and thowe it on the counter like roadkill and slam some dollar bills down, then count the change and snatch up their sack and be gone—and never look at me if they could hep it. No *howdy* or *thank you* or *bye*. Nothin'."

I couldn't help feeling sorry for her. Through her hair I could see first one eye, then the other. "Did you just not open up one morning? I mean, how'd you do it? What about all the stuff that was in the store?"

"Some of it's still in that storeroom. I got cases of Spam been there over twenty years. Prolly still good as it was the day it was canned."

"No giant liquidation sale? No going-out-of-business sale?" Annie was big on liquidation sales.

"Naw, little sister, I just decided to keep what I had on hand.

Sold some of it to other store owners, but I wudn't gon' give it away to them people that'd been tacky to me, for sure, and that's what it woulda amounted to, givin' it away."

"Why didn't you sell it and just take off for someplace else?" Annie asked. "That's what I would have done."

"Little sister, look at me." One eye was visible through a split in her hair. "I am a old woman now and I was a old woman then. I don't ever remember bein' anythang much *but* old. This store kep' us tied down here ever day of the year except for Sundays and New Year's Day and Christmas. And even then Daddy'd set right in there drankin' and piddlin' with somethin' or other, ready to wait on anybody that needed somethin', and everbody *knowed* he'd open up for'm too, which meant we might as well of stayed open. There was too much work for me to do around here to even thank about going someplace. Where would I go anyhow? I never went anywhere much at all."

"What about family?" Annie was beginning to get into this story.

"Wudn't but one person—there was a far cousin lived over on the other side of Trinity, but he never done nothin' but try to beat us out of stuff."

"And your grandparents?"

"Nope, little sister. Daddy's folks lived way over in Georgia, and I never heard much of anythang about them. They died young, I 'spect, and Daddy didn't have no brothers or sisters. Momma's people was somewhere in—I believe it was Arkansas—but she run away to marry Daddy and they never so much as sent her a card. They disowned her. We was alone."

Gradually her story unrolled. After her mother died and her father bought the store, that was the end of whatever life she might have had, she no more to him than any other beast of labor, though she hastened to add that he never was abusive to her, in any fashion, except that he swore a lot when he got drunk. She cooked and sewed and gardened and kept up the living quarters of the building, and he tended to the business and building and kept their old truck running.

"I guess I was everthang to him—wife and daughter and son. I mean, don't get me wrong about the wife bit. It wudn't like that. He never touched me in that way. Just that I kep' the place up, like a wife, in addition to everthang else there was to do."

"And you never thought of just up and leaving?" Annie asked.

"A-course I thought about it. Many a time when I was younger. When them handsome travelin' salesmen would come thoo here and talk about places like Dallis and Houston, a-course I thought about it. But after we take'n over this store, I never went anywhere atall past Lufkin, where I'd go a few times a year maybe, except for the one time I got to go to Houston and stay in a real hotel. The store was all there was for me."

I cocked my head at her. "You said you were married once."

"Yep. That's when I got to go to Houston, the day I got married.

"He blowed in off the highway one early sprang day in a black Chevrolet truck," she said, a lean young seed salesman carrying a leather satchel and dressed in gray slacks and light-blue sports coat with a bright tie with roses on it, sat on a Coke case and had a lunch of crackers and potted meat and a cream soda and spent the entire afternoon telling her about all the places he'd been. Her father was off in Trinity tending to some sort of business and was not back when it started getting dark, so she closed the store and invited the young salesman to stay for dinner, since he seemed comfortable with her and she with him and he wasn't in a hurry to leave. She kept thinking her father would soon be home.

As dark settled in, she knew that she would be spending the night alone, since her father refused to drive after dark. Sure enough, along about eight o'clock, after the two of them had finished their meal of fried chicken and vegetables, an old farmer from down the road dropped by to say her father had called from Trinity and asked him to drive over and tell her that he had had trouble with the truck and wouldn't be able to get it fixed until the following day, for her to lock up and open the store the next morning as usual. He'd see her sometime that afternoon.

She hadn't been alone an entire night her whole life, so she went into a panic and decided that it wouldn't be such a bad idea for the young man to spend the night there, unless he had to be getting on.

"He give me his finest grin and said, 'No ma'am, I don't have nowhere to hurry off to. You want me to stay here and keep you compny?' And I said yes, 'cept that by the time the word was out of my mouth I wudn't sure which I was scareder of, spendin' the night alone or spendin' the night in the house with him. But I'd already tol' him he could stay, so he excused hisself and went out to his truck and brought all his seed racks in so that nobody'd steal'm. He even take'n the coil wire off his motor so nobody could steal the truck. Careful sort, he was. I halfway expected him to jack it up and take the wheels off."

They sat up talking at the kitchen table a little while and he had quite a bit of her father's whiskey, drinking it out of a little stainless steel cup. He spun out story after story about what it was like being on the road, things that had happened to him, about how sorry most folks were and how lonely he felt, how he longed for a wife and permanent home.

She motioned over her shoulder. "I got that cup up there in the cabnet yet. I never did even warsh it. Still got his germs on it, I rekkin."

Along about nine o'clock he started stretching and talking about going to bed, so she suggested to him that he sleep on a pallet in the middle of the main store or in the storeroom. He said that he'd be pleased to sleep in the room with her on her father's bed, which she had told him about, but she said she didn't think that was a good idea, so he chose the storeroom, where he'd be a little closer to her in case she needed him. He said he'd leave the door open and for her to leave the bedroom door cracked. That way he could hear her if she needed anything.

Annie looked at me and smiled. "This has the ring of a conventional traveling salesman story."

"Let her get on with it," I said.

She rolled up her father's mattress from the little steel-frame single bed he slept on in the corner of the bedroom and laid it out in the storeroom for the young man and made it up for him with fresh sun-dried sheets and her father's pillow. Then she went to the bathroom and got ready for bed, it being quite late for her, and the man went in the bathroom after she was out. She could hear him flush the commode and then run a bath.

"It was like a pitcher show or some kinda dream, I'll tell you, knowin' there was a strange man just on the other side of that wall nekkid and in the tub I'd just took a bath in. A man that had been places and was goin' places tomar. I could hear him splashin' around and singin' some kinda little song, only he kep' it soft. I remember thankin' that it sounded like a nasty song. I just couldn't make it out."

After his bath the man tapped on the door and told her again to keep it cracked so that he could hear her if she needed him. When she was sure he had settled onto the pallet in the storeroom she got up and opened the door a few inches, blocking it on both sides with a pair of her father's boots so that it couldn't swing either way without waking her up.

"So what happened?" Annie asked, way forward in her chair. Her eyes were wide and glittering.

"What you'd figger would happen. What happens in ever story you ever heard about a travelin' salesman. Halfway thoo the night, best I could tell, I woke up with him settin' on the bed with me strokin' my back. He said I musta had a bad dream and called out in my sleep."

"Did you?" Annie asked.

"I *bet* you I didn't. Or if I had one, I sure couldn't remember it—and I always remember my dreams. I laid there awake for what musta been hours after I first went to bed. My heart was just goin' crazy, knowin' he was on the other side of that wall. Then I dozed off, but I sure don't remember havin' no bad dream and yellin' out about anythang.

"Y'all gon' have to pardon me for the way I'mon tell this, but y'all married and know what I'm talkin' about, and, besides, I ain't never had a chanch to tell this story before. So here y'are. There he was with his hands all over me, layin' beside me buck nekkid and kissin' me from my head to my feet. And then he had his—you know, his *thang*—in my hands and he asked me to rub it for him, and I didn't know what else to do, so I rubbed it like it was a dog's head, just sort of pattin' it—felt slimy as a snail and hard as a rock—but he said no, I had to put my hand around it and hold it just so and pump it back and forth, and I couldn't believe it at the time but it seemed to get harder and bigger the more I pumped until it was like a piece of pipe with a trailer ball on the end of it, and next thang I knowed he done squirted all over me."

Here we were into heavy porn with a strange woman in the middle of nowhere, and she seemed not at all sensitive to the fact that we were there. "And then what did he do?" Annie asked.

I gently, ever so gently, moved a leg against one of hers, but she pulled hers away.

"Exactly what you'd figger agin. He kep' kissin' on me and then got a finger—you know, *there*—and then got hard agin, and this time it was the real thang we did. He pinned me back on that bed and pulled off my drawers and spread my legs and he gored me good."

I was watching Annie. "*Gored you good*," she said and giggled. "What a way to put it. Sounds like a bull."

"He *was* a bull, let me tell you. He wudn't a real big man, but I rekkin he needed a woman bad. He gored me good. But it was my first time, so . . ."

"Your first *time*?"

"A-course it was, little sister."

"How old were you?"

She looked at me a few seconds. "Old enough to know better." She reached and slid open a drawer behind her and pulled out a crumpled pack of cigarettes and a large box of wooden matches. "Would y'all mind it I had one of these?"

Annie shrugged. I shook my head no. "It's your house. Fire away." That was one hell of a choice of words, with the pistol within swooping distance.

She worried out a cigarette, pitched the pack on the counter, and struck a match. Her hair swung perilously close to the flame as she leaned into it. The cigarette tip flared and glowed. I could see one eye glinting through the crack in her hair.

She blew a billow of smoke out over our heads. "Been tryin' to quit these thangs. Ain't had one all day, but I been wantin' one real bad."

Annie winced. "Those things will put you in an early grave."

The old woman locked eyes with her. "You listen here—I am healthy as a horse and have been my whole life. I don't know about nobody else in the famly, but I have always been healthy. Except for a goiter I got once."

"A goiter?" Annie asked.

"You prolly don't even know what one is. But it come up on my neck. I didn't even notice it till Daddy ast me one mornin' what that knot was on my neck that looked like it was big as a egg. Then I felt it for myself."

Annie was studying her with serious eyes. "A goiter? What the hell is a *goiter*?"

The old woman just ignored her and went on. "Over the months it got bigger'n bigger till I felt like it was the size of a rump roast. Then Daddy tol' me one day we'z goin' to have to take care of it because people was talkin' and it was spookin' the little kids that come in. You'd thank I was totin' a bastard baby, the way he made me feel about it." She took a deep drag and exhaled.

"Tommy, what the hell is a *goiter*? What an awful sounding word."

I just shrugged. What I knew about goiters would balance on the head of a pin.

"Some ladies from one of the churches off over there a few miles come in one day, ministered to me and tol' me they was a preacher in Marshall that could heal that thang quick as a wink, easier than castin' out a demon, but Daddy said he wudn't havin' no preacher messin' around with it. Said he'd just as soon let a mule take a look at it. He finally take'n me to a doctor in Beaumont that cut the thang off.

"Yonna see the scar?" She stretched out her neck.

Annie looked away, and so did I. All I could think about was how glad I was that we had already eaten.

"No, ma'am," I said, "but thanks. The smoking is fine. Go right ahead. It's OK. Won't bother us a bit. Now, come on, how old were you when this happened with the guy?"

She turned the cigarette around and pointed the lit end toward her face and studied it. "I was twenty-seven."

"Jesus!" Annie slid her chair away from the table. "And you were a *virgin*?"

"Little sister, watch yer language. You cain't use the Son's name thataway. Them was different days. I didn't know what he was doin' to me or what I was doin' back, but I had a good idea. I just wudn't sure. My daddy never tol' me a thang about sex. All I knowed was that a man was on top of me and had somethin' in me and it hurt and it didn't hurt. My head was spinnin' like crazy. He done his bidness and that was it. When he was thoo he went back to the storeroom and not five minutes later I could hear him a-snorin.'"

"Well, did he take precautions?" Annie asked. "You know, did he use a—" She was leaning forward on the table with her elbows, her face in her hands.

"You mean did he use a—naw, he never put nothin' on. He might of had one, but he never put it on. It was meat on meat. Believe me." She gave Annie a shrewd look. "It was the days before women started totin' rubbers in they purses."

Annie avoided my eyes.

The morning after, the young man had breakfast with her and apologized for what he had done, said that he had been on the road a long time and just lost his head. But he told her that he was not married and didn't even have a girlfriend and that he liked her a lot, so he would like to see her again his next trip through.

"Said he needed to talk to my daddy about puttin' one of his seed racks up in the store anyhow and he'd see me in just a few days."

"Did he come back?" I asked.

The young man did come back by that next week, ostensibly to sell seeds. He stayed late, after her father had shut the store for the night, ate supper with them, and then to the surprise of both announced that he had given the whole matter a lot of thought and decided that he wanted to marry her, to which her father, who had had several strong whiskeys by that time, responded with a roar of curses, declaring that he could not afford to lose the only dependable help he'd ever had at the store—and right then and there he told her that she was a joint partner and that she couldn't just up and leave him. All the while she had not had a chance to say a word.

When she finally spoke, she told the seed salesman that she could not leave her father, but that she thanked him for his very kind offer.

Well, he had apparently come unprepared to accept rejection and proposed that they marry anyway, that he would buy a place near there for them to live, and that he was "headquartered" in Huntsville and would go on living there until they could work things out—she could stay with her father at the store and he'd get over to see her as often as he could.

She had told her father about the salesman spending the night there, quite naturally saying nothing about her bedroom experience with the fellow, but seated at the table with them that night the old man surmised soon enough that in his absence there might not have been any seed selling going on at the store, but there certainly had been some seed *planting*, so fearing the worst from the suspected union, he agreed to the marriage, shaking the man's hand and hugging his daughter and, after suggesting that he might be willing to give up a corner of the property for them to build a house on, he left the room in tears to crawl into his bottle for the evening. She and the young man went out and sat in his truck a little while talking. He tried to lay her across the seat and have his pleasure, but she resisted. She told him that her father might come out with a shotgun if he saw them doing it in the truck. Finally he kissed her good night and left for Huntsville.

"Two weeks later we was married right here in the store by a JP—Christopher Collins take'n Ludy Dowdle to be his lawful wedded wife and off we went on a honeymoon to Houston. Lord, that was the crownin' jurry trip of my life."

I cleared my throat. "Dowdle? I thought your name was Autrey. That's what the painted-over sign says out front."

"We never changed the name of the store when Daddy bought it. He said that woulda been bad luck."

Annie nodded. "Did you have a wedding dress and all?"

"Had my momma's weddin' dress. And veil and garter. And Chris, he brought in a big cake. He looked so nice in a dark suit. He was a good-lookin' man, let me tell you. Dark, curly hair, face pretty as a boy's." She smiled and tossed her head. "I still got the little plaster bride and groom somewheres."

"Were there lots of people?"

"No, little sister. Just me and Daddy and Chris and the justice and a couple of customers that happ'n to be in the store. Daddy got drunk as a skunk early that mornin' and was still slobberin' drunk when we drove off for Houston that afternoon and drunk when we got back the next day. I found him out in the pasture with the goats—they was eatin' grass all around him. When I got him up, there was his outline in the grass that he was layin' on.

"When we come back from Houston, Chris dropped me off at the store and said he'd see me the next weekend, and he was off on the road agin. He was true to his word. As a matter of fact, he come by ever weekend for three or four months, and ever time he'd show me a new drawin' of the house he had in mind. And then it got to be twice a month, then once a month, and finally by the time we'd been married about ten months it petered out to nothin'."

"He quit coming?" Annie asked.

"Yep. Him and Daddy didn't get along anyhow. When he was here Daddy slep' in the storeroom on his mattress and me and Chris take'n my bed. Daddy tol' me I wouldn't believe the racket we made in bed. Chris grunted and moaned a lot—I might of did a little bit myself—and he didn't mind if the bed slammed up against the wall either.

"It just didn't work out. Daddy'd get drunk and stay grouchy the whole time Chris was here, wouldn't even use the bathroom with him in the house—he'd go off down in the woods—and they'd argue about this and that, pertickly about how slow Chris was in gettin' a house started. And he'd jump on me about the noise we made in bed. Said it was white trash the way we carried on. He'd get real drunk and yell at me and Chris and even customers, if they rubbed him the wrong way. Them wudn't good times.

"One day Chris left and he never come back. We learned later he was havin' relations with women all over East Texas and might even been married to two or three, so Daddy just set me down at this table here." She reached out and slapped the Formica top. "Set me down and said that he declared the marriage nulleded and voided and that was that."

"You never got a formal divorce?" Annie asked.

"Naw. Daddy's word was gospel here. His castle and his kingdom, like he put it, and what he said went."

"And what happened to your . . . to Chris?"

"Well, little sister, he got kilt about four years later. Run into the end of a bridge out in the country south of here and a two-by-six oak railin' come thoo the windshield of his truck and went clean thoo his chest. Take'n his spine plumb outta the skin on his back, they said, almost de-boned him like a chicken. A-course, I never seen it. Never would of even knowed about it except that somebody come by and tol' Daddy. Had a nigger woman with him that didn't have nothin' but a dress on, nary a stitch of underwear— kilt her too. She went thoo the windshield and landed way out in the creek and went to the bottom. Straight road and no sign of other traffic. I just figgered he had his mind and maybe his hands on somethin' besides drivin', how come he hit that bridge."

"Did you ever hear from his family or anything?" I asked her.

"Nothin'. I ain't sure they ever knowed about me. He never said a word about'm, except that they lived over in Louisiana somewheres."

"What about his house in Huntsville?"

"Well sir, we wudn't never for sure that he *had* any propty in Huntsville. He never take'n me there. Besides, Daddy said he was prolly just staying in a boardin' house and might of had a bunch of other wives, so it was better to leave them rocks unturned, that one snake had already crawled out and there might be others that we knew not of."

"But you might have inherited something, being his legal wife. . . ."

"Little sister, when Daddy said we wudn't goin' to pursue it, that was the gospel. He did haul what was left of the truck back here and fixed it up and sold it. And he got a whole lot of seeds out of the deal. Nothin' on Chris anywhere that pointed to a bank where he might of had money. It was like he just come out of nowhere atall."

"But surely there was an address for the seed company he worked for...."

The old woman cleared her throat and looked at me, then at Annie. "That is all I have got to say about it."

Annie's eyes were rimmed with tears. Now her leg was against mine, pressing lightly. "That's such a sad story," she said.

"Maybe so. But he was already dead, far's I was concerned. I had done turnt to the store, put all my days into doin' what Daddy couldn't or wouldn't do. Many a night layin' back there on my bed I thought about that man. Only man that ever loved me. Only man I ever give my body to."

She stood at that and picked up the pistol, laid it on the counter, and turned to the sink and pushed her hair back. She splashed water on her face and dried it, but when she turned around her eyes were red and puffy.

Annie shifted in her chair. "And you spent the rest of your days here at the store?"

She sat back down at the table but left the pistol on the counter. "Yep. Lotsa fancy fellers come in here over the years, but I never found no interest in one agin. Once bit, four times shy, as they say."

"What finally convinced you to close the store after your daddy died?" I asked.

"No customers mostly. I was losin' more'n I was makin'. Like I say, they put the freeze on me. Why, they threw their garbage out right there in my driveway. Rolled dead calves and hogs and stuff out in front of the place. One time they was more than two dozen buzzards feedin' off of a cow somebody left in my driveway. Them black bastards—excuse the language—was roostin' on top of the buildin'. I finally shot the buzzards with the shotgun and sloshed coal oil on the cow and burnt it up. They just treated me terrible, and I ain't talkin' about the buzzards."

One dark morning in November, a few months after the old man died, she got up early—way before the sun, as she put it— and lit the heaters, fired up the wood stove, and put on some coffee. The weather was threatening, with a front due in with probable ice and sleet, maybe snow. She sat at the kitchen table drinking coffee and thumbing through a *Progressive Farmer* until the place had begun to heat to a comfortable level, then walked and opened the front door and stood a long time looking at the churning sky and up and down the narrow strip of asphalt that wound off into gray winter-stark trees splashed with the green of pines. There was no traffic. The only sound was the sweep of wind through the trees.

"Stood there lookin' down that lonesome old road and thought about how it seemed that whatever direction you went in you run into trouble and I didn't rekkin that road went to anyplace I'd want to go and how it didn't look like nothin' ever changed from week to week and how I was makin' about a five dollars a day profit, if that much, and all them people hatin' me the way they did—you know, people don't ever forget trouble that comes from money, even if they the ones caused it. The store was warm and I had everthang I needed to get by, so I just said, 'At's it, folks, go get yer bread and gas someplace else.' I didn't see no sense in workin' my tail off for people that didn't appreciate it. And that very mornin' I shut them gas pumps off for good and fetched out my big ladder and climbed up there and painted over the sign, with it sleetin' to beat the band. I had ice all in my hair time I come down the ladder. And it had started to snow. I remember that I left the heaters on all night and it snowed real deep for the first time since I was a little girl. The store looked like a birthday cake the next mornin', all humped with snow and froze over. It was the first time I ever thought it looked purty."

"That was the end of it, huh?" Annie asked.

"Yep. I drawed in my horns, as they say. From what we had in the bank and what I sold off from the store supplies and the insurance money I got when Daddy died, I had enough laid back and the place was already paid for. Had cows and chickens and goats and plenty of pastureland and garden space. I just decided I was gon' look out for myself, let the world go on off someplace else. I sold all the stuff I wouldn't need to a couple of other store owners and just kep' the rest." She motioned toward the huge front room. "Boxed up the stuff I figgered I could use and turnt the main store into my living room. Brought in that couch, moved the desk in there, put up pitchers, made it look like a house."

She frowned and gazed at the glowing tip of the cigarette. "All the time we was here we never had a couch or a living room to put one in. It was a store to him, not a house, but I always wanted a house back, like we had when I was little. I was bound and determined to have me a living room *and* a couch. Even if I was the only one that ever set on it."

At this point Annie asked for another Coke, and I nodded the same for me. The old woman rose from her chair and dumped some ice in glasses this time, poured up our Cokes, and put them before us with napkins. She left the pistol on the counter. When she had taken care of us, she sat back down, keeping her chair well away from the table where we sat.

"You call yourself a survivalist. What—"

"Yessir, a survivalist is what I am. Keep plenty of food on hand. Got my animals and garden—"

"What about other stuff you need?" Annie asked. "I mean, you have to go to the store."

"No, little sister, I don't. Got the mailman for money bidness. Sometimes I might go into Lufkin for clothes or somethin', go t'bank or what not. Propane man comes by with gas coupla times a year. But what I need, I got a nigger that comes by and checks on me ever so often, 'bout once a week, and he goes and gets it. He's about my age, only he don't know for sure how old he is. Close to my age, though. Got arthritis real bad. He takes me wherever I want to go, or he goes and buys the stuff for me and brangs it here. If they's somethin' needs doin' around here I cain't do, I pay him to do it. Like run the tractor. He cuts up wood for the stove and stacks it for me. Good man, better'n any white man I ever knowed."

Annie smiled. "Y'all don't—I mean, with him about your age and all—"

The eye that blazed out at her from between the shags of hair told me I'd better divert the subject and quick. "Will that truck run out there?"

She swung her head at me. "Lord, that thang wouldn't run *any*where."

I waited for her to smile or something, but she went on, "I 'spect the tars done rotted off of that thang by now. It ain't run in six, eight years. Rust in the gas tank. No way that thang would run."

Annie had pulled her feet up beneath her. She looked so young and so pretty. I wanted to reach and touch her, but she avoided my eyes. My mind kept going back to those few minutes in the car when I held my hand on her leg. I could still feel the heat.

"Just exactly what are you surviving *from*?" Annie asked.

The old woman had been slowly nursing the cigarette along, and it was now well into the filter. She leaned and pitched it into the sink and ran a little burst of water. "Mind if I light up another one? Talkin' and smokin' goes together."

"No, smoke doesn't bother us." I lied, since Annie despised smoking in any form. "You sure you don't have any beer or whiskey or something. Talking goes better with those too."

"Done tol' you, I won't tolerate that stuff in the house."

"For him, everything goes better with whiskey," Annie said.

"At's what my daddy always said too."

I shrugged and sipped my Coke.

"Well, little sister, about the survivalist bit. I can understand why you'd be askin' that, what with the Rooskies all done for—if that ain't some kinda trick up they sleeve to make us relax. But they's all kinds of thangs people have got to keep their eyes open for. Terrism and stuff like that. For years all we worried about was bein' blowed up by atom bombs, but I never did thank too much about that, because if they as big as we been tol', wouldn't be no survivin' them atall anyhow. If I'd a-thought we could, I'd have me a big cellar dug out there in the side of that slope." She jerked her thumb toward the rear of the building. "No, it's yer own people you got to worry about."

She fished another cigarette out of the wrinkled pack and lit it and added to the blue haze that hung over the kitchen. A deep rattling cough shook her shoulders. Holding the cigarette package out to the light, she squinted to see what was left in it.

"You might not believe it, but I'm still smokin' on cigarettes that was left over from the store. They was hunderds of cartons back in the storeroom. One month I'm the Camel Lady, the next Marlberry, then Salems. Had'm all. People'll tell you they go stale, but they don't. Or if they do, I ain't noticed."

We nodded. Salem Lady indeed. I could believe that. Annie's eyes were red-rimmed, but she no longer winced at the smoke.

"Over the years here we was robbed seven times by thugs out of Houston, or at least that's where we figgered they was from. Seven times. You know, they don't come in and announce they're so and so from so and so and hand you a card, and when they leave they don't tell you where they're goin' to. They come in wavin' guns and demandin' the money from the drawer and Daddy always give it to'm. Until one day—this was in the late sixties—a big nigger come in, staggerin' drunk, and said he wanted our money, which Daddy opened the drawer and give him, but he hit Daddy upside the head anyway with the barrel of his pistol. It was a big black one, like this'n, I remember it well." She leaned back and laid her hand on the pistol.

"Hit him for no reason atall. Just laid back and swung it and it sounded like somebody hit a hog in the head with a sledgehammer. And then he was gone and Daddy layin' there on the floor bleedin' like a stuck pig. I don't thank he was ever quite the same after that nigger hit him. I mean, it wudn't like he had brain damage or anythang from it. It was like his whole attitude toward people had done changed. Like that big barrel uncorked him and let somethin' out I didn't know was there. I don't know whether it was because it was a nigger done it or because Daddy didn't do anythang to get hit for. I don't know. I just remember when he got up he had a terrible look in his eyes, the kind you see in people's faces in pitchers of a war-tore land, and I got his head warshed off and bandaged—Lord, he was bleedin' but he wudn't sayin' ary a word. He went into the bedroom back there and come back with his shotgun, a old J. C. Higgins twelve-gauge pump, and take'n it out to the toolshed and sawed the barrel off as far back as he could without cuttin' the magazine tube and cut the stock off with his handsaw just back of the handgrip and wrapped it with black tape. And he take'n a box of shells down off a shelf and slid that gun under the counter loaded to the brim with number-one buck. Never said a word the whole time, but I knowed what he was thankin'."

"What's number-one buck?" Annie asked. "I don't know what—"

"It doesn't matter," I said. "That's just a kind of shotgun shell for shooting deer."

"I'll tell you what number-one buck is, little sister. It's a shot-gun shell that's got sixteen pellets in it in the twelve-gauge, sixteen little balls of lead about the size of a English pea. And some people do use'm for deer. Only what Daddy shot with them shells was the next two robbers that come thoo that door in there tellin' us to give up our money. The first time it was a wild-eyed nigger high on somethin' and carryin' a baseball bat, which he drawed back to hit my daddy with on his way to the cash register. Daddy got off three shots quick as you could say *Jack*—"

I grinned. "As in Jack Robinson?"

"No, you just would have got the *Jack* out. We done been thoo this Jack Robson stuff." She drew her hand into a curl and pre-tended to work the slide of a shotgun. "*Blam, blam, blam.* It was like somethin' out of a pitcher show. Blowed him clean thoo the screen door. Take'n him right outta one of his shoes. I can walk in there and show you right now where some of them buckshots pit-ted the wall."

"No thanks." Annie was watching the old woman's hand motions. "I get the picture."

"What did the Law say?" I asked.

"The *Law*? The Law didn't say nothin'. There wudn't nothin' for'm *to* say. Where was they when that nigger come in here to rob us? That bat had two holes in it, the screen door had five, the nig-ger had twenty-seven, proof enough he was holdin' the bat and where he was standin' at. The rest of'm hit the wall, I guess, but I never counted'm. Sixteen balls in a number-one buck shell. That's forty-eight balls big as a English pea. Like a hailstorm hit'm."

"And the next one?"

"The next what?"

"The next robber."

"Well, sir, this time it was a piece of white trash from Louisiana somewhere passin' thoo to Lord knows where. White or Cajun—wudn't a nigger. Drove some kind of old green car. Pulled in and got out with a raincoat on even in the dead of summer and it hot and the weather chrystial clear and walked in, but Daddy already had his eye on him, and he had done seen that he was totin' somethin' under the raincoat, so he went behind the counter and waited and when the guy come in Daddy tol' him to turn around and go right back out, that he didn't want no trouble, but the guy started up with whatever was under his coat—turned out to be a sawed-off double barrel—and he was close enough that the whole charge hit his head, and Daddy take'n most of it clean off. Wudn't but one shot that time. Didn't need but one. High on dope, Daddy figgered, since *any* fool ort to know better'n to try to face down a twelve-gauge."

"Jesus." Annie hid her face in her hands.

I glanced at the pistol. "I guess we've heard enough about that."

"Word got out after that and we never was robbed again."

"And I take it you don't intend to be."

"No sir. You got to keep the drop on people, else they'll get the drop on *you.* Folks got to get up powerfully early to beat me to the draw, I tell you. Like if I had just invited y'all in here like compny, Annie Oakley here might of whipped a little silver pistol outta her purse and shot me and Duke dead as ce-ment and take'n everthang on the place."

"Lady . . ."

"It's all right." I nudged Annie with my foot. "So you're a survivalist."

"Yep."

"Is that why you don't get the driveway fixed?"

"Yessir. It gouges out a little more ever time it rains. From time to time the county'll come in and dump some red clay and gravel that they haul in from somewhere, but I let it warsh out agin. Nobody got no need to drive up out there. I don't pump gas and I don't sell feed and groceries. The propane man lugs a hose over from the shoulder of the road."

"It's sort of a moat, huh?"

"Well sir, I don't know what a mote is, except the *Bible* mentions somethin' about gettin' one in yer eye," she said, "a beam or a mote, it says."

Annie said, "I think he's talking about a different kind of moat, one that runs around a castle to protect it."

"All I know's that the ditch keeps folks outta my driveway."

"You know," Annie said, "this seems like an awfully lonely way of life. What'll you do when you get real old and weak or sick and can't take care of yourself?"

She leaned and patted the pistol. "That's what friends is for. This here's my best friend, besides Duke. When the time comes, I'll know it and I'll do somethin' about it."

"But there's no love in your life," Annie said. Her eyes were soft and filmy.

The old woman took a long last drag on the cigarette and pitched it into the sink. "There's love here awright. The only kind that makes any sense atall. That's the kind that me and Duke got."

"You call that *love*?"

"Yes'm, I do. All the other kinds got strangs attached to'm. My daddy loved me because he had to. That's what daddies do. And mothers. And the rest of yer famly, if you got any that you know about. What Chris felt for me was some kinda love, I guess, but only for what he got out of it. I thank the road got to him bad and he needed somebody he could come home to. I 'spect most marriages is like that. Only Chris had lots of women he was goin' home to. Friends love you as long as it works to their advantage. But what me'n this dog got is the only real love there is. If I didn't feed him, he'd go right on lovin' me. If I kicked his butt ever day and starved him, he'd go right on lovin' me. It's the way thangs is between us."

"What if he bit you or ran off?" Annie asked.

"He wouldn't," she said, leaning down and stroking the dog's head. He had lain quietly all the while. He rolled his eyes up at her.

"But if he *did*?"

"Little sister, if he run off, when he come back I'd tie him up and beat him till he wouldn't run away no more."

"What if he bit you?"

She put a cold eye on Annie. "He wouldn't, but if he did, I'd blow his ass to Kingdom Come, pardon the language."

Annie shook her head. "Kingdom Come—wherever the *hell* that is—must be awfully full of shot-up people and animals. But if you love him—"

"Little sister, if he run off or bit me, it'd mean he had went crazy. It wouldn't be Duke no more, because Duke wouldn't run off and he wouldn't bite me. Don't you see?" Every time the dog heard his name he would blink.

"I'm trying," Annie said. "Jesus, you're cynical."

"I don't know what sin's got to do with it. I don't see no sin in it atall. It's just the way I got it figgered. But you ain't got to worry, because dogs just ain't like that. They ain't like men."

She removed the last cigarette from the flattened pack, lit it, and inhaled deeply. The room was heavy now with bluish-white smoke. "Lord, I don't know when I have smoked like this. Guess I'll go into a carton of Kools next. That'll make me the Kool Lady." She laughed and hacked. "Had it figgered that what we had left over would last me to the grave." She had moved a cereal bowl over beside the sink and started flicking her ashes in it.

"The grave is where they'll send you," Annie said.

"So what?" The crone drew deep, thrust out her lower lip, and let the smoke rise slowly out of the curtain of hair that fell across her face.

"It looks like your hair's on fire."

"Well, it ain't, little sister. You sure you don't want a cigarette? These is prolly '80 or '81 Marlberrys. Rekkin cigarettes get better with age, like wine?"

"I doubt it. So whatever happens, you'll survive?"

"Yessir. Used to be everbody was afraid of the Russians and built bomb shelters, but it ain't Russians or Chinese or A-rabs or nobody else over the wide water we got to worry about. What's comin' is worse. Much worse." She tilted her head so the hair cracked like a curtain and stared at me with a hard eye. "When it comes, it'll be in the form of white trash and Meskins and niggers boilin' up outta Houston or down from Dallis. Maybe a big har-rikin will tear thoo here or somebody will dump a couple of atom bombs on us, maybe one of them big chunks of ice from outer space will hit, or there might be a race war. But somethin' will happen and all hell will bust loose—pardon the language—and then it'll be the have-nots against the got-mores."

She blew a great blast of smoke between me and Annie. "And I intend to keep what I got. When the time comes, I'll be blazin' away at all them starvin' people, the niggers and Meskins and white trash up from Houston that'll be trying to take this place."

Annie grinned. "Why would they want to come *here?*"

"They'll have to go *somewheres*. They'll come here to tote off all the stuff I've stored up, my guns and food. To get my tractor and the gas I got stashed, my two cows and the goats down there. My chickens." She motioned toward the woods behind the building. "You mark my word, young people. This here world ain't got long to last. We near the end of times. The Bible tells about it." Her body was wracked by a violent cough. "Near the end of times, boys and girls," she wheezed.

The conversation lapsed at that and for long minutes we just sat there while the old woman quietly smoked and Annie and I self-consciously played with our hands on the table. I looked up at her a couple of times, but she avoided my eyes. The dog deeply sighed and scratched himself, his foot making a rasping sound on his belly. I noticed how chilly the kitchen was, though the sun had been beating down the way it does in September in East Texas. The rain and cool front had apparently taken all the heat out of the blocks. Of course, we *were* scantily dressed.

Then Annie sneezed one of those petite little sneezes that women do and the spell was broken. The crone snapped her head up and flung the filter of the finished cigarette into the sink. "I rekkin it's time to shut this place down for the night. Ain't been up this late in a long time."

She stood and pushed her hair back so that her face broke completely free of the dark shroud. She didn't appear so very old then, just worn and tough, the way people who smoke over a long period of time eventually look, her forehead quite smooth, with delicate wrinkles fanning out from the corners of her mouth and eyes like something that has been stretched too much and let go. Her eyes were puffy. She leaned her elbows back on the counter and studied us.

"You know, I have come to like y'all. I just don't get to talk to people. But you ain't told me one thang about yerselves, except that yer headin' to Houston to see about a little girl that has been hurt."

"There's nothing to tell that we haven't already told you," Annie said. "And that's the truth."

"Little sister, I don't know what kinda wall y'all done put up between yerselves, or what kinda moat—that what you called it?—you dug between yerselves, but I know it's somethin' there. I'd suggest you do yer dead-level best to tear it down or fill it in before you cain't get across it anymore. Bein' alone is—" She coughed violently. "Bein' alone. . . ."

She picked up the pistol and pointed toward the door at the end of the room. "Now, little sister, you go on in there and do yer stuff in the bathroom and be quick. You come on back out and yer man can go in."

"I need to take a bath."

"No ma'am. The drain on the tub is rusted out—I done tol'

you that. Water just goes everwhere, and I ain't about to mop up after you."

"Where do *you* bathe," Annie asked her.

"That ain't none of yer bidness, little sister. I might go in the creek down yonder, all you know. Or hose off in the yard. It ain't none of y'all's bidness."

"May one of us please go to the car to get our overnight bags? I'll go, or she can. But we need those bags."

"No sir. Yer in for the night, like I done been over. Make do."

"You don't happen to have any toothbrushes left over from the store, do you?" Annie asked. "I'll *buy* one from you."

"She's got her own money," I explained.

The old woman glanced at me and then at Annie. "Well, they's prolly boxes of'm off somewheres, but I cain't lay my hand on'm tonight. Just go on in there and make do. You can use the brush that's in there or put a little dob of toothpaste on yer finger and rub yer teeth with it. It'll do just as good a job as you can with a toothbrush."

"Yes'm." Annie got up and ducked around the pistol. "I'll make do."

While Annie was in the bathroom the old woman fed the dog and poured him a fresh bowl of water. I studied the two of them crouched in the corner of the room. While he ate she stroked his back and talked softly to him the way a little girl would talk to a doll. The dog's tail wagged in rhythm with her hand.

Then Annie whispered and motioned me to the bathroom door. "*Yer* turn. But I wouldn't use that monstrosity on the back of the sink. I don't know whether it's a brush for teeth or for toilets. Just *make do.*"

The bathroom was stark, like one you'd expect to find around the side of a service station. A lone bulb jutted out above the medicine cabinet, nothing hung on the heavily painted concrete block walls but a towel rack at the end of the tub and one near the lavatory. No pictures of Jesus, nothing. A clothes hamper sat on one side of the sink and a small white porcelain gas heater sat on the other. I wanted desperately to open the medicine cabinet and see what she kept in there, but I figured it would all come tumbling out and I'd have that .44 shoved up to my head.

I peed in the brown-ringed commode, kneeling and aiming up along the sides of the bowl so that I wouldn't make a lot of noise. I've always hated to hear men pee like bull elephants when there are women nearby, like they are proving something with their torrent. Women are not generally impressed by that, I think.

When I contemplated my face in the mirror, I realized that I looked closer to the old woman's age than to Annie's, though we were only a little over five years apart. Jesus, what a mess. What a day. I splashed cold water over my head and face and dried off with the face towel on the rack. It smelled vaguely of Annie's perfume. I held it to my face a long time.

My teeth felt mossy, so I decided to try the old paste-on-the-finger trick. I damned sure wasn't going to use the old woman's brush. With an enormous, odd-shaped head—one of those designed to clean dentures *and* teeth or perhaps scrub a tub out or clear the cleats of a boot—it lay obscenely on the back of the lavatory in a thin sheen of water and beside it, curled up like something dead and desiccated in the road, was a Colgate tube, the old thin-metal kind that you can't get anymore. I couldn't tell whether Annie had used the paste or not, but assumed that she had, so I squeezed out a little bird dropping on a finger and worked the paste all over my teeth and gums, rinsed, and spat. My mouth felt better, but what it needed was a good wholesome flushing with Jack Daniels. One more glance at my face and I returned to the kitchen.

"Now here's the deal," the old woman said when I had taken my seat. "I'm puttin' y'all in the storeroom for the night and lockin' the door—"

"What?"

"Easy, Annie Oakley. That's the way it's gon' be done. That way you got a place to sleep for the night but you ain't no threat to me."

"We're not a threat to you anyway," Annie said. "I don't understand you, you crazy old woman. You treat us nice one minute and like criminals the next. We have been sitting at your table talking to you like friends. You can't lock us up in there all night. What if the place were to catch fire?"

"Well, it ain't in all the years it's been here. Why would it catch a-fahr now? Less'n y'all go to playin' with matches in there. Besides, this buildin' is made out of ce-ment blocks, in case you ain't noticed, and ce-ment blocks don't burn."

"No," I said, "but what's *in* a concrete block building will burn and the roof will burn. I'll bet that roof's got three inches of tar up there. It would be an inferno."

"It ain't a-goin' to burn atall less'n you start a fahr in there. But there ain't no need to argue. You are goin' in that room and I am padlockin' the door. Ain't no more discussion about it."

Annie shoved her chair back and stood, her fists on the table top, her face fierce. "You cannot make me go into any storeroom with him to spend the night, you harpie. I'll not be locked up like a Goddamned dog—"

"You watch yer language, little lady." She had picked the pistol up and held it casually in her hand, arms crossed. "You are goin' in there, and you are goin' with him and I am goin' to padlock the door. *And that is the gospel according to Ludy Dowdle!*"

Annie hammered her fists on the table and sat down and dropped her face into her hands.

"It's OK, Baby," I whispered, rubbing my leg against hers, "come on." She moved her legs away.

"Look, folks, I don't what the prollem with y'all is, but you gon' have to get over it for tonight, because I ain't got but one safe place to keep y'all and you are both goin' in there and that is *that*. All there is is Daddy's old single-bed mattress, which two people can fit on, if they lay straight and still, but if y'all don't want to sleep on it together, one of you can sprawl out in the boxes or beside the mattress while the other one sleeps on it. That's up to y'all how you work it out. Me, I'm ready to put myself and that dog to bed for the night. Now, on yer feet."

"This is house arrest!" Annie yelled.

"And this is a *.44 magnum*." The crone raised the pistol and motioned us toward the hallway. She pointed a finger at the dog, who had finished eating and was watching us with interest. "And that's a purty big German shepherd that'll hep you along, if you need it. Now get on down that hall and to the left."

I snatched Annie's hand and pulled her out of the chair and behind me into the hallway. Just past the bathroom was a door to the right, which I assumed was her bedroom, then the hall turned left.

"First door there's yer room," her voice came from behind us.

"Where's that go?" I pointed to another door at the end of the hall.

"At's a room full of old tars and battries and boxes of hoses and belts and Lord knows what all. Just junk. It ain't fittin' to stay in, and I cain't lock it up."

"You have tires in there?"

"Well sir, what you drivin' won't fit none of them tars, and they are *old*, like I said. Wore out. Some of'm got holes. Some plumb rotted. Daddy just never throwed nothin' away. Ain't nothin' in that room you'd be interested in. Now open that door and go on in."

I noticed a heavy steel hasp as I twisted the knob and swung the door open. The thin shaft of light from the end of the hallway stabbed the dark, cluttered room. There were boxes everywhere, of all sorts and shapes and sizes with just enough room for the door to swing back.

I stepped forward into the room and turned around and slid my hand up and down the wall for a switch. "Where's the light?"

"Ain't nothin' on that wall. They used to be a strang hangin' down from the bulb up there but it broke a long time ago. I just ain't got around to fixin' it."

Annie balked at the door and put a hand on each side of the facing like someone bracing herself against falling into a well. "I am not going into that room without a light."

"Yes'm, y'are. I'll thowe you a flashlight in d'rectly, after I get you some sheets. It's warm enough you ain't gon' need a blanket. Then you can get yerself a place cleared for that pallet."

She put her hand in the middle of Annie's back and pushed gently at first, then firmly. Annie's arms folded back and she stumbled into my arms. She tried to pull away, but I kept her in a tight embrace as the door slammed to and rebounded to a thin crack through which I could see the dog sitting just across the hallway watching.

"You stay right where yer at till I get back. I'm gon' get you some sheets and stuff. Keep a eye on'm, Duke."

"Just relax, Annie. Hold still."

"Turn me loose, bastard."

"Relax, Annie, just relax." I maintained my grip.

She stopped struggling and leaned her head against my chest while the old woman bumbled around somewhere down the hallway, then the door swung back and in the pale sliver of light she slid a stack of neatly folded sheets into the room. I could smell the sun. On top of them lay a green flashlight. She closed the door and I heard her slide a padlock through the staple. The lock clicked shut.

"Now," her voice came through the door. "You can see with that flashlight to get you a place cleared. Over in the corner to yer left, if you still lookin' at the door, is a rolled-up mattress that you can make yer pallet with. Just stack them boxes anywhere you want to. Most of it's just junk anyway. That sink's over to yer left too, in case you want some water. I don't want you to make a whole lot of noise, now, or it'll keep me and Duke on edge. He'll be just outside this door. It ain't no skin off of me whether y'all sleep together or not or whether you sleep atall, but I don't want you makin' a whole bunch of noise. People *and* dogs got to get their rest out. Now, good night to you. I'll knock on the door when I got breakfast ready."

At that her feet shuffled off down the hallway and the sliver of light beneath the door zipped up. The room turned very, very dark.

SIX

Even before the strip of light beneath the door disappeared and the old woman's steps died off and put between us once again the great silence only estranged couples can know—a cold and impenetrable, unhuman silence—Annie had pulled away. In unmerciful dark, like the inside of a lidded cauldron, we stood a long time within arms' length of each other not talking, not touching. Finally my eyes began to adjust and from some dim source of light behind me I could vaguely see her outline against the whitewashed door, a small familiar statue chiseled out of stone. In the awful silence of that room I could hear her breathing, shallow and swift, like a frightened child. The vision of a wood nymph swam through my mind.

The first sound was her impatient voice asking, "You want to turn that damned flashlight on? I'd like to know what kind of dungeon we've been thrown into here."

I felt around and found the flashlight and flipped it on. Its pale beam played over a room maybe twenty by thirty feet, constructed of the same drab concrete blocks as the rest of the house and sloshed over with whitewash sometime ages past. Cobwebs, ancient and sooty, billowed along the ceiling and draped down the walls. The room was filled with boxes of every size and sort, beginning just beyond the sweep of the door and stacked in graduating height almost to the ceiling along the walls. Some were dull, ordinary cardboard boxes, others had panels of bright color and flashy logos; some were still factory sealed, some had tops gaping open with the contents, mostly old clothing, lolling out like obscene tongues. Everything was coated with a sepia dust. Clothes and canned food, cigarettes, magazines and newspapers, accumulations of plastic bags, great clutches of coat hangers.

"Jesus," Annie whispered, "this is like the Haunted House at the fair. Jesus."

On the back wall the slope of boxes dipped in the middle to allow light from a small barred window, up high, the way they are in the jailhouses in old westerns, and to our right a slender corridor wove round to a ponderous white porcelain sink fastened to the wall.

"My God, Tommy, we are in *jail*. Look at the bars on that window." I could feel her breath on my neck.

"Well put. I guess you'd call this the Davy Crockett National Forest Prison."

"And we never did a damned thing."

"They all say that."

She actually laughed then, a quick giggle. "At least we're not looking down the barrel of that cannon."

"Yeah." I swung the light beam across the slope of boxes again and blew toward the ceiling and the cobwebs rippled. "What a mess."

"It reminds me of the way you used to keep your study. You know that this room is probably alive with spiders and roaches and rats . . ."

"Be glad for what companionship you can find, my dear. We're all in this together. What it reminds me of is the way the first people who came into this God-awful country must have felt, with the door, so to speak, closed and locked behind them and nothing before them but trees, only what we're facing is boxes, a forest of them."

Her hand touched my back. "Tommy, what do we do?"

"I don't see that we have many options. What do you suggest?"

"No, no, you brought me here. *You* decide."

"Well." I handed her the light. "We do what they did. We hack out a place in the wilderness to camp. You hold the light while I try to clear out a spot big enough to put a mattress in." I bent over and hoisted a box and laid it on top of some others and shoved it hard until it balanced enough to stay.

"Forget the mattress bit. I am not getting on a mattress with you. Even if I have to sit on the floor and lean against the door all night."

"Fine with me," I grunted, moving another box. "Nobody says you've got to lie down on the Goddamned thing. Lean against the door if you want to, but we can spread the mattress out and you can sit on one end and me on the other and we'll pretend it's a lifeboat and we're adrift somewhere waiting for help."

"That's a pretty fair analogy." She swung the flashlight around the room. "Did you see the mattress?"

"No, but she said it was rolled up in the corner to our left, looking toward the door."

Annie pointed the light in that direction and there the mattress was, rolled and clenched in the middle with a piece of rope. Its upper half slumped over like a tired old man.

"Garrgh, that thing's filthy," she said.

"I'll try to roll it out. It might not be so bad. Besides, we've got sheets to cover it with. Gotta shift a couple of more boxes first."

When I determined that I had a place large enough to unroll the mattress, I scrambled over a pile of boxes and got it and untied and unfurled it. Dust rose and engulfed me, coating my arms the way fine flecks of snow whirl and settle onto figures in one of those little snow globes when you tumble it.

"That's pretty bad," Annie said. "We'll both be sneezing."

"Let's get a sheet over the damned thing, trap the edges underneath. That'll do it."

She laid the flashlight on the floor and after helping me spread and tuck a sheet over the mattress, she set the folded sheet in the middle between us and settled onto her end. All the while she was careful to keep her blouse pulled down as far as it would go. I didn't give a damn about what I was wearing. If anything showed, tough. I sat down on my end.

"Better turn off the light," I suggested. "Save the batteries."

She switched the flashlight off and we sat in the dark at opposite ends of the narrow mattress, but we could have been a universe apart. It was all so totally unreal, the sequence of events that brought us to that point, like the feeling a person must have when he finds himself adrift in a night sea, one moment the lights and music and sounds of the throbbing ship alive with beautiful people, then nothing but the black sea on which the puny boat sits almost motionless, like a slender mattress in a dark, silent store-room somewhere in the middle of a wilderness—and at the other end of his boat or mattress or universe sits a stranger who is now no longer a stranger if for no other reason than that she shares his present fate. I could hear her softly breathing.

She sneezed and sniffed. "My God, here I am in the Davy Crockett National Forest Jail with my favorite person for a cell-mate."

"And you say so without a trace of irony. You can sleep out there with Duke, you know. Or in the room with her."

"No thanks. I'll take my chances here. At least I know the nature of the animal I've been locked up with. I can predict his behavior pretty well. But I won't sleep."

"Suit yourself." A gust of wind tore over the roof and slashed through the treetops. I could feel the air pulse in the room like a breathing thing.

"What a crazy night," Annie said. "One minute I was scared absolutely out of my wits, the next I was joking along with the Medusa, like she was my grandmother. Jesus, what a character. First, she's waving that pistol around and threatening to blow our heads off, then she's serving us egg sandwiches."

"It reminds me of absurd drama. Did you ever read any in college?"

"A little. *Waiting for Godot*, a couple of others. One called *No Escape* or *No Exit*, something like that. That's about it."

"I mean, the absurdists stretched reality about as thin as it could be stretched, even past the point of breaking, and I kept feeling like we were on a stage with her—"

Annie laughed. "And the dog was the audience."

"Well, as the Duke, he should have been swaggering on stage with us. 'Howdy, pilgrim,' he'd say."

"I'm glad he didn't have a more active role. I kept thinking about those big teeth of his."

"The better to eat you with, my dear."

"I'm not sure which one I was more frightened of—her or the gun or the dog. The three of them, though, whew. . . . Tommy, what in hell are we going to do in this filthy place for eight or ten hours, however long it is before the sun comes again?"

"Damned if I know. I'm not sure I can sleep in here either. You know that whatever built all those cobwebs is probably still living in here somewhere."

"Oh, that is very reassuring. Thank you so much."

"Sorry. My bad."

"I can see stars through the window," she said.

I looked, and beyond the bars the night sky shone.

"It's like a picture somebody has hung on a wall, a painting of stars the way a prisoner might see them."

"It's a very realistic painting," I said. "Like the painter might really have been in that jail looking out at night and he remembered very well what he saw."

"Or painted it while he was there."

"And if our painter decided to do a self-portrait at the time he painted that jailhouse window, he might very well paint a man and a woman dressed in their underwear and shirts sitting on the opposite ends of a little mattress and it would become surreal."

"Completely absurd," she agreed. "Tommy," she said softly,

"this whole day has been ridiculous. It really is like the theater of the absurd. Nobody—*nobody* could outdo this. I mean, we had a real gun pointed at us, ready to shoot . . ."

"I could see the tips of the bullets," I said. "The mean kind, *hollow-points*."

"*Holler*-points," she corrected me, "and a dog big enough to eat us for breakfast."

"Owned by a real-life witch."

"Medusa," Annie said.

"Without the snakes."

"Oh, they're here. She probably keeps them in this room."

"Were you as scared as I was?"

"Tommy, I don't know how scared you were. But when she made us crawl into that dark room, yeah, I was scared to death. And humiliated. I was just *mad* as hell while we were outside, especially when she made me dump my purse."

"Yeah, I'll just bet you were. Having to dump out your rubber. What a touch of class."

"The condom's none of your business," she fired back. "You don't know how long it's been in there. Nothing I do is any of your business—"

"Keep your voice down."

She lowered her volume a bit. "Had the rubber been opened? Was it *used*? Did you look at the expiration date?" I could tell by her movements on the mattress that she was big-time agitated.

"No—not even you are desperate enough to keep a used rubber."

"Well, all right, then. But, mister, let's get this straight: I can do whatever I want to with my life. You have no control over it. If I want to buy a backpack and haul a gross of condoms around with me, a whole year's supply, it's my business."

"That would average out to around three times a week," I said.

"What are you talking about?"

"A gross is 144. You'd be screwing almost three times a week."

"Just shut up, Tommy. If I wanted to use a gross a *month*, it wouldn't be any business of yours."

"That would be roughly five times a day. I don't see how you'd work all that in. You'd sure have to be more interested in sex than I remember you being. What kind of diet—"

"Can we talk about something else?"

"OK," I said, "let's try this: have you ever had a gun pointed at you before?"

"My God, no. I haven't even *seen* many guns in my life. Daddy had a shotgun, but I don't think he ever had a pistol in the house."

"That was weird, looking at the gray heads of those bullets, knowing that one could come down that barrel if her finger slipped. They had little holes in them. Hollow-points, you know. Designed to spread open when they hit flesh and bone and tear up everything they touch."

"*Holler*-points," she corrected again. "I guess that means they make you holler when they hit you."

"If one of those hit you, I doubt you'd have enough life left in you to holler."

She shifted on the mattress. It was too dark to tell for certain, but I think she pulled her legs up and was resting her chin on her knees. My night-adjusted eyes could now just barely make out small light spots on her blouse, the white squares in the gingham.

"The gun really didn't scare me that much," she said. "It was too absurd to be frightened of. It's like the Devil the way the preachers used to describe him, with a forked tail and horns, bright red and all. The image was too ludicrous for me to take him seriously. For some strange reason, I—the gun just didn't register much. I kept looking at it and thinking that it wasn't real, that it was made out of plastic and wouldn't really shoot. You know, that it just *couldn't*. That big old black pistol in her tiny hand. And that face that I couldn't see the eyes in. She'd tilt her head one way and you'd see one eye, then the other through that greasy hair. Like she was one-eyed and it kept shifting around. Now, that was spooky."

"Something else that was spooky, too—when she made us pull our clothes off. I mean, really, she knew damned well we weren't carrying a weapon in or under our clothes. I think she was getting her jollies watching us strip down."

"I thought the same thing."

"Truth is," I said, "I thought for a while she was going to make us screw for her, have her own porno show."

"You'd have gone for it too, wouldn't you?"

"Well . . ."

"I felt your hard-on when I came out of that faint."

I was glad she couldn't see my red face. "Jesus, Annie, it's been a long time."

"Not nearly as long as it's going to be. It would have been a tough choice, deciding whether to let her shoot me or let you fuck me."

"Keep your voice down, Annie. She'll be back in here if you keep on."

"That old hag can go straight to hell for all I care. She's the one that got us in this mess. No, your *stupidity* got us in this mess, but she's an accomplice."

Now she was up on all fours facing me. I swear I could feel her heat. "Do you mean to say that if that old woman had held that gun to your head and given you the choice of lying back and letting me screw you or taking a bullet through the head, you'd have chosen to die? Do you despise me that much?"

"I said it would have been a tough choice, but realistically I probably would have clamped my eyes shut and put my mind off someplace else and treated it like any other rape. Let you and her get off on it. Then I'd have gotten over it."

"I don't know whether to believe that you hate me that much or—"

"Believe it—I hate you that much."

I sat back again. "This room seems to be hotter than the others. Even the kitchen wasn't this hot. Would you mind if I took off my shirt?"

"Tommy, it's dark in here, so why should I care whether you take off your shirt or not. Get comfortable. But for the sake of common decency leave your shorts on."

I slipped my shirt off, stuck my glasses in the pocket, and rolled it into a little ball and laid it on top of the folded sheet. "The sun must spend a lot of time on this wall. Gotta be the southwest wall. No, it'd have to be . . ."

"Don't go analyzing it too much," she said. "I don't care what direction the wall's facing. It's not that hot in here to me. Just stuffy. I mean, the only air we've got is from that little window and what comes under the door."

"Thank God for early cold fronts. It could be hot as hell in here in September."

"I'd leave God out of this. He didn't have anymore to do with that cold front than He did with getting us in this mess."

We were silent a few seconds. "Do you still believe, Annie."

"In what?"

"In God. You know, the way you used to?"

"I don't know what I believe anymore, Tommy, just what I don't believe. I don't believe in the goodness of the world anymore, and I don't believe in the sanctity of love—it's just chemistry and cells, glands, and nothing more. I'm not bold enough to not believe in God, but I'm not sure I *do* believe, either. That make any sense?"

"A little. You're getting cynical as all hell."

"Well, I prayed for Allison last night and on the way down, if that counts in my favor. It's what you do when you don't know what else to do, which dilutes the belief factor just a little, wouldn't you say? I used to pray that we could have a child. Used to even pray that we would stay together. Used to pray for *you*. I hope the prayers for Allison are a little more effective."

The wind was really kicking up. It whined across the building and I could hear somewhere not very far off the sound of it rushing through trees. There was no sound at all in the room except our shallow breathing.

"It happened so fast," I said.

"What did?"

"The split. You know, between us."

"Did not. You're not remembering right. Men never do. I put up with your screwing around for nearly two years before I moved out. And we were at each other's throats all the time. Jesus, those months seemed like an eternal hell to me."

"Didn't to me."

She didn't say anything to that. The dog had moved against the door to sleep. I could hear his deep breathing and sighing, an occasional whimper. Another gust of wind tore through the trees and moaned across the roof and the room pulsed.

After a long silent while she said, "Well, I'm through talking about that. Let's climb up to that window."

I flashed the light on and played it over the boxes between us and the back wall. "It'll be tough to do it quietly, but we can try. You really want to?"

"I've never looked out a jailhouse window before."

"All right. Let's try it."

The first box I stepped on collapsed like something filled with feathers, but the next one was firm and the second layer held me like a ledge of stone. It was a stack of boxes of canned goods of some sort that must have gone all the way to the floor, but the labels were so faded and coated with dust that I couldn't be certain what was in them. I could make out a few: Del Monte and Dole and Underwood. When I reached my hand down to Annie, she pushed it away and clambered up behind me. It was like a miniature mountain climbing expedition, finding a handhold here, a toehold there, hoisting and bracing, but soon we were kneeling on a large rigid box that brought our faces to window level.

"What are we on?" She rubbed her hand over the box.

"I don't know. Something solid in it, though." I blew across the surface and shone the flashlight on it. "It's a folding stairway, like those you use to go into an attic. Disappears so that the bottom of it is flush with the ceiling. It's upside down and we're on the ply-wood-bottom side of it."

"Tommy, what in God's name would she be doing with one of these? Does she even *have* an attic?"

"No. This place is one level and has a flat roof."

"Maybe her daddy sold them here."

"Must have. Totally useless to her, I'd say."

"A disappearing stairway . . . ," Annie mused. "And upside down at that."

The window opening, maybe a couple of feet wide and a little better than a foot high, was just large enough to accommodate our heads without requiring our faces to touch, though my shoulder was tight against hers. There were four bars evenly spaced across it, embedded in concrete at top and bottom. Annie had grasped two of the bars and pressed her cheeks to the knuckles of her thumbs.

"Jesus, Tommy, it's exactly like a jail."

"Might *have* been at one time. Lots of these old buildings did double duty of one sort or another."

"There may be ghosts of murderers and rapists and thieves haunting these walls," she whispered. "Who knows who might have looked out past these bars?"

"I'll bet you Chris did. Imagine ol' Chris lying on his back down there staring up through that window at the stars and won-dering whether he ought to go in there and jump her bones, or maybe sitting right here where we are looking through these bars, and nowhere in his mind the image of the bridge railing that would someday rip through his chest and take out his backbone."

"That was such a sad story, Tommy. Not about him—he deserved it—but about her."

"What do you mean, deserved it? No man deserves that kind of awful death."

"He was a philanderer, Tommy. Messing around with women all over East Texas."

"Goddamn it, you don't know that. That's just what *she* said about him. She might have been the only woman he was ever with."

"Well, if you're going to use that line of argument, there might never have even *been* a Chris."

"I believe that part. I don't know about the other."

"Well, what about the black woman who was killed with him with nothing but a dress on?"

"She might have been a hitchhiker, for all we know, Annie. If there *was* anyone with him."

"Might have been, but I'll bet he was having a fling with her. And I'll bet it was a black woman with nothing on but a dress."

"Even if he did have a black woman without underwear in the truck with him, do you think he deserved to die for it? You seem to have the notion that he made her get in the truck without panties on or that he took them off. How do you figure that he deserved to die for it?"

"If the fates allow it, fine."

"Fates hell. Annie, we don't even know that there *was* a Chris, and if there was one, that he died that way. He might still be alive somewhere, selling seeds."

"No. It just made too much sense, the manner of his death. It seemed appropriate. Too bad the black woman had to die too. No telling how he was stringing her along."

"Bloodthirsty is what you are. You women would assign the death penalty for cheating."

"Tommy, that old woman in there had all her hopes riding on *one man*, a stranger from off the road, blown in like something on the wind. She'd waited all that time, maybe not even knowing what she was waiting for, waited all that time and along he came and that was it for her when he left. That one shot, that one chance at love with a man. Only I doubt that she knew that was her only shot. She must have dreamed there'd be others."

The night was savagely starry, with no trace of a moon, and the wind rode the trees over like some great unseen northern force. I could hear it whipping through them and see their silhouettes dancing against the sky, and beneath them the pale, starlit pasture sloped away to a dark line of trees.

"God, Tommy, this is so eery." I could smell toothpaste on her breath. "It's so dark. So quiet. If that wind weren't blowing, there would be no sound at all. Just us breathing."

"I remember a time when that was enough, can't you?"

"Well, that was a long time ago. A lot of whiskey has passed over the rail of your bridge since then. You're damned lucky you haven't been shot through by a railing with Betty Dunbar beside you, holding a pizza and not wearing her teeth *or* panties."

"Please stop it." I grabbed her by the shoulders and turned her to face me. "Annie, did we burn the bridge? I mean, is it completely, utterly burned?"

She shoved me away. We were now on opposite ends of that

rectangular box smaller than the mattress, kneeling, squared off against each other like two fighters wearied to their knees. Damned if I can understand how a starlit sky can generate enough light for you to see the details of someone's angry face. I used to wonder about where the light came from in movies during a night scene. Now I know. Once your eyes adjust, it just doesn't take much light from the outside.

"Tommy, *you* stop it. I told you I don't want to talk about that anymore. That's the kind of crap you start when you've been drinking. You're not even *drinking*. Now, if you want to look out the window with me, get yourself focused on the real world. The real world is this cluttered, filthy room and what you and I can see out there. It's you and me and an old woman and a dog. There is no we, no us. I don't like you and there's no common ground between you and me. If I had had any say-so at all in it, I wouldn't be here and you know it. And to answer your question, the bridge is burned so completely that even the ashes have washed away—there's no trace of it, no evidence it was ever there, no charred timbers sticking out of the muck, *nothing*."

"Annie."

She thrust her face toward mine. Our lips were not six inches apart. God, I wanted to grab her and kiss her.

"Don't try to start up anything with me. I am over you. Do you understand me?"

"Yes. I. . . ."

Then her voice softened. "Tommy, please, we've got a long night ahead of us and it looks like we're going to have to spend it together, whether I like it or not. And that's OK, as if I had any say in it. Please respect me enough not to go on with this. I don't want anything else to do with you, and I don't want to talk about *us*. OK?"

"OK. I'm sorry, Annie. It's just that I haven't had a chance to talk to you in so long. I thought—"

"Then don't *think*, Tommy, if your mind is inclined to go in that direction. Let's just play this night however it goes. We can sit up here on this upside-down disappearing staircase a while and watch the sky and then crawl back down and talk about whatever. I don't mind that. Or we can crouch up here by the window and talk all night. But I don't want to talk about *us*. There *is* no us."

I extended a hand. "OK. Respect it is. I'm focused on the present. History's history, the bridge is totally burned. We'll talk about whatever you want to talk about."

She hesitantly put her hand in mine and the electricity shot through me again. I pumped once and withdrew mine.

"You know," I said, "we've been so absorbed with this absurdity here that we've completely forgotten why we're here."

"Maybe *you've* forgotten. I remember that we're here because of your stupidity."

"No, I grant you that. I mean, we're here—we're heading to Houston—because of *Allison*."

There was no sound in the room as the awful truth of what I'd said sank in. In the blurred insanity of the past few hours I had given little thought to Allison, to the dear child whose plight had the two of us paired up once again, as if in a season of miracles something glorious had happened, something that wasn't supposed to, that couldn't. And I figured that she hadn't thought about Allison either.

"God, I feel awful, Tommy. You're absolutely right. That child just got crowded out of my mind, shoved out like a piece of furniture that I didn't want up there anymore." She reached and laid her hand on mine, then drew it away. "Let's talk about Allison."

And so we did. For over an hour, I'm sure, though I never checked my watch, mainly because I couldn't make out the time—my glasses were at the bottom of the heap in my shirt pocket. We sat on that box, from time to time kneeling to look out our jailhouse window, and talked about Allison, the golden child of our golden time together, the child who bound us, as children do. Listening to Annie talk about her, stopping to wipe her eyes with the sleeve of her blouse, I realized how much she had meant not just to me, not just to Annie, but to the couple that we became because of her. And the analogue was clear for the first time—the compound that we were before, two separate elements, was only as strong as one of the elements; she blended us into an alloy, stronger than the compound and stronger by far than the elements, either one apart. And then, when she went out of our lives. . . .

"She is such a beautiful child," Annie concluded. "And I love her with a passion. I just hope . . . I just hope."

"I know, Baby," I said softly, "I do too."

"Tommy, this is getting maudlin. I'm rummaging around too much in the past, and when I do, I bump into *us*, and there is no us anymore. I just can't do this."

"Well, it was good to get it out. To talk about it."

"And we have. Now we've just got to hope she's going to be OK."

We sat then and watched the night sky through our prison

window and listened to the wind. It came in gusts. It came from far off, like a great wave toward a beach, gathered strength, roared through the trees near the house, and swept over us and down toward the dark mass of trees at the bottom of the pasture slope. There it roared again, its sound finally tapering off in the distance, and silence settled on us until the next wave came. It was almost like a living thing racing across the landscape, hellbent for the Coast, wave after wave after wave.

The wash of air was chilly, so I suggested to Annie that perhaps we'd better think about how we were going to sleep. It had to be close to midnight.

"I don't feel like sleeping, Tommy. I don't know what I want to do, but I don't want to lie down and go to sleep in this creepy room, with spiders and roaches and God knows what else."

"What do you want to do then? I mean, our options are fairly limited. We've seen the sights out this window. Tennis and golf are out. This late the pool's closed."

"I told you, I don't know. You're the one who brought me here. *You* suggest something."

"Well, we've talked about Allison. Neither one of us wants to go on with that, and you sure as hell don't want to talk about us . . ."

"Not going to."

"So what do you want to do, if you don't want to lie down? I mean, if you're worried about me, don't—I won't mess with you."

"Oh, I'm not worried about that, big boy, as she called you. I'm just not sleepy. I seem to be running on some kind of weird energy source, like I've had eight cups of coffee."

"It's adrenalin," I said.

"Maybe, but it's not going to let me sleep."

"So what . . ."

"Tommy." She reached and tapped my leg. "Are you at all . . . aren't you at all curious about what's in all these boxes?"

"Sure, I'm curious."

"Then let's take a look. I'm just dying to know. Jesus, if she's got a disappearing staircase in a building that doesn't have an attic, there's no telling what else she's got in here. Frankly, I'm intrigued by the old bat and the stuff in her castle."

I flashed the light around the cluttered room. "Just where the hell would you suggest that we start?"

"Well, most of this looks like cases of food and stuff, but shine the light back over here, behind me, in the corner. There're some shelves with boxes that have handwriting on them. Maybe it's personal stuff."

"Annie, we can't get into her personal things."

"Of course we can. I'll bet those boxes haven't been touched since they were put there, and I doubt they'll be touched again. She won't know. Come on—let's *do* it."

"This is crazy. But if you want to. . . ."

In the pale beam of the flashlight we worked our way across the high ledge of boxes we were on, sinking down in some, finding some as solid as concrete, until we were within reach of the boldly lettered boxes on the top shelf. The rest of the shelves were below the level of boxes stacked against them. Most were labeled Bills and Receipts and Tax Records, the earliest dating 1954.

"Damn," Annie said, "the best ones must be down below. All I see is financial stuff and canned food. She has to have hundreds of boxes of Spam and beans and all kinds of food here."

"Enough for a store, huh?"

"Yeah. And I'll bet some of it dates back to the fifties."

"Well, don't look for a challenge here. Come on, Annie, let's go back to the window or to the mattress."

She grabbed my arm and forced the flashlight beam lower. "This looks like personal stuff stacked in here, though, so let's try to get some of the junk cleared away so we can see what's on the shelves lower down."

"What we're going to do is find ourselves looking down the barrel of that .44 again or scrambling to get away from that damned dog. Annie, the old bat is bananas. There's no telling what she'll do if she catches us at this. Why don't we either go back to the window or climb down to the mattress?"

"Or why don't we see what's in the boxes on these shelves? Don't you have any curiosity about you?"

"I'm curious, yeah, but I'm cautious too. We're rummaging through her private stuff here. She might just come in and kill us."

"No," Annie said. "They always wait till dawn, remember? She'll give us each a Marlberry and stand us against the back wall out there and shoot us. With Duke as witness. It's a noble enough way to go. Then she'll *berry* us out in the goat pasture."

As I held the flashlight she pried out a couple of large, light boxes and set them aside. "The label says *cloths*. Probably clothes, don't you figure?"

"Yep," I said. "I doubt that she can spell *Duke*."

"Well, she can for sure spell *Financial Statements* or her daddy could—this box is from 1967. And *Progressive Farmer*. She's kept all these old magazines."

"She seem very progressive to you?" I asked.

"No," she grunted, shifting another large box. "*Re*-gressive, just like everybody else in East Texas."

"Why don't you let me in there to do that? You hold the light."

"OK, big boy, if you insist, and if you're not too scared of the big bad witch."

Annie took the light and directed it into the depression where she had extracted boxes. I could now see boxes on the third shelf from the top, but all of it still looked like financial records, bills and receipts from decades ago. A fine sepia dust coated everything. It boiled up and settled on us as I moved deeper into the pile.

"I swear, Annie, I'm going to start sneezing in a minute and wake up her and the dog."

"I know. I've been breathing through my blouse to keep from it."

I turned and looked into the light. She had her blouse pulled up and clamped over her nose and mouth. Her neck was arched like a bird sleeping with its head under a wing.

"I don't see any reason to go on with this, Annie. There's nothing here but bills and stuff. Nothing of any interest."

"Let's look through some of *that* stuff, then. It would have to be fascinating. We can see how much money the store made, what all they sold. We might even be able to figure out what she's worth."

"Now, as bored as we might be in here tonight, Annie, I am not going to spend the next six or eight hours reading over old financial reports on this place. If you want to, have at it."

"There's got to be something interesting, Tommy. Some personal things. Some love letters or something. Keep on. One more layer at least."

"*Love* letters? Can you imagine what kind of love letters she'd write? She can barely *talk* the language, much less *write* it."

"One more layer? Please."

"OK. OK." I opened a couple of smaller boxes packed with sweaters and gowns. Then two big boxes of snippets and rolls of every kind of fabric imaginable, the kind of stuff that women would use to make quilts with. Another box of damned magazines.

"Annie, I am just not going to go on with this."

"What does that one say?" She pointed to a long, flat box with something written on it that I couldn't make out.

"Hell, Annie, I don't know, but to gratify your curiosity, I'll open the Goddamned thing." I pried it out and laid it beside her. It was so light that it had to have been clothes. She reached and tore the tape back a couple of feet and shone the light inside. She pulled the tape back some more and opened the flaps.

"Oh, my God, Tommy, it's her *wedding stuff!*"

"You are kidding."

"No, look here." She rose to her knees and lifted a long white dress with her free hand and shook it out. It was so white that the reflected glow of the flashlight brightened the whole room.

"Put it back, Annie."

She laid the dress aside and reached into the box. "Look here, Tommy. Look here. It's a picture of the two of them."

I squinted and held my face close. The photograph, framed in cheap wood, had to have been taken out behind the house. A corner of the building came into focus to the left and a light-colored truck sat in the right background. The newlyweds, starched and stiff, stood like plastic figures on a cake. The man, tall and lean with short jet-black hair, had a hard look, unsmiling, his eyes fixed somewhere above and to the left of the camera, as if he were looking off into the distance. The woman likewise seemed to be looking beyond the camera, her face slightly tilted. Their arms were straight down at their sides, the way children sometimes pose for photographs when they've been told to stand very still until the camera clicks.

I leaned across her shoulder. "So there *was* a Chris. Jesus, Annie, she wasn't half bad looking."

"You don't have your glasses on, but you're right, she wasn't. And neither was Chris."

"Time hasn't been very kind to her."

"Tommy, wait till time has dragged you through the bushes as long as it has her. See what you look like in thirty or forty years. Of course, it'll never happen, because there's a bridge railing out there waiting for you, gon' take yer backbone clean out. Ol' Betty Dunbar'll be catapulted through the windshield wearing just a dress, pantiless, won't even have her teeth in, and they'll find her belly up in the river still clutching a piece of Super Supreme, with anchovies."

"You have to be a bitch, no matter what, don't you? Now, let's put this stuff back."

"No. Hold the light." She handed it to me and kept pulling things out of the box. "Oh, here's her *veil*. And even her shoes. Tommy, this is so sad. Every real dream she ever had is in this box."

"Annie, that's overdramatization. Put that stuff back in there and let's get off this stack of junk."

"Tommy, look. Shine the light." I did. "It's her *garter*." She held up the little pink ruffled band with blue flowers sewn to it. "This is so *sad*. Her garter."

"Annie, put it back."

She looked at me, her eyes shining. "No. I'm taking *this* with me. This is going to be my souvenir of a night in prison. By God, I have earned at least *this* much. She'll never know it's gone." She sat back and slipped the garter over her left foot and slid it up her leg, stopping halfway on her marvelous white thigh. She thrust the leg up like a dancer. "What do you think?"

"Looks great," I said. "But how will you get it out of here in the morning?"

"Stuff it down in my panties. Whatever, I'll smuggle it out."

"I think you ought to put it back."

"No. And you can take that light off my legs now. You've seen enough."

"I don't have my glasses on, remember?"

She left the garter on her leg and carefully replaced the picture and dress and other things she had taken from the box, then smoothed the tape across the seam. It wouldn't stick, of course, so she pushed the box over to me and told me to put it back where I pulled it from. "Stack another box on top of it," she directed. "That way she won't be able to tell it's been opened."

"Yes'm."

I trapped the light between my upper arm and side and repositioned the wedding box and pulled another box down on top of it. It was then, just as I was getting ready to turn and ask her for the third time whether she wanted to go back to the window or down to the mattress, that the beam fell on the side of a wooden crate with a large black bird printed on it, beneath it some faded words. I squinted close. *Old Crow.*

"*Old Crow.* Oh, my God, let that be what the label says it is," I whispered, then dislodged the box from those stacked around and on top of it. I swung it up beside me. One of the wooden slats on top had been pulled loose and something removed from the crate, leaving a socket in the straw it had been packed in. Like a kid at Christmas, in an ecstasy of fumbling I pushed my hand down into the straw and grasped the top of a bottle and pulled it out. I held the flat brown bottle up toward Annie and trained the light on it.

"Old Crow," I said. "I've got almost a whole case of Old Crow half-pints here, packed in straw. Must be—no telling how old this stuff is. I'll bet she has no idea it's in here."

"Oh, sweet Jesus," Annie muttered. "I cannot be-*lieve* this. All we need now is for you to get roaring drunk. Tommy, put that back."

"Not on your life. You had your fun. Now I'm going to have mine." I replaced the bottle and yanked the crate up and cradled it under one arm, holding the flashlight in my other hand. The light trained on the slope of boxes before me, I carefully made my way down to the mattress and set the crate on it. I whispered back up to her: "She threw me in the briar patch, the old bat. Now, you can crouch up there on that mountain of trash, or you can come down and drink with me, but this boy is cracking a seal, right now."

I set the other sheet and my shirt aside and positioned the crate in the middle of the mattress and after removing two more bottles spread the sheet over it, forming a small table. "You wanna come down and party?" She was still on the stack of boxes by the shelves. I could barely make out her form against the ceiling.

"No. You go ahead. I'm going back to the window."

"Suit yourself. But this night will go a lot better *with* whiskey than without it."

"One of us needs to keep a clear head," she whispered. "And keep your voice down."

"A clear head for *what*? Like we're going to be able to reason our way out of this? Bottom line, little sister, is that we are locked in here for the night, we're not going anywhere—we damned sure aren't going to be driving—and the preacher's not likely to drop by for a visit. Why the hell *not* drink?" I uncapped a bottle and held it to my nose, breathing deep the potent old whiskey fumes. "Oh, this is the real *stuff*. Aged Old Crow. *Really* aged. Wooden crate. Packed in straw. God-*damn*, it must be fifty years old."

I touched the bottle to my lips and sipped. It stung all the way down. I sipped again. This time it stung but little, forming in my stomach a nugget of warmth from which even before my third sip I could feel tentacles of sensation radiating. "Come on down, Annie. Just a couple of sips. You'd be surprised what a little nip'll do for you." I could see her head against the backdrop of stars beyond her barred window. I tilted the bottle again.

"OK," she said after she had worked her way carefully down to me, "I'll have a couple of sips. It's something to do." She settled onto her end of the mattress and I passed the bottle to her.

"Careful," I said. "It's strong."

"So'm *I*." She tilted the bottle back. My eyes were accustomed enough to the dark now that I could see her very white hand around the dark bottle. She made a little sucking noise when she drank and the bottle sizzled as she let air past her lips. She handed the bottle back to me.

"Well?"

"*Jeeeeesus*," she hissed. "That's liquid *fire*. I need to chase that. God, Tommy, Holy Jeeees . . ."

"That wasn't a sip. You guzzled. When we empty this bottle, I'll fill it with water and you can chase."

"You empty it. I'll wait till I have water."

"You're going to force me to finish this?"

"At's right, big boy," she said. "Thank you can handle it?"

"You sound just like her."

"*Meant* to."

I took three stiff belts and the spot in my stomach grew larger and more wonderfully warm with each delivery. My fingers were tingling. I felt warm all over. I held the bottle out to Annie. "Here. Go on and have another go. *Sip* it. Don't guzzle the damned stuff. It won't burn nearly as much the second time."

"No. I've got to chase it. I feel like I've swallowed a sparkler." She pushed my hand back. "If you don't want to finish that bottle off, just dump out what's in it. You've got a whole case here—"

"Not quite. There was a bottle missing."

"Big damned deal. You can't drink all this tonight anyway, so just dump whatever's left in that bottle and fill it with water and open another one."

"Annie, I know we can't drink all of it tonight. I intend to take the rest back with me."

"And just where the hell are you going to hide it? In your shorts? What are we talking about, eight or ten bottles?"

"Probably. It's packed in straw, so I'm not sure. But I'd guess six or eight are still in the case."

"You can't smuggle eight bottles of whiskey out of here. Not unless you want to hide them the way they smuggle drugs. As big an asshole as you *are*, I don't think that many would fit. Look, just go dump that and get me a bottle of water or I'm not having another drink."

"All right, all right." I stood up and the dark room spun. I steadied myself against the door and shone the light down the little corridor that led to the sink. "Shoooooeeeeee. Off on a God-damned water run."

I leaned against the sink and took another good shot and started to pour the rest in the sink. *I just can't fucking do this. It's desecration.* I tilted the bottle and slugged the rest of it and turned the creaky handle. A puny stream of water came. I ran it a few seconds to clear any stagnant water that might have been in the pipes and bent over and sipped from the stream, then filled the bottle and capped it.

"This water's got a lot of iron in it," I said when I settled back onto the mattress. I passed the bottle to her. "Tastes like my grandparents' water used to taste. Gotta be well water. Deep water too." My head was whirling.

"It does," she agreed when she'd taken some. "And of *course* it's well water. Where else would it come from? The Davy Crockett National Forest Municipal Water System?"

I uncapped another bottle of Old Crow, swigged, and held it out to her. "Maybe from that swamp."

"Nope," she said, "it's well water. Got a lot of minerals of some kind in it for sure."

For a long while we sat in the dark room wordless, passing the bottle back and forth across our little table. She'd take a sip from the Old Crow, then one from her bottle of water, pass the whiskey to me, then I'd slug the Crow and hand the bottle back to her. In no time at all I was deliciously drunk and the room grew more and more cozy.

Annie never was one for drinking, except for those bad days before we split. She'd take a glass of wine at dinner occasionally, and a couple of rounds of champagne at parties. Sometimes she'd have a mixed drink with me if she'd had a really rough day. That was about it. So I was a bit surprised that she'd take the Old Crow. Of course, she *had* had a really rough day.

"You know," she said, "if anybody had told me twenty-four hours ago I'd be sitting in a jailhouse in the middle of the Davy Crockett National Forest drinking whiskey with you, of all people, tonight, I'd have called them an absolute fool."

"They'd have been absoluuuute fools *to* have said it. But you know I didn't exactly envision the day like this either. By now we should be in Houston scowling at each other across a hospital waiting room instead of passing a bottle back and forth on a mattress."

"Yeah. If I'd even sit in the same room with you." She spun her hand around her head. "Whew, Tommy, I am really *feeling* that stuff. Nothing much in my stomach to dilute it. The real tip-off is that I don't hate you nearly as much as I did a little while ago. Maybe I'd better quit while I'm ahead. Or while I've *got* one. Or behind. Or while I've got one."

"Suit yourself," I said, "but I'm going on with it."

"Oh, what the hell. Gimme that bottle, big boy. Won't hurt not to hate you so much for one night. I can pick it up again tomorrow. Onliest time I can remember drinking whiskey straight like this." She took the Old Crow and this time took a real swig, following it quickly with water. "*Yow–sheeeeeuuuut.* That Old Crow is flying all over my body."

"Yeah. I'll be cawing here in a minute." I slammed down another swallow.

"You know," she said, "if I'm liking you more as I drink, it must be that I like you more than I think." She giggled.

"That's a cute rhyme, li'l sister." I felt like a real ocean was tossing the mattress now.

"Thank you, mister. More than I thought I did, I should have said. Hey, that almost rhymes too. Lordy, it's *rhyme time*! I mean, if what they say about drinking is true, that the real you comes out when you're drinking, then—"

She interrupted her sentence with another sip. I was reeling, so by that point I wasn't fully digesting what she was saying, but I was certainly feeling better about her. "Me too," I said. "Me too."

"Me too what? What are you saying me too to?" She laughed.

"*Shhhhh.* You're going to wake up the old woman or Duke."

"I don't care about that weird pair. I said too-too, like a train."

"No, that's choo-choo," I said.

"The sound of a train blowing its whistle is *toooo-toooo*, not *choooo-chooo*. But what did you mean, saying *me too*?"

"Just me too. I'm liking you better too. That's what I meant."

"Oh," she said. She handed the bottle back. "It's about gone. Maybe we'd better not open another one. It wouldn't do for us to start liking each other too much."

"I think we should—have another, that is. Hell, they're *little* bottles, not much bigger than the ones you get on airplanes." I unscrewed the cap on another and held it out to her. She took it and drank. In the dark I could hear her swallow. She chased it with a slug of water.

"Wow. I'm not sure I even *need* the chaser now."

"I can't feel it going down anymore," I said. "I've cauterized my esophagus, I think."

"Oh, that sounds serious," she said, laughing again.

"I did that one time in college. Drank a guy under the table with straight vodka. Nearly burned my esophagus up."

"Did you win?"

"Yep. He passed out and I kept on a-drinkin'."

"What'd you win?"

"Five dollars."

"Five fuckin' dollars. And burned up your esophagus? That was dumb. You know what a new esophagus costs?"

"Guys do dumb things in college."

"*Guys* do dumb things until they're stretched out under an undertaker's lamp." She was getting louder and louder. "By the way, have you ever heard of a 'sophagus transplant?"

"Shhh, shhhh. Come on, Annie, keep it down. She's gon' come in here and shoot us."

"Fuck her *and* that dog. We didn't ask to be put in here for the night. If we can turn it into a party, it's no business of hers."

"That Old Crow's made you downright courageous, little sister. I'll bet that gun or Duke would sober you up real quick."

She was quiet a few seconds. Then: "Let's fuck with Duke."

"What the hell are you talking about, Annie?"

"He's right outside this door, you know," she said.

"I know that. I been drinkin', but I still got a grip on reality."

"Put your ear to the door and you can hear him snoring."

"I thought that was her."

"No, it's him. Lean down here and you can hear him."

"No thank you," I said. "You go on and listen to him snore, if you want to. I don't give a shit whether he's outside the door or not, and I don't care whether he's snoring or not. I just know I don't want to mess with an animal that big."

"You got something better to do?" I could tell in the faint light that she was looking at me. Her head was tilted to one side.

"Not really. But for God's sake talk a little quieter."

"Air you go, a-takin' the Lord's name in vain agin. The sky's gon' split plumb open and thowe a lightnin' bolt down on you and melt you like a hunk of lard. Be just a puddle of grease, and this mattress will suck you plumb up."

I tilted forward on my knees and nudged her. "Mute it. And quit talking like her—it's spooky."

"Let's fuck with the *dog*."

"Got a better idea," I said. "Let's you and *me* fuck."

"I'm not *that* drunk," she said. "Don't start that shit, Tommy. I'm beginning to have fun, but I'm not going to lose my head. Let's mess with the *dog*."

"Why?"

"Because he's the only one who hasn't had any fun tonight. He didn't even get a negg samwitch. Let's *mess* with him."

"Goddamn it, Annie," I whispered, "he's big enough to tear that door down."

"Can-*not*. A bulldozer couldn't tear that door down. It's made out of iron." She reached and yanked me forward. "Feel it. It's cool. It's iron."

"Steel."

"I don't give a damn whether it's steel or bricks or sticks or straw or *gingerbread*—no dog alive could get through it. Not even a wolf. Get me a coat hanger."

"Annie, *no.*"

"You are chickenshit—or worse, a *corny-dog*—if you don't get me a coat hanger."

"Jesus Christ, Annie. The only thing about getting you drunk is I never know what you'll do." I rolled off the mattress onto my hands and knees and rummaged around and found one of the clumps of hangers and finally managed to slip one out of the tie that held them together. "Goddamn things," I seethed. "I hate coat hangers." I held it out to her. "Here. Go ahead and poke his ass, if that's your idea of fun. But if you get that bastard barking and wake up that old woman. . . ."

There was almost an inch of clearance beneath the door, enough so that with her hand flat she could shove it at least to the knuckles. The dog was apparently lying directly against the door, because when Annie inverted her hand and pushed it under the edge, she said that she felt his fur.

"Then why don't you diddle him with your hand?"

She took the coat hanger. "Because I want to take the hand with me if and when we get to leave this place is why, big boy. I'm not *that* drunk."

She squeezed the coat hanger into a long probe and slid it under the edge of the door, working it back and forth and farther beneath the dog, who took a deep breath and grunted and shifted positions. I could hear his collar scrape across the metal door.

"Wake up, you big bastard," she said. She was on her knees, her face low against the door. I could vaguely see her cute little ass thrust up. "Duke. Oh, Duuuuuuuke. Dukey, Dukey. Wake up, Duuuuuuuuuukeeeee." The sound prickled the back of my neck. She sounded like a ghost.

Suddenly the dog growled and I heard his feet scrambling against the tile floor. Then the hallway reverberated with horrendous barking and the dog flung himself against the door. Annie recoiled across the mattress into a stack of boxes while I drew the flashlight back in defense, uncertain whether the door would keep him out or not.

"See, Goddamn it," I yelled over the clamor of the dog, "I *told* you."

The old woman's voice came from down the hallway. "Shut up, Duke! Just shut up. Get on away from there. Get in that kitchen." I heard her whack the dog with something and he retreated, growling, his nails making clicking sounds on the tiles.

"Now y'all *listen*, in there." Her voice came from beneath the door. "I don't know what you done to get him so upset, but it better not happen agin. Y'all done woke me up twice't with all yer noise. I'm a old woman and I got to get my rest out. Now, you settle down and go t'sleep. Y'all actin' like a couple of kids. I ort to take a switch to you. You better not get me up agin. And you let that dog alone, whatever it was you done to'm."

"Yes'm," I said. The dog was roaring in the background.

"Yes'm," Annie echoed.

"I *mean* it, now. Behave yerselves."

"We're *being hayve*," Annie whispered.

The old woman smacked the door with her open hand and padded off down the hallway. "You shut up and get yer black ass in here," she yelled. The dog stopped barking and I heard her door close.

I listened carefully a full minute to see whether Duke had returned. "I don't hear him. Maybe she closed him off in the kitchen."

"Or put him in the room with her." Annie still had not moved back onto the mattress. She was balled up by the boxes where she had taken refuge.

"You can relax now, I think."

She crawled back onto the mattress. "I thought he was coming through that door. It sounded like a wolf."

"I don't know what a wolf at the door sounds like, but I figure pretty much like what we just heard."

"I haven't been chewed out like that since the last slumber party I had, when I was fifteen years old."

"You had it coming," I said. "I told you you shouldn't mess with that damned dog. If he'd gotten to us, we'd have been chewed worse."

"Now, Tommy, just how long do you figure it's been since he's been that excited? Or *her*, for that matter?"

"Or us. I suspect we'll *all* remember this night a long time. She and that dog'll be talking about it for years to come. 'You 'member that night we had thatere couple from Shrevesport in the storeroom, Duke. God, they was a noisy pair.'"

"She wouldn't say that."

"And why not?" I asked.

"Because she won't take the Lord's name in vain. Remember?"

"Oh yeah. Forgot myself." I felt around for the bottle. It was amazing how my mind had cleared. "Ready for another drink?"

"You bet. Maybe it'll get my heart back down where it's supposed to be. Shoooo-eeee. Gimme that bottle, big boy."

I took another drink and passed the bottle to her. "Air y'are, li'l sister."

She took a sip and handed it back. "What do we do now, besides keep swapping spit?"

"We could swap spit another way."

"Forget it, Tommy. I told you, I'm not that drunk."

"Want to go back to the window?"

"Sure," she said. "Like you say, the pool's closed."

As quietly as we could we made our way up the slope of boxes to our disappearing staircase and sat for a long time with our chins on our hands staring out at the night sky. The wind had died down and there was no sound, save an occasional night bird down by the woods. I had my face pressed to the bars and could feel her shoulder against me, and when she moved a certain way her hair would brush my cheek. I detected a faint trace of her perfume.

"Look, Tommy. There is something down there," she said, "down by the woods." She lifted her hand and pointed through the bars, her pale finger clearly visible against the dark trees.

I looked where she pointed and at first saw nothing but stars above the black wall of woods, no glow of a town anywhere, just a vast belly of space sprinkled with points of light as if someone had fired a shotgun through funeral crepe and hung it against the sun. And then I could see it too, something white moving at the edge of the pasture and very near the woods, like a ghost, floating, a filmy gauze trailing out behind, or like a woman wearing a long white dress and skimming just above the ground. Or a child with wings. It moved fast, then slow, stopping as if to listen or look, then zigging and zagging like it was pursued by something or was pursuing.

"What *is* it?" she asked.

"Shiiiiiiit, I don't know. It's not like anything I've ever seen. It's not moving like an animal or a person, but it looks like a woman or a child dressed in white. Look, it's going into the woods."

"Maybe it's a ghost."

"You don't believe in ghosts."

"I never have," she answered. Her hand was now clenching my upper arm. "But neither would I have believed any of the craziness since we left Lufkin."

Then it disappeared, apparently into the woods.

"Maybe this changes things. There is something down there at the edge of those woods, and we both saw it, and that makes it real. If what has happened here happened only to me, you would not believe it, and if it happened only to you, I would not believe it. But it happened to both of us."

She pulled her face from the bars and looked at me.

"And because we have seen the white thing down there, Annie, it is real, it exists, if only to us. Because of that thing down there, because of this room and the old woman, there is an us again. You can't deny it."

"Yes, we saw *something*," she said quietly, "but it doesn't really change things. And I can deny *anything*. We both know it's just the whiskey and the crazy-ass circumstances. What we saw and what I said. I just wish to hell I was sober—or drunker. You bring any of the whiskey up with you?"

"Yeah." I handed her the bottle. She drank and gave it back and looked out the window again.

"Well, it's gone," she said, "whatever it was."

I looked again, but there was nothing but stars and dark woods. "But *we* saw it, didn't we?" I settled back onto the box.

"Like I said, *we* saw *something*," she said. "But I'll bet if we'd been sober we wouldn't have seen it. I wish to God I'd been sober."

"Annie, I don't see stuff like that when I've been drinking. I might act goofy and I might forget what I've done, but I do not see ghosts when I drink. And neither do you. What the hell could it have been?"

"I don't know," she said softly, "I just don't know. It looked to me like a woman in a white wedding dress. But it was probably just—whadda they call it?—marsh gas or swamp gas. But it wasn't a ghost and it wasn't a woman wearing white."

"I'll bet it was the ghost of ol' Chris," I said. "Bet he haunts this place."

"Or maybe the black woman who was in the truck with him."

"Naw, it was white."

"How do you know Negroes don't come back white as ghosts? You ever heard anybody talk about a black one? How would you see one at night?"

"Maybe they get laundered, you know, bleached. Hell, I don't know. It could be the ghost of her father."

"That looked like a dress it was wearing," Annie said.

"Maybe he cross-dressed. Whatever, it was just another crazy-ass thing in a crazy-ass day."

"It was one for the scrapbook, for sure. Jane and Tony will never believe this."

"I'm not sure we ought to try to explain it to them. Maybe this is something to keep to ourselves."

A car passed on the road and we both rose to our knees and watched headlights spear the dark, slice through thick trees, and disappear, its tires whizzing on off out of hearing.

"My God," she said, "that was a car. A *car*. There *are* other people out here."

"Sounded more like an old truck, but somebody had to be driving it, so I guess you're right. Whatever, they're gone now."

"They didn't even slow down."

"Why would they?"

"Because our car's out there. If they live back in here, they'd have to know it was somebody in trouble."

"*Our* car?"

"*Your* car, asshole."

"I'm glad they didn't stop. They'd probably have popped open the trunk and taken everything."

"Call *me* cynical," she said.

After a few more minutes of watching and listening at the window, I asked her, "Annie, what part of today was weirdest to you?"

"You mean besides just now? The white thing down by the woods? That was as weird as it gets."

"Besides the thing, whatever it was."

"I don't know," she said. "Probably having to crawl into that dark room on all fours, like a dog. That was the scariest, for sure."

"I was scared too, but the weirdest was that damned striptease she made us do."

"That was the part you liked best. You couldn't keep your eyes off me."

"Like you didn't look too!"

"I didn't *stare* at you, Tommy. I glanced is all. But you *stared*."

"And you acted like you were watching a porno film when she told that traveling salesman story."

"Well, hell, it *was* exciting, at least for her. Getting laid like that her first time, getting herself *gored good*—"

"If she was telling the truth. For all you know, she might have done tricks in New Orleans for a living."

"No, I believe every word she said."

"Me too," I said, "right down to the part about ol' Chris getting speared by a bridge rail, the poor bastard."

"I did look." She giggled. "We both know it's the whiskey talking here, but you've still got a cute ass."

"So do you. And beasties."

"God, I forgot about you calling'm that. You sure got an eyeful while I was stretched out across your lap."

"Yep." My head was spinning with whiskey. "I enjoyed that."

"Pervert. You'd enjoy looking at the titties on a dead woman."

"You weren't dead."

"You'd have looked if I *had* been."

"Probably."

"Did you touch me while I was out?"

"Aw, come on, Annie, what do you take me for?"

"You laid your hand on my leg while we were drivin' down here, when you thought I was asleep. I take you for a *pervert* is what."

Even reeling with the whiskey, I could feel the color rising in my face. "You were *awake*? In the *car*?"

"Oh yeah, I was awake."

"Then why'd you let me do it?"

"I just wondered how far you'd go, wondered at what point I was going to have to slap the shit out of you."

We were leaning against the wall passing the bottle back and forth, taking little sips now. It seemed to me that we were beginning to venture into perilous waters, and I wasn't sure I needed to be any drunker. "Well, you could have stopped me if you didn't want me to do it."

"I wanted to brush you off like a blue fly, big boy, but I was intrigued to see what you were up to, how far you'd go. I mean, it wasn't as if a stranger was laying a hand on me. It was a man who slept with me for years. But if you had made a move any farther up my thigh, you'd have seen great big ol' white stars all over yer heaven."

"Now, whatever you think of me, you gotta know that I—"

"What did you want to touch me for?"

"I don't know, Annie. I just did. I never got over . . ." I adjusted myself on the upside-down disappearing staircase and leaned toward her face, clearly visible in the pale glow of the night sky from the window. "Annie, I fucked things up is what I'm trying to say, I guess. God, woman, I still *dream* about you, almost every night. And every woman I've been with since I left you, if we got around to bed, it was always you I fantasized about, the times in the back seat of the car, at Gulf Shores in a tent, on your momma's bathroom floor before we were even married."

"You must have a hell of a good imagination, if you can fancy Betty Dunbar was me . . ."

"Why the hell do you keep bringing up Betty Dunbar? I didn't say anything about Betty."

"You said—"

"Forget what I said."

"That's easy enough. I could always do that without any trouble."

"Come on, lighten up. I'm baring my soul here."

"You recall that I don't remember my dreams," she said quietly. Her tongue was having a bit of coordination trouble now. "So I'm sure I've dreamed nice things about you since the split, but I don't remember'm. I mean, there've been times I could recall little bits and pieces, and when I woke up in a bad mood, I was sure you were responsible."

I nodded, then realized in the dark that she probably couldn't see me. "I guess I was."

"Sometimes I wake up with a vague sense that I've been dreaming about children. I always feel warm and tender. . . ."

She hesitated a long time. "But empty, with an inde . . . indefinable—ooh, that exercised my tongue—longing, the kind you get in the spring as a child, when the weather's finally warmed up and the trees have greened and flowers have popped out all over and the air's heavy with their smell."

I touched her hand, then interlaced my fingers with hers. She didn't resist. Then I pulled mine back—no need to push my luck. "I wake up sometimes feeling like that myself. Only the dream I was having was of you. Of *us*."

"You know," she said, her voice soft and slurry, "the one positive thing that I remember about you, sonofabitch that you were in every other imaginable way, is that you were always so damned gentle. Even when we were fighting along toward the end. You never hit me. Not with your hand or your fist or a broom handle or anything. You never ever hit me, and I liked that about you." She hesitated a few seconds. "Because there were times when we were really fighting that you probably had a right to take a broom to me."

"Well, that would have been one of the times when you'd have been justified blowing my head off with a .44, one of those times when I'd *made* you mean, and I always understood that. You've heard me say it before—every sorry woman is that way because some sorry man has made her that way. Every woman in prison is there because some guy dragged her into a crime or pushed her into it or left her so destitute she had to steal, or because he was so mean to her that she finally snapped and blew his brains out with a shotgun. And every woman that's mean to her kids is that way because she's not big enough to take her frustration out on the sorry-ass man who's making her life miserable."

"It's when I get to thinking about your attitude toward women that I realize why I fell in love with you to start with, except that you never met a woman in your life you didn't half fall in love with. You felt sorry for her or she was too beautiful for you to quit thinking about or whatever. My God, it was as if you had a divine duty to take an interest in them. Have you ever your whole life been a full month without being in love with a woman?"

"Not since I was twelve. In the first grade I started having crushes on girls because I never had seen any but a couple of cousins before I started to school. I remember vividly swinging on the playground in first grade singing 'You Are My Sunshine' to a girl named Sandy Collins, a pretty little brown-haired girl whose parents had money and lived in a big ranch-style house just outside the little town we lived in. And there were others who took my breath away when I looked at them. Teachers, too. Lord, I have been infatuated with some teachers. But one day when I was twelve I had an almost mystical experience with a girl—well, not *with* her, but I never forgot her and I never forgot that day."

"You never did tell me about it, did you?"

"Probably not. Hell, I don't know." Jesus, my head was spinning. There was very little whiskey left in the bottle. "You want the spit in the bottom?"

"No. I'm ready to slack off this stuff for a little while. I don't want to throw up. Cap it."

"I didn't bring the cap up here."

"Then pour it out the window."

"Naw," I said. "If it's my spit, I swallow it all day anyway. If it's yours, I don't mind. I've had it before." I finished off the bottle, then slid it through the bars and let go. It clunked onto something below, but it didn't shatter.

"How poetic," she said. Then: "Tell me about your love affair at twelve."

So I told her about it. I had ridden my bike to the county fair in Mississippi one afternoon—they always let us off half a day in September the Friday that the fair was in town—and spent two or three hours roaming the stalls and riding bumper cars and the Ferris wheel and stayed until after dark for the big-top performance. I was hanging around behind the big tent just watching all the bustle as crews got things ready for the big show, and this beautiful slender girl, probably my age or maybe a little older, came out of a silver trailer, one of those shaped like a loaf of bread that you see even today being pulled along the interstates. Exiting behind her was a muscular man with hairy shoulders and back and powerful-looking arms and legs. He had on a tight-fitting outfit, pants and muscle shirt, gaily colored and simply glittering with what I guess was rhinestones, and she was wearing a silver one-piece bathing suit, or it looked like a bathing suit, so tight I could see the outline of her ribs and nipples no bigger than mine and the little cleft between her legs, and when she walked past I could see the track of her spine and shoulder blades, which seemed to me like the beginnings of wings that any second might sprout out of her back like an angel's and she'd go flitting off into the night sky.

The man was talking softly, reassuringly to her and pointing at a wire that was strung between two poles. He was holding his large hands just so, then turning them, and he took her hands in his, swallowed her slender white hands in his great hairy-backed dark ones and swung her up and over onto his neck and back down. She landed light as a feather and smiled up at him. They walked over and looked up at the wire and support poles from which it was strung. Every movement she made reminded me of water flowing, a liquid silver sheen. Her feet seemed not even to touch the ground, just flow over it, and though the man's feet made deep prints in the sawdust, hers made none.

The man climbed the pole—it had metal stirrups like a telephone pole—and tested the wire and, finding it to his satisfaction, descended and nodded at the girl and they walked past me toward the trailer. She smiled at me as she brushed by—I could not have moved if God had commanded it—and I stared straight into the bluest eyes I'd ever seen and have ever seen since.

"When the show began," I continued, "I watched her climb the pole behind him and they took their places on a little platform high above the rings, and then when the music really swelled . . . and, Annie, I remember the music to this day." My lips were troublesome and my tongue kept getting in the way, but I softly whistled the tune.

When the music reached a crescendo, she spread her arms wide and slipped across the wire smoothly, like a skater, pivoted on the opposite platform, and skated back across to his open arms. She was so graceful, so perfectly tuned to the wire. Then he walked across, using a pole for balance, his weight bellying the wire so that he went downhill, then up. He crossed again and joined her on the little platform, where she was standing first on one foot, then the other.

Annie was listening intently to my story with one elbow propped on the window ledge. "Whistle the tune again."

"If I can get my lips to work," I said. "It went like this." I whistled it softly again.

The man put his hands on the girl's shoulders and moved her before him, his back to the tent pole that the platform was attached to. He had laid his balancing staff at his feet. In one incredibly swift motion he spun her around, grabbed her hands, and flung her out into the air in a broad arc and she landed astraddle his neck. Stooping, he picked up the staff and moved out onto the wire as she spread her arms above him like a protective angel. Halfway across she dropped her hands to his shoulders, shot her legs and body straight out and up, and stood inverted above him as he inched toward the opposite platform. She scissored her legs, then held them together and balanced by one hand on his shoulder.

"They did everything but *fly*, Annie, I fell in love right then and there for the first time."

"You fell in love with the costume and the music and the magic," she said.

"I fell in love with all of it, the evening, the music, smells, but most of all with her. The rest of it was special because of her. She was—well, without her none of the rest would have mattered, would have stuck. I rode my bike home in the dark, with just the moonlight keeping me out of the ditches, and I'd have gone to bed and to sleep and that would have been the end of it, except for her. That night I seemed to be moving through some sort of magic kingdom. After I left the highway and got on the little dirt road we called the Pig Trail that led over to the gravel road we lived on, there was nothing in the universe but me and that moon and her and that song on my mind and lips. The whole moon-bathed world was humming that tune. I felt like I could have pedaled a little faster and pulled back on the handlebars and I would have left the earth forever, just sailed across the sky like those kids on their bikes in *ET*."

"You fell in love with an ideal."

"Yes. I think so. We all do, don't we? I mean, you said yourself that love is just—what did you say? Chemistry and cells? Glands? But the ideal is the most important part of it. You've got to have that. If someone had told me that that girl was an angel, I would have believed it. If those little shoulder blades had suddenly sprouted out into wings and she had flown across the tent, I would have believed that too."

It was all light and music and the silver sheen of her costume and her face, perfect in every detail. Sky-blue eyes, a brush stroke of color on each cheek, hair the color of sun-bleached straw. The drift of carnival air, redolent with the smell of cotton candy and candied apples and popcorn and pine sawdust and cigarette smoke, the faint odor of animals, an occasional trace of perfume, the sounds of chattering children and far in the background the roar of the midway with its barkers and rides. It was a moment frozen forever in my memory, and for weeks I dreamed of her and that night and filled my waking hours with thoughts of her. Her against that canvas sky, the light thrown back dazzling from her silver costume, her with her arms spread, little feet sliding across the wire, eyes intent on the opposite platform. A little girl who didn't even leave tracks in the sawdust.

"Oh, Annie, she was something. Something. And I never saw her again, never even knew her name."

"Do you ever wonder where she is now?"

"Sure," I said. "I don't like to think about it, though. I'd rather keep her twelve years old and free of gravity, an angel on a wire, silver and beautiful in a world that was all light, light, light."

"Gravity got her," Annie said. "Bet on that."

"I know."

"She's probably had a parade of sorry-ass carnival men by now. Five or six kids. Shaped like that trailer she came out of, hair growing out of warts on her face, her skin the color of that old woman's in there from smoking. Cusses like a sailor. Dips snuff maybe. Couldn't walk a straight line across a room without stumbling."

I laughed. "You can sure trash out a woman. For all you know, she might be as slender and pretty as you and still zipping across wires somewhere."

"You really think I'm pretty?" She was deliciously drunk.

"Damn, Annie, you don't have to ask that. You've always been the most beautiful woman I've ever known."

"Then why did you go and fuck things up? Why did you go after other women? Every damned emotional cripple out there with tits and a twat was fair game for you. Why, Tommy? What the hell was the fascination? I am intelligent. I have a college degree. I was good to you and never cheated on you. I am pretty—you said so yourself. Why did you go and fuck things up?"

I didn't answer. I couldn't. How does a man explain that sort of thing? *Is* it explainable? Shame and regret settled in my stomach like a stone. I had repositioned myself at the window, beyond which the sky was one vast carnival of lights, stretching on forever. The tune was still on my mind.

"You know," she said, "if that old woman in there had two eyes, you'd probably fall for her."

"What do you mean, if she had two eyes?"

"She doesn't have but one eye. It moves around, but there's just one. She tilts her head one way and the hair cracks open and there's the eye. She tilts it the other and the hair cracks open, and there's the eye, like it just slid across her face. Did you ever see two eyes?"

"Yeah, and you did too, when she pulled her hair back for you, and when she washed her face at the sink and turned around. And one other time."

"OK. Point is, that's the kind of woman you fall for. It beats the ever-loving hell out of me how the two of us ended up together."

"I thought you had just one eye for a long time. I guess that's what did it."

"Har-har," she said.

"You sure looked good out there tonight with your clothes off."

"You were a sonofabitch to look, an even greater sonofabitch to stare at my breasts with me passed out."

"I would have been a stupid sonofabitch not to."

"I knew you looked. You probably *touched* them too."

"Annie, why do you still wear your rings?"

"What?" I caught her by surprise.

"Your rings. I noticed this afternoon, or yesterday, whenever the hell it was, that you still wear your rings."

"I don't have my rings on, Tommy."

"I could see the light band of flesh where they were. You took them off this morning, didn't you? Or yesterday morning. Jesus, we're outside time now. And I saw the little ring box fall out of your purse."

She snorted. "Well, what if I *do* wear them? They keep guys from hitting on me. They think I'm married and they don't mess with me so much."

"You *are* married."

"That's a *legal* condition, not domestic." She seemed to be sobering fast. "And we could sit here in the damned dark all night and discuss my rings and it wouldn't solve the problem at hand. What in the hell are we going to *do* in here, Tommy? I can't sleep in this room. What's in here with us? Snakes, lizards, roaches? Worse? And what in God's name is that white thing down by the woods? Ghosts out there, God knows what in here. When I stop to think about what's happening to us, I get scared as hell. How do we know she'll let us go in the morning and not just have our car hauled off and dumped—"

"*Our* car?"

"*Your* fucking car," she seethed. "I slipped up again. She might just have some redneck come along and haul it off and strip it down and dump what's left in the river."

"And do what with us?"

"That is my point, Tommy. We don't know what she'll do with us in the morning."

"The whiskey's wearing thin. I'm going down to get another bottle."

"That might be a good idea."

I left my end of the upside-down disappearing staircase and scrambled down the mountain of boxes to the mattress, found the case, and took out another bottle. There were still five or six, maybe more, nestled in the straw, far more than it would take to send us off into never-never land. I climbed up to her.

"Here y'are." I uncapped the bottle and passed it to her. She drank deep and handed the bottle back to me.

"That helps," she said. "I cannot believe I'm drinking so much and not throwing up."

"You're not even chasing it anymore."

"Don't have to. I can't *feel* anything. I'll pay hell for this in the morning, if in the morning ever comes. Where is the water anyway?"

"You left it down there."

"Whatcha mean, *I* left it down there, white boy?"

"You were the one with the water. You're the one who needs it."

"I'm gon' need some soon," she said.

We passed the bottle back and forth a few more times and said nothing. The room was so deathly quiet that I could hear her swallow, gasp, and exhale each time she tilted the bottle and drank. No sound came from outside, nothing. I swear I could hear our hearts beating.

"Annie."

"Yes?" Her voice was soft again.

"How many guys have you been to bed with since we split?"

"You saw the rubber in my purse. It's obvious that I go prepared. Jesus, Tommy, throngs of them. A *gross*. I've lost count."

"Come on, Annie."

"Tommy, if you only knew. . . . Would it surprise you terribly if I admitted that I've made love to two men since you—since we split up?"

"Yeah, it would."

"I figured that. Especially since you've had dozens of women. And don't deny that."

"I've been to bed with a few. But I was careful."

"Hell, big boy, I don't care whether you were careful or not. I'll bet you can't even *remember* how many. We both know that you were prolly drunk every time you screwed one. Were they all sluts like Betty? By the way, I hope you double-rubbered with her."

"You can't shake Betty, can you?"

"You were the one that shook Betty, big boy. And Betty is a *type*, not an indi-indi-invijul, with liberty and justice for all."

"You can't even talk, you're so drunk. *Invijul*—in-di-vid-u-al has more than two syllables."

"And Betty Dunbar's got more than two tits. One's hangin' where her nose goes."

"You're getting vicious, Annie."

"Wudn't that cute? Where her *nose goes*. She's got a nose like a—whaddaya call'm? That flies have? Probitus, probiscuit? Oh, shit . . . *proboscis*. Like a fly. That's it. I bet you had to push her proboscis aside to kiss'r."

"Cut it out, Annie, OK?"

"Air you go now, big boy, callin' me Annie Oakley."

"For God's sake, Annie, tone it down—you're gonna wake that old fool up."

"Air you go agin, a-takin' the Lord's name in vain."

"Annie . . ."

"Ya know, Tommy, if somebody told me I could even be awake after that much whiskey, much less capable of talking and not throwing up, I'd say they was—they *were* lyin'."

"It's the adrenaline. It negates the alcohol or something. I don't know how it works, but I ought to be stretched out cold as a turnip on that mattress."

"Well, I'll tell you what, big boy—"

She didn't finish the sentence. She reached out and grabbed the bars and pulled her face up to them.

"Do you see something?"

"No. Thought I heard another car comin'. Needed air anyway. Don't see *ary* a *thang* in any direction. At's the strange thang. Seems like I'd be seein' more'n one white thang down there, the shape I'm in. Seems like there'd be more cars, real or imaginary. Don't see nothin'. No elephants neither, pink or otherwise. No cars. Hit's lak we're in the middle of the Davy Crockett National Forest or somep'n."

"You've got her language down pat."

"My name ain't Pat, big boy."

"Whon't we go back down to the mattress?"

"You're talkin' like her yerself, big boy. God, I love that—*big boy*. You're about average, I'd say, maybe a little smaller than."

"You're comparing me with two guys? That's what you said, two guys. Unless you lied."

"Yeah, two. But they were *above* average. Longer, thicker, longer lasting—"

"I get the point. You don't have to rub it in."

"Sorry, big boy. Actually, they were quite ordinary in every way. I just wanted to get on yer goat or get yer goat or however that sayin' goes. Got somethin' to do with a goat."

"So I'm in the race, huh?"

"You'da stayed the whole pack if you hadn't fucked up. There wasn't another hoofprint on the track until you fucked up."

"What is *this*? You on that virgin kick again? Both of us know you were not a virgin when we got married."

"Was too a virgin. Been diddled, but that was it. And if you hadn't been so Goddamned drunk that first time, you'd have reconnized virgin territory."

"I still don't believe it."

"Don't believe it. I don't care. I don't owe you anything."

"You can't tell me that . . ."

"I c'n tell you anything I want to tell you, but it's the God's honest truth that you were the first guy to ever penetrate me with a penis. What a way to put it, to *penetrate me with a penis*. Sounds like pinning a bug to a display board or something."

"I always thought you were lying about that to make me respect you more."

"Well, hell, back then I might have told it to you for that reason. I sure as hell got no reason to tell you now unless it's just the plain truth. If I had screwed the football team and half the senior class and the janitor and his deaf-mute brother, I'd just be happy as hell to lay it out for you, so to speak, give you every little detail, be fuckin' proud of it, but the fact is it never happened. Some layin' on of hands, but that was it." She laughed. "That sounds religious."

"I'll be damned." I held the bottle up to the window and looked at the stars through the amber glass. The whiskey was better than half gone. "I always thought you were lying about that."

"Wouldn't have made any difference if you'd believed me or not."

"You never know."

"I gotta have some water. And I gotta pee."

"Shoooo. Me too. That's one little detail we didn't figure on."

"Who ever plans on *that*? If we hadn't been drinkin', we wouldn't have that to worry about. You got no problem anyway. You can just whiz out the window. The advantages you boys do have. But what the hell am *I* gon' do?"

"Now, how am I going to get myself situated so that I can piss out that window? It's too near the ceiling. I'd have to curl up like a worm . . ."

"You could get up on your knees and heist your leg, like a dog."

"I'll go in the sink," I said.

"Fine, but what about me?"

"Well, damn, Annie, there's got to be something down there you can pee in, a jar or something, a bucket maybe, and we'll pour it in the sink. Or maybe an Old Crow bottle."

"An Old Crow bottle? Now, maybe you could squeeze yourself into the neck of one of'm, but I can't begin to imagine a woman being able to pee into one in broad daylight and stone sober, much less in the dark and drunk as a skunk. Jesus, you ought to understand female anatomy better than that."

"You ready to go down?"

"I'm ready to go, period. These ain't tears in my eyes. Boy, that came on fast."

We made our way slowly down the slope of boxes. Behind me Annie was making all kinds of ridiculous noise and giggling as she descended.

"Shhhh. You're gonna wake her up."

"Shhhhhhhiiiiiiiit—I don't care. If I don't get to pee soon she can go ahead and kill me. It would be more merciful than drowning. Or maybe she could call a highway petro-le-um. I swear to God thas the way that guy with the broom back in Lufkin said it, highway *petroleums*."

"That he did. Highway pe-tro-le-ums. But I still think he was joking."

"Naw, naw, Tommy, he wudn't joking."

She bumped into my back and settled onto her end of the mattress. "Home again. How nice. Just the way I left it. All cozy. Home from the mountain. Now, how about finding a container for me, big boy?"

My head was whirling as I made my way through the dark corridor of boxes to the sink, but there was nothing on or underneath it that she could possibly use as a receptacle. Not even a fruit jar, which would have been tough enough to target sober, much less in her condition. I felt all over the floor and among the boxes, but there was nothing.

"I couldn't find a thing," I said when I got back to the mattress.

"Well, shit," she said. "What am I going to do? I am not going to pee on the floor, even in here." She was quiet a few seconds. "What about getting a can of vegetables or Spam or something and open it and empty it out. I might be able to hit a can. Couldn't be much tougher than aiming for a Dixie cup when you give a sample. Tommy, why do you rekkin they call them Dixie cups anyway? I never saw one in my life that had Dixie anywhere on it. Why not a Betty cup or a Chris cup?"

"I don't think I'd worry all that much about Dixie cups right now, and if you mention Betty one more time, I am going to let you go ahead and explode. By the way, just how the hell would I open a can? Anything stashed in here wouldn't have a pull-tab on it, and I'll bet the Spam is so old that it wouldn't be the kind with a key attached to it."

"Oh, Lord, my kingdom for a *can*! And I mean either kind."

"If *you* don't *can* it, you are going to get us shot. You need to go bad enough, you'll pee on the floor. I damned sure would. I'd pee anywhere I had to if I had to bad enough."

"There's another one of those big differences between you and me. I don't mind dying with dignity."

"If you get to needing to bad enough, you'll go on the floor. Just wait and see. Too bad you can't pee in a bottle, the way I can."

"If women could do that, we wouldn't be much fun for y'all, now, would we?"

"Good point," I said. "I've got an idea, though."

"What? Hurry with it."

"If you can get up on the sink . . ."

"Jesus, Tommy, how can I do that, drunk as I am? I don't know whether I could balance on the *floor*."

I took the flashlight and made my way over and shone it on the sink. "It's big, heavy," I whispered back to her. "Hung up there with what looks like lag bolts into the blocks. The damn drain is cast iron and would probably hold the thing up by itself. If we can get you up there, you can squat and go right in it." The sink was an enormous porcelained cast-iron affair with a curled lip like a bathtub, probably a foot deep and two feet square with the spigot coming out of the wall just above it. It was mounted high, almost to my navel, probably put there for washing dirty hands after working on cars.

"I can move a box over for you to step up on and get on the

sink itself, or stack them high enough for you to squat over it. I'll hold you steady."

She started giggling.

"What the hell's so funny. Do you need to go or not? You start giggling and you're gonna pee in your panties. Hurry the hell up and make up your mind. I got my own problems."

"The absurd drama has kicked back in big-time here. My estranged husband, a man I hate with a passion, is going to hold my hands while I pee in a sink in a friggin' jailhouse in the middle of the Davy Crockett National Forest? We couldn't in ten thousand years have come up with a story this ludicrous. I mean, think about it. Lying in your bed last night—or night before, time's just gone away for me—lying in your bed whenever you was last in it—*were* in it, Goddamn, I keep talking like her—what are the chances you could ever have imagined what we've been through over the past six or eight hours?"

"I'm not sure yet that it's really happened. I'm wondering whether we're not back in Shreveport having a shared nightmare in our separate apartments."

"Might be, except for one thing."

"What's that?"

"Reality always kicks in, sooner or later, and tells you you've got to go pee. What I'm feeling here is not the stuff of dreams. It is a big-time *gotta-go-pee* feeling. So lead me over there, big boy, and let's just see what we can work out."

So I groped my way back over and grasped her hand and pulled her to her feet. As we stood on the mattress she dropped her head onto my chest and clung to me.

"Whoa. Let me steady myself first. God, my head's goin' round. Tommy, I might get sick."

"Just hang on. You'll feel better in a minute. And you're not the only one who's dizzy here."

"Egg san-wich and milkshake. Ohhhh, that'd make a mess." She giggled. "But not like corny-dogs, all down the side of the car."

"Come on. Don't even think about corny-dogs, as you call'm. Take a deep breath and hold it down."

"How long?"

"How long what, Annie?"

"How long I gotta hold my breath down."

"Arright, damn it, go on joking. I'm going to piss."

"OK, OK," she said. "Lead on, big boy."

I led her slowly over to the sink. "Now, just stand here while I get some boxes stacked. You want to squat on the sink or on some boxes in front of it? You know, so . . . so you can—"

"So I can hang my butt over the sink?"

"Yeah. You put it so much better than I ever could."

"I'll try the sink itself, if you think it'll hold me."

"I suspect you could hold a circle piss on this thing, it's so big."

"You put that so much better than I ever could. What's a circle piss?"

"Guys stand in a circle and piss in a ring in the sand. See who can write their complete name first. It's just a game."

"I guess *Bo* would have a leg up on *Wellington*, huh? Sorta like a circle jerk, huh?"

"Not really. But where'd you hear about *that*?"

"Girls hear about that kind of shit. Guys standin' in a circle jerkin' off, seeing who can get jack-off first."

"You can sit," I said. "Or squat or kneel or lie on your back. You don't necessarily *stand*."

"Whatever. I'm sure you've tried it all ways. It's disgusting. At least as bad as a circle piss. Y'all really got it made with them-ere toys of yers. You can have all sorts of fun. Get to write yer names in the snow and sand and everthang."

"I haven't seen enough snow in my lifetime to write my name *in*."

"Well, you cain't have everthang."

"Y'all really can't stand not having one, can you?"

"If we did have one," she said, "we'd control them, which is more than y'all can do. Would you please *hurry the hell up*?"

"Goddamn it, it's dark. And while you've been standing there, I've been moving boxes."

"How come you don't go get the upside-down disappearing staircase and rig it up so I can climb up there comflit—comforbly. Com-fort-a-bly. Damn it, Tommy, I'm so drunk I can barely talk. Get some boxes stacked. Hurry!"

With her holding the light, I finally fished out enough boxes of canned goods, half of them Spam, and lined them up in front of the sink to make a pretty good, firm staircase: three on the bottom, then two, then one.

"My God, the pyramids musta gone quicker."

"You wanna do this?"

"No."

"Then shut up." I stood up on the first box, weaved a bit, then stepped off.

"There, that'll get you up to where you can get on the rim without any trouble."

"Tommy, I'm so dizzy I don't think I can climb the boxes, much less balance on that sink."

"I'll hold your hands."

"Not likely. Have you ever tried to pee with somebody holding your hands?"

"Then maybe you can hold your arms back and brace against the wall."

"I'll try that. I'm taking my blouse and panties off, though. I don't want to splatter them."

"Fine with me."

"Tommy, you turn that damned flashlight off right now, and if you turn it on while I'm up there, I will brain you with it when I get through."

So I flicked it off and laid it on the floor.

She took off her clothes and put them on the bottom step of the boxes and gave me her hand and I helped her climb up and position herself on the rim of the sink. It was so dark that I got only the vaguest sense of the shape of her body against the white porcelain basin, though God knows I was trying. That damned flashlight had dulled my night vision.

"This is absolutely insane," she hissed, pulling her hand free of mine. "Crazy as hell. My dinni—my dignity's just gone right down the drain, so to speak."

"Can you manage?"

"Yes. By holding my elbows against the wall. But that God-damned faucet is gouging my back."

"Can you rise above it?"

She laughed, then was silent a few seconds. "I don't know that I could ever sink any lower, pun intended. This has got to be one of the most humiliating things I've ever done."

"What can I do?"

"Nothing." She grunted and adjusted her position. "I'm OK. Just go to the mattress and come back when I tell you to. Leave my blouse and panties where they are and go on back. And leave that flashlight. I'll call you."

"Yes'm. It's on the floor right beside the first box."

She managed to reach around and turn the water on to drown out any sounds she might make. I made my way to the mattress and kneeled down, my back to her, and stared at the dark ceiling. The water seemed to run forever, then abruptly hushed and there was only silence behind me. I turned and saw her form against the wall, crouched on the sink like a little girl behind a bush.

"Tommy, you've got to come help me." Her voice came in a tremulous whisper. "I can't—I can't move. I'm too Goddamned drunk to get up, and my legs are locked."

"Well, I'm not sure what help I'll be, but here I come." I stood and slowly weaved to the sink. My head was reeling. "Shooo-eeee, little sister, I am so screwed up."

"Me too. My legs won't work. Can you see me, Tommy?"

"Hell no. It's black as the inside of a Goddamned whale in here, woman. Quit worrying about it. I've seen everything you've got. I doubt that anything's changed that much in three years."

"I don't care. I don't want you to see me naked anymore."

"Like that's some kind of big deal. Fuck it. Do you want me to help you down from there or not?"

"Yes."

"Well, hold out your hands."

"I can't."

"What do you mean, you *can't*?"

"I'm holding myself up with them, Tommy. My legs are locked. I can't straighten them out enough to get off this Goddamned sink, and I can't move my hands, because if I do, I'll fall down *in* the Goddamned sink. Do you get the picture?"

"Pretty much. The flashlight would help."

"Tommy, I swear to God that I will kill you with whatever is at hand if you turn that flashlight on me."

"Fine. What do you want me to grab then? Your proboscis?"

"This is no time for your humor. I don't know what you can do, but you've got to help me down from here."

"Well, did you pee?"

"Yes, if it's any of your business. That is what the hell I got up here for."

"OK, OK. Settle down. I'm not in the best condition to solve a problem, but it seems to me that the only way I'm going to get you off there—and you got to get off quick, because if you don't, I've got to piss in an Old Crow bottle or off in the boxes or past your legs—is to grab you under the arms and lift you off."

"Then do it. But you keep your hands to yourself."

"Would you listen to what you're *saying*? How the hell am I going to lift you off there if I keep my hands to myself? If I wanted to, if I didn't have to piss so bad, I could get up on these boxes and nail you right there on the sink. Or at the very least turn the flashlight on you and have myself a good look. Lady, you are awfully vulnerable to be giving me orders."

"Tommy, please don't shine the light on me."

"Give me some credit for decency, Annie. I'm not going to turn the light on or grab your titties or pussy or anything else. Just relax and let me help you off that sink so I can *piss*."

"Fine," she said. "Lift me off."

So I reached out and slid my hands in her armpits and hoisted her off the sink and swung her lightly onto the makeshift staircase. For one brief instant I could see the little girl in silver again, hear the music from the fair.

"There y'are. I was a gentleman, wasn't I? Never touched anything I wasn't s'posed to."

"Yes," she said quietly, wrangling with her blouse and panties. "Quite the gentleman."

"Now, kindly go to the mattress before I hose down this end of the room."

She disappeared into the dark and I stood on the middle step of our makeshift stairs and peed into the sink, trying to hit the little dark round spot that I knew was the drain. I was too unsteady to do it properly.

"Be sure to flush," she whispered.

"Yes'm." I turned the spigot on and ran the water for quite some time, directing the stream with my hands so that the whole basin was well rinsed.

"Well, now," I said, kneeling on my end of the mattress, "that was a memorable experience, wasn't it, mingling our urine in a jailhouse sink?"

"Urine and mine," she said, laughing. "Thanks for getting me down."

"You sure were an easy target up there. I could have taken

advantage, with you drunk and legs spread and locked like that."

"But you didn't try to. I'm grateful, because you saved me from a murder charge. I'd have beaten you to death with an Old Crow bottle when I did get down."

"My knowing that is what saved you," I said.

"Thanks, Tommy. Seriously. I was about to die. My legs just cramped up and—"

"You're welcome."

"I was wondering while you were peeing in there whether Chris pissed there." She giggled. "There I go again with a rhyme. Chris pissed."

I laughed. "Naw, he had bathroom privi . . . privileges. That might have been a sobering experience, but I still can't talk right. But we know he slept on this mattress."

"I'm thirsty," she said. "For water."

"Me too. Hand me that bottle."

"It's empty."

"You drank all of it?"

"Jesus, Tommy, I sipped on it for hours. Why didn't you get a drink while you were over there?"

"Why didn't you?"

"Because I had just peed in the sink is why," she said. "You can rinse it out, but you still *smell* it."

"All right, then."

"You gotta go fill the bottle, Tommy."

"Yas'm. Hand it here." I took the empty bottle. "But I'm using the Goddamned light."

"Fine. I'm dressed."

I stood and went back to the sink by flashlight glow, rinsed it again, then drank from the big iron spigot and refilled the bottle and capped it.

"Try it in the dark," she whispered.

"Try what?" I still had my back to her.

"Turn the light off and try to find me in the dark."

"Jesus, Annie. As many trips as I've made to that mattress, how could I *not* find you, unless you're planning to crawl up there in the boxes somewhere. There's only one path to that spot. You gon' stay on the mattress or what?"

"Yes. But keep the light off."

"All right, here I come." I switched off the light and stood braced against the sink, my head wheeling, trying to make something of the absolute dark before me. The adrenaline had settled down and I could feel my buzz again. At first I couldn't even see stars through the window, but gradually little points of light appeared. There was nothing before, around, or above me but pitch black. I bent over and slid my hand along the sloping wall of boxes and stepped forward.

There was nothing to it. In a few careful little steps I felt my end of the mattress and kneeled down on it. "Here's the water." I held the bottle out before me. She took it. "It's good stuff. Got enough iron in it to pick it up with a magnet."

"And here's the whiskey," she said. "I never thought I'd admit it, but it's pretty good too."

The Crow was decidedly lighter. "You haven't been wasting time, have you? I've never known you to drink like this. You ought to be out-cold drunk by now."

"Nope." I heard her chugging water. "Not out cold, but damn sure drunk." She giggled. "Thanks for the water."

"So what was the bit about me finding you in the dark, another one of your crazy little games?"

"You haven't found me yet," she said.

"I know where you are. You're on the mattress."

"You haven't found me yet."

"What the hell do you want me to do, *tag* you?"

"Until you've touched me, you haven't found me."

"OK. If that's the game." I felt for the whiskey case that sat between us and swung it to the side. "You've always got to have some kind of game going."

"You used to love my games."

"Yeah, well, if you remember, they got pretty damned nasty toward the end."

"Those weren't games. That was for real. And you got pretty nasty yourself."

"Let it rest." I reached out and groped in the dark but my hand closed on nothing. It was so dark that I couldn't even see the little white checks in her blouse. "Are you still on the mattress?"

"I tol' you I was. Hand me the flashlight."

I held it out and she took it and laid it on the floor somewhere beside or behind her. I crawled forward and reached again, this time dropping my hand on her knee. "There you are. Tag, you're it. So what's the big deal?"

"Is that all you want to touch?"

I sat back on my legs and stared at where her voice was coming from. "Annie, what are you up to?"

"I've got a little gift for you." She thrust something out to me.

I took a bundle of some kind of cloth into my hands. "What is this?"

"My clothes."

"Annie, I don't know what's going on here." I separated the blouse from the panties and held them before me like I was weighing them. Then I held them to my face and breathed deep.

"I've been scared all day and now I'm drunk and naked in a dark room with a strange man and I'm not sleepy, so I want to play with this strange man."

"What do you want me to do?"

"I don't want *you*, Tommy Carmack, to do anything. Tommy Carmack is back in Shrevesport. I want the strange man in the dark, the man I cannot see, to do something."

"OK. Fine with me. You don't know me. I'm a stranger. Sell seeds out of my Goddamned truck. Hell-bent for a deboning by a bridge railing someday, with a pantiless black woman beside me. What can I do for you, lady?"

"You've got to take this garter off."

"What garter?"

"What damned garter *would* I be talking about? How many you figger are in this room, Mr. Seed Salesman? I've got it on my leg. Take it off."

"You're kidding. I know what's up. You've found a machete or a meat cleaver, and when I reach over there, you're going to whack my hand off."

"If I had a machete or cleaver, I'd already have whacked off something else of yours. But I wouldn't do that to a stranger unless he did something that made me hate him." She shoved her leg out and touched my knee with a foot. "Remove the garter, Mr. Seed Man."

"Or you've found a snake or spider, and when I get my hand up there he'll bite me." My head was reeling. I turned and looked at the stars, then into the blackness where she was. "How about letting me turn the light on?"

"No way. With the light on it would be *you*, not some strange seed salesman. Besides, you saw more of me in yonder when she made us undress than you're ever going to see again."

"But you want me to take the garter off your leg?"

"At's right, big boy. Jes' reach up here and do it. F'yont to, you can play like yer Chris and we're in a hotel room in Houston. You done peed in the sank or out the winder and come to the bed to take this here garter offa my laig."

"No, thank you. I'll play like I'm me and you're you." I closed my hands around the foot that was touching me. "This the leg?"

"You're either a strange man or the game's over."

"All right, Goddamn it. I'm a strange man. I'm the Seed Man. Now, is this the leg?"

"No, that's a foot. My leg's attached to it, and the garter is on that leg."

"Look, I've been doing some pretty heavy drinking here, lady, so let me get this straight before I make a move—you want me to reach up your leg and take off the garter."

"Well, for God's sake, do I have to e-mail you the *instructions*? That'd be downright impossible in this place, come to think of it. Maybe I could lean over and tap it out on the door in Morse code. If I knew what the hell Mr. Morse's code was. And how do you rekkin he come up with it? By the way, how come he didn't use the telephone like other people?"

"Jesus, you are such a smartass. And you sound just like Miz Ludy."

"Meant to. She done growed on me. Wow, I'm really gettin' good, ain't I?"

"Arright, the Seed Man cometh."

"And you are not going to make a move that I don't tell you to make, Mr. Seed Dispenser. Understood? I will break this bottle acrost yer head if you do any more than I tell you to do, the same as I would do if my estranged husband touched me. If you touch anything past that garter. . ."

"You and your damned power games."

"I remember one time a bunch of us girls were sitting around at a slumber party talking about boys and what they'd do just for a chance to see one of us naked or lay a hand on one of us, much less fuck us. One of my girlfriends told about what she made this guy do once. They were at his house while his parents were gone, and she made him put on lipstick and rouge and a pair of his momma's panties and bra—just for a feel of one of her breasts. And I remember I said to her, 'You can't make a boy do that!' My best friend, Carol Pemberton, looked at me real hard and grinned and said, 'Annie, you'd be real surprised what a girl can make a boy do.' So I've got a pretty good idea that you'll do anything I want you to do. Now, are you willing to play my game or not, stranger?"

"OK. Deal. This mean I get to feel your breasts?"

"Do and die. You get to touch me, though."

"You want me to take that garter off is all, right?"

"My God, I really do have to write out the instructions, don't I? Find me a frigging pencil and pad. How did you ever get in the seed bidness anyhow? You ort to of stayed in the field behind a mule. Just slip your hand up my leg until you touch the garter, Seed Man, then take it off. Don't you dare go any farther up that leg or they'll be pickin' pieces of the pitcher of a crow out of yer brain tomar."

"I gotta have another drink before I take off on this trip. To steady my nerves." I took a swig. "Wanna drink?" I asked.

"Might'swell." She took the bottle. "Don't see what difference a few more coals on the fahr can make." I heard her swigging and making that sizzling sound.

I think that if I had been sober I could not have removed the garter, my fingers would have trembled so. My hands closed gently around her foot and moved upward, as if they were smoothing on a stocking, my thumbs side by side, fingers wrapped around the leg and touching until the swell of her marvelous calf, touching again just at the knee, then separating as they moved slowly up her thigh. God, what wonderful legs! I could feel the heat of her body radiating in the dark. Goosebumps popped up all over her. Then my thumbs touched the ruffled edge of the garter and I stopped.

"You're there," she said.

I nodded and took a deep breath, hooked my fingers around the garter, and eased it off her leg.

"Well done. OK. That's it for tonight. Hand me my clothes. If we're still here tomorrow night, we'll play another game."

"Annie, come on. You can't quit now."

"You're gettin' mighty familiar, stranger, calling me by my first name. I thought you didn't want to play my game." She giggled. "My God, I rhymed again."

"I didn't say I don't want to play the game. You've just got me so fucking confused. You won't even be civil to me for three years, and now you're buck-naked in the dark with me and I'm taking a garter off your leg."

"I thought you'd like the game, Mr. Seed Man."

"I *do* like it. I just don't know what you want me to do."

"I want you to do what I *tell* you to do. That's all."

"I did."

"And you did great, big boy," she said in a husky Mae West voice. "Now take your shorts off and put the garter on your leg."

"Annie, what the hell—"

"Just do it, Tommy Turnipseed." She bumped me with the empty whiskey bottle. "Open another one."

I reached and pulled out another bottle, uncapped it, took a swig, and handed it to her. "Here. But I'm not sure you need to drink any more."

"I'll drink all I want to, thankyouverymuch. Now off with the shorts and on with the garter."

I had no idea where the game was going, but the throbbing between my legs told me it didn't matter, that it was certainly more fun than I'd had in a long time with a woman. The whiskey, a woman I was now sure I was still in love with naked on a mattress with me in a pitch-black jail cell in the middle of a great wilderness, a big black dog, and a crazy old woman with a revolver big as her arm—what a witch's broth. And if she wanted me to be a traveling seed salesman, that was fine too. I'd be happy to leave some seed with her. I slipped off my shorts and pulled the garter to mid-thigh.

"OK, I'm naked," I said, taking a deep breath, "and the garter's on my leg, but it's cutting my circulation off. I didn't know these things were so tight. I'm damned glad the light's not on."

"I'd like to have a picture—uh, *pitcher*—of this to remind me of this night the rest of my life."

"Don't worry, you won't forget this night ever. Now what do you want me to do?"

"I get to take the garter off you. Stick out the leg it's on."

I did as she ordered. "And if you want to, you can go past the garter."

"No way. I know what's up there. And I know some of the places it's been. All you seed salesmen are alike. You spread yer seed everwhur."

"Annie, what's this all about? Are you teasing me just to torment me? You know, it used to be these little games of yours led to sex—"

"It's something to *do*. And, believe me, it won't lead to sex this time. I mean, if you have a better plan for passing this crazy-ass night, lay it out on the mattress."

"No. No. Go ahead and take the damned garter off." I waved my leg in front of her. "But keep your voice down. If we wake that old woman up, there'll be hell to pay."

As her hands moved up toward my knee, not touching skin but so close I could feel the warmth of her fingers, goosebumps sprouted all over my body. Jesus, I wanted her to seize me and do what she used to do. She slipped the garter off. Yow, she was quick.

"Now what?" I asked. I could feel her shifting positions on the mattress.

"I've got it back on, just a little higher. This time you've got to take it off with your mouth."

"Holy shit, Annie, I can't take this. I'm about to lose it."

"Y'mean yer egg san-wich?"

"No. I mean—"

"I know what you mean. It won't go off on its own while you're awake, Tommy. Just don't touch the damn thing. Don't pull the trigger. Control yourself. Or if you can't take it, go and jerk off in the sink and we'll call it quits."

"I'll control it," I said.

"Good. Now take the garter off with your mouth." She touched my knee with her foot.

I bent over and kissed the top of her foot and ran my tongue lightly over her instep and up to her ankle. She didn't stop me, so I kept on up her calf, working slowly, barely touching her leg with my lips and tongue. She had goosebumps all the way up her leg, I was sure all over her body. Then I stopped and returned to a kneeling position.

"Why'd you stop?" she asked.

"I need a drink. This is hard work. Have you got the bottle?"

"Yes." She handed it to me and I took a swig. I kneeled in the dark silence a long while trying to get my head straight.

"You ready to get back to it?" she asked.

"You in a hurry?"

"No. I just . . ."

"I'm a player in this game, too, you know. I'm not just a damned footman you can order around."

"You're the *Seed Man*. Not a foot man. A poder . . . podda . . . some kind of damn *podologist* or *poddatrician* or whatever they're called. Goofy-ass name for a foot doctor, if you ask me. Looks like somebody specializing in pods would be into seeds or goiters or something."

"Whatever, are you ready?"

"Yeah. But believe me, big boy, I can hold out if you can."

"Think so, huh?"

"Looky here, Mr. Seed Man, maybe we'd better just put our clothes back on and behave. You drop by next time you're in these parts and we'll play another game. You mus' have bunches of fine women out there jes' waitin' for you to come by and leave some seed."

"No, no. I'm happy here. Back on the job." Before she could move I had my mouth on her leg, working my way up toward the garter with lips and tongue. She bristled with bumps again as I moved higher and higher. I didn't know where the garter was, but it was higher than it had been before—that I could tell—and so was I. When I was about two-thirds up her thigh I felt it with my tongue.

Removing a tight garter with your mouth is far more difficult than a person might imagine. Unlike taking one off with two hands, where you can grasp and pull both sides down with even pressure, with your mouth you can pull only so far, then move to the other side and pull. It's damned tough. Every time I repositioned my mouth and gripped the garter with my teeth, she tensed. It had to be from pleasure, because I sure as hell wasn't hurting her. Finally I got it over her knee and past the full part of her calf and it came off and I was there on all fours, the garter dangling from my mouth like a dog's plaything.

"Well done, Mr. Seed Man." Her voice was sultry. "I wish I had you around to undress me like that every night."

"That can be arranged," I said.

"Now I get to take it off you with *my* mouth."

"Holy shit, Annie—"

"You cannot call me by my name, stranger. I could be anybody in the dark and so could you. And we're both drunk as the wind. So I might be the woman in white from the woods down there for all you know, and you might be a pulpwood hauler fresh from the Dairy Queen in Lufkin or a seed man from Huntsville. Neither one of us is going to remember much of this in the morning, if anything. Let's have another drink or two, and then I want you to put the garter on your leg and I'll try to take it off with my mouth."

So we sat on our little mattress adrift in that dark sea, all around us boxes like flotsam from some great wreck, a square of star-sprinkled night sky looking in on us, and passed the bottle back and forth. My knees touched hers. There was no time, no light, no world beyond those four walls, only the two of us in deeper and deeper whiskey oblivion moving suddenly into each other's arms, the garter flung aside, the dog and old pistol-waving woman forgotten, the anger and bitterness gone.

I remember my lips closing on hers, hers loosening and her

tongue running wild against mine, then me falling forward onto the mattress with her beneath me.

"Oh, God, I wanted this," she panted. "I am so drunk, Tommy, but I wanted this, I *wanted* this."

"Me too" was all that I could manage before I lost myself completely in her.

SEVEN

Dawn comes round no more slowly in East Texas than it does anywhere else, unless you happen to slip into a drunken slumber just before the sky lightens. Then dawn does not come at all. The morning is simply not there, as if it never existed, and the night before it is just a blur.

You wake slowly, at first seeing nothing but a square of deep bright-blue sky with black bars slashing across it vertically, then the slow stirring of recognizable shapes of boxes, over on the wall a sink, and an age-soiled cobwebbed ceiling softly billowing with pulses of air from the window. The room is faintly chill, and you wonder first where you are and what the day is, then the week and month, nothing focusing easily in the fog you are lying in.

Then you remember that it is September in the Deep South, where September is merely an extension of summer. You hear far off, as if in another world, a car passing and closer by the noise of a kitchen in use—a utensil clanging against a pan, cups and plates rattling, the tinny sound of silverware. Someone coughing. A hag's cough. You smell coffee and cigarette smoke and some kind of meat frying. And then the day comes back, and the place, and you are aware that there is someone lying with you.

We were wrapped together in a sheet, which still bore the clean, fresh smell of the sun. Annie was breathing softly against my chest, my chin resting on the top of her head, and she had one arm around me from beneath and one over the top, embracing me the way a child would a large stuffed toy. My right arm lay across her waist, left curled around the top of her head and down her back, and my hand rested between her shoulder blades. Our legs were intertwined.

Within the confines of my hammering head the night tried to fall slowly into place the way a jigsaw puzzle does, little pieces snapping together properly to form familiar shapes, start a simple scene—sitting in the dark at the window on an upside-down disappearing staircase talking about an injured child, passing a bottle of Old Crow back and forth on the mattress, watching a ghostly form at the edge of the woods, harassing the dog beneath the door, the old woman yelling at us. And then the puzzle grew troublesome, with pieces that did not fit, tabs ill-formed, improperly cut, nebulous, shadowy pieces that seemed not to belong anywhere. A scrambled scene with a garter, a sink, a seed salesman, then real or imagined passionate love in the dark. The picture sagged utterly out of shape, like a Dali painting.

I lifted my arm and tried to focus on the watch. My glasses were in the pocket of my shirt, wherever that was. It might have been ten o'clock or three, but the sun seemed awfully far up in the sky. As long as Annie slept, I refused to move, to get my glasses or get a drink of water, which I needed bad, or to pee, which I needed worse. It was like a dream I didn't want to awake from, wrapped up with her again, her face against my chest the way I remembered it, the feel of her legs clamping mine, the smell of her hair in the morning, as if the last few years had never happened. Even with a cottony mouth and insistent bladder, I would have been content to lie there with her all day until the sun settled back down and we entered again the region of the dark where miracles happen.

With as much stealth as I could in my condition manage, I lifted my right arm and slid my hand beneath the sheet and down her side, not pausing until I had reached the middle of her thigh. She was gloriously naked. When I moved my hand back up, she shivered and moaned. I tried again, my eyes clenched shut, to piece together the night before. Then I drifted off.

"*What?*" Annie's head was thrown back, her face scowling up at the door. "What in hell do you *want?*" She had rolled away from me and clutched the sheet to her chest.

The old woman hammered again. "Y'all got t'get up in there. Hit's afternoon awready. Y'all a-goin' to sleep all day long? I thought you had somewhere to get to. And you quit cussin' me."

"All right, all right." Annie pulled the sheet around her as she got up. She just stood there, looking bewildered. "God-*damn*," she sighed and dropped back to her knees. Her face was puffy, her eyes mere slits.

I was suddenly aware that I was lying there completely naked before her, so I snatched up the edge of the bottom sheet and pulled it from beneath the mattress and flung it across my middle.

"Sorry about that, Annie. I'm sorry."

"Well, Jesus, Tommy, what difference does it make anyhow? I can't see shit."

The hammering came again. "Y'all get *up!*"

"We're *up*, Goddamn it! Just give us a minute. And how about throwing our clothes in here?"

"I told you about cussin' me, little lady. You want somethin' from me, you gotta be nicer."

"All right," Annie yelled back at the door. "Please throw us our clothes." Then, quietly, "You old bitch."

She was weaving around on her knees, both hands to her face. She kept the sheet pinned tightly about her with her elbows. "Holy shiiiiut. My head. My head. Oh, God, my head."

"Lie back down, Annie. The hell with her. We got squatters' rights now. Just lie back down."

"Don't want to. We gotta get out of here while the sun's up." She spread her fingers so that her eyes peeped through. "Where's my stuff, Tommy? My panties and blouse?"

"Search me," I said. "I didn't pull them off of you. I don't know where anything is. This is as much your place as mine."

"I will never drink again," she said quietly. She yanked the bottom sheet around and lifted up the corners of the mattress. "Get off the fucking mattress so I can find my stuff."

I scrambled onto the floor. With one arm clutching the sheet about her, she flipped the mattress over onto the boxes.

"It's on the other side of the whiskey case, I think." I pointed behind her. "We must have—"

She stood up, wobbling, and collapsed to her knees again. "I'm going to throw up." She wound the sheet tighter about her and

307

got up and shuffled down the corridor of boxes to the sink, stuck her head under the spigot and drank. The staircase was still in place, so she dropped both hands onto the lip at one end of the sink but kept the sheet clamped by pressing against it. "Maybe not. Maybe not. But I've sure as hell got to go to the bathroom."

"You want me to help you back up there?" I asked from the mattress.

"No, I do not," she said to the wall. "I want you to get your clothes on and let me get dressed." She turned her head around toward the door and yelled, "Where are our *clothes, old woman*?"

"Give her a second, Annie. I think she's gone to get them. And don't antagonize her."

I heard the padlock unsnap, the door cracked open, and a gnarled hand slipped through, clutching the rest of our clothes. "Yer shoes is still out yonder by the front door. You c'n hose'm off or take a hoe blade to'm d'rectly."

"Yes'm," I mumbled.

"Soon's y'all dressed, I'll get you fed. Hit'll be a late breakfast, if that's all right with you."

"Close the God—just close the *door*," Annie yelled.

"Y'all come on out right away now, y'hear?"

"Yes'm," I said.

The door closed and I heard her padding off down the hallway. I turned to Annie. "You could still get us shot. Lighten up. You OK over there?"

"No, I am not *OK*. I don't figure I'll ever be *OK* again. I feel like—I just can't put it into words, Tommy. I feel like she *looks*. Just leave my clothes on the mattress and go on to the bathroom while I get dressed. But be out of there quick."

"You gon' throw up?"

"I don't know what I'm going to do, but whatever it is, I can manage it by myself." She was still holding herself steady with her hands, her head bent over the sink. "My esophagus feels like it's been scalded with a blowtorch, and my stomach's got a bed of hot coals right in the middle of it."

"At's right poetic, little sister," I said and tried to laugh. I couldn't. It came out a dry hack. I stood and wrapped the sheet around my middle and made my way slowly over to the other end of the sink. My head was spinning wildly. "Mind if I get some water?"

I stuck my mouth beneath the spigot and turned the handle, letting that cold, iron-tinged water snuff out the fire in my stomach. I let it run all over my face and hair, sloshed it over my arms.

"Why don't you just crawl up there and take a shower?" she said.

"I would if I'd fit."

"It's the new thing in bathrooms. Two-foot square. You do everything right there."

"Air you go a-rhymin'," I said, trying again to laugh. My head was zinging.

She merely scowled. "If you're through, would you mind getting on out of here so I can get dressed? Is all my stuff there?"

I looked. "Yeah. Your bra and pants."

"Where are my panties and blouse?"

"I told you, over there behind that whiskey case. I think. Wherever you put'm. Hell, I'll look."

I went back to the mattress and kneeled down over the case. The heads of four Old Crow bottles leered up at me from their straw nests. I shoved the case aside and found my shorts and shirt and her blouse and the garter, but her panties weren't there. I slipped the garter into my pants pocket, stood and dressed, and put on my glasses. She stood clenched to the sink.

"Your panties aren't here. The rest of your clothes are on the mattress. I'll go on to the bathroom."

"Where are my *panties?*" she whispered hoarsely.

"I don't *know*, I told you. They're not with our other stuff. You're the one who pulled them off last night. I never touched them. Whatever *you* did with them is—I don't keep up with'm anymore, Annie."

"I handed the damned things to you. You did too touch them. So where did you put'm?"

"I just don't know. I thought—"

She waved an arm impatiently. "Just get dressed and get on out of here. I'll look for the damned things."

"I *am* dressed," I said. I slipped the half-empty bottle of whiskey into my back pocket, took one more loathing look at the four Old Crow heads and, after being certain that the dog wasn't waiting just outside, stepped through the door.

After a quick trip to the bathroom, where I finished up by running a toothpaste-coated finger over my teeth and gums and tongue, I walked into the kitchen. The old woman was sitting at the table in a fine blue haze, smoking, a cup of coffee before her. I saw nothing of the pistol or the dog.

"Thought y'all wudn't never gettin' up."

"We slept in," I said.

"You didn't sleep atall until I got up around five. I never heard nothin' like the noise that come outta that room." She studied my face. "You look like you been run over by a logtruck."

"I *feel* like it. Where's Duke?"

"Got him locked up in my room. It wouldn't do for y'all to get near him this mornin'. I don't know what you done to him last night, but he was as mad as I've ever seen him. He would of tore that door down if I hadn't of locked him up with me."

"I thought you put him in the kitchen."

"Naw, I put him in bed with me. He'd of tore up this kitchen. It take'n me half a hour to calm him down. He don't like compny anyhow, not that he's ever seen that much of it. What in the world did y'all do to him to get him goin' like that?"

"I didn't do anything to him," I said. "He must have had a bad dream."

"Ain't nary dream got him goin' like that."

"Where's the pistol?"

She grinned. "Close by."

I heard Annie slam the bathroom door.

"Y'all want somethin' t'eat, I imagine." She motioned to the oven. "I got some ham fried up and some biscuits made, a boiler of grits. They probably stiff as ce-ment by now, but you can get'm down. I'll scramble you some eggs, if you want me to, or fry'm. Whatever."

Annie's voice came from the hallway: "Tommy."

I got up and walked to the bathroom door, cracked a couple of inches. "What?"

"Go get my makeup bag out of the car," she whispered. Her breath smelled of toothpaste and stale whiskey.

"What makes you think she's going to let me go to the car? And what in the hell are you worried about makeup for?"

"Just *tell* her you're going. I am through with her bullshit and with yours. We are breaking out of this joint as soon as I get ready, come dog or goiter or hog leg or hag."

"What if—"

"*Make do*," she said, and closed the door.

I went back into the kitchen. "She wants me to get her makeup bag out of the car."

"What does she want makeup for? If I looked like her, *I* wouldn't wear it." She pointed into the big room. "Yer keys and stuff are on the coffee table. Go ahead."

"Thanks," I said. I glanced toward the hallway. "Duke's locked up. Right?"

"Yep."

I opened the bandana and filled my pockets with what had come out of them the evening before and stepped through the doorway into a shockingly brilliant day. The sun was fierce and the pines such a glaring green that I had to narrow my eyes to fine slits to see anything. My head was pounding as I walked way around the cut to the car, my feet smarting from the sharp pebbles of the drive. The little spare had collapsed completely, so there was no hope of driving anywhere. I popped the trunk and rummaged around until I found what I presumed to be her makeup bag, confirmed by the fragrance that yawned from it when I unzipped it. The bottle of Jack Daniels squatted obscenely in a corner of the trunk. I laid the makeup bag on the roof of the car and dug out her sneakers. I hadn't brought along any other shoes, so I was stuck with the muddy ones.

When I rapped on the bathroom door, Annie's hand shot out and took the bag and the door slammed to.

"You're welcome," I said and went back to the kitchen.

"In a foul mood, ain't she?" the old woman said when I had settled at the table.

"Yeah. Had a bad night."

"Didn't sound too bad to me, what I heard of it. Rough maybe, but not bad."

"What *did* you hear?"

"Heard enough. You want some coffee?"

"Yes'm, please. And some orange juice, if you've got it."

"Got some froze. But I can mix it up."

I had two glasses of orange juice and a large mug of coffee while I watched her bustle around the kitchen and Annie finished up in the bathroom. The throbbing in my head was beginning slowly to subside, but my body felt wrung out, as if some great beast had snatched it up and twisted it into a tight little ball. The cells had to fill with fluid again. My hands trembled each time I lifted the mug to my lips.

Annie's voice came suddenly from behind: "OK, where's the gun?" She brushed past me and sat down. It is simply amazing what a woman can do with makeup. She looked almost as fresh as she had when I picked her up, but I knew what was going on inside her head. Her hair was wet.

"Don't figger I need it nomore." She set a glass of juice and a mug of coffee before Annie and stood with her back against the counter. "Y'all ain't nothin but a couple of kids. I never heard so much racket in my whole life as y'all made in that room last night. Gigglin' and knockin' stuff around and messin' with the dog."

"You ever heard tell of a slumber party?" Annie mumbled after setting down the empty orange juice glass.

"I heard tell of'm, but I ain't ever been to one. If they like what y'all had, then they misnamed. Far's I know, y'all didn't *slumber* all night long. But it sounded like you done everthang else."

"We slept a little," I said.

"Well, *you* look like you ain't *ever* slep' before. And I bet that room's a mess."

"A *mess?*" Annie managed, talking into her cup. "There's one hell of an understatement—and it was a *mess* long before we took up residence there."

"You c'n find yerselves another hotel next time then, if you ain't satisfied with the 'commodations."

"I 'spect we might do just that," Annie said. "Where's the frig— where's Duke?"

I corrected her: "You mean, where's Duke *at?*" She shot me a look and seemed to smile behind the cup.

"Got him back in my room. He ain't in no real good mood this mornin', bein' as y'all kep' him up all night."

"Yeah, well," Annie said, "his snoring bothered us for a while too. Right outside that door."

"Honey, that wudn't nothin' compared to the noise y'all made later."

"Let me ask you something."

"Yessir?"

I looked at Annie, but she kept her eyes on the cup, slightly crossed. "We saw something down there by the woods late, real late, probably after midnight sometime. It looked like somebody dressed in white. A woman maybe. Or a little girl."

"I don't know nothin' about it."

"Maybe we imagined it," Annie said. "It looked more like a ghost than a woman or child to me." She narrowed her eyes at the old woman.

"Must of imagined it. Wouldn't have been no ghost or woman or girl down there with them goats. And it *sure* wudn't me. I don't go out of this place after dark, less'n I *have* to."

I persisted: "You've never seen anything like that down there?"

"Ain't seen no woman or ghost, no. Nothin' like that. Seen some mighty big pigs down there. But they was black. You sure it wudn't a pig? Or a goat?"

"No," Annie said. She was staring into her cup again. "It wasn't a pig or a goat. It was white and it wasn't either of those."

"Well, maybe it was a sheep got in the pasture. They done that a few times before. Them sheep's almost white."

"Wasn't a sheep," Annie said.

"Coulda been swamp gas."

"It wasn't—"

I reached my foot out and tapped her leg. "Let it go."

"Y'all was drankin' in there last night, wudn't you?"

"What makes you think so?" I asked.

"I could smell it from under the door last night, and when I opened the door this mornin', the smell almost knocked me down. And you both got it on yer breath this mornin'. That toothpaste ain't covered it up."

"Yes'm. We were drinking," I said.

"You found a case of his whiskey, didn't you?"

"Yes'm. I did."

"Y'all didn't have no bidness rummagin' around in there. That's *my* stuff. What else did you get into?"

Annie blew across her cup. "Nothing. We just sat on an upside-down disappearing staircase and looked out the window."

"You was in my stuff. That whiskey would have been deep down. I heard y'all diggin' around in there, movin' boxes. What else did you get into?"

"I told you, nothing." Annie's eyes were stony. "We didn't get into anything else."

I started to say something about the box staircase, then decided against it. She could try to figure it out for herself.

"I knowed there was one or two cases of that rotgut left in there somewheres. I'm glad you found it. When you leave here, I want you to take whatever you didn't drank."

I nodded. "Yes ma'am. I'd love to."

"I don't think he'll be drinking any of it today."

"For a fact, little sister," I said. "For a fact."

"I guess we can leave this morning?"

"Yes'm, you can. Only it ain't mornin'. I 'spect y'all will want to eat somethin' first."

I glanced at Annie, who kept her eyes averted. "*I* would. I don't know about her."

"What about you, little sister? You want somethin' t'eat?"

"Might as well. God knows when we'll get to a restaurant. My stomach feels like it's feeding on itself. And if y'all don't stop that *little sister* crap, I am going to throw up on this table."

I patted her hand. "It's OK, little sister." She swung a foot but missed me.

"By the way, the spare is flat," I said.

The old woman, busy at the sink again, nodded. "I seen it earlier. Flatter'n a pancake."

"Oh, great," Annie said. "So how in the hell are we going to get to some place to use a phone?"

"They's a couple lives down the road a half a mile or so," the crone said, cracking eggs into a bowl. "Just around the next main curve down there. They got a phone. Seem like nice people."

Annie stared coldly at me. "Do you mean we could have driven another half mile last night and gotten to a phone?"

"At's a fact. Now you got to walk it. Less'n y'all gon' drive on the rim. Yer tar's flat."

Annie looked at me. "Don't y'all figure I have that straight by now? But that's fine. I'd be happy to walk half a mile to a telephone," she said. "Or a mile. Or five. Barefooted or with my clunkers on."

"I brought your sneakers in," I said.

"How sweet." She was staring back into the cup, her eyes crossed. "Big boy."

We had our breakfast—ham and eggs and grits, biscuits, more coffee and juice—while the old woman sat with us very slowly nursing a cigarette, a Salem, judging from the package lying by her elbow. She would tilt her head one way for a while studying us, then the other, alternating eyes as if one tired and she had to press the other into service, like a bird watching something too bright for it to examine for long.

Annie started slowly with breakfast, taking greater interest in it as her stomach quieted. "I would assume," she said, finishing her grits, "that we may walk out that door anytime we want to?" She pointed over her shoulder at the doorway that led to the main store area, the living room, as the old woman had described it.

"You can leave when you git ready. I ain't a-holdin' you. Yer purse is in there on the coffee table with the shades and bandanner and all. In y'all's condition you prolly gon' want to wear yer shades most of the day."

"I 'spect so." Annie rose and picked up her plate and silverware.

"I'll take care of all that," the old woman said. "Y'all got to get on. It'll take a while to get somebody way out here to fix yer car, less'n the Simms feller down there at the trailer has got a tar that'll fit, and I bet he don't."

"We'll make do," Annie said. She followed me into the large room, where she slipped on her sneakers and loaded her purse.

"Little sister," I whispered, "don't forget your protection."

"Fuck you," she mouthed and pulled the scarf over her head, tied it, and put on her sunshades.

The old woman stood in the kitchen doorway. "You look just like you did when y'all come in here." She looked at me. "Only *yer* a little worse for the wear."

"I'll take that as a compliment, both ways," Annie said and pushed through the screen door. "Are you coming, big boy?"

"Yeah, little sister, right behind you." I stepped through the doorway and picked up my shoes and knocked them against the side of the building, but the mud was still too wet to break off. I held one in each hand. They felt like bowling balls.

"Throw'm in the trunk. Mine too," Annie said, "and let's go." She started down the edge of the road, purse clutched under her arm, then stopped.

"My feet are too tender to go barefooted. I'll just walk the mud off." I sat down in the gravel and squeezed my feet into the heavy shoes and took Annie's to the trunk and pitched them in. She watched from the shoulder.

The old woman was shadowed in the doorway. "We were wondering—earlier, yesterday." I pointed to the pitiful little shrub that grew by the door. "What kind of bush is that?"

"At's a Jerusalem thorn bush," she said, "like the burnin' bush in the Bible."

"Does it bloom or anything?"

"It blooms ever seven years. Leastways, it's sposed to."

"When's it supposed to bloom again?" I asked.

"I don't know," she said.

"When did it bloom *last*?" Annie had come up beside me.

"It never *has* bloomed that I remember."

"Well, how long have you had it?" I asked.

"It was here when we moved in."

"But—"

I could see her shaking her head. One dim eye peeped through the streaked mass. "At's what we was told it was. A Jerusalem thorn bush. Blooms ever seven years."

"Why not every two years or every ten?" Annie scowled at the little bush. "Why an odd number like seven?"

"Why seven is what I kep' on astin' my daddy. And he never

said nothin' except it was a Jerusalem thorn bush and we gotta wait and see. I keep a-waitin' for it to bloom but it never has. It pops out in leaves like everthang else in the sprang and grows like any other bush, but it don't bloom. Just does what you see it a-doin' now. Sets there by the building and does what it's supposed to do, only it don't bloom, like it ain't figgered how to count or what to do when it gets to seven. If it has bloomed, it done it too quick for me to see."

"Maybe you should water it more often," I suggested, "or fertil-ize it."

"Or teach it to count," Annie said.

"Whoever told my daddy about it said we wudn't supposed to do anythang to it. You just let it alone."

"Make do," Annie said. "You just let it make do."

I shook my head and waved and started toward the road, casu-ally looking off past the building toward the line of trees along the bottom edge of the pasture, where a small string of goats seemed to float in the heat waves. The sun was bearing down. Annie stared at the doorway a few seconds, then walked over and stood directly in front of the old woman. I kept walking slowly, looking back. Annie held out her hand and said something, but I was out of hearing and on the blacktop, my eyes searching for the trailer.

A few minutes later I heard her sneakers whispering on the pavement beside me, but she kept her face pointed straight ahead.

"What did you say to her?"

"It was a woman thing," she said. "You wouldn't understand."

"You could try me."

"I've already tried you."

We walked along in silence, I in my mud-shrouded shoes, she in her sneakers, and the old building slid around the bend. On either side of us the woods thickened and closed, and I felt once again like I was looking down the barrel of a gun.

"Wanna talk about last night?" I finally said to her.

"No."

"Why don't you take off that scarf? Your hair looks fine."

She ignored me, and for what seemed like a hell of a lot more than half a mile we walked in silence, her feet whispering on the asphalt, mine clumping until finally the mud started sloughing off, leaving a little trail of chips and slivers behind us, the way a logtruck does pulling out onto a highway. Her eyes stayed on the road ahead, watching for something, for anything. I swept mine from pavement to trees to pavement again. Around a broad bend came an opening and, announced by a little picket fence and fruit trees beside a late garden, a long white trailer emerged from the green.

"Thank God," Annie said, stepping up the pace. "Thank *God*."

When after nearly an hour the man from the auto club arrived, Annie stayed with the couple at the trailer, sitting on a back deck sipping iced tea and talking, while I rode with him to the car. In a matter of minutes he had jacked it up and removed the worthless spare and thrown it into the trunk. While I leaned against his truck and watched the man work, from time to time I glanced at the building, but there was no sign of the old woman. Not even a curtain moved.

"What in the world was y'all doin' back in here, if you don't mind me asking so?" The mechanic had hauled the damaged tire from my trunk to the front of the car. He was kneeling over it examining the gash.

"We were on the way to Houston—took a wrong turn back up there on 94. I ran over something on the highway, a metal bracket of some kind."

"You sure did, on both counts. There ain't nothin' back in here but. . . ." His voice trailed off as he rummaged around in his toolbox, then put the tire on some contraption on the back of his truck. He worked the tire off the rim, put on the new one, and inflated it.

"Them little donut thangs ain't worth a shit."

"Tell me about it."

He held up the gashed tire. "Ort to just throw this at the edge of the road," he said. "Nobody'd notice it, for sure." He flung it onto the back of his truck.

"What I'd do," he said, tightening the nuts on the wheel, "when I got back to civilization, is throw that little sombitch away and get me a real tar to go in the trunk. I went and put some air in it, but I guarantee you it ain't gon' hold."

"I'll do that," I said. I was sitting on the back bumper of his truck watching.

After we had finished the little paperwork that had to be done, he asked, "That your whiskey back there?"

"*What* whiskey?"

He pointed to the rear of the car. I walked past him and there the Old Crow case was, sitting on the gravel. I took a bottle out of the straw and handed it to the mechanic and put the case in the trunk and closed the lid.

He held it up to the sun and wagged it back and forth, nodded, and grinned. "Man, that's some old shit there, for sure. Ain't seen one of them wooden cases like that in twenty or thirty years. And them bottles packed in *straw*. Bet it's good, ain't it?"

"Yeah," I said. "It'll do the trick. But go slow—it's high octane."

"I sure appreciate it," he said, getting in the truck. "Best damned tip I had in a while." He got in and drove slowly off toward Lufkin. Before he disappeared around the bend I saw his head tilt back and the bottle rise.

I looked at the building once more and got in the car, started it, and eased off down the road. Annie met me at the couple's mailbox and got in. They waved from the little deck and held their iced-tea glasses up like they were toasting us.

"Goin' to Houston, little sister?" I asked, grinning.

"Just drive, big boy," she said.

"Have a good chat?"

"Yes. They were nice. I called Jane while you were off with that guy. They wouldn't even take money for the call. She'd just gotten back from the hospital. Allison's alert and doing much better. All she's talking about is getting to see us again. That news has done more than anything else to clear my head."

"Did they wonder where we were?"

"Of course they did. They kept trying to call us in *Shrevesport*. Did everything but send out the highway *petroleums*." She laughed at that and leaned her head against the glass.

"What did you tell her?"

"Told her we had car trouble and had to spend the night on the road."

"You didn't tell her where?"

"Now, Tommy, that would have taken a while, wouldn't it? I just told her we stayed at somebody's house, and they didn't even have a *telephone*. I'm not sure she believed that part of it."

"Did those folks back there say anything about the old woman?"

"Just that she keeps to herself. They know very little about her. Didn't even know her name."

"Did you mention the ghost?"

"Of course not. Why would I do something stupid like that? It was probably a pig or sheep or something. Or just the whiskey. Let's just forget about last night and the ghost. Have you got a spare in case we blow another tire out?"

"Yes'm. The same one that saved us before. Only this time it's probably already flat."

"Jesus, Tommy. You Goddamned cheapskate. If we have another blowout, I swear I'm abandoning this car and hitching on into Houston."

"Say, I hate to change the subject, but did you ever find your panties?"

She spun her head toward me. "What the hell is that to you?"

"Just wondering."

"Well, the answer, for whatever it's worth, is no. I don't know where they are. Up in the boxes somewhere, I guess, or under one. But I sure wasn't going to spend a whole lot of time in there looking for them."

"So you're sitting there. . . ."

She gave me a look.

"Somebody will find them, ages hence. They'll pick them up and shake off the dust and cobwebs and hold them out to the light and wonder whose they were and how they came to be there."

"And there would be no way under the sun they could ever begin to imagine the story behind them." She was looking out the window at the wall of woods sliding past.

"They'll hold those panties up and never know that they belonged to Annie Oakley, who once spent the night there." I twisted around and removed the garter from my pocket and pulled it up onto my bicep. "I brought you a souvenir." I flexed my muscle.

She turned her face toward me. "My God, I wondered what happened to it. I guess you have the panties too."

"No. I swear I don't know what happened to them." I flexed my muscle again. "Wanna take it off?"

She laughed and slipped the garter off my arm and put it in her purse. "Thanks. I think I'm going to have it matted and framed, and I'm going to hang it on the wall at the foot of my bed so that every day I wake up to the reminder of the most insane night of my life."

"I have the Old Crow case. I'm going to use it for a nightstand or something." I held up the bottle I'd stuck in my pocket and looked at the trees through it. They swam slowly by in the amber.

"You went back in there?"

"No. She set it out by the car."

"She jes' don't want no whiskey in her castle."

In no time at all we came to the road we were looking for, FM 2262, and I jammed the accelerator to the floor and squalled right out onto it and headed east toward 59. God, I felt free now.

"You nearly hit that car back there," Annie said, turning in her seat.

"What car?"

"The one with the blue lights on right behind us."

"What the shit—"

I looked in the rearview mirror, and sure as sin in the inner city, there was a Goddamned patrol car behind us with his lights on.

"You ran that stop sign like it wasn't there."

"What damned stop sign?" I asked her.

"The one you ran."

"Smartass."

I pulled over and stopped on the shoulder. The patrol car stopped behind me and an officer got out and put his hat on and reached back and pulled out a clipboard.

"It is a fucking *highway patrolman*," Annie said.

"What?"

"A highway patrolman. You ran a stop sign right in front of a highway patrolman."

"A highway patrolman? I thought we agreed that they didn't come down in here."

"Well, they do now." She was looking at him over her sunshades as he approached and motioned for me to roll down the window.

I did as he directed.

He leaned and looked in at us.

"Howdy, sir. I don't suppose you happened to see that stop sign back there that you just ran right through."

"Uh, well, no sir, I wasn't aware of one."

"Well, it's there and you ran right through it. Matter of fact, you didn't even slow down. How about you show me your license and proof of insurance, please sir?"

I fished my wallet out and fumbled for the license.

"Exactly how often does the Department of Public Safety or whatever it is y'all are called come down in here?" Annie asked him.

He leaned way down and squinted in at her. "Ma'am?"

"What in the world is the highway patrol doing down in here? This is barely a road, much less a highway."

He straightened up. "Well, we got jurisdiction on any of these roads. But to answer your question, I was headed over to 59 to help with a traffic prollem over there. They got a prollem on the highway."

"We heard tell," Annie said.

I glanced at her and grinned and handed him my license and proof of insurance.

"What you folks doing down in here?" he asked.

"Headed to Houston," Annie said.

"To Houston? Why in the world—you sure are taking a strange way. You from Shrevesport, and you're going to Houston this way?"

When he pronounced it *Shrevesport*, I almost burst out laughing, but I kept a firm grip. I could see Annie biting her lip.

"Yessir. We took a detour," she said.

"Y'all sure did. Y'all know how to go from here?"

"Yessir. We spent the night with my husband's aunt, Miz Ludy Dowdle. They're real close. Just back up 357."

"Name's Dowdle? I don't know of no Dowdles down in here."

"Husband's name's Duke," I added.

Annie nudged me. "Now, Honey, admit it. They just shackin', Officer. It's one of them modern relationships."

He nodded and grinned. "Yes'm, I understand."

Then he stood back from the car and leaned down and looked at us. "You know, y'all seem like mighty nice people, so I'm just gonna cut y'all some slack and get on over to 59." He handed me the license and insurance card.

"Thank you, sir," Annie said. Then: "How in the world do y'all manage to cover all these roads in the middle of nowhere. There can't be that many of you."

"Aw, sometimes it's tough, ma'am, but we make do."

When he said that, all the tension that had built up over the past almost twenty-four hours rose in my throat like a gigantic bubble of gas and I simply roared, and she was laughing with me, and then there was no stopping it. We were out of control. I dropped my head down on the wheel and put my hands on the dash and laughed until tears were flooding from my face. I don't know what she was doing besides laughing, and I really don't know how long it went on, and I frankly did not really give a damn whether the officer reconsidered and wrote a ticket.

"Look here," the officer finally managed to get through to me, "you people are—what is wrong with you people? What is so *funny*? Y'all ain't been drinking at this hour, have you?"

328

"No, no, no sir," I managed, trying to draw in enough breath to try to go on living. "It's, uhhhhhh. It's just a jjjjjoke." Uncontrollable laughter again. "Just a private joke."

"Well, you just count yourself lucky. I hope y'all get to Houston OK."

Through the tears I watched him as he shook his head and walked back to his car, got in, and headed east.

"My G-G-God," she said as he drove past us, "my God in heaven. You nearly ran over a highway fucking petro-le-um and there couldn't have been one within fifty miles of here when we needed him."

"At's the way the turnip bounces, little sister. Soon's I get my face wiped off and can see again, we'll head on to Houston."

"And he didn't even give us a ticket!" She exploded again, and so did I.

Then we were sprawled back in the seat, laughing our asses off. And it went on and on and on.

She was still snickering a little when we finally got our breath back. "What a catharsis! I needed that. I don't think I've ever laughed as hard in my life. *We make do. We make do!* I swear to God, if I ever hear that again, even in church or at a funeral, I will simply lose it."

In another mile we passed a house, then two more and another. "Annie, I think we may have struck civilization again."

"Not quite," she said, "but we're getting there."

My hand hooked casually over the wheel, I said to her, "Do you remember everything that happened last night?"

"In thatere jailhouse?"

"Yes."

"All of the early stuff, sure, before we got into whatever bottle we got down to before things got fuzzy. Sitting on that upside-down disappearing staircase talking. Talking about Allison. I remember the white thing. And more talking. And fumbling around in those dusty boxes. Jesus, Tommy, I felt like we were grave robbing when we got into her wedding things."

"Do you remember peeing in the sink?"

She laughed. "Of course. You can't forget something like that, even when you're drunk out of your mind. I'm glad nobody got a picture. I felt more undignified than I ever have in my life—and more helpless. Buck-naked, squatting over a sink, legs locked, it dark as sin . . ."

"Drunk."

"I've already admitted that—drunk as a skunk."

"By the way," I said, "there was a camera mounted in the corner of the ceiling, aimed toward the sink. Looked like it was infrared too."

She slapped my arm. "Yeah, the one hooked up to her computer."

Then I asked what she remembered about the garter business.

"I don't remember all of it. Just drinking whiskey and playing around in the dark with you and that garter and pretending you were the Seed Man. Then we started drinking again. I don't remember anything much after handing that bottle back and forth a few times. Once it quit burning my damned throat and tongue, I didn't even pay attention to how much I was drinking. I just got goofy and passed out, I guess."

"I think we both passed out. I remember the sink business and messing around with the garter, and I think I remember . . ."

"I'll bet you don't remember any more about it than I do. I sure don't remember a damned thing after—"

"Annie, did we—I mean, I'm pretty sure."

"Did we *what*?" She was glaring at me over her shades.

"Come on, Annie, you know what I'm driving at. Did we—"

"Did we *screw*?"

"I—"

"You mean you don't know?"

"No. I mean, I think so. I keep getting little flashes of it."

"How much *do* you remember of it?"

"Annie, after I took the garter off your leg with my mouth, which I remember vaguely, everything from that point on is gone. You said it yourself, you know how I get. I don't pass out, but everything up here is dead." I tapped my head. "It started coming alive again this morning, when I woke up naked wrapped up in that sheet with you. Like I say, I get flashes, little pieces of it, like pieces of a puzzle."

"Well, not *everything* on you was dead, big boy. Or if it was, it had an amazing resurrection. Yeah, Tommy, the party went all the way."

"But if you don't remember . . ."

"Tommy, a woman knows when she's been fucked. And I mean that literally and figuratively. You didn't use a rubber. You left *evidence*. Jesus, what a fool you can be sometimes. Even if you had used one, I would have known. A woman knows things like that. She knows when a man has been in her. Besides, I remember enough about it to know."

I studied the road a few seconds. "Are you OK about it then?"

"Hell, I don't know, Tommy. The whole thing was fantasy, from the very second we crawled through the door. That wasn't us on that mattress last night."

"Of course it was us."

"I got crazy drunk, which I should not have done, but I don't know who did the initiating and consenting. I haven't been that drunk since our first date together. And I sure as hell wouldn't have gotten that way with any other man." She snorted. "That ought—*ort*—to tell me something. *What*, I don't know, but something."

"I'm sorry. I just don't know what to say except I'm sorry." I hesitated. "And that I still love you, Annie. I honest to God do. And I don't mean just because we slept together. You enchanted me the whole afternoon, like you used to do when we first started going together. Fainting the way you did—the way you lay back in my arms with just your panties on. The way you got along with the witch. Messing with Duke with a coat hanger. Starting that garter business. Peeing in the sink. You just *enchanted* me."

"Well, I'm not enchanting now. I'm just the same old me, I'm afraid, and we're back to ground zero. By the way, I calculated it a little earlier, while we were walking back there. It would be a perfect time for me to have gotten pregnant. It would be just my damned luck. . . ." She turned her face away from me. "Just my fucking luck to get pregnant after years of trying with you."

"Well, we both know how slim those chances are."

"I'm much more worried about the other."

"The other?"

"Disease, Tommy, disease. You've been with all kinds of women since me."

"And you've been with other men. So that goes both ways."

"But they used protection."

"So did I."

"Not last night you didn't."

"I'm not talking about last night. You are the only woman I haven't used a rubber with since I was in high school."

"You're not lying?"

"No, I swear."

"And you double-rubbered with Betty?"

"Stop it, Annie."

"Back to the real world for sure."

She kicked off her sneakers and drew her feet onto the seat. "What a nightmare all that was. What a *night*."

After a while I asked, "What do you think that thing was we saw down by the swamp?"

"Tommy, my head's still screwed up, my stomach's screwed up. I don't want to think about anything for a while. Do you *mind*?"

"Well, as we know from the experience of less than twenty-four hours, life can take some crazy twists. Maybe we're destined to be back together."

"Tommy, I'm afraid we don't know anything about anything. I thought I was strong, in control of my life. And I thought I had you neatly pegged. Now I'm just confused. About everything. Let's *please* just stop talking. I'm going to take a nap."

"I sure would like to know what that white thing was."

"Well, whatever it was," she said, curled up in the seat, "we'll *never* know, unless maybe you'd like to go back and check it out some night."

"Would you like to go back? I mean, someday."

"I don't know about that. Probably not. I'd rather just leave it all just as it is. Perhaps it's better for us to wonder about it. Maybe knowing what it was would—well, it would be better not to know."

"Still. . . ."

Then we were on 59, headed south in a steady stream of traffic.

"Something else I was thinking," she said after a few miles, "while I was putting my makeup on in that God-awful bathroom. That toothpaste tube and toothbrush made me want to throw up." She had rotated in the seat and moved her shades up on her forehead and was looking at me.

"I got to thinking that what it all boils down to is food and sleep and sex and going to the bathroom. Not necessarily in that order. That's all life's really about. Everything else is just fluff, glitter, and what our imaginations make of it. Airplanes and satellites and cars and televisions, computers. Telephones. All our toys. We surround ourselves with them, but they're just momentary distractions. We come into the world without those things and we go out without them. Allison lying down there in the hospital—it may be that she wouldn't have made it without some wonderful machine hooked to her, but in the end it's her body, it's nature, keeping her going. And her love for us might have helped. For her it's just food and sleep and her bodily functions. And if her body and mind didn't have the will to do it, none of the machines, those doctors' toys, would have any bearing on the outcome. In the end none of that can save us."

"What about hope and love and memory," I asked, "whatever

they are and however they factor in? Don't we have to have those?"

"I'll bet Allison did. *Does.* But they're not always there for us. Sometimes I think it's better if there's no memory at all."

"This sounds awfully cynical, Annie."

"I don't mean for it to. It's just the way things are. There's Allison at the beginning of her life and that old fool of a woman back there at the the end of things. Our toys mean nothing to her either. Not even a damned telephone! Food and sleep and going to the bathroom and the *memory* of sex—that's what her world's boiled down to. You know she heard everything we did last night. She said as much. I'll bet she was down on all fours outside that door with her ear to it."

I nodded and watched the road. "She's got Duke."

She smiled. "Yeah, at least she's got Duke."

"Sad."

"All our toys, all our dreams, Tommy. But food and sleep and sex and going to the bathroom—that's reality. You know, I keep talking about last night being a dream, but *reality* is what we went through last night, even with the whiskey—that room and what happened in it could have been anytime over the past hundred years. Hell, two hundred. A thousand, five thousand. Could have been in a stone jailhouse in Mexico or Spain or almost anywhere in the world, yesterday or a thousand years ago. You and me, a little food, that *iron* water, whiskey, peeing, sex, and sleep. Not one of our modern toys on the scene. That was rock-solid real, what happened last night, Tommy, however looped we were."

"I don't quite know what to say to that."

"You don't have to say anything. That's just what I was thinking," she said.

"I guess we're somewhere between Allison and the old woman."

"Yes," she said quietly.

We drove along a while without talking.

"What did you say to her? At the door?"

"I told you, it was a woman thing."

"Annie, come on."

"She asked me whether it was true about Allison—the *hurt girl*, as she put it."

"What else?"

"I *thanked* her, Tommy."

"Thanked her?

"Yes."

"For what? For not killing us? For not turning Duke loose on us last night? For feeding us? For what?"

"I just thanked her. I shook her hand and thanked her."

"God, women are weird."

"Goes to show what you know," she said. Then: "I told her that I thought I saw buds on that thorn bush."

"You told her what?"

"You heard me. I didn't actually see any—or at least I don't think I did—but it just seemed like the right thing to say. Who knows, the Goddamned thing might be loaded with blooms come spring."

"My God, women. . . ."

She straightened up in her seat and rolled the window down.

The slipstream was playing lightly with her scarf, lifting and tossing little strands of hair around the edge of it. "One thing I do know. One decision I've come to. From the past three years and from what we went through last night."

"What?"

"Just this—whatever this life's all about, whatever it comes down to in the end, whatever reality's out there waiting for me—I don't want to face it alone." She turned away from me and rested her head against the back of the seat, her eyes toward the towering wall of trees that slid past us. "And a dog won't do the trick."

I looked at her. "What does that mean?"

"Tommy, I'm just not sure what it means. Let me alone for a while. I want to sit here and think, maybe try to nap. I feel like I'm in some old woman's body, and it needs rest."

I drove along in silence then, trying again to piece together the details of the night before, but things just wouldn't lock into place. They kept shifting and contorting. From time to time I glanced over at the beautiful woman curled up in the seat beside me. I started to reach and touch her but didn't. Things seemed to be going right.

In a few miles as if by magic the woods broke open to a convenience store and laundromat, a cluster of houses with neat lawns and shiny cars in the driveways. Two towers rose against the shocking depth of the sky, and beyond them the vapor trails of jets crossed. Then there were small towns and swarming traffic. It was as if the night before had never happened.

Annie breathed soft and deep, lost in some dream, her face turning slowly toward me as I drove south, taking in that panorama of color and shape and light that a few hours earlier I thought I might never see again. When next I looked at her she had removed her scarf and the shades and I could see the deep blue of her eyes. The sun was over far enough in the sky that it slanted in and emblazoned her hair.

"You awake?"

"Yes," she said. "The open eyes give it away?"

"What are you looking at?"

"You."

"For how long?

"Not long."

Then she rose and leaned and kissed me lightly on the cheek.

"What was that for?"

"Just felt like it, big boy."

"About tonight. . . ."

"What about tonight?"

"Well," I ventured, "Jane asked whether I wanted to sleep at the house."

"And?"

"I told her yes."

"She asked me the same thing."

"She did?"

"Yes."

"So what did you tell her?"

She had propped her feet on the dash and leaned her head back. She was staring at the ceiling. "I told her yes."

"So. . . ."

"So let's just wait and see how things shake out. How about that?"

A passing truck buffeted the car. I slid my hand over to touch hers. Our fingers met and twined and she lifted her head and smiled at me. Then I put my hand back on the wheel.

"I know what we saw last night," she said. "Down at the edge of the woods."

"What?"

"It's something that can't be named, Tommy." She squeezed my hand. "Neither one of us can name it. But you know too. We both know what it was."

I nodded and breathed deep. She reached and took my hand in both of hers, enfolded it like a seed.